Reeling in Time
with Fish Tales
Mono Fulfillment

Capt. Brian E Smith

Published by:
Southern Yellow Pine (SYP) Publishing
4351 Natural Bridge Rd.
Tallahassee, FL 32305

www.syppublishing.com

This is a work of fiction. Names, characters, places, and events that occur either are the products of the author's imagination or are used fictitiously. Any resemblance to actual persons, places, or events is purely coincidental.

The contents and opinions expressed in this book do not necessarily reflect the views and opinions of Southern Yellow Pine Publishing, nor does the mention of brands or trade names constitute endorsement.

ISBN-10: 1940869242
ISBN-13: 978-1-940869-24-7

Front Cover Design: Taylor Nelson

First Edition
Printed in the United States of America
August 2014

Dedication

This book is dedicated to those who have given their time and resources to take another fishing.

Contents

FOREWORD vii

Introduction ix

Chapter 1 - Push-Button 1

Chapter 2 - Isthmus? 16

Chapter 3 - My Pond 30

Chapter 4 - My First Trophy Fish 42

Chapter 5 - The Pier 51

Chapter 6 - Speckled Pink 68

Chapter 7 - Catfish Ladies 89

Chapter 8 - Head Boat Monkeys 108

Chapter 9 - A View from the End of My World 124

Chapter 10 - The Ranger Station 145

Chapter 11 - The Walk 164

Chapter 12 - The Skiff 191

Chapter 13 - Black Drum Beat 214

Chapter 14 – Part I - Patchwork Trout 231

Chapter 14: Part II - The Patchwork Expands 240

Chapter 15 - Spanish as a Second Chance 250

Chapter 16 - Cobia on the Mark 258

Chapter 17 - The Fox is Pushed into the Henhouse 291

About the Author 297

FOREWORD

Captain Cefus McRae

It was an early summer morning when I first met Capt. Brian Smith; and from the moment we shook hands I knew this guy was passionate about fishing. It was pure serendipity that he was the only charter guide in Steinhatchee, Florida, who had an opening that day. There were four of us... two dads, and their two young sons who would be experiencing their first time fishing offshore. The boys were anxious to catch a big fish on a morning that was hot and humid with a chance of thunderstorms in the forecast. The seas were flat calm and we made good time to our first stop to catch bait. The boys did the bait catching and Capt. B cheered them on, unhooking the pinfish and re-baiting their hooks. His comments to the kids, even when they tangled lines, were always positive... and patient. He would offer instruction in a fun way that kept a smile on the boys' faces, and he had a playful manner that keep them excited, even when the fishing slowed down.

With the live well full, Capt. B situated the kids in seats where they could get a good view and set the course for offshore waters. The further we went, the darker the skies became and we finally dropped anchor on a place that Brian called his *Magic Spot*. The kids beamed and jousted for positions at the back of the boat. We had been fishing for just a few minutes when the first rumble of thunder was heard in the distance, followed by a distinctly cool breeze. Time to reel in and go.

The kids were obviously and justifiably disheartened. No big fish today. We made it back to the dock as the bottom fell out. Raindrops as big as Ping-Pong balls and hail that covered the docks. There wasn't much to do except say our goodbyes and thank Brian for the effort. Brian cleaned the boat quickly with the help of the rain, said goodbye again and left. We figured that was that, so we ate lunch at the marina's Tiki Hut. After lunch, the rain subsided as we were trying to come up with a game plan of what to do for the rest of the day with two energetic ten year olds. Just then, the phone at the bar rang. It was Brian calling for me. The conversation was short and to the point. "You guys want to go fishing?"

That clinched it for me. This guy, who I'd never met and might never see again, cared enough to do his best to give us a fun day on the water. He didn't have to do that. But Brian went the extra mile and gave two very happy boys and their dads an awesome fishing adventure.

With that as background, you now have some insight into Capt. Brian Smith... his character and his passion for fishing. *Reeling in Time with Fish Tales* is a chronology of fishing stories and life experiences that ultimately steered Brian to his career as a charter captain. They are stories that most folks can relate to, whether you're an avid angler or simply like a story where the good guy gets the girl. And woven into each story is fish-catching knowledge that can help both the novice angler and the old salt on their next fishing excursion. *Reeling in Time with Fish Tales* is more than a series of anecdotal fishing stories, it's a reminder, and proof, that life is a journey with lots of serendipitous moments.

Each chapter blends valuable, practical fishing tips with a wonderful life-story featuring familiar characters we've all known during our own growing-up years; from parents and uncles to best buddies and girlfriends. Brian's story brings back memories of our own innocence of youth and the lessons we learned as we grew up; such as the adventures and mischief with a best buddy, the anxiety of a first date, moving away from home and beginning to carve a life on your own. *Reeling in Time with Fish Tales* chronicles those life experiences that led Brian down the path to a place called Steinhatchee, on Florida's Big Bend.

Until I read this book, I had only known Capt. B, the charter captain. After reading it, I now have insight into what molded Brian Smith into the man that refused to let a rainstorm disappoint a couple young boys on their first offshore fishing adventure.

Captain Cefus McRae
"Nuts & Bolts of Fishing & Boating TV Show"

Introduction

I've been fishing since as far back as my memory allows. Beyond memory, there are yellowed photos of me holding a stick with a string attached beside some forgotten creek. I was at Uncle Tom's fish camp Burgoo Hollow, West Virginia, with my mom and family, while Dad was serving the Army, in Korea. Uncle Tom *tainted* me with fishing from my start. I wouldn't deny it, because indoctrinated in the ways, means, and joys of fishing was what being with Tom Redman was all about. At my early age, I was vulnerable; he imprinted my life.

Uncle Tom fished for trout, catfish, or any other fish that swam through West Virginia, with the passion that any woman would love to receive a fraction of from her husband. The *kiss and tell* fish stories he told were better than the fishing trips themselves. Uncle Tom had the gift of story, lightly seasoned with concoction strongly spoken in hillbilly. He illustrated on the kitchen table with whatever coffee cup, salt and pepper shaker, pack of smokes, lighter, teaspoon/fork/knife, bowl, or plate, ashtray, pocketknife or piece of food fallen off a plate; he needed to make the trout stream run through Aunt Clara's kitchen. I've listened to most of his stories more than once, but each time, I thought, if I lifted up the coffee cup, a trout would flounce on the table. He could resurrect a fish from long ago. He made it so fresh you could not only smell its odor on your hands but also the earthy aroma of moss on the rocks and the organic bouquet of fallen leaves on the autumn bank. You could hear the rush of water tumble over rocks (salt and pepper shakers) with the seasonal chill that made your feet cold at the table. When Uncle Tom passed, a lifetime of stories was buried in an insufficient fishing hole.

My father took me fishing as I grew up in Virginia Beach, Virginia. He realized I was tainted from Uncle Tom, he understood I enjoyed fishing more than I enjoyed anything else. He liked wetting a line as well and saw fishing as an opportunity to spend time together; memorable moments with his only child. Dad understood the importance of one-on-one time well ahead of the coined term *quality time*. His graveyard shift at the Postal Service made early morning fishing trips a sacrifice on his part…, more than I realized at the time. Now, I know how valuable his time was for us; our time spent on watery banks remains my fondest memories growing up.

Likewise, reminiscences of fishing with family, and friends as close as family, are recollections I treasure, though the fish we caught are mostly forgotten. Time on the water was indeed special, a brief period of one's years etched in each mind for a lifetime.

This first volume includes a collection of stories that progress through my life, starting as a young boy with Dad. I age through each chapter. The conclusion is when I start fishing professionally. Lightly salted with real life humor and heavily seasoned with reality. I write in hope that you, the reader, can identify with me at that particular time in life. Loosely hidden in each chapter are learning tidbits about fishing, some are actual techniques, others are simple thoughts; both are inserted to help you enjoy the sport of fishing more.

Uncle Tom naturally spoke so well that listening brought vivid life back to long ago people or fish, as well as, an account of his living history. Words are more important than we realize: words of praise from a parent, kind words said by a friend, tender words from a lover, perhaps a sermon in due time. Additionally, who hasn't been touched by lyrics from a special song? I hope the words I chose for these stories bring you fond memories and, perhaps, challenge you to make your own stories with those you care for. Enjoy the read.

Capt. B

Chapter 1 - Push-Button

The parking lot was empty, except for our car. Covered picnic tables dotted the lakeshore. Several uncovered tables were clustered around a nearby small playground area. Seagulls had gathered around a covered picnic table on a point of land where the lake cut back into a cove. Most of the gulls lay on the ground, either sleeping or preening, while others stood amongst them. I didn't know if they were on guard or just looking for some mischief, but they looked, to me, as if they were up to something. A few had perched on the gazebo roof. From first look, they appeared to be painters, patiently painting the roof, one white spot at a time.

Dad starting unloading the fishing gear from the back seat of the car. On top of the fishing tackle and bait, he placed the two fishing rods we were to use.

"Champ, always load the fishing poles last, they'll be on top of the rest of the stuff and are less likely to get broke," Dad gave a quick lesson.

He leaned the fishing rods against the car. His was a six-foot spinning combination. It looked fancy, especially, next to my fishing rod, a short stick with a pistol grip and a Zebco® 33 spin/cast reel. He said that style of reel had caught more fish than all other type reels combined. It looked like an old hand-crank pencil sharpener; he called it a push-button. Dad had given me the push-button the week before. He took me in the yard to *practice fish* that same day.

"How am I going to catch a fish in the yard, Dad?"

1

"Champ, really you're not."

"Then… why am I fishing in the yard?"

"You're going to practice casting, not fishing."

"Dad, people will see me in the yard with a fishing pole and think I'm stupid."

"Don't worry about what people think because most of the time they don't think things through in the first place."

"I'll still look silly, won't I?" Dad smiled, and then moved the practice to the back yard.

In the back yard, Dad explained the reel as he got it ready for practice fishing. He pushed the button in the back of the reel, releasing the fishing line. To keep the line from going down inside a little hole in the front of the reel, there was a piece of plastic attached to the end of the line. He pulled twice as much line out of the reel as the rod was long, and then turned the handle a quarter turn forward. The reel made a clicking noise, and that action stopped the line from coming out any more. He cut the piece of plastic off the end of the line with his pocketknife, putting that in his pocket. Then he took the end of the fishing line and threaded it through each of the hoops—he called the hoops the eyes of the fishing pole—and out the last one, which he called a tip. After all of that, he tied a 3/8 oz. bell sinker to the line end. The sinker looked like a tiny bell made of lead.

"Champ, did you see how all that worked?"

"Sure, Dad." That wasn't the truth, but I figured I'd learn how to do it on my own later.

"Champ, wind the sinker so it hangs about six inches from the tip of the pole." He showed me as he went through the motions. "Then push the button in and hold it in with your thumb. Keep the rod straight with your arm, bringing it over your shoulder to about the ten o'clock position." He stopped his arm and said, "Right like this."

I acted as if I wasn't watching all the way, but I was paying full attention out of the corner of my eye.

"Quickly move your arm and swinging the rod forward to about one o'clock, let go of the button, like this." When he did that, the sinker sailed across the yard and my head snapped around to watch it fly. It was a small baseball on a string!

"Let me try it, Dad!"

"Watch me, one more time first." Either he liked doing it, or he was just showing off, because the next cast went further than the first by a long shot.

I couldn't wait for him to reel in that chunk of lead to give me a turn. Finally, after forever, he gave me the rod. In the blink of an eye, I thumped myself in the butt with the sinker on the back cast, and then flung the rod several feet in front of me during the forward cast. I had let go of the button and the rod, which then bounced and cart wheeled across the ground. I rubbed my butt as I ran to the rod to see how badly broken it was. Embarrassed and ashamed, I picked up the rod. Except for some clumps of dirt and grass, the rod and reel were fine.

"Dad, this thing is bullet proof!"

He smiled, "But it will sink."

Those words calmed me down. He told me to slow down and add speed as I learned. Ten or fifteen minutes later, I was flying the sinker all by myself. Each cast being better than the last!

While I practiced, Dad got a metal garbage can lid. He put it on the ground ten feet in front of me.

"Let me see the rod, Champ." I gave it to him and on his first cast, he plinked the sinker off the lid. "Now, you do it." Nine shots later, the sinker plinked the rim of the lid. Davy Crocket on the fishing pole I was!

"Now, do it three more times," said Dad. The last two hits, I made in a row. He walked up and moved the lid five feet further away, saying, "Hit that three times." After I did that, he moved the lid five more feet away, and after the lid was thirty feet away, he left me on my own.

An hour later, the sinker sailed across the yard, way past Dad's longest shot. It sped high over the chain link fence, crashed through the leaves of the trees behind the house, ricocheted off some large branches, slammed against an exposed hickory root, and tumbled along the ground into some leaves. *Wow, I'm already so much better at this than Dad*, I thought, until I reeled in a ten-foot section of fishing line with no sinker attached to it.

"Dad, the line broke and the sinker is lost in the woods."

"Champ, anything but water that touches that line puts peewee cuts in it. The grass is nicking away at your fishing string with each cast. Feel

3

the end of the line with your fingers. Do you feel how rough it feels between your fingers?"

"Yes, sir" and I nodded.

"Check your line every now and then, and when it feels rough, cut out the bad line and re-tie with fresh smooth line." He tied on another sinker, showing me a simple overhand knot, and gave me two extra sinkers to put in my pocket along with his pocketknife.

By the time we finally got to the lake, I was more than ready to cast anything other than that sinker, such as a lure, bait, or whatever, all the way across the lake, just to impress Dad.

Once the fishing rods were out of the car, Dad pulled out a knapsack that had our lunch, drinks, a loaf of stale, white bread, and some other stuff. The bait came next. The cricket tube contained a few dozen crickets crawling from one end to the other. The worm bucket was a three-pound coffee can half-filled with garden soil and crumbled leaves with a couple of handfuls of fat earthworms mixed in. Finally, a good-sized Plano tackle box.

The earthworms we dug up from our garden. Dad told me the best worms were under the weed patches, so be sure to dig there. It took only ten turns of the shovel to produce several dozen wiggle-worms. It was cool to dig up the worms the day before we went fishing, but what was really neat was Dad's worm bucket.

He ran both ends of the coffee can through a can opener to form a metal tube. He put a plastic lid at each end to close both ends. Each lid he punched with plenty of holes using a nail. Toward one open end of the can, he punched two holes across from each other using an ice pick and a Phillips head screwdriver, to open up the hole. Afterwards, he strung a section of small rope through from the outside in and tied an overhand knot on the inside bitter ends to form a simple rope handle.

"Don't swing the bucket around, son, the bottom lid will fall out," he cautioned.

"Dad, why did you knock out both ends of the coffee can and not just the top?"

"Do worms dig up or dig down?" Dad asked.

"Down, right?"

"You're right, Champ, but in this magic can the worms will always

4

crawl to the top on one side or the other." He didn't fool me with the magic can bit, but Dad always had a reason for doing things.

"Dad, tell me why you told me the best worms are found underneath the garden weeds?"

He smiled and said, "There is more than one way to weed a garden."

Four days before going fishing, Dad took me out to the garden; he was toting two large Russet potatoes. He took his pocketknife and cut both potatoes into thin slices, giving me a handful of slices, saying, "Put a slice or two under every old board, brick, block, garbage can, garbage can lid, and especially under the sheets of plastic we used to cover the tomatoes."

Dad's gone nuts having me hide potato slices like Easter eggs, but I did as told. This was so strange I was afraid to ask. Once I hid the potato slices, we walked away, no words about it. I was really confused.

The day before we went fishing, after we dug the worms, we stood in the garden.

"This is a cricket tube, son." It was a cylinder made of hardware cloth, about twelve inches long and four inches in diameter. One end tapered to a half-inch funnel hole with a cork in the end. To keep from dropping and losing the cork, it had a knotted string stapled on the end loosely tied back to the tube. The other end of the tube was blunt. Dad showed me that it had a sleeved cap to secure that end made of the same hardware cloth as the tube.

"Is that some kind of cricket trap, Dad?"

"No, this is where you put them after you catch them."

"Catch 'em? I don't see any to catch"

"Look under that garbage can lid where you put the tater slices a few days ago." I flipped the lid over and black and brown *popcorn* started hopping up off the ground. I took two quick steps backwards and heard Dad and Mom laugh.

"Mom?"

She had snuck in behind us and said, "Grab 'em, Babe, grab 'em." I jumped in like a chicken on a June bug. I swatted at one, missing. Then one hopped on me; I grabbed myself and it hopped off. Finally, I slapped one to the ground.

"I got one, Dad!" I picked up my hand to find cricket goop. The rest got away. I turned to Dad with a forlorn look.

"Champ, you got to be ready, sitting on go when you flip the lid. In addition, you have to pick a target. In other words, don't get distracted by a whole bunch of jumping crickets, pick out one and go for it, but do it gently. Remember, you're a giant compared to tiny crickets. Do that once more; remember you only have two hands, so most of the crickets will escape to go fishing another day. I'll help also so we'll have plenty of crickets to fish with."

"What about Mom, she can help, right?"

Dad smiled, "I don't think so, Champ."

The crickets were fun to catch. Mom seemed to have the most fun just watching us cricket-cowboys. The crickets hopped. We hopped. I paid attention to what Dad said. I was getting good at catching two crickets each flip-over. In a competitive spirit, I tried to match Dad in the number I caught, but it became obvious that he had done this a time or two before. In half an hour we flipped over everything I'd hid a potato slice under. We had a good number of crickets in our tube.

"Champ, did you notice the little notches missing from the edges of the tater slices?"

"Yes, sir."

"Crickets like to eat potatoes and we used potatoes as bait. I'm not as crazy as you thought, am I?" He had read my mind!

Dad slid the cricket cage in the top of the knapsack before slinging it across one shoulder. As he bent over to get the tackle box, I grabbed both fishing rods and the worm bucket.

"Which way, Dad?" He struck out walking toward the point where the birds were. When we were still a good way off, some of the gulls began to call and screech. The ones lying on the ground got up. Strangely, some of the ones on top of the gazebo commenced to paint. When we were within a stone's throw, the entire flock flew off. By the sound, they didn't like us breaking up their party.

I started running. "Champ! Don't...." The bottom of the worm bucket fell out. "You can't run with the worm bucket."

"I know, Dad, I forgot." We scooped up the worms and soil, putting the bucket back whole.

On the point where the gulls were, Dad set up camp on the picnic table, under the gazebo. He took the worm bucket from me and set it on the table, doing the same thing with the fishing rods. Next, he pulled the cricket cage from the knapsack setting it beside the worm bucket. The loaf of stale white bread, he put at the other end of the table over the top of a few sheets of old newspaper he brought. The next items were two cans of whole yellow corn and a hand turn can opener.

"I hope that's not our lunch, Dad."

"Just fish food, Champ, fish food." I was watching intently, because Dad had an agenda of some sort.

"Come on," he said, grabbing the two cans of corn and the can opener and moving to the end of the table with the bread. He spread three sheets of newspaper out to form an eighteen by twenty-four-inch rectangle. He set the cans of corn on the windward corners to keep the slight breeze from blowing the papers. He took the top eight slices of bread, including the heel, and put them in the middle of the paper.

"Son, get up on the table and help me do this." I did as he asked.

"When are we going to fish, Dad?"

"Give me five minutes; we're making a fish-call! Here's what to do…" He took a slice of bread between both hands and began rubbing his hands back and forth. Mini-crumbs rained down like snow. "Rub it lightly so you won't get big clumps," he warned.

Four minutes later, we had a pile of tiny breadcrumbs in the middle of the newspaper. Dad rolled the paper into a cone and folded over the pointed end several times.

"Hold this straight up, Champ," he told me as he took a can of corn and the can opener. He cut the lid so it was hanging on to the can by a thread of metal. He drained the corn juice on the ground. "Let's switch." He gave me the corn can and took the cone of newspaper with the breadcrumbs. We walked down to the left side of the point together. By snapping his wrist sharply, he scattered breadcrumbs five to ten feet off the bank as we walked along the water's edge until the breadcrumbs ran out. We backtracked along the shore doing the same thing with the corn in a more hit and miss pattern. Dad used the lid as a choke to keep all the corn from going out in one toss.

Some pretty white ducks were swimming toward us when we were putting out the corn.

"You have to use a fish-call that sinks quickly, otherwise you're putting out a duck-call, and a duck-call, when fishing, can lead to trouble," Dad told me. The ducks swam around where we had tossed out the fish-call, but soon lost interest when there was nothing for them.

"When are we going to start fishing, Dad?" I repeated.

"Let's go get the fishing poles and bait; I'll explain the fishing rigs while the fish-call works." He picked up my fishing pole from the picnic table. "Do you know what this is and what it does?" He pointed to a pencil-shaped piece of Styrofoam pinned to the fishing line.

"It's the thing that lets you know when you have a bite, right?" I asked.

"You're headed in the right direction." He went on to tell me by many names such as cork, float, bobber, tip up, and even a strike indicator by fly fishermen. He explained that bobbers come in all sorts of shapes and sizes, depending on their application, and always to use the smallest bobber necessary. However, the important thing to remember is that they all do the same job, and that is to keep the fish bait suspended in the water at the depth you want.

"How do you set the depth, Dad?" I asked.

He explained that most fixed bobbers have the fishing line pass through the middle and use a wood or plastic peg to pinch the line and bobber together. He showed me the peg on my bobber, and how by removing the peg, the bobber could slide up or down to change depth.

"Today, we're going to be fishing close to the bank. The water is three to four feet deep, so we set the bobbers to keep our bait two feet or so below the water."

"This is called a split shot," as he pointed to a BB bump of lead pinched on the fishing line six inches above the hook. "Son, what does it do?"

"It makes the bait sink, Dad," I said with confidence.

"You're right, but it also makes the end of your line heavier so you can cast further. Champ, if you put too much lead under your float, what will happen?"

It took me some time before my eyes popped wide open, "Sink!" He gave me a high five.

"Hooks are important, Champ." He told me hooks come in more

shapes and sizes than bobbers do. "We'll talk all about hooks later, but in a nutshell...," he said, "you need to create balance. You have to consider the bait you're using and the fish you're after or most likely to catch. For example, today, we're fishing with small bait for hand-sized bream, so the hook needs to be on the small side. Keep in mind, bream tend to inhale the bait deep, so a long shank hook will help with hook removal." He pointed to the hook he tied on our lines "Champ, this is an Aberdeen #8, it is strong and small enough to catch bream, yet light enough so the bait we're putting on remain alive and act natural." I know I had a glazed look on my face when Dad said, "Champ, I just planted a seed in your noggin so one day you'll figure it out without realizing you had even given it thought. Just remember balance."

Dad cut the lid off the other can of corn before we walked down to the shore with the worm bucket, cricket cage, and tackle box. We set up on the left side of the bank where Dad started the fish-call. He flipped the worm bucket upside down, taking off the lid. Sure enough, the worms were on top. He ran my hook twice through a fat worm.

"Go ahead and toss it out." When he dropped that green flag, I fired off about thirty feet of line from my reel toward the middle of the lake. With a slight smile and nod he said, "Been practicing, I see!" I smiled back and said nothing, just glad he noticed. He pinned a worm on his hook, flipped it just ten feet from the bank and the bobber sank.

"Too much sinker on your line, Dad," I grinned when I said it. He pulled a fat bream out. My face spoke for me.

"You over-shot the fish, Champ. The fish-call brought them to us. Reel yours in about twenty feet." I did it with speed and my bobber sank. "Set the hook, Champ!" I heard him say as I ran up the bank past him. I stopped at the picnic table. That poor fish had left a slime-trail in the grass for the first fifteen feet before it ran out of slime.

"I got 'em, I got 'em!" I squealed, jumping as if I were a gold medalist of some sort, raising the fishing pole in the air, Stanley Cup style. Dad came along in a minute, fish in one hand, fishing pole in the other. He dropped both down, grabbing me up.

"Way to go, Champ!" We celebrated that bream as if the International Game Fish Association (IGFA) were honoring my catch!

Dad and I walked back to the lake with our fish still dangling from

9

our fishing lines. Dad pulled a nylon stringer from his tackle box. The stringer was just a heavy cord with a metal ring on one end and a four-inch metal spike crimped to the other. He unhooked his fish first. While he still had his fish in hand, he slipped the metal spike underneath the gill plate, out the fish's mouth, and ran the spike back through the ring to secure his fish to the end of the stringer. Holding the spike end of the stringer, he tossed his fish into the lake, dropped the spike end, and stepped on it, holding it solidly to the ground.

"Champ, let me show you something." I came up to him with my fish that was barely flipping and worn out. A foot above the fish, Dad pinched the line between his thumb and forefinger on his right hand. Using his left hand, he formed a circle around the line with his thumb and forefinger; he then slid his left hand down the line and let it form over the fish until he had a firm grasp on the fish with just its head sticking out from his hand. "Did you see how that worked?"

"Dad, you just grabbed the fish; what's the big deal?"

"Watch." He let go of the fish. "Did you see that?" He pointed out that when he let go, the fish stuck its dorsal (top), pectoral (side), and pelvic (bottom) fins out. "Those fins are sharp as needles; they're a defense mechanism to protect the fish. As long as the fish doesn't have teeth, sliding the fish through your hand like this—he did it again—brushes the fins down so they won't poke you."

"It's always something new, isn't it, Dad?" I sighed.

"Let's do some more fishing!" And we did! The game was on, no more explaining things. Well, almost. He told me to reel the fish in and not take it for a sprint up the bank again.

Dad pinned a couple more worms on our hooks and we couldn't finish a sentence before one cork would be yanked down, then the next. It went on and on as long as there was bait in the water. Some of the fish were big enough to go on the stringer, but most were a bit smaller and we tossed them back. It didn't matter what size the fish was; every one of them was fun to catch.

"What about those crickets, Dad?"

"You're right, Champ, I've been a touch lazy. We went through the trouble to get them and bring them. Let me show you how to use them correctly. When I have a bird in the hand, it is hard to go for the one in the bush, Champ. The worms were catching fish so well, I kept using them." The cricket tube was lying next to the worm bucket. "Quick, let me show you something." I could tell by his tone and action that this wasn't going to be a long drawn out lesson. Dad had fishing fever.

"Pull the cork, shake one of the critters down the funnel into the palm of your hand, then loosely close your hand around the cricket, turn the tube pointy end up, and replace the cork. Always replace the cork or you'll end up on a cricket rodeo. Shake your hand with the cricket in it toward the thumb to motivate the cricket, between your thumb and forefinger. Champ, this takes feel; feel that comes with practice, not explanation."

He jostled the insect about in his hand until it lay face down on his forefinger underneath his thumb. "Come close, you have to see what I'm doing." I leaned over his hand, watching him take the hook with his other hand, turn it sideways and slip it forward, toward the head, underneath a hard flap that covered what I would call the cricket's neck. "That part is called the collar." He guided the hook halfway under the collar, then turned it up and gently wiggled it until it punctured all the way through. Using the fishing line, he lifted the cricket away from his hand. The cricket squirmed in the air, firmly attached to the hook.

"Champ, that cricket doesn't know it's hung on a hook. It's not hurt and it will behave naturally. Whenever possible, hook live bait so the hook does the least amount of damage and the live bait acts natural. Generally, natural action produces more bites."

"Imagine if you will, Mom sends us to Browns' Turkey Farm to pick out a turkey for Thanksgiving. Given the choice of all the birds, would you pick out a big, strutting, pretty turkey or would you pick the dirty one, limping along the fence line?"

"Dad, I don't like to think about hurting a turkey, but I get what you're saying."

"Champ, think about all the effort we put into collecting the live bait and getting it here in good shape; why would we go through all that trouble just to kill it right before we need it most?"

"Dad, there is more to this fishing thing than I realized, isn't there? There's always something more than meets the eye. The guys on TV make it look easy, hauling in fish after fish."

11

"It's the same way with anything you're going to do well, you not only have to know what you're doing, but why you're doing it the way you are."

Together we flipped our crickets into the lake. You could see the crickets slowly sink. Their little legs paddled as they went down. Flash! A tea-saucer sized something sped by, took my bait before my eyes, and yanked my rod tip down before I had a chance to do anything.

"Reel, Champ, reel!" I was on it.

"It's a big one, Dad!" That fish darted left, right, up and down, and then again. At times, I couldn't reel; at times, I forgot to reel. Somehow, after what seemed forever, I managed to get the fish close enough so Dad could get hold of the line, bringing it in the rest of the way.

"Dad, that's the biggest one!" The bream weighed almost a pound. I jumped in Dad's arms "I love crickets!" Over Dad's shoulder, I noticed a fish flopping on the shore. I hadn't noticed, but he had caught a fish while I was dancing with mine. It was bigger than mine was, but he was happier for me.

He took my fish off, put another cricket on my hook, and sent me fishing. By the time he had his on the stringer, I had another bream on the bank. It was a good one, too.

"Champ, we got twelve or fifteen fish on the stringer. I think that is plenty for dinner. Let's start throwing them back."

"I don't care, Dad; I'm having fun just catching them." We spent the next hour or so feeding the fish crickets until we ran out of crickets.

"You ready, Champ?"

"Sure, Dad."

"Give the rest of them a treat; sling this corn in the water." Handful after handful, I peppered the water with corn. I wondered why we didn't use it when fish started to come in and eat the corn as it sank. *Oh well, at least I found out the corn was good bait, too.*

The last two handfuls I scattered around the picnic table to make amends with the gulls. A flock of gulls hovered around as Dad and I picked up our stuff from the table. He carried most of the gear and I had the fishing poles and worm bucket.

"Dad, I think the birds are still ticked off; one just painted my head!" He wiped my head off with his handkerchief, laughing all the while.

12

At the car, Dad popped the trunk, putting the fish in a five-gallon bucket he had inside it. He put the rest of the fishing gear in the trunk, too. In the front seat, he tossed the knapsack, and then he arranged the fishing poles in the back seat.

"Hop in, Champ!" We had our lunches of lukewarm Coke, Fritos, and PB&Js in the car on the ride back to the house, while I gave a recap of every bream I'd caught.

"Do you remember that one, Dad, that took my fourth worm and ran to the middle of the…?"

At home, Dad told me to dump the worms back in the garden. While I was doing that, he carried the bucket of fish to the backyard picnic table under the maple tree. Then he carried a scrap piece of plywood to the table, while dragging the garden hose with a nozzle behind. I was waiting at the picnic table when he came back around with a shovel, sharp knife, fish scaler, and a big plastic bowl.

"Jump down, Champ." As I did, he wet the table and board with the hose and took the fish from the bucket, sliding them off the stringer onto the table. The bucket, he sat on the bench next to the plywood.

"Champ, today you just get to watch, but in short time this is going to be your job, understand?"

"Yes, sir." I had my hind-end up on the table, mopping up some water with the seat of my pants, watching every move he made. First, he took the fish scaler and scraped the scales from each fish. There were thirteen bream. Scales flipped around everywhere, some even got in our hair! Second, he cut a semi-circle around the pectoral fin, toward the head before cutting the head off. He put the heads in the five-gallon bucket beside him.

I thought, *This isn't girl stuff, for sure!*

Third, he ran his thumb in the body cavity to remove the guts, which he put in the bucket, too. Last, he rinsed each fish with the garden hose and put the cleaned fish in the big plastic bowl.

"Did you see how that worked, Champ?"

"Yes, sir."

"Now, take these fish guts and bury them at least a foot deep in the garden. I'll take these fish and knife to your mother. When you're done with that, wash down the table and bucket, and put the plywood and hose up, OK?"

"Yes, sir."

"Be sure to turn the water off, too."

By the time I finished, Dad had already put the rest of the fishing tackle away. He was busy doing something so I watched TV, drifting off quickly. Mom woke me up for supper.

Mom had put most of a bag of corn meal in a paper sack, then she'd drop in three or four fish at a time, she'd shake the bag until the corn meal covered the fish. She eased them into a cast-iron pot, half-filled with hot peanut oil, cooking them until they floated up, golden brown. With tongs, she put them on an oblong platter, layered in a few sheets of newspaper with a top layer of paper towels. On the side, she made French fries, coleslaw, and home-canned green beans. It was a heavenly smell.

We held hands as Dad said grace. I was happy he didn't go into a long prayer. After *Amen*, my hand shot to the fish platter. I grabbed the top fish, fingers telling me it was the last one out of the hot oil.

As I juggled it back to my plate, Dad said, "Hot, Champ?"

"Yes, sir, but I just couldn't wait!"

"Honey, eat it slowly, so you won't choke on a bone," Mom told me. I watched and did as Dad did. He used his fork to work along the backbone, and then flipped one side of the fish over to expose the meat. Steam rose off the fish. He picked the meat away from the skin. They were so delicious. I ate three fish. I believed every piece I ate I'd caught. I told Mom about the whole day at the lake, even told her about the bird painting me.

"For goodness sake, go take a bath!" Mom said, making a face.

"Good night, Dad."

"Good night, Champ."

"Thanks for taking me fishing today."

"We'll do it again soon, OK?"

"Sounds good to me."

He didn't know it, but that first fishing step directed me on a long, joyful journey, which has enriched my life with adventure, experience, knowledge, friendship, and love.

Thanks again, Dad. Today is my forty-seventh birthday and the thrill of fishing has lasted, getting better with each new trip. The memory of that first Push-Button and my dad's fishing lessons will be a treasure in my mind, always.

Chapter 2 - Isthmus?

"Champ, you ready to go fishing?" Dad was shaking me awake. It was still dark outside. Six o'clock came early. Mom and Dad put me to bed on time, but he didn't know I flounced there until after two o'clock, thinking about going fishing. My head just wouldn't turn off. In the morning, my head was still half-asleep, but I didn't complain.

Mom had laid out some fishing clothes for me the night before. I slipped into my most worn out pair of shorts, pulled that ratty T-shirt over my head, stuck my feet in blue-ringed athletic socks, then worked my feet into the old funky Chuck Taylor's that needed a retread about 3,000 miles ago. I took a moment to fold the socks down below my calves. I always felt goofy with socks riding up to my knees.

I stumbled to the bathroom, splashed water on my face, looked in the mirror, and just put a ball cap over my uncombed hair. The rest of the bathroom business I hustled through.

"I made you an egg sandwich, Champ. It's in the car with a cup of OJ," Dad told me as I came in the kitchen.

"What about the fishing gear?" It was missing from the living room where we put it by the front door. Last night I helped Dad rig the poles. Well, actually, I went through every gizmo in his tackle box, asking the what, how, and when, with each trinket.

"I loaded everything before I got you up," Dad said.

In the front seat of the car, my head fit just underneath the half dozen, rod tips jutting over the backrest. I ate the egg sandwich and drank

16

the OJ en route.

"What do you think we'll catch today?"

"Well, I'd like to bring home a mess of catfish, but we might tangle with a bream or big carp along the way." He went on talking, but my eyelids fell down shortly after I downed breakfast.

I woke when Dad opened the car door. Right in front of the windshield was a big lake. I quickly hopped out and looked all around. Day was breaking. Four of the brightest stars still dotted the sky, slowly washing away as the sun rose. Wisps of pink, cotton candy clouds strung along the skyline, with streams of bright sunshine vaulting upwards from the east, silhouetting the trees while bathing their tops in brilliance along the western shore. I was caught up in the wonder. It was like God coming. A light onshore wind brought the odor of the lake to me, smelling good and natural. I could smell the sweet hint of a plant in bloom. It was the beginning of a perfect, early summer day.

"Want to give me a hand with this?" Dad popped off and brought me back to reality. He had already laid out six fishing poles against the front of the car. He pulled his tackle box, worm bucket, knapsack with our lunches, and a five-gallon bucket half-filled with stuff out of the trunk, putting it all on the ground behind the car. He placed the worm bucket inside the five-gallon bucket, and slung the knapsack over one shoulder.

"Champ, will you grab the tackle box and a couple of those fishing poles?" He picked up the bucket full of stuff and met me at the front of the car where the rods were.

"Why do we have so many fishing rods, Dad?"

"I'm going to show you when we get to the fishing spot."

"Which way is the spot?" He started down a dirt path through some scrubby bushes, me following behind.

"Put the fishing poles over your shoulder, son, so the tips won't get hung up and break off in the bushes." I'm glad he said that because I was coming close to catching the tips in the bushes, while looking at everything, not paying attention. I thought he must have eyes in the back of his head. We hiked a quarter mile. From what I could see, the path went down the middle of a spit of land that separated the main lake from a small bay to my right. The path dead-ended on a point. At the point,

17

there was a thin cut of flowing water connecting the main lake to the small bay behind. On the far side of the bay, a canal came in. Looking up the canal from the point, it meandered and then turned out of sight. A sloping, sandy beach went all around the point.

Dad sat the bucket down, slid the knapsack off his shoulder, and spread the poles out so they leaned individually against some bushes. I sat the tackle box down and handed him the rods I carried. He leaned them against a bush as well.

"Champ, do you know what an isthmus is?"

"Sure, *this mus* be the place we're going to fish." Dad broke into laughter until his eyes watered. He stumbled over to blank-faced me, squatted down, put his arms around me, drew me close and rolled back in the grass still laughing.

"I love you, son." We sat up on the grass together enjoying the moment. "Great answer, but let me tell you what an isthmus is." He spelled it out for me, then took a stick and drew a map on the ground, starting with where we were.

"This is the point of land we're sitting on," pointing to the map with the stick. "A narrow neck of land that connects two larger pieces of land is called an isthmus. This really isn't an isthmus now, but it once was before the water eroded this channel on the end. I still call it an isthmus because I remember when."

Dad jumped up, saying, "Let's get ready to fish." He took his pocketknife out and cut a pencil-sized limb from a weeping willow tree. He whittled it until all that remained was an eighteen-inch stick with two trimmed branches forming a Y on the thin ends. He whittled six of those sticks. At the waterline, he shoved three of the sticks in the sand, fat end down, facing the main lake. One stick faced the left side of the channel toward the main lake at the end of the point. He stuck one at the end of the point directly at the cut. He angled one stick toward the bayside of the point on the right. The sticks were evenly spaced about fifteen to twenty feet apart.

Dad called to me, "Help get the fishing poles." There were five medium, light spinning rod outfits and my push-button Zebco® Dad gave me a year or so ago. I grabbed two poles, Dad got the rest, and we walked back to the shore. Working left to right, Dad put the butt of the fishing rod in the sand and leaned the pole against the stick, so that the pole rested in the crotch of the little branches.

"Champ, notice that you lean the poles so the reel doesn't touch the ground," Dad said. He continued along, setting a pole in each of the sticks. He placed my push-button on the left side toward the main lake on the point.

We went back and brought the big bucket of stuff, knapsack, and tackle box, down to the shore. Dad had us set up midway between the two end poles; we could see each fishing pole from that vantage point. He pulled the worm bucket out of the big bucket and flipped it upside down. Then he took out a can of corn and a can opener and cut the lid off, putting the lid in the big bucket. We walked down to the left fishing pole, the one farthest away.

"Hold out your hands, Champ." As I did, he dumped some corn in my cupped hands; the juice ran through my fingers. He shook some corn into his right hand and tossed it as far as he could into the lake.

"Toss a little here and there, son, as we walk the bank." Dad, with his right hand, and me with my left, tossed corn in the lake all the way to the last fishing pole.

"Fish-call, Dad?"

"You bet, Champ; it costs pennies, takes but a moment to do, won't ever hurt and may just lure in the catch of a lifetime!" Dad said excitedly.

We returned to base camp. Dad tossed the empty corn can into the five-gallon bucket. Going back to the lake, we squatted at the water's edge and washed our hands.

Dad pulled out a plastic bag full of hotdogs, pre-cut into thirds. He picked out one section, closed the bag, and walked down to the last fishing pole on the left as I followed behind him.

Dad stopped, saying, "Hold this hotdog for me, and I'll take a moment to explain the fishing rig."

Even though it would seem I was just interested in catching fish, I really liked it when Dad took time to explain things to me. I learned a lot when I listened, right from the first time he started teaching.

"Notice where I secured the hook, Champ."

"You hooked it on the pole hoop; I mean on the rod eye," I blurted. He drew my attention closer, pointing out that he had hooked it secure to

19

the eye-brace, not the eye itself.

"Never secure a hook to the eye because the hook can chip or burr the inside of the eye, and that tiny bit of damage can shave the line, eventually causing it to break."

He released line tension, by quickly opening and closing the bail, loosening the line, freeing the hook from the eye brace.

"This is a simple slip rig," he continued. He passed the ten-pound, test main line through the ring of a 3/8 oz. bell sinker, then tied it to a barrel swivel with an improved clinch knot. The swivel keeps the sinker from sliding all the way to the hook. He tied a two-foot section of thirty-pound, test leader to the other side of the swivel. At the end of the leader, a 1/0 long shank, offset hook was tied.

"A catfish, or any fish for that matter, is apt to drop the bait if it feels the resistance of the sinker. The sinker isn't fixed to the line with this rig. The fishing line passes through the sinker so the fish doesn't feel the weight at all." He demonstrated that on the shore by putting the rig on the sand and telling me to pull on the hook. "Did you feel the sinker?"

"No, sir," I replied.

Dad asked me for the piece of hotdog. I watched as he inserted the point of the hook down the center of the link until it met the bend of the hook out the side of the wiener, pulling enough of the hook out, embedding the point in the other center end of the hotdog. Next, he held the hotdog in one hand and gently pulled the leader away, tightening up the bait on the hook.

"Remember how I showed you, and toss this toward the middle of the lake." I'd been practicing in the yard with the spinning rod, so I flipped the bail over after pinching the line against the rod with my forefinger. Slowly I lowered the rod behind my shoulder and with quick motion, I snapped the rod forward, releasing the line about the one o'clock position. The sinker went ten yards and hit the water. The hotdog landed an additional fifty feet further out.

"Nice try, but we have to keep the bait and hook together so the fish get the point, if you get my point," Dad said. I reeled in, Dad got another hotdog section. "This time, toss it out a little more softly, Champ." The second time was the charm.

With patience, Dad said, "Now, set the rod in the forked stick like I showed you." I did, making sure the reel didn't touch the ground. He came behind me, flipped the bail open, and let out just enough line so that a loose swag of line bowed down from the rod tip. Then, at the reel, he pulled some line to the ground and covered it with a small scoop of sand, leaving the bail open.

"What's that all about, Dad?" He told me that when a fish picks up the bait it would take the line, making the line straight from the tip to where it enters the water. When the slack line is gone, more line can run out by pulling the line free from the sand. The fish will feel very little resistance as it enjoys its last meal. If the bail was closed, a big fish could drag the rod and reel into the lake before you could get to it. *He's pretty smart*, I thought.

"But what would happen if all the line was pulled from the reel and we didn't notice?" I asked.

"If you don't pay good enough attention, you lose the rod or go for a swim," Dad smiled.

With the next pole, Dad just formed a two-inch cube of Velveeta cheese around the hook and I let it fly. We began to set up the rest of the poles.

On the third pole, he threaded kernels of corn on the hook until the corn ran up and covered the hook eye. I reared back and sent that one to the moon!

Pole number four, my push-button, was baited with three fat earthworms and cast to the lakeside of the channel. I picked the earthworm bait for my push-button rod.

At the fifth pole, I thought Dad had cut his finger. Blood was running between his fingers dripping from his hand.

"Dad, are you OK?" He opened his hand to show me a bloody chicken liver.

"It looks ugly, but the catfish will follow that blood trail to the bait." He hooked the liver on three times and I flipped it to the middle of the channel. He rinsed his hands off in the water.

For the last pole, Dad brought a Tupperware bowl of homemade fish bait we made the night before. It was a mixture of flour, cinnamon, sugar, and water to make dough. It came out stiff, yet sticky, and it smelled like something from the breakfast table.

If I were a fish, I'd eat that, I thought. Dad formed a golf ball sized dough ball around the hook. I pitched it in the bay as soon as he was done.

All the rods were fishing, and it was a waiting game from there on out. Dad sat on the five-gallon bucket, placing the worm bucket in its shadow, so the worms would stay cool and comfortable. I sat on the tackle box. Our heads turned left and right, watching the poles for a bite. From a distance, we looked like we were watching a slow motion tennis match. We talked about a lot of things.

My curiosity got the best of me and I asked, "On this whole big lake, why did you pick here to fish, Dad?"

"Habitat diversity, Champ." He pointed out that water moved out of the small bay, past the point and into the lake. "The neck of land forces the water to move through a narrow channel and the moving water carries baitfish with it. That means a lot of fish food in a small area, so fish stage-up around and in areas like this to get an easy meal. Furthermore, even slow moving water cuts into the bottom over time, making deep holes. Sometimes fish move into deeper water because it's a little warmer or cooler making them more comfortable. In a nutshell, places like this offer many opportunities to find the fish without having to move around."

"Look at the line on my push-button, Dad!

"You're right; a fish is taking the bait. See the line starting to straighten out." He said that as we ran for the pole.

"What should I do, Dad?"

"Keep the rod tip low to the water as you pick up the pole, turn the handle to click it in gear, and wait for him to pull the line tight, then set the hook."

"That's a lot of stuff to do—" I had the rod in my hand when the line began to tumble out the front of my push-button.

"Champ, click it in gear!" I turned the handle a quarter-turn, engaging the reel. Excitement had strengthened my grip; otherwise, the push-button would have been snatched from my hands. I held the rod up and commenced reeling. The rod tip was yanked down, pointed to the lake.

"What's that noise…? What's that noise the reel is making?" The reel was making a ratcheting sound. I looked at the reel, noticing that the line was going in the opposite direction. Somehow, I was reeling out instead of in! I was screwing up the biggest fish of my life! The faster the line reeled out, the higher the pitch of the reel.

"It's the drag, Champ, it's the reel drag. When you hear the noise, stop reeling, when you don't hear the noise, reel smoothly. Trust me; I'll explain later." The reel surprising me, too much information, a big fish, all at the same time, had my mind spinning. My body determined that my mind was no longer capable of handling the situation! My body took over, becoming a reel monkey to the background music of *Flight of the Bumblebee.*

God must have wanted me to have that fish because it was nothing short of a miracle when it wallowed up close enough for Dad to step in shin-deep with one foot to get the line and pull the fish up on shore. He dragged it up high on the beach and hugged me.

I grabbed his neck and blared in his ear "That's the biggest fish of my life; let's go show Mom!"

The fish was a four and a half-pound channel catfish that made the mistake of craving worms for breakfast that morning. Dad put the fish on a stringer, tossed it in the lake, and tied the stringer to a peg of good driftwood he had driven into the sand.

During the excitement, Dad continued to scan the other fishing rods for a bite, but nothing had happened.

"Time to re-group," he said, as he reeled in the left rod, the one most distant from the point. The hotdog bait was still in good shape. He pulled up the forked stick and pushed it back in the sand right next to the stick that held my push-button. Effortlessly, he tossed the bait in the lake close to where the water from the channel flowed.

"Hey, you're cheating," I quipped.

"No, Champ, I'm sighting-in our fishing rifle. The wide pattern of fishing poles we started out with were set that way so the fish could tell us where they were hiding. Were they cruising the open flats in the lake, near the channel, in the channel, or in the bay? Though one fish doesn't indicate much, at least, it is something to go on," Dad was explaining as he pointed here and there in the lake, doing some *show and tell* fishing.

"We need to look at your push-button and go over the function of a reel drag," he said while sitting on the five-gallon bucket, holding my little push-button in his hands. "Look at the fishing line." Horribly curled up, it was almost in knots. "Let's take care of this situation first, OK?"

He cut the line above the swivel at the knot with his pocketknife. The sinker, he put in his pocket. The hook, leader, and swivel remained as one piece, which he laid straight at the base of the bucket he sat on. Handing me my rod, he said, "Push the button for me," as he began hand-stripping the kinky line from the reel until the line came out smooth. A nip with the knife and the bad line was gone, wadded up, and put in the five-gallon bucket.

"Dad, the hotdog pole!" I yelled.

Dad *hot walked* to the pole. I watched as he, in one single motion, picked up the pole by raising the reel from the ground while keeping the rod tip in the same position, down. He flipped the bail closed, sweeping the rod straight overhead when the line came taut. The rod tip arched downward and the reel drag chirped a bit while Dad was playing the fish in. Halfway in, the fish got mad, making the line squeal off the reel. Not reeling, he kept his rod at the one o'clock position, occasionally dipping his rod hand when the fish surged. When the reel stopped squealing, he started pumping the fish back in by quickly reeling as he lowered the pole to where it was horizontal to the ground, then he would gently raise, not jerk, the pole back to the one o'clock position and start over. At no time did he allow slack in the line. He was just like the TV guys, but this was real! It was exciting to watch it live. In a few minutes, Dad had a two to three pound catfish flopping around at his feet.

"Let me show you something, Champ."

I put the push-button down butt first into the five-gallon bucket before running over to him.

"These catfish have three sharp spines on them; one fin on the top and one fin on each side." He pointed out the dorsal and two pectoral fins. "Some people use a rag or glove to handle them, but if you take your time and do it right, you can use your bare hand." Dad held the fish up so it dangled from the fishing line; then he carefully wrapped his other hand around the tail below the spines. At first, the fish squirmed and rolled around, but in seconds, the fish was used to his touch and calmed down.

"You have to come from the belly-side so as to avoid the top spine,"

Dad said. With that, he slipped his hand gently up the fish to where one pectoral fin was between his forefinger and middle finger, and the other fin was behind his thumb. He clutched the fish firmly but far from a bear grip. A downward twist and the hook came free with a popping sound.

"Champ, bait my pole with a hotdog and toss it out where it was, please. I'll put this fish on the stringer." We met back at the five-gallon bucket where Dad quickly took the sinker from his pocket, threaded it on the line, tied the swivel back on, and said, "Now, let's finish our talk about the reel drag."

He explained to me that the reel drag is a clutch that allows line to slip from the reel when there is a certain amount of pressure on the fishing line. The purpose is to give line from the reel before the line breaks from the force of the fish. It is an adjustable system regulated by turning a small wheel on the reel. Backwards makes it more slippery, forward makes the drag firm. Dad did a *show and tell* for me. He explained that you can catch big fish on light line because of the reel drag.

After the lesson, he baited the hook with three good worms saying, "Here you go; you know where to cast it."

As I walked down to make the cast, the line on the hotdog pole twitched.

"Dad, come quick, the hotdog is working again." The bait had been out there just five minutes. I cast out my push-button as Dad walked over to the hotdog pole.

"You get it, son."

"Really?" I did just as Dad did, but it took a couple minutes before the line shot straight. I set the hook with an up-sweep of the rod. The battle didn't take long, because the fish didn't take any drag. Dad was taking off a two pound catfish when he noticed the cinnamon dough pole was having line walking off to the bay.

"Champ, go get the pole across the point!" I raced up the beach, took a short cut across the point, hopped down the beach on the other side, and picked up the rod. Two seconds after flipping the bail over, I swept the rod up and set off a rocket. Line sang off the reel, startling me how fast line was coming off the spool.

"DAD!" I could see some of the bare spool when the line stopped going out. I began pumping and reeling the fish like I saw Dad do. The reel job was slow; the fish felt so heavy! Dad came up as I was making progress.

"Keep up the good work, looks to be a big one."

"Yeah, Dad, this is the biggest one so far."

Halfway in, the fish took a spirited run back into the bay. I held the rod up and let the line peel off the spool.

"Great job, Champ!" That comment made me feel real good. Several long minutes later the fish was zig-zagging up and down the shore.

"It's a big carp; hang in there," Dad yelled. I was getting tuckered out. Finally, Dad was able to take the line, lead the fish up on the beach, and grab it. There, standing before Dad was the greatest fisherman in the world!

Dad picked up the fish from underneath the gill plate and big belly, stating, "This fish must go ten or twelve pounds."

I thought it was well over twenty pounds, but I was new to the game asking, "Is that a world record?"

"No, but it's still a good fish." Dad told me to run over to the tackle box and bring the camera back. He hardly blinked before I returned. After briefly explaining the how-to-hold-the-fish instructions, there was an ear-to-ear smile in front of the camera.

"We're going to let this one go, Champ."

"What are you saying, Dad, this fish is huge."

"We have got to show Mom!" He pointed out the set of sucker lips on the fish and told me that carp are bottom feeders. The bay was shallow, and at the time, didn't have much water exchange, he didn't want to eat a carp out of that water. I put the carp in the water like putting a baby to bed. At that moment I had mixed emotions, but one strong swish of the tail, splashed water all over my face and the moment was over.

"Dad, the corn pole!" The rod was whipping up and down. Dad took off like a criminal with a police K-9 behind him. Just before he got there, the rod hopped up in the air and arrowed into the lake. Dad ran out of land, but that didn't stop him, into the lake, he went. In a semi-dive, he came up with the butt of the rod in one hand in a great spray of water. Dad followed the fish out in water up to his thighs.

26

"Champ, get the push-button!" That command snapped me out of his action movie. I got to the push-button and fought a two-pound catfish in but never took my eyes off Dad. He had gained control of the situation. Fighting the fish, while sloshing back to shore, he was in a real fish war. I had dragged my fish back to base camp and met him at the water's edge. He handed me his wallet and I stuck it in my underwear.

"Watch out, son," he said, signaling to back away. He used his pole to sweep the fish on shore. His catfish could eat my catfish.

"Hold the pole, Champ." He grabbed the fish with both hands, carried it up the beach, and dropped it in the sand near the five-gallon bucket. Plopping down on the bucket, he gasped, "Please, get me a soda out of the knapsack, son." Back in a flash, I opened it for him. "I almost lost that one."

"Yeah, Dad, the fishing pole was in the lake!"

"I was talking about the fish, son."

"Yeah, me too," I faked the right response.

"How big is that fish, Dad?" He looked at it hard for a spell, taking a slug from his soda pop. "A good fifteen-pounds, if it's an ounce." For the next ten minutes, he drip-dried while I gave him the replay as the fish film rolled in my mind.

Dad looked at his watch, realizing the battery got wet. "Champ, I don't know what time it is, but what say we give the fish our bait, except for the worms, gather up our belongings, and eat lunch in the car on the way back home?"

With the knapsack across his shoulder, Dad had four fishing poles, the five-gallon bucket with the worm bucket in one hand, and the stringer of fish in the other hand. I had the tackle box and a couple of poles. I walked behind him up the dirt path. I thought how it had been an exciting morning, watching that big catfish tail kick up dust as we went along. It was a morning I'll never forget.

In the car, I told him, "I can't wait to tell Mom about you going in the lake and catching that big catfish. I can tell her, right?"

"Sure, but you have to tell her about your giant carp, too."

"Oh, I'm going to tell her everything, do you want another peanut butter sandwich?" A short time later, the car hardly came to rest in the drive before I hopped out and ran in the front door of the house.

"Mom, Mom, come see what we got!" I ran out the garage door. The shovel hung on a wall nail; I grabbed it off in flight. I passed Dad on the side of the house as he was taking the fish out to the picnic table to clean them. On the top of the bucket, Dad had laid the worm bucket. I picked it off the top and carried, it like a football, to the garden. Worms are one thing you can bury and not feel bad about. While in the garden, I dug an extra hole for the fish carcasses.

In the shade of the maple tree, Dad had the scrap of plywood, garden hose, big plastic bowl, knife and pliers ready on the picnic table. Pliers? I'd find out about that after getting Mom. I ran square into her when I cornered the house. She stopped me with a hug.

"I wanted you to see the fish before Dad got hold of them!"

"Sugar, that's what I was coming to see. I heard you when you raced through the house. Why are your father's clothes damp?"

"He ran into the lake like an elephant, Mom. You should have been there. Come on!"

"Honey, why are your clothes wet?" Mom asked.

He started, "Well—"

I interrupted, "Here's your wallet." I reached down the front of my shorts and pulled it out of my underwear. That set the stage for a funny recap.

Dad began cleaning fish, starting with the smallest, as we spun stories for Mom. We were dragon-slayers returning to the queen's court with tales of battle for her amusement.

"Watch closely, Champ." Dad, using his sharpest knife, slit the skin all the way around the catfish head. The fish was still alive. It flipped occasionally. I had some difficulty watching, but I understood that the fish had to die for us to eat. It made me feel good that Dad had thrown good fish back to live on once we had enough to eat.

He grabbed the head and worked his way around the cut, using the pliers to roll a short flap of skin away from the meat. He then got a good grip on the head with his hand and the roll of skin beside the dorsal fin with the pliers and forcibly pulled the skin down to the tail. It was like taking off a wet T-shirt. In one smooth motion the catfish was naked. Dad took a huge knife to lop the head off. Using a small knife, he cut the belly open by inserting it first in the poop hole, then running it forward.

28

With his fingers, he pulled the guts out. Skin, head, and guts went in the five-gallon bucket. Dad placed it in the big plastic bowl after rinsing the body with hose water.

After all five fish were dressed, Mom took the fish in the house, and Dad cleaned up the picnic table area. I buried the guts and stuff in the garden and rinsed the bucket out.

Years later, I was a teenager in love. One Friday evening, I drove a young lady down to the lake to watch the sun set. It had been such a long time since I had been there. I thought the shoreline might have houses on it by then. Our area was in the midst of a development boom. I was happy to see the lake as I remembered. We got out and walked down the dirt path to the point, hand in hand. At the end of the path we stopped. She was prattling on while I was looking out on the lake, re-winding the mental film of my dad running down a catfish with a fishing pole attached to it.

"What are you looking at? The sunset is over here."

I turned and noticed something I had overlooked, though I had fished there many times since Dad and I first came. There were six big willow bushes growing at the water's edge. Two bushes faced the main lake, twenty feet apart. One bush was growing to the right of the point toward the bay. One bush overhung the water at the end of the point. In addition, two bushes grew, side by side, on the left of the point toward the channel where the catfish are.

Chapter 3 - My Pond

In the cover of darkness, our headlights poked a hole down a short, pure sand passage that for most was unknown; and those who passed before us would have just as soon it be forgotten. I got out of the car with a flashlight and walked the headlights into the black hole. I walked back toward the car, stopped short, and began to use the flashlight beam as a pointer. The U.S. Army had laid down segments of perforated, metal track to allow military vehicles movement across the deep soft sand. Wind-blown sand had covered much of the track and some sections were deep under the sand, caused by the weight of heavy vehicles. Jagged metal ends popped up here and there where heavier trucks had damaged the segment edges. My job was to help Dad keep the car on the track so we wouldn't be stuck and to avoid the sharp ragged metal edges to keep from popping a tire. The first part of the road was the worst. Once we crested the small hill in the middle, it was easier to coast down to an oak hammock where roots and moisture made the sand firm enough to drive on.

Sequestered under a low blanket of live oak branches and tucked in behind an ancient arrangement of sand dunes, the sunrise appeared, as if someone greater than us simply turned the dimmer up and things slowly began to illuminate. It didn't take us long to unpack our gear. We had three medium light spinning outfits and two canvas creels. The creels were identical with a multitude of pockets and pouches that were semi-organized with an assortment of lures and fishing paraphernalia. Armed like the platoons of soldiers that had rehearsed warfare amongst these dunes before us, we geared up to assault the fish.

The pond was just down a slope from where we parked. From our vantage point close to one end, you could see all the way across the width of the pond in the light of dawn. If you looked just right, you could see a reflection of light off the water at the far end. Vapor steamed a foot high off the pond, resembling a loose roll of cotton insulation, padding the surface. The pond was an oblong oval with a couple of small sandy points jutting out across from one another, roughly halfway along the length of the pond.

Once we got out from underneath the trees, there was a wide, well-rutted, sandy strip, obviously used as a course during maneuvers. The strip undulated left and right, making its way around the pond with many side trails coming in where two sand dunes dipped down together. Six or eight high struts across the strip got us to a sparse band of coarse clump grasses, scrub oaks, and individual mature pines that naturally fenced the pond. Swathes of young weeping willow trees rimmed much of the shoreline. Their limp branches draped over the water, the longest of which swept the surface in the faint breeze. Where the bank was a bit higher, a big pine and thickets of oaks grew to the water. Subtleties in elevation, sometimes less than a foot, made big changes in the vegetation. By taking notice of the vegetation at the water's edge, you could tell where the lake gently sloped verses where the bank dropped off to deeper water.

We were there in the midst of spring. The morning air still had crispness to it, yet the mid-day sun was strong enough to make shorts and a T-shirt most comfortable. I was dressed, waiting for such to occur. The air was infused with the fragrance of new growth. The kind of smell you get when your nose is close to a fresh garden salad—a salad with just a hint of pine—breathing tasted good.

Dad and I had developed a routine; he would start fishing his way around the pond to the right, and I would start fishing my way around the pond to the left. We would meet somewhere in the middle on the other side with a, "how'd you do?" Then we'd fish our way back around the pond together in the direction of whoever caught the most fish. We had our own quiet time, and we had shared time. It worked for us.

I always started fishing where rainwater had washed out a part between the willow trees in the near corner of the pond. I stepped in the gully away from the pond. Dad taught me to sneak up on water. It is heartbreaking to anxiously rush in to wet a line, and realize with a boil of water that your haste cost you an opportunity to tangle with a fine, eager fish that was waiting right there at the water's edge.

At the back of the gully, I crouched down, jabbed the butt of my spare rod into the sand with a Snagless Sally® tied on. The rod in hand had a small Pop-R. Top water fishing at the break of day has, and always will cause a restless sleep the night before. Here I was, living the moment that kept me awake longer than I wished. Fresh eight-pound line ran through the eyes of my rod. I greased the reel two days before the trip. I ran the hooks across a stone yesterday evening during final preparation.

While scoping the situation, I was hoping the puff of wind from right to left wouldn't make an impact on my cast. New growth had narrowed the free air space between the willow swaths. On the other hand, was I just jittery on the first cast? Hope, anticipation, and apprehension swarmed in my head as I tried to quell my nerves enough to make the cast, without having the fishing line so much as touch anything but clean, fresh air.

From a squat, I flipped my wrist forward. The Pop-R sailed backwards between the willows, trailing loose coils of line. I watched intently. My free hand cupped by the reel spool; line slapping my palm like a feather. A split second before the lure splashed down, I pushed my palm against the spool, stopping any more line from coming off and at the same time, straightening the line that was in the air without recoiling the lure. The line floated gently down, splitting the gap. It was the perfect cast. I was proud of myself. There is far more satisfaction in fishing than merely reeling in a fish.

Concentric circles rippled from the lure fifty feet from the rod tip. I let it rest on the surface until the ripples dissipated. The lure was in open water, next to nothing, floating over a sandy bottom. Four times, I softly frog swam the Pop-R five feet forward by holding the rod with the tip down and rhythmically flicking the tip while taking up the slack with the reel. Work it five feet and let the lure rest, the water still. One more frog swim and the lure came to rest fifteen feet from the bank.

Pinching the line between the thumb and forefinger and Jell-O jiggling the rod tip, I kept the lure stationery but caused it to vibrate like a nervous animal approaching a known ambush point. I stopped; the lure silenced. Long seconds passed. Glug... glug, the popper sounded. Two short, sharp wrist snaps forced the lure ten inches closer in two motions that had water spritzing forward from the concave face of the plug. A prolonged pause, then a subdued four-foot frog-swim brought the lure within ten feet of the sand. I vibrated the Pop-R five seconds or so and stopped. Spiritless, it sat atop the water. Slowly I pulled the lure another foot toward me, ending in a slight flick that sprinkled a few tiny drops of water from the face. I was ready to vibrate the lure again when a brick splash fell from underneath the plug.

I must have hypnotized myself with the lure's motion, because I didn't respond to the strike until the line yanked the rod in my hand. The fish set the hook itself. Hooked together, we both jumped in spasm upon realizing it. The bass vaulted in a cinematic brief tail-walk and shuttering headshake with its mouth agape, showing the Pop-R latched in the corner of his mouth. The flared gill plates flashed the brilliant red of the gills behind it with each head twist. Oddly, the belly-flop re-entry was naturally graceful. Before my eyes was a live replay of the slow motion film footage from every bass fishing TV program I'd ever seen on rainy Saturday mornings.

I played for the fish. The fish danced. The fish surged. I dipped. During two moments of stage fright, the fish ran for dark weed cover. I applied as much pressure as I could stomach to bring her back to the limelight. The torrid dance brought us closer to near exhaustion, the music slowed. The explosive moves were now alluring wiggles and flirtatious flips. The final note ended in a captivating, sliding embrace. In a lip lock, I held her up to the sun. Iridescent body scales scattered the low morning light. I cupped her motherly belly in my hand. Translucent fins, trimmed in black, were her lace. She dripped cool water. I looked into her eye. She looked back. She was beautiful. She gave me everything I'd dreamed of last night. Carefully, I laid her down in the pond. Her tail sashayed through my open fingers, taking her back where she belonged.

As I watched her swim away, I noticed something I hadn't seen from the back of the gully. There, just off the bank, in a foot and a half of water, was a sand saucer, sixteen inches in diameter. She was expecting and had helped make a nursery. I had invaded her nest with my Pop-R. She instinctively tried to kill the intruder like good mamas do.

I stood there, silently feeling good about my decision to give her back. She carried the future. She carried my future fun. I looked back at the nest and she was there, standing guard, in her foxhole.

I took off running through the deep sand to Dad. He wasn't far away. Panting, I said, "Let's not keep the pregnant ones! I just let a five-pound girl go. It felt great."

"I let a big one go already, too, Champ," Dad said.

"OK," I smiled, and ran back to my gear.

I picked up my two poles and creel and walked to the next clearing. As I did, I thought about what a great start to the day it was. A perfect cast, good work with the lure, a heart stopping strike, and picturesque moments with a big bass right off the cover of *Outdoor Life*. I had the best feelings going on inside of me, especially knowing I had given my girl freedom. She freed my spirit. Things come around full circle in life; sometimes you have to wait for it, but that day gratification was instant, thankfully, because I was too young to understand time.

My next stop was a pocket-sized slight up bump of sand between the willows on the near shore width of the pond. My feet felt the lumps of large roots from years ago, before my time where, perhaps, a big pine had been. It may have been destroyed with a lightning strike, and the roots had maintained the elevation stalling the invasion of willows. Regardless of whatever happened in the past, now it was a place to push through and get in a cast.

The casting spot was tight and I found myself draped in a spider's web of willow branches. Willow branches hung over the first three to four feet of bank. You couldn't get the angle to cast the lure so it ran parallel to the bank cover. It was a messy place to fish, but sometimes you could pick up a bass just by doing the best you could. In the past, I had tried an array of lures only frustrating myself with line tangles and lure hang-ups. A Snagless Sally® or Texas-rigged worms were the snag free options.

I decided to try a white Snagless Sally® with a gold spinner. It is exciting to watch this lure flashing just under the surface and then disappearing in the black hole of a bass's mouth. Fan casting from the left to the right, it took until the last cast to the far right, when a small buck bass turned the lights off on the golden spinner blade. A quick animated air dance and I was able to sweep the spring suitor through the veil of limbs. The hook popped out easily. He was back in the pond before actually knowing what happened.

I wanted another top water tussle before the sun got too high, making the top water action fade away like the shadows. There was another cloaked sand lump with limited casting space before the corner of the pond, but I skipped it. Just around the corner was one of my favorite spots to fish.

Forty feet around the corner of the pond stood a massive pine tree on a jut of compacted sand that stuck a dozen feet into the pond. Around the base of the pine was a light scramble of scrub oaks and smilax vines, which grew to the water's edge. On the northwest side of the pine was an opening two people could stand in. That spot had a lot of shade time. If you couldn't tell that by the dimness of light, you could certainly tell by the smell and feel of a carpet of damp moss under your feet. The odor would catch you on the approach. A clean, earthy aroma coming up from the ground that added to the outdoor experience more than I realized at the time, because to this day that fragrance takes me back, through the years, to that spot on this big earth.

Coming in through the shade, I didn't feel as strongly about keeping hidden. I came in slow and crouched a bit, but I didn't worry about throwing a shadow across the water.

I dropped my creel and laid my pole with the Snagless Sally® over it, such that the reel wouldn't get any sand in it, some five paces away from the opening. If there was an instrument that could measure the energy vibe coming off me when I stood in the opening, ready to flip that Pop-R into battle, it would be pegged on overload. The shadowed waters were an oily slick calm in the tiny cove. Out beyond the shadows, where the sun struck the water, bits and pieces of vapor snaked upward from the surface. The end of the pond, where I had just fished was now awash in sunlight. The willow leaves, flickering about in a puff of wind, strew sunbeams off their waxy surfaces. The scene, spiced with the flavor of the moss, was primordial.

I flung the Pop-R into the soup, slightly to my left from the ten o'clock position and several feet past the point where the big pine stood. The lure landed in the sun. The sound of the lure hitting the water, changed the mood. I let things get quiet again. A couple of frog-swims and the Pop-R was floating outside the point, close to the bank, five feet from where the shadow line fell. I Jell-O jiggled the lure in place and it looked like someone had slung a two-gallon bucket of water from the left side onto the plug. We were on! The fish and I connected. The bass put on a wildly energetic dance that had an unusual amount of airtime. I had my feet off the ground at times, as well. The fish wore itself out fighting air. The dance was fantastic to watch, but short-lived. It weighed about a pound and half to two pounds. I decided to put that boy on the stringer.

I fan-cast the entire cove with the Pop-R twice after that. Each cast had the same degree of hope and anticipation as the first cast. One cast, along the far right bank, came to a close with a sucking sound from the back end of the lure, followed by a slow angled descent toward open water. I set the hook on an overstuffed blue gill. The fish was a scrappy fighter, using the width of its body against me, no acrobatics to the fight, just a sub-surface, kiddie roller coaster ride. It weighed almost a pound and went on the stringer with my bass.

I had spent a little less than a half hour there, enjoying every minute. In that time, the sun had climbed well above the tree line and the shadows shrunk. The air temperature was comfortable as I collected my gear, the two fish, and moved on to the next spot.

The next spot was actually a collection of spots along a straight forty yard section of pond bank that had a perceptible rise in elevation. If you didn't notice the big one to two foot uplift, you would certainly notice that the willows were replaced with clump grasses and sparse, gangly scrub oaks along the bank. Furthermore, there was just a thin line of aquatic vegetation growing next to the shore before the sand bottom dropped to four to six feet of water. In the past, I hadn't caught many bass in this stretch. However, since you had to pass by it anyway, it was worth putting in some speed casting for blue gill as you went along.

The Pop-R had lost its magic in the full light of day, so I changed it out for a Beetle Spin® with a white body and red belly dot. That Beetle Spin®, the size and shape of a safety pin, sporting a tiny silver spinner blade, was a natural bream-killer, which was fantastic in this pond because of the natural balance. There were enough bass and catfish to keep the bream population from exploding into a million runts with at least a third of the bream caught worth keeping. It wasn't unusual to take a couple of bluegill at, or a bit more than, a pound.

By choosing to use the medium light spinning gear with eight-pound test line, I was able to cast the miniature lure a fair ways, opening up the blue gill action to me. Heavier tackle or bait casting gear was the equivalent of me walking across the sand in shackles. I had learned that the hard way on a previous trip. One broken line ago, and I thought, *It will never happen again.* I returned with heavy artillery spooled with twenty-pound test. What I got was a frustrating exercise drill around the pond, relearning to pick the right weapon for the job, which made the task a lot more fun.

Pitching the Beetle Spin® out parallel to the bank, it plopped down fifteen to twenty feet off the shore. I'd let it sink to the bottom, and then steadily reeled it at a pace that kept the flash of the blade just visible under the water. Small bream would fly in and knock the lure to one side or the other. Large blue gills simply consumed it. On light tackle, a blue gill is a spirited adversary. I picked up six quality blue gills and many throw backs in that stretch of sand bank before I found myself on a high point of land midway along the length of the pond. From that vantage, I could see Dad working the bank at the far end. We waved at each other.

On the point, I stood a good five feet above the pond on a bluntly triangular sand dune that gently sloped down away from me. The bank was steep; the water dropped off quickly. Inches above the water, a line of wiry bushes clung to the slope with their branches protruding a couple of feet over the pond. Atop the dune, a wild, low thicket of vegetation entangled my feet. If you took a moment to look at the vegetation, a strange growth pattern appeared. You could see how blowing sand groomed the plants back as the wind carried it up the dune.

From where I stood, I had historically caught very few fish, so I saved my casting time and walked down the slope to where the shore and the point joined. There was a small clearing where you could toss a bait, parallel to the wiry bushes going out to the point, then work to the far left down the length of the pond bank from the wedge shaped cove. I started to the right at the wire brush and fan-cast to the left using the Snagless Sally®. A buck bass picked off the lure halfway down. He was a good dancer, but small. Another larger buck bass took the bait on a random cast in the main lake, making my stringer.

I kept glancing to my left while I was fishing the cove. About the ten o'clock position, twenty-five yards down the shore, and thirty or so feet off the bank, a small, weathered fragment of a large stump protruded several inches above the surface. During a drought, I once saw the whole stump. It was perched on a hump of sand not much larger than the stump itself. Sand had eroded from under two sizable prop roots on both the right and left side. The big roots tapered into a snarl of smaller lure grabbing root branches. Except for when it was high and dry, I had always had a big fish encounter at the stump. I had to get there before Dad. A twinge of guilt hit me when I thought that, but I'd deal with it later.

Hot-footing my way to the clearing in front of the stump—I made the clearing myself—I cut the Beetle Spin ® off in stride, stuck it in a small creel pocket, fumbled around for a quarter ounce bullet sinker and worm hook. I had to stop to thread the bullet sinker on the line and tie on the hook. As I was looking down at the hole in the weight, I noticed a black coil by the trunk of a willow tree. When I looked at the coil, the middle opened white and hissed!

Crap! I was flash frozen to the warm sand with a humming bird heart rate, staring at a cottonmouth moccasin that was less than five feet from me. One more step and it would have bit me. *Now what? Do I slowly back away? Do I jump backwards? Do I use my fishing poles to scare the snake? Do I call for Dad? Do I kick sand at it and run? If I'm bitten, Mom's going to have a fit and never let us come back to fish.*

My thoughts ran amok; I thought on... *I'll have to use my shirt as a tourniquet to slow the flow of venom. Dad can help me around the pond to the car. He may have to carry me in the deep sand. We'll have to leave our fishing stuff somewhere in the sand. In the car, we can speed to post headquarters, and they'll issue an Army helicopter to fly me to a hospital where some Trapper John MD would give me anti-venom and save me. I'll have a cool scar I can show off the rest of my life!*

Then... the snake left. It crawled into the lake. Apparently, my fairytale story was even too much for the snake. Snakes don't tolerate nonsense.

In my race to fish, I had ignored Dad's warning to keep an eye out for snakes. The warming sun had brought them out for a spring sunbath. I was the fool that disrupted the snake's good time. To my left was a big patch of clump grass. I was still motionless as I scanned all around the base of the clump. It was clear. I pivoted about and peed all over it. It felt good. The pressure was gone!

Rooting through the main pouch, I pulled an eight inch June Bug colored Jelly Worm from a plastic bag and rigged it weedless, Texas-style. Quickly glancing left and right for snakes, I slowly rushed into the clearing in front of the stump. My entrance was announced with a boil of water three feet from the bank. I had just spooked a big sow bass propped up on a sand saucer nursery. Taking a deep breath, I realized I was still rattled from the snake, yet anxious to throw the worm toward the stump.

A plastic worm has probably caught more bass than any other lure, but there is something about seeing the strike of any fish. I went with the Snagless Sally® for the first series of casts. Launching the spinner out past the right side of the stump, I started slow reeling the moment the lure got wet. You could see it approaching the stump, wobbling as it came through the jumble of roots. Released from the roots, it flashed a couple more times until it went over where the sand dropped off. A black streak took it to the right. I set the hook. The bass vaulted like the picture on the cover of *Bassmaster Magazine.*

"Get 'em, Champ!" I heard Dad call out. Between the stump and me, it cut back left, digging deep at an angle to the bank. The head poked above the surface as it fought back toward me. In a crazed headshake, the fish tossed the Snagless Sally® limply into the pond. The fight was over. The fish's memory had lasted, obviously.

I caught two more fish off that stump. Both were keepers I put one on the stringer. Dad walked up on me with a nice stringer of bass and blue gill. We exchanged how things went on our individual march. I told him about the snake. He told me I did the right thing by not moving.

"Snakes naturally want to escape from danger. Standing still let him do what he wanted to do," Dad said. I shook my head up and down when needed, acting like that was my plan from the beginning. I didn't tell him about sprinkling on the grass afterwards.

"Look, son!" He pointed at a big mamma bass suspended over her nest. "Get your worm pole."

In an effort not to spook her off again, I slow motioned to my pole like a scene from an old Kung Fu movie. I could hear the background music in my head. Standing back away from the bank, I flipped the worm underhand, over the nest. She flinched at the noise, but didn't move away. I inched the worm into the nest, and let it lay dead center and watched. She swam backwards, tilted down, and picked up the worm in her mouth. I spastically jerked the pole up to set the hook only to hit Dad in the chest with the worm. Worse yet, I had to duck out of the way so it could hit him. Thud was the sound behind me.

"I'm sorry, are you OK?"

Dad was rubbing his chest when he said, "I'm fine, but you have to let her carry the bait off the nest before setting the hook." She was still there. I worked the worm to the same spot. She picked up the bait. I waited. She moved off the nest.

"Now, Dad?"

"Go ahead." I jerked and the worm shot between us like a bullet into some clump grass. Once I reeled it in, we saw the back third of the worm was gone. She wasn't eating the bait, but merely taking out the trash. We both tried everything we had, short of snagging, to catch her, but she wasn't interested in what we had to offer. She was on duty. You don't eat on duty. We left her alone.

We walked back the direction Dad had come from, pitching bait in here and there, just talking and walking. Dad made sure to show me where he had found a fish nest. He showed me a working wasp's nest. It was a big one dangling from a willow limb over the water. After we walked past it, I picked up a pinecone and threw it into the tree. I didn't hit the nest, but the disturbance caused a buzz of activity that sent Dad and I double-timing across some soft sand.

"Why'd you do that, Champ?" Dad asked breathlessly.

"I don't know. It was like my arm took over." We both laughed. The fish were coated in sand we had kicked up. At the next clearing, we rinsed them in the pond.

At the car, we took the fish off the stringers, putting them in a five-gallon bucket that was in the trunk. We split a big bottle of RC Cola Dad had on ice in a small cooler in the back seat. Dad shook the ice from the drink cooler onto the fish in the bucket. Except for the fishing poles, we put all our gear in the trunk and closed it. The fishing rods went in the car.

"Before we leave, Champ, let's spend a minute to police this area." The old soldier from yester-year—twenty years of service—needed to clean up behind some reckless recruits. The new soldiers had had a party and left a clutter of empty beer bottles/cans on and around a picnic table. We picked them up, even the big chunks of broken bottles, and put them in a fifty-five-gallon drum that was near the table. I didn't like having to pick up behind somebody, but it did look much better once we finished. It only took a few minutes to make things right. Dad was happier, though disappointed in the men who left their mess for others to pick up.

He told me, "A real soldier wouldn't do this." It was a hint for my lifetime.

On the way home, we stopped at a Burger Doodle and washed up in the restroom. Dad got us a hamburger, fries, and a Coke to go. I told Dad about the snake a couple more times, telling him not to mention it to Mom each time I brought it up. She'd get nervous over any snake and might throw a *momma-block* on Dad about fishing with me at the pond. She loved us so much, but she didn't need to know everything. It would be best to omit some trip details for everyone's good.

I cleaned the fish when we got home. Dad put away the fishing gear. We had fish that night for dinner. It was good. The best taste, for me, came from knowing we had released the best fish we caught back to the pond and not the kitchen.

There, in their pond, they spawned and live everlasting. As far as I know, her great-grand fish await my Pop-R. Fish are far more than food. Thirty some years have passed, and she, the one guarding her nest, still satisfies me. I remain content with the choice I made as a young man. I've made the same type of decisions during the years since. It is still good. I'm just as happy releasing a fish as when I ran across the sand to tell my father I let her go. Pure fishing satisfaction doesn't always end-up passing across the tongue.

41

Chapter 4 - My First Trophy Fish

"Come on, we're going to Aunt Quida's house!" Mom told me to my total surprise. It was a three-mile ride I didn't want to make. She didn't give me time to make an excuse why I couldn't go. In my opinion, listening to two women talk, about everything I didn't care anything about, would waste a gorgeous, summer afternoon. They could talk for hours, say goodbyes for half an hour in the doorway, go home, and then talk on the phone for an hour, or more, that evening. Don't get me wrong; I loved Uncle Russ and Aunt Quida and their daughters Cindy, Ann, Cathy, and Suzy. They had been friends since Dad and Russ were in the Army decades before my time. After Dad got out of the Army, he moved Mom and me to Virginia Beach, Virginia to be near to Uncle Russ, Aunt Quida, and the girls. They were as close as or closer than the family we left in West Virginia. Nonetheless, sitting around listening to two women talk was not something a young boy likes to do. Besides, Uncle Russ was at work and the girls were out, so it was just Mom, Aunt Quida, and I in the house. It didn't take long for me to become bored out of my mind.

I presently found myself outside, walking down a typical middle class neighborhood street, kicking a rock along with me. About a quarter mile from Aunt Quida's house, there was a small bridge that crossed over a canal three times the size of a good ditch. Heading for it, I am drawn to water like the proverbial moth to the flame.

One side of the bridge had a pedestrian walkway. A third of the way across, I stopped and popped my head over the railing. I noticed a beer can washed up against the rocks placed to prevent erosion around the bridge. It was making a soft, peaceful pinging sound. The brownish water slowly moved down stream, carrying with it a scattering of anything that would float, including some grass clippings, leaves, and a light peppering of trash blown into the water from here and there along the meandering stream. Tiny minnows flickered in wads around the rocks, looking for food.

I wondered if they would eat bread, so I walked back to Aunt Quida's house to get a couple slices of bread for the minnows. They gave me the remains of a loaf of bread in the sack. The ladies were so involved in conversion that they didn't even ask what I needed it for. With a "Sure, honey," they just handed it off. In less than a half hour, I was back looking at the minnows in the canal. I rubbed a slice of bread between my hands as Dad had shown me at the lake. Crumbs rained down upon the water. Three or four clumps of bread dropped down with the crumbs. In a minute, the minnows had gobbled up the crumbs. The miniscule pieces of bread would disappear in the minnows when they swam up. The big clumps were slowly floating away in the flow, rung with feeding minnows, like cows around a slow moving hay bail. I bent over to get another slice of bread and something caught the corner of my eye. I popped my head over the rail to see a ring of water where a clump of bread used to be. Half a slice of bread I rubbed between my hands, before hastily breaking the rest of it into four pieces and letting it fall in the water.

The crumbs disappeared right away. A wad of minnows were working over the biggest piece of bread when they all scattered away, only to come back in a few seconds. I watched closely and they scattered again and didn't come back. A big fish came up in front of the bread and slurped it off the surface! *Wow! What was that?* Breaking up two more slices of bread into random sized chunks, I tossed them on the water without making crumbs. I watched all the pieces at once. My head and eyes darted back and forth from one white ball of bread to the next, as if I was watching three tennis matches at the same time.

A fish came up behind one piece and slurped it down. I broke up the last three slices and put them in the water. In minutes, several large fish began feeding on the bread. Sometimes I could see almost the entire fish in the water. It was huge. Every one of them was ten pounds or better. I had found a mother lode of big fish. I couldn't believe so many big fish were available so close to my house, and nobody knew about them. Apparently, many people went over the bridge in a day's time, but nobody had the opportunity or inclination to look over the railing.

Ideas started flying around in my head. First thought; I needed to get back here immediately with a fishing pole and a loaf of bread. Big fish, so close to home, and I didn't need a boat I didn't have in the first place. I was Christmas morning excited.

How would I land the fish? The fish were too big to lift from the water up on the bridge, using just the fishing line. The line would break before the fish was out of the water. I ran around to where the bridge abutted land. It wasn't a mountain goat trail, but tricky. For a twelve-year-old boy, it wasn't bad. I quickly figured out a path to take and what rock to stand on to get the fish on land if things should happen as I planned. My mind was still a rush, figuring out the details, while riding back home with Mom, but I didn't mention what I was thinking about.

"Are we going over to Aunt Quida's today?" I asked Mom the next morning. She gave me a strange look to a question she thought I would never ask.

"No, we're going shopping together tomorrow," Mom said, and asked, "Why?"

"No reason, just wanted to know," I nonchalantly replied. That bit of information meant no free ride to the bridge, so I had to apply plan B, my bicycle. *I'll ride over this evening after supper.* Passing the math through my head, I figured I could hump it there in fifteen minutes or so.

***

"Did you taste it?" Dad asked, referring to supper.

"I guess I was real hungry. I'm going for a bike ride," I said as I headed out the garage door. Secretly, I had rigged a medium weight, spinning rod that afternoon for fishing from the bridge. Rigging consisted of tying a number four bait holder hook to the end of ten-pound test main line. I decided to use bait holder hooks, thinking the barbs on the back of the hook shank would better hold wet bread on the hook.

Mom's garage freezer was missing one loaf of wheat bread. I snitched it, stuffed it in my fishing creel, and set the creel in the sun to thaw the loaf all afternoon.

I thought holding a fishing pole in one hand while peddling, would be awkward travel, slowing me down. Something I didn't have time for, even though the summer days were long. So that afternoon I had tied the fishing pole along the horizontal bar between the seat and the handle bars; the reel hung just forward of the seat, and the rod tip rode above the front tire. I looked like Sir Lancelot on joust with the fishing pole jutting out the front of the bike. I didn't care what it looked like, because it worked great for me at the time. I believe we're all given a small invisible booklet of crazy idea tickets at the beginning of life, and one ticket may be pure genius, but we can't be too humble or ashamed to use the tickets in public in order to find the one that pays off. Think about it; somebody pulled a ticket that said "Pet Rock" and went for it.

The sound of the garage door closing was what I heard, after quickly grabbing the creel with the bread, hooks, bobbers, and other stuff already in it and hopping on the bike. Ten hard peddle pumps had the bike up to optimum cruise speed. I wove through the neighborhood streets, trying to guess the best crows-flight to the bridge. Twice, I found dead ends, but within fifteen minutes, I skidded to a stop at the foot of the bridge. I leaned the bike against the guardrail, hurriedly opened up the creel, took out the bag of bread, fingered two slices of bread from the bag, tore them to chunks, and tossed them in the water as chum. I next untied my fishing pole from the bike.

With hook in hand, I ripped the middle out of a slice of bread. I gently inserted the hook in the middle and lowered it over the railing. A gust of wind came from under the bridge, blowing the soft piece of bread off the hook into the canal. I ripped the middle out of another slice of bread, but this time, I kneaded a small piece of the center into dough and stuck the hook in the doughy part. I lowered it to the water, but in a matter of seconds, the bread became mushy. The hook sank through the middle, carrying with it a booger of dough. A fish skinned that piece of bread off the surface as I was bringing up my hook. That made a frustrating situation more frustrating to me. Now, I laugh thinking back; that bread not staying on a hook was a memorable frustration in my life. I didn't know how carefree I was. That was then.

I looked on the ground at the two rings of crust. It came to me. The crust is tougher than the middle. I took the corner of crust off one of the rings and inserted the hook flat in the corner so it ran through the crust twice. It held fast. I lowered it over the rail into the water, watching as minnows began to nip the edges. The hook hung from the bread corner. I pulled line from the reel, so the bread would free float naturally in the light current. A lazy V wake came from down current toward the bread. The minnows scattered as a pair of lips protruded above the surface. I yanked. The fish slurped the bread down. I untangled the hook from a patch of weeds around the guardrail. Frustration, coupled with anticipation, spiked with a touch of fear, lead to a premature hook set. I got the hook untangled, checked the line for nicks, and tore off another corner of crust. My hands were shaking, trying to pin the bread on the hook like Barney Fife looking for his bullet in his front shirt pocket. I managed to get bread on the hook with just a prick to my finger. The bait was back in the water with a taint of my blood.

"Brian, relax!" I said to myself aloud, while sucking the blood from my fingertip. I slung my head back and forth to see if anyone was around to cash in my crazy ticket. It was cool; there was nobody within earshot.

I watched my bread intensely. Minnows came around it. The current was slowly moving the bread downstream. Where the bank cut back from the rock riprap, a small eddy formed. My bait was doing slow laps around the faint vortex. I gingerly pulled on the line in an effort to move the bait out of the sluggish whirlpool. The bait was just out of the influence of the eddy when the hook pulled free. The bread floated five feet past the eddy when a set of lips sucked it down.

I walked out on the bridge an extra pace or two to set my next bait out a little further from the bank. That simple adjustment, might allow my bait to flow downstream, without the eddy drawing it in. Minnows gathered as it floated gently down the stream. The popping noise you get when your straw sucks the bottom out of thick milkshake came from directly under my bait. It was gone in a pop.

The fishing line, floating on the surface behind the bait twitched, and then shot down. The line tightened quickly. I don't remember if I helped by setting the hook or not, but I do remember the rod being bent double in my hands. The power of that fish was far more than I expected. Line peeled off the reel against a firm drag.

Calm down, calm down, I kept thinking to myself. This was the biggest and most powerful fish I had ever had strike my line in my life! Solo, ten feet above, and fifty feet away from the object of my desire, I was inventing bridge fishing on a need to figure out basis. A car passed by in the heat of my battle, but I didn't realize it until the horn tooted.

"Get 'em, son," a man yelled out the window. It broke my concentration. Strangely, I felt somewhat heroic, in an embarrassing way. In a blink, I was back to the fish at hand. The fish swam across the canal to the right, then stopped, and ran back to where it came from. Tense minutes passed with each give and take of the line. It took time, but I managed to work the fish to the bridge. The fish was giving its last efforts directly below me.

I have to get around the guardrail and down on the rocks to land this fish. Somehow, I needed to play out enough line to give me room to swing around the guardrail, while keeping just enough tension to hold the fish, but not so much to pull the fish against the rocks, where it would surely breakaway. Things were getting complicated! My mind was racing faster than my body could respond.

The fish surfaced semi-tilted to its belly, and lay cradled in slow moving brown water. *I won! I won!* I thought, as I was moving off the bridge toward the bank. However, with a headshake, the thin lip skin that had tethered the fish and I together tore, and the hook fell away. The fish wallowed off, exhausted. I stood in silence at the end of the bridge, my mind screaming. *Nooooo!* Nevertheless, it was over. The biggest fish of my life was gone. I had no words for my disappointment. Like the words that you search to say to a dear friend at a funeral, the silent, uncomfortable moment ends in a long wet-eyed hug. Crushed, I reminded myself it wasn't nearly that bad. I was young.

What did I do wrong? How could I have prevented that? What should I have done differently? There was no one there to get answers from; I had to figure it out on my own.

I decided to try casting from down on the rocks. From there, I wouldn't have to worry about making the trek down from the bridge. If I started where I needed to finish, it would eliminate a large part of the problem. It made sense, but it was near impossible to cast a quarter-slice of bread. It was like throwing a kite against the wind. It just wouldn't work.

In addition, I had the sensation that the fish were aware of my presence. The fish were accustomed to the car noises crossing over the bridge, but weren't used to a shadow figure next to them on shore. For some unknown reason, I felt unwelcome on the rocks. I trusted my little voice and left.

I needed to get the bread from the bridge, carried by the current to the fish. What would happen if I lowered the bread from the bridge then swung around the guardrail before the fish took the bait? When I tried it, however, a loop of line formed as I moved around the guardrail, down on the rocks. The line loop produced enough resistance to either usher the bait next to the rocks or pull the hook from the bread. That idea didn't work either.

I needed to fish from the bridge because it was the only way to be effective. When a fish was hooked, I had to manage my way quickly, around to the landing rocks, in the early part of the battle. That was when there was enough line out to let me swing around the guardrail.

The letdown taught me that if the fish was too close to the bridge, I had painted myself into a corner with fishing line. Nevertheless, would there be a next time? At least I had a game plan, if it happened.

I tore the centers out of three slices of bread. The big centerpieces, I broke into quarter-sized wafers and trickled them over the bridge to form a loose chum train. A big hunk of corner crust was the caboose, carrying the hook. I watched and waited, playing out line from the reel so the caboose kept up with the bread train in the sluggish current. The lead locomotive piece of bread made its way down the canal, carrying an entourage of minnows. The second piece of bread slipped down the canal with its following of minnows, as well. The third piece vanished off the top of the water, sucked up by a Mick Jagger set of lips. As was the fourth, fifth, sixth etc… the crust was the next in line. Rhythmically, on by one, they disappeared.

I flipped the bail over, letting the slack line play out before setting the hook with the upward sweep of the rod. The pole doubled over with an explosion in the middle of the canal. The fish bolted down current taking line, squealing the reel drag. Holding the rod high in the air, I hip-swung around the nearest part of guardrail like working a pommel horse in the gym, watching the fish as I went down the rocks. I stumbled when a rock the size and shape of a bowling ball rolled under my foot. Reflexes kicked in so fast I impressed myself, but I realized from there on I had to watch where I was going until I made it to the water's edge. Balancing on the rocks, I took up line when it was given to me, letting line go when the fish demanded. Twenty feet off the rocks the sowbelly got the first glimpse of me. It got scared, bolting straight down the canal for thirty some feet. The spool on the reel burned around. I touched the revolving spool with my index finger to assist the drag. It was the first time I had ever done that. Instead of fumbling with the knob on top of the spool to adjust the drag, I simply applied light pressure with my finger; pressure I could apply or take away at any time with a fine and infinite adjustment. I had learned how to do something important in fishing during a need to figure out situation. I learned how better to play a fish, using a spinning reel.

After a few minutes of easy give and take, the fish was worn out. Exhausted, lying on its side, cradled in a form-fitted, low lump of brown water close to the rocks. I was standing near my pot of gold, it was just out of reach. It was going to be a delicate situation getting the fish from the water without tumbling in myself. The rocks were far from a sandy spot on which to slide the fish up. I had to think about things before doing anything stupid. With my right side facing the water, I held the rod horizontally with the rod tip four feet directly over the fish. I squatted down, tilting the rod tip up and backwards, while pushing the rod away from me, as far as my left arm would reach. The fish slid across the surface of the water toward me. My right fingers gently slipped under the gill plate of a very tired fish. I stood up heaving a fifteen pound, plus, carp from the water.

It was awesome! I set the rod on the rocks and took my left hand to support the tail section. It was awesome. Armored in huge, thick, hard scales, and colored brilliant orange with brownish black trimmings, it was a beautiful specimen. The eye was a large white marble with a big black pupil. The fins were overly sturdy. The mouth was a reddish protruded toilet plunger that disturbingly, sucked at the raw air. I had to look away from the mouth to admire the rest of the fish. After thinking about it, I realized what I found hard to look at, the mouth. It did have form, and function for a fish that sucked up its food. A short straw for a mouth was the perfect feeding tool.

I held my first trophy fish, for me, and there was nobody there. Alone on the rocks below a bridge on a drainage canal, I was as proud of my fish as any of the saltwater guys I'd seen photographed at a marina with their citation fish. I thought about taking it home to show Mom and Dad, but that would have been an ordeal on a bicycle. There was no need to kill the fish anyway. I held the fish straight up and down with my right hand still under the gill plate and leaned it against my leg with the tail just touching the ground. It came up to my hip. I became excited at the thought of me saying, "and it was this long," while marking my hip with my finger. I bent over and put the fish back in the water. In a couple of seconds, it swam off in a lazy manner.

It was a perfect moment for reflection, but I was young and the only thing on my mind was getting back up on that bridge and getting another fish. That evening I caught two more carp that looked like brothers of the first fish. Twelve minutes before hard dusk, I pulled myself away from the bridge, readied my bike with my joisting rod, and peddled off to home.

I cruised into the driveway to find my dad finishing some yard work. He looked at my two-wheeled, rod-carrying contraption and smiled.

"What have you been doing?" he asked.

I hopped off the bike and answered, "I've been catching trophy worthy carp by Aunt Quida's house," with as much brazen inflection as I felt I could get away with.

"You got some big ol' carp, Champ?"

I answered John Wayne style in a twelve-year-old voice, "Yes, sir," then blathered on and on like Mom and Aunt Quida on the phone, telling Dad about the big fish and how I figured out how to catch it. He listened to things I ranted about three times as night fell on my recollections. He put his arm around me as we walked into the garage light.

"So what do you think about that, Dad?"

"I think you're growing up, Champ."

Chapter 5 - The Pier

The tires crackled over the sun bleached oyster shells that paved the parking lot. We could hear them crunch loudly because the four-fifty-five air conditioner completely stopped blowing when we turned in. Nowadays, most folks have never heard of the antiquated four-fifty-five AC, but back then it was standard on most all vehicles. You see, for the air conditioner to work, you had to roll down all four windows and have the car moving at fifty-five miles per hour or better. It would even style your hair as you went along.

Worn-out railroad ties delineated parking places in the oyster shell lot. Trucks and cars packed the front of the lot. As we rode by, I noticed many of the license plates were from out of state. I imagined those vehicles belonging to a small slice of the summer vacation crowd enjoying a day of fishing from the pier or head boats.

The back of the lot had plenty of empty spaces. We inched toward the back as the summer heat poured in the open windows like an invisible wave pushing out the air and bringing the faint odor of creosote from the railroad ties. Mr. Sullivan pulled in the first available spot. We couldn't wait to get out of that *rolling oven*. The sun reflected off the white shells, blinding us when we got out of the shadow of the car's interior. Sweat beaded up on our skin within the first exposed minute. In the next minute, it was running down our foreheads, the back of our necks, and forming a growing stain under our arms and in the middle of our T-shirts both front and back. It was a strangling heat; the kind that puts those wavy lines in your eyes.

"Well, boys, let's get unloaded," Mr. Sullivan said to Gilbert, his son, Johnny, a neighborhood friend, and me. He unlocked the trunk of his well-broken in, five-tone LTD. It popped open with an un-oiled creak. Inside the cavernous trunk were one small cooler, one large cooler, a five-gallon bucket with tackle and towels, and four small, dirty fishing rods with round reels covered in greasy dust and grit.

Mr. Sullivan grabbed all four poles, the five-gallon bucket, and started walking toward the front of the parking lot. He stopped, turned, and said, "Close the lid when you get the coolers out and hurry up."

It took two of us to lift the small cooler from the trunk. Gilbert and I sat it on the ground and opened it up. Inside were six half-gallon milk cartons, a plastic gallon jug of tea, four Styrofoam cups and what looked like peanut butter and jelly sandwiches stacked in a bread bag.

"What's with the milk?" I asked Gilbert.

"My dad saves the cartons and uses them to make blocks of ice in the garage freezer. He says it's better than buying ice," Gilbert replied.

I picked up one carton and said, "They're heavy."

"Yeah, I weighed one using my fishing scales once, and they weigh four pounds apiece," Gilbert said shyly.

"That's fifty pounds of ice," Johnny popped in.

"Not quite, but with the tea, sandwiches, and the cooler, it's pushing forty pounds," I said.

"What's in the big cooler?" Johnny asked. Gilbert and I heaved it out of the trunk and gravity took it to the ground in a hurry. We gave each other blank stares before raising the lid. Inside were two five-pound boxes of frozen squid, two small plastic bags of frozen shrimp, and twelve, stacked, milk cartons. Quick math brought the load to sixty-five pounds.

"Your dad wants us to carry all this on the pier?" Johnny asked, in disbelief.

"Why didn't we drop it off up front?" I asked.

"That's the way my dad is," Gilbert replied.

We formed a three-boy chain with coolers in between us. We'd hump it toward the pier for as long as the guy in the middle could last, then put down the load and shift one to the left, and continue with a new guy in the middle position. We were in sweat-soaked agony by the time we made it up to the pier house where Mr. Sullivan waited.

"What took you boys so long?" he said, turning away, smiling. He handed the man behind the counter a ten-dollar bill. The man gave him back four bucks and some change. I noticed the fare was a buck a head for us kids. I also noticed the wall of fishing tackle, the stacks of bait buckets, shelves randomly stocked with sun block, cheese and peanut butter crackers, T-shirts, cases of Vienna sausages, dusty bottles of hot sauce, big straw hats, cigars, candy bars, and other stuff. Everything looked like it had been hanging there for a long time. The dust was a dead giveaway. Along one wall was a good-sized refrigerated case with a small section of soft drinks and a big section of beer, mostly Budweiser in cans. One of the bottom shelves had empty beer flats filled with plastic bags labeled, Bloodworms. You could see the red worms through the clear plastic, wadded up in a creepy ball. Every free space on the walls, posts, shelves, and counters had faded photographs of people with fish, taped or thumb tacked to it. I kept going from one photo to the next, until I was interrupted.

"Brian, the man needs to stamp your hand with a pier pass," blurted Mr. Sullivan. The man had stamped the back of everyone else's left hand with a smiley face symbol. When I raised my hand to be stamped by the unshaven, apishly hairy, fat man in a skintight, used-to-be white tank top, I was shook by the smell of body odor, strong cigarettes, and stale beer. I looked at him as he was stamping my hand; his mouth was agape. The teeth he had left hung down from his gums like dried kernels of rotten corn. Strings of elastic spittle connected the top and lower jaw in the corners of his mouth.

"There you go, kid." I took off for the door!

Gilbert and Johnny were already on the outside post of the cooler train. I was happy to get the middle position and leave the pier house. We could see Mr. Sullivan well ahead of us when we started out on the pier. Each of us boys gazed down what had to be the longest pier in the world.

"How far we got to go?" Johnny asked. "He usually starts fishing near the end," said Gilbert. Somehow, I knew that was going to be the answer; that's why I didn't want to ask the question.

Fortunately, a good sea breeze blew across us when we were just a short way out on the open pier. It felt like a cool fan, but thick with the smell of salt water. It felt great. We stopped to reposition. I loved that breeze as we weaved in and around people, trashcans, light poles, coolers, gobs of tackle, and other miscellaneous stuff one finds on a fishing pier. It was my first time on a fishing pier and everything was new and fun for me to watch. We stopped again to reposition. I quickly learned to hold my breath when down-wind of pier trashcans. People threw unused bait in those cans instead of tossing it in the water and letting the fish eat free. The surprise odors of hot, rotten shrimp, squid, fish, or a blended smell will garner a gag reflex. We stopped to reposition once more. The weight of those coolers was wearing us out. They must have been gaining weight with each step we took.

Mr. Sullivan stopped just short of the end of the pier on the left side. We were so thankful he stopped. We dropped the coolers down next to the wooden bench we were going to fish by. Johnny and I flopped down on the bench.

"You boys tired already?" Mr. Sullivan asked, as he smiled and turned away.

"You guys want some tea?" Gilbert asked.

"Sure," said Mr. Sullivan. Johnny and I gave Gilbert the good call look and hopped up to help him. Gilbert handed his dad the first cup of cold tea. We three gulped down two quick cups. I noticed the jug was half-empty when Gilbert put it back in the cooler.

"Mr. Sullivan, what are the guys fishing for at the end of the pier with those long fishing poles?" I asked.

"Kingfish and sharks," responded Mr. Sullivan. I wanted to ask more about it, but he seemed to have an agenda that didn't have anything to do with kingfish or sharks. Nevertheless, those cluster of fellows concentrating on what lay beyond the end of the pier stuck in my mind. That question I'd asked Mr. Sullivan about, the activity on the end of the pier, was the beginning, soon to become an obsession for me.

"Boys, here's how it works," Mr. Sullivan said boldly, before going on to explain how to fish from the pier. All four rods and reels were identical. He picked out one, grabbed a rag from the bucket, and began to wipe the dusty grit from the rod and reel. The rod was a white, forty-two inch long, stiff, solid fiberglass stick, about the diameter of a pencil from the tip to where it joined a metal pistol-grip reel seat that ended in a short cork handle. The rod had a tip and two small metal eyes tied to the pole with red and white thread. The reel was a Penn No. 77. The body of the reel was made of dark brown plastic. Light green plastic handle knobs adorned the crank. Metal tubes spanned across the spool, fitting the two sides of the reel together. The reel foot was made of metal. The fancy part of the reel was a small, round metal button on the left side of the reel that, if pushed forward, would make a clicking sound when the spool turned forward or backwards.

"That's the clicker," Mr. Sullivan pointed out, then told us never to use it. There was no lever to take the spool in or out of gear. It was direct drive. The handle spun backwards when line was played out. When you wanted to reel in, you turned the handle forward. It was as simple as it gets. It looked like a toy.

"This is a bottom rig." Mr. Sullivan explained, pulling one from the bucket. It was a store bought gizmo about eighteen inches long. It started with a barrel swivel and ended with a snap swivel. A thin plastic coated wire connected the two. Two light twisted wire arms, about six inches in length, dangled out from the main plastic coated wire. One was fixed with beads and crimps to stay at the top, and the other beaded and crimped to hang at the bottom. The two little arms could spin around on the main wire.

"Where are the hooks, Mr. Sullivan?" Johnny asked.

"I'm getting to that part, give me a minute, Johnny," Mr. Sullivan shot back. With that said, Mr. Sullivan pulled a long plastic sleeve, which looked like a see through envelope with a piece of heavy construction paper inside from the bucket. Mr. Sullivan flipped it around showing us. A line up of leadered hooks was on the side with writing. He carefully pulled one out so as not to tangle it with the rest of the hooks. I'd seen hooks like that in stores but never bought any. Dad told me it was a lot cheaper to make our own.

The leadered hook was medium-sized, with a long shank, and had a loop tied at the other end. Mr. Sullivan pushed that loop through the loop at the end of the little wire arm on the bottom of the rig, then slipped the hook through the fishing line loop and pulled on the hook. The leadered hook was looped to the end of the little wire arm. I called it the loop-to-loop knot for lack of anything better. He did the same thing for the top wire arm. I noticed the store bought, leadered hooks were cut to size for use on the bottom rig. They fit just right so they didn't tangle. Next, Mr. Sullivan pulled a two-ounce triangle sinker from the bucket and linked it on the bottom snap swivel.

"That sinker is called a pyramid sinker for obvious reasons, boys. It is made to hold bottom in some strong current," Mr. Sullivan informed us.

"Gilbert, get me that box of squid from the cooler." Gilbert handed his father the box of squid. Mr. Sullivan took the frozen squid over to the fish-cleaning sink set up on the pier banister to the left of the bench.

"I like fishing here because it is close to the sink. You can stay cleaned up a bit," Mr. Sullivan told us. Then he said "Don't drink it, it's saltwater pumped up from below the pier." There was the reason he picked here to fish. He ran water over the frozen squid to thaw out the top layer. The squid were of uniform length, approximately eight inches long, and stacked tightly in the box like cord wood.

"Gather around the cutting board, I'll show you guys how to do this." We three kids stood around him like a litter of puppies. Mr. Sullivan explained as he went along. He first pulled the head from the body and set that aside. Next, he ran his short fillet knife inside the body cavity all the way to the pointy part of the squid's tail and pushed the point of the knife through. In one motion, he sliced through one side of the tubular body from top to bottom and the body unfurled flat on the cutting board. He then scrapped what little guts were there away with the blade of his knife and flipped them in the ocean. A triangle piece of flesh lay before him. With the knife, he cut half-inch strips the whole length of the squid.

He pulled twelve more squid from the box and put them on the cutting board, saying, "Put the box of squid back in the cooler, Johnny." He laid down his knife on the cutting board with the squid.

"Ya'll cut these up and rig your poles and I'll show you how to hook the bait when you're ready," he said, grabbing the head and one squid strip. Gilbert and Johnny started snatching the heads off and cleaning the squid. I watched Mr. Sullivan.

He walked over to the bench and laid the squid strip on the top of the pier banister. He held the squid head in his right hand. The bottom hook was inserted in the back of the head and directed out the front in the middle. The tiny tentacles dangled down below the bend of the hook, hiding it in the bait. He punched the top hook through the end of the squid strip, turned it around, and stuck it back in the bait for a double hook up. The squid strip hung straight on the hook like a rubber worm.

Mr. Sullivan held the rod over the banister and lowered the rig into the sea. The reel's little green knobs back-wound for a long time. The bait must have just hit the bottom when he jerked it, commencing to spin the tiny handle round and round. In seconds, he swung two fish back over the railing. They were twelve to fourteen inches long and silver.

"What are those, Mr. Sullivan?" I asked. He had the top fish in his left hand working the hook free

"They are croaker. Brian, open the big cooler lid for me." I did as told, and the first of many croakers went in the cooler. The second fish made its flight into the cooler and I went to close the lid.

"Son, don't worry about closing the lid."

That statement set me in go fish mode. I had my rod and reel wiped down and rigged up in a hurry. Gilbert and Johnny were horsing around with the squid, so I took the liberty to break into the bag of shrimp. I busted a shrimp in half and put a chunk on each of the two hooks. By the time I had all that done, Mr. Sullivan had tossed four more fish in the box. I slid the small cooler over to the railing so I could stand on it and lean over the top of the banister like Mr. Sullivan. Pole in hand, leaning over the banister, watching the waves far below, I took my thumb off the spool and let the rig plummet down to the water. When the rig hit the water a snarl of fishing line billowed out of my reel.

"Put your thumb on it, put your thumb on it, Brian!" yelled Mr. Sullivan. I was a statue when a big thumb pressed against the spool, stopping the accident from getting any worse. I felt so stupid.

"Reel this one up and then we'll work out this bird's nest" Mr. Sullivan said, gruffly. His rod had two fish on it when he handed it to me. I reeled them up but didn't feel too good about it. I took off the two croakers and put them in the cooler before walking over to Mr. Sullivan. He was picking and pulling on the fishing line. In a few long minutes, he had the line smoothed out.

"Remember you have to keep light pressure on the spool with your thumb so you won't get a bird's nest." He warned me.

"Thanks for the help, Mr. Sullivan," I quietly said. I looked over at Gilbert and Johnny and they were gesturing me the silent monkey dance. I felt like a dumb monkey.

My rig still had the shrimp on the hooks, so I stepped back up on the cooler and cautiously lowered my rig into the ocean. A salty gust of air climbed in my face as I watched the rig go in the water. As soon I felt it hit the bottom, I put my right hand on the handle. As soon as I did that, I could feel the fish popping the bait. I set the hook and speed-reeled the fish all the way to the tip of the rod and flung them over the banister onto the pier. I laid the rod down on the deck and squatted over the flopping fish, getting them off the hooks and in the cooler.

My bait was gone, so I went for another shrimp when I heard, "Use the squid, it will last longer." Those words came from Mr. Sullivan who had been watching me the entire time.

Gilbert and Johnny laid a gob of squid on the bench end and put a small wet towel over the bait strips. I wondered why they put the bait where we might end up sitting on it so I asked Johnny.

"Mr. Sullivan told us to put it there because if we left it on the cutting board or up on the banister, the sea gulls would carry it off and eat it," Johnny said. I looked around the pier and saw dozens of sea gulls perched up around the sinks, trashcans, and those fishing. They were sitting, waiting for a fast food opportunity. The sky had eyes. The wet towel was to keep the food hidden, as well as to keep the sun from baking it dry, I guessed; I learned.

I took two strips and pinned them on my hooks. Mr. Sullivan was steady putting fish in the box while Gilbert and Johnny were just getting started. Up on the cooler I went and down went my bottom rig. Again, when the bait hit the bottom, two croakers instantly picked it up. It went on like that for an hour. Gilbert and Johnny tried to go to the other side of the pier, but Mr. Sullivan called them back.

"Why can't we fish on the other side, Mr. Sullivan?" Johnny asked.

"Son, the tide has just started coming in."

"So," quipped Johnny.

"On the other side your bait will get washed up under the pier and get hung up."

I thought, *Things aren't as random as they first seemed.*

For that hour, we were all picking up fish as fast as we could get the bait to the bottom. I'd never experienced fishing like that. It didn't even feel like fishing. If you had enough skill to get bait to the bottom, without making a mess, you could always catch a fish. I found myself totally in the moment. The heat was gone. There was no wind. There were no odors. I was entirely alone amongst many. The bounty of fish had reduced my world to the tiny area between the banister and the fish cooler on a big pier propped out over an endless ocean. Once Mr. Sullivan asked us to pull the bait out of the fish box and put it in the food cooler, shifting the ice blocks over on top of the fish. We had to shift the ice blocks on top of the fish a second time, before the action began to trickle off and it stopped all together.

"Boys, let me see your fishing poles," said Mr. Sullivan. He had already gotten his gear ready to travel. He took Gilbert's first, pushed the clicker button forward, slipped the bottom hook over the top bar on the reel, and wound the fishing line tight. It made several loud clicks before snugging up. After tightening each pole, he picked up the five-gallon bucket and headed down the pier. "Ya'll get the coolers and find me about half-way down the pier," he said, walking off.

We three boys stood in silence, looking at one another before Johnny looked into the fish cooler and said, "This ain't cool."

The fish cooler lacked but few inches from the top of being full. The fish weren't big, but it doesn't take long when four people are putting fish in the box at a quick and steady pace.

"Now what?" Johnny asked exasperated.

"Pull the plug on the cooler and let's drain the water off," Gilbert said. He had been here before. About a gallon and a half of water and slime fell between the slits in the pier before becoming slow drips. Gilbert put the plug back in the cooler. Then he opened both coolers up and began to put some blocks of ice in the food cooler to reduce weight from the fish box.

"We need to get rid of this tea and let's eat the sandwiches, too," I suggested.

We took a minute to wash up in the sink before eating the sandwiches and tea.

"Man, these sandwiches are all mashed up," Johnny exclaimed, pulling them out of the bread bag. He was right, for the blocks of ice slid around in the cooler and pressed the sandwiches into some unique shapes, none of which resembled a sandwich. We ate three modern art, peanut butter and jelly sandwiches and passed the tea jug around until Johnny noticed a string of PBJ awash in the tea jug. Each of us blamed the other for the backwash. We dumped the rest of the tea between the slits in the pier boards, and the jug was tossed in the closest trashcan.

"We better hurry up and get down the pier, my dad will be waiting," Gilbert blurted out.

"We ain't going to be hurrying nowhere," I responded. We put Johnny in the middle of the cooler train and started down the pier. Making it less than ten feet, a gravity storm hit the fish box, sucking it down to the pier.

"Maybe three of us can carry the fish box and come back for the food cooler," Gilbert suggested.

"Where is the third guy going to grab the cooler?" I asked.

"Hey, kids!" a man's voice came from the other side of the pier. In retrospect, the voice may have come from above. "You can use my pier cart to haul those coolers down the pier if you promise to bring it back," said a middle-aged man we had never seen before.

A collective "Thanks, mister!" came from us. He emptied his stuff out of the pier cart onto a bench. The pier cart was a forever-borrowed rusty shopping cart with six short sections of galvanized pipe sized and staggered so the top of the pipes were always at the height of the basket top. The man helped us lift and position the big cooler across the cart toward the rear and the small cooler on the front of the basket. He loaned us a piece of quarter-inch line to tie down the coolers. Working together, we formed a web with the line by running the line through the basket and over the coolers so they couldn't move, much, forward, back, or side to side. It was a godsend! I told him it was easier to fish on the other side of the pier where the tide wouldn't wash his bait under the pier.

He smiled, and said, "Thanks." We rattled our way down the pier smiling at folks like young men driving a snazzy car.

We found Mr. Sullivan a bit more than halfway down the pier on the left hand side. I didn't notice earlier, but he had wadded up the squid in the wet towel and put it in the bucket before he walked back down the pier. When he got to where he wanted to fish, he emptied the stuff from the bucket on a bench. Using the bait from the rag, and the empty bucket as a makeshift cooler, he wasn't waiting on us to get started fishing. The bucket was half-full of fish when we got to him. He lifted the fish cooler from the pier cart after we untangled it from our web of line. As he lifted the small cooler, he asked where we got the cart. We told him the story. He coiled the line neatly, putting it in the bottom of the cart.

"Be sure and tell the man thank you," he said, as Johnny drove the cart back up the pier solo. Gilbert flipped the fish cooler lid open at his dad's request, and his dad sloshed the fish from the bucket on top of the fish in the cooler. The cooler was just about full to the brim.

Gilbert and I started fishing with Mr. Sullivan. The action was as fast as it was in the beginning at the end of the pier; all three of us tossing in singles and doubles as quickly as we could get bait to the bottom. In a matter of minutes, the big cooler was full of fish and ice. The lid would just close tight.

"What are we going to do now, Mr. Sullivan?" I asked.

"Open the lid on the small cooler and take the food and bait out." Gilbert threw the Styrofoam cups in a trashcan and I set the bait on the bench next to his dad. When Johnny returned, all four of us ganged up on the croaker. The steady thud of fish landing in the cooler was like a slow, heavy rain on a tin roof. It was a quick thirty to forty minutes before the cooler was as full of fish as it could get. It ended when Mr. Sullivan told us to stop fishing. All three of us had to throw the fish we had on the line at the time back in the ocean. Mr. Sullivan had to throw some of the fish on top back in order to squeeze the lid shut. It was fun tossing fish off the pier. I wondered what the fish were thinking as they sailed through the air before belly-flopping home. They were the lucky ones with a thrill ride.

Mr. Sullivan walked over to some folks fishing nearby and gave them our leftover bait. When he returned, we were washing the form fitted slime gloves from our hands with a water hose.

"Why did the fish at the end of the pier stop eating and the fish near the beach start eating, Mr. Sullivan? And, how did you know?" I asked.

"Brian, fish at the end of the pier never stopped feeding. You see, the school of fish at the end of the pier was the same school of fish at the beach; they just moved closer in with the incoming tide. We moved along the pier to follow the fish in the tide."

I stood there with my mouth agape, like the man at the pier house, thinking about what he just said. The only thing I knew about tide was it only worked in saltwater, and it would come in during the day and leave during the day then repeat at night. Where it came from or where it went was a mystery to me, and I sure didn't know it could carry fish. It was a good thing to know. That was when I learned fish move with the tide.

"Take your sinkers off your rigs, boys." While we were busy doing that, Mr. Sullivan came along to each of us and cut the leadered hooks off our rigs with his knife.

"You don't save the hooks?" I asked.

"Brian, I've tried, but they end up rusted out by the time I use them again. Besides, they tangle up in everything if you leave them on. It is not worth the hassle." He showed us how to hook the snap swivel to the reel after cleaning the rig off.

"Ya'll stay here till I come back; don't goof off," he told us, as he picked up the fishing poles and five-gallon bucket and walked down the pier.

When he was out of earshot, Johnny blurted, "Those coolers are heavier now than when we carried them on the pier! How are we going to get them to the car?" He was right! I was eyeballing around for a kind looking person who happened to have a pier cart or anything with wheels, but there was nothing within sight.

"What are we going to do, Gilbert?"

"I don't know," he said. "I thought you and your dad came fishing here before?"

"We have, but we only bring a small cooler."

"Do you think we should go ask that guy to borrow his pier cart again?"

"Johnny, what are you doing?" Gilbert and I asked in unison.

"Cooling off." Johnny was hosing down with the sink hose. It was a great idea, considering we were thirsty, out of tea, boiling hot, and faced with what seemed to be an overwhelming task. Gilbert went to the hose on the other side of the sink and started doing the same thing. Then they started hosing me down. I fell to the pier as if I was being shot, and they soaked me down. Boy, it felt good, especially with the sea breeze. That had to escalate into a water fight; and it did.

Occasionally, someone nearby would be hit with a stream of water, but nobody minded. It felt that good. Of course, when Mr. Sullivan sneaked up on us, on an open pier, in broad daylight, and caught us in the midst of goofing off, nobody came forward and told him it felt good.

"What are ya'll doing!" barked Mr. Sullivan. The hoses went silent. We three boys stood board straight in silence. Everybody around us was silent, waiting and watching to see what was going to happen next. Even the gulls stopped screeching. The world stopped. The only sound was that of running water still flowing from our short pants, splattering on the pier. I'm not quite sure it was all just water either.

"I can't believe I can't leave ya'll alone for ten minutes without some antics! You're going to get in my car sopping wet!"

"Dad, we were just cooling off."

"Gilbert!"

I noticed Mr. Sullivan had rolled a hand truck with him and then I loved that man who was yelling at us. Mr. Sullivan put the large cooler on the bottom, and then put the small cooler on top.

"You wet rats ready?"

"Yes, sir," said in synchronicity. Mr. Sullivan eased the hand truck back and started rolling it down the pier. We quietly followed behind, puppy fashion.

Gilbert whispered to Johnny, "It's all your fault!"

"Yeah, but don't it feel good?" He was right, it still felt good.

At the pier house, Mr. Sullivan stopped, gave Gilbert a couple of bucks, and told him to go buy four Cokes. Johnny went with him as I rolled on with Mr. Sullivan. The car was parked at the entrance with the trunk popped open. He set the small cooler in the trunk and then he heaved the large cooler in the trunk. He sure was a strong man!

Gilbert and Johnny came scrambling down with the drinks. Mr. Sullivan shut the trunk, told Gilbert to roll the hand truck back to the pier house, and slid behind the steering wheel. Gilbert ran back in a couple of minutes and we boys hopped in. We sat still, with shut mouths and the windows rolled down, anticipating the air conditioning. Mr. Sullivan pulled away and asked us if we enjoyed fishing from the pier. That broke the ice.

We started briefly talking about feeling the fish bite, then exaggerating a guess of how many fish each of us caught. A belch here and there from the Cokes was the only thing that interrupted the chatter. The ride over to the Sullivan's went by so quickly. It seemed like minutes before Mr. Sullivan was backing the LTD through a gate on the side of his house to a picnic table in the back yard. I thought about how many fish we caught from another perspective, then. The fun was over and work about to begin.

Mr. Sullivan popped the trunk, set the coolers by the picnic table, and started getting things and people in motion. He told Gilbert to get two fish scalers and two sharp knives from the kitchen.

He told Johnny to carry the water hose over to the table, "and this time, manage not to get wet," he said in jest.

He told me to get two five-gallon buckets from beside the house and a shovel from the garage. I brought the buckets to the table, and he pointed out the garden in the corner of the backyard. I knew what to do, but not exactly how big a hole I should dig. Mrs. Sullivan brought out four big glasses of iced tea with Gilbert. She said she'd hug us later and went back in the house. By the time I had dug a good-sized hole in the ground, Mr. Sullivan had organized a *Henry Ford de-assembly line* at the picnic table. A custom fit, well-used, sheet of plywood lay atop the picnic table with a clean open cooler, the size of the large cooler we brought on the pier, on top of that at the far end. The small cooler set atop the large cooler at the other end, on the ground. It was open, ready for business to begin. Two metal fish scalers were placed on the table across from one another, close to the cooler of fish. Two knives sat next to the open, clean cooler across from one another. Between the scalers and knives, draped the water hose. One five-gallon bucket sat on the picnic bench seat just forward of the clean cooler on the table. The other five-gallon bucket was the same way but on the opposite side of the table. The only things missing were the line workers.

Before production began, Mr. Sullivan told Johnny and me that Mrs. Sullivan had called our parents and told them we'd be home after we finished cleaning the fish. I thought, *this is going to take forever, plus some. Johnny and I ain't getting home for quite a while.* Mr. Sullivan may have adopted us into a fish labor camp!

"Gilbert, you and Johnny start scraping the scales off the fish and pass them down to Brian and me to cut the heads off and gut them. The scales started flying; heads lopped off, bellies slit open, and guts rooted out with the scrape of a thumbnail at a steady pace, but slightly slower than the scaling process. Mr. Sullivan was cleaning the fish a bit faster than I was, but I was racing to keep up. The clean cooler was loading up with dressed croakers. When ice was stuck to the fish from the fish cooler, we rinsed it with the hose and dropped in the cleaned fish cooler. Every now and then, someone would grab the hose and give the table a quick rinse of fresh water. The five-gallon buckets filled up with heads and guts.

"Gilbert and Johnny, go dump the buckets in the hole," Mr. Sullivan told them. He and I had a backlog of fish anyway.

They returned and set the buckets back up, saying, "Dad, the hole ain't big enough."

"Go dig another hole then." Gilbert walked off with the shovel, and Johnny resumed scaling fish, solo. When Gilbert came back, we were steady working, with less than a dozen fish in the bottom of the small cooler. We cleaned those remaining quickly.

"Gilbert, rinse that cooler out with the hose," Mr. Sullivan told his son, as he walked off. He returned a few minutes later with a jug of bleach and a rag. Gilbert was relieved of cooler cleaning when his dad took hold of the cooler and dumped the residual water on the ground. He set the small cooler atop the large cooler upright, tossed the rag in it, splashed a good glug of bleach on the rag and in the cooler, and squirted in some extra water. Then he thoroughly wiped the rag around the inside and outside of the cooler and dumped the wash water out. He closed the lid and set the small cooler on the ground beside the larger cooler.

"When I lift this big cooler up, Gilbert, you slide the smaller cooler underneath." Before he did that, he said, "Johnny, go dump the gut buckets." Johnny ran both gut-buckets to the new pit and came back in a flash.

Mr. Sullivan opened the lid to the big cooler and we were back in business scraping scales and gutting fish. The cleaning tempo resumed with a smoother rhythm. With the second cooler, I was able to keep up with Mr. Sullivan cleaning fish. Either I was getting better or it was good to be young. The second cooler, even though it was larger, emptied in about the same amount of time as the first, smaller cooler. A couple of gut-bucket runs by Gilbert and Johnny and the fish cleaning was over. Amazingly, all the fish that took up two coolers of space fit in a single, large cooler after being cleaned. We couldn't close the lid, but they fit without falling out.

When we saw the bottom of the big cooler, we thought the work was over. We were wrong.

"Gilbert, rinse out the big fish cooler and wipe it down. Johnny, rinse off the table when Gilbert is done with the hose. Brian, go dump the rest of the guts and cover them up. And be sure and clean the buckets when you're through." Mr. Sullivan kept us all hopping. In ten minutes, we boys had finished our jobs. Mr. Sullivan took the two empty coolers and gave them each a quick rinse with the hose. He then sat the coolers, with closed lids, on the picnic table bench seat, on the opposite side of the table where he was working. The cooler with the cleaned fish, he carefully dumped on the table then rinsed that cooler out well afterwards and set it with the other two coolers on the bench seat.

"Boys, fish around, and pick out the chunks of ice and bring them to me," Mr. Sullivan said. Back in the slime we went, getting a few pokes from the fish fins as we hunted. When we found a chunk of ice, we brought it to him. We'd hold it in our hands while he rinsed it off, and then put it in a bucket. The big blocks of ice were now small chunks, but I was still impressed at how long block ice lasted. Crushed bag ice would have long ago melted away, but Mr. Sullivan's milk carton, ice idea was smart.

After sorting out the ice, Mr. Sullivan turned the hose on the pile of fish. The firm spray had slime, blood, and left over scales pouring off the ends of the picnic table. Twice he stopped and had us stir the pile of fish around. By the end of the third rinse, the fish were very clean.

He gave the closed coolers a quick rinse then said, "Gilbert, go flip the cooler lids open." Mr. Sullivan had arranged the coolers so the cooler lids opened out away from the table. "Ya'll boys come over here now," said Mr. Sullivan.

"Johnny, the cooler on the far end is yours. Brian, your cooler is in the middle and, Gilbert, ours is on this end," he directed. "When I toss a fish in my cooler, ya'll toss a fish in your coolers, OK?" said Mr. Sullivan.

"Cool, a fish toss," Johnny said. Mr. Sullivan grabbed a fish and flipped it in his cooler. We all did the same with our coolers. We got in a rhythm and the fish were flying. It was disappointing when we got down to the last two fish. Mr. Sullivan told Johnny and me we could have them. He and I picked up a fish apiece and tossed them in Mr. Sullivan's and Gilbert's cooler as a thank you. Mr. Sullivan divided the ice in the bucket between Johnny's cooler and mine. Gilbert toted their cooler of fish into the house for the bagging process. Johnny and I put our coolers in the back of the LTD, while Mr. Sullivan rinsed the table and area around the table. We washed up with the hose as best we could. Fish smell takes soap, water, scrubbing, and time to get rid of.

Johnny and I said goodbye to Mrs. Sullivan and Gilbert before loading up in the car and taking the short ride to our houses. It had just turned dark when Mr. Sullivan pulled into my driveway. My dad came out and met us at the car. The men talked a bit as I carried the cooler in the garage with Johnny's help. Mom was going to bag up the fish and put them in the garage freezer. I came back out and thanked Mr. Sullivan for taking me fishing. I told Johnny I'd see him around. Going back in the house, I felt tired. For the first time, I realized there could be a lot of work involved in the fun of fishing.

Chapter 6 - Speckled Pink

I was excited. I was more than excited. Fully adjusted to the darkness in my room, my eyes watched the old digital alarm clock flop over number 12:57 a.m. *I've got to go to sleep. Are my two fishing rods ready?* They had fresh line, fresh grease, the drag was smooth, and they were fully rigged the way Dad taught me to do it. *Do I feel sleepy? No, I could go run laps at the moment. What about my tackle? Hooks, sinkers, bobbers, jigs, Rapalas, Jelly Worms, Bullet Weights®, Snagless Sallys®, Hula Poppers (big and small), finger nail clippers to cut the fishing line, knife, swivels, extra fishing line, leader line, and.... Did I remember the plastic worm hooks? Yes, they are next to the Bullet Weights®. Let me go through the list again just to make sure. I'm not tired, but I've got to get to sleep.* Mentally I went back to the tackle list another time, and again, and again.

The buzz of the alarm clock at 5:30 a.m. was shocking. The tackle list worked like counting sheep for me. I crawled out of that warm bed and put on the jeans, T-shirt, and an over shirt that I had laid out the evening before. The first stop was the bathroom to take care of urgent business and wash my face. In the kitchen, Dad was over the stove scrambling eggs in the bacon grease. He is such a morning person.

"So, today is your big day to go fishing with Mr. Poe in his nice bass boat?"

"Yes, sir," I said in a yawn.

"You don't seem too excited about it, Champ. Go ahead and drink your orange juice. Mom packed you a lunch last night before she went to bed." Mom isn't a morning person and I'm just like her. The best time of day is in the morning, but I just wished they started a bit later.

At 5:55 a.m., I was leaning against the door jam, looking out the screen door, keeping an eye on my two fishing poles and tackle box that I set by the maple tree in the front yard. I had my jacket and my ball cap from last year's Little League team on. Well worn, the hat had both sides of the bill bent down to look cool. It had a distinctive odor of boys' play juices rung around the sweatband. I was poised in the door, anxiously waiting the day in a sleepy state of go.

Six o'clock sharp, Mr. Poe coasted to a stop at the edge of the yard. It looked like an eighteen-wheeler out front, with the amber running lights adorning the top of the truck cab, down the running boards and continuing along the trailer, ending in two big red brake lights mounted a good foot higher than the gunnels of the boat. The lights reflecting off the freshly waxed truck and shiny aluminum sixteen-foot bass boat, made the rig look much larger in the darkness than during the day.

"He's here!" I announced to Dad. I ran outside with my lunch bag in one hand and grabbed my two poles and tackle box with my other hand. I sat my bag lunch on the bow of the boat, while I stepped up on the trailer tongue to put the fishing poles and tackle box in the bed of Mr. Poe's truck. Dad had followed me out. He shook hands with Mr. Poe.

"Champ, come here," Dad said, and then started chatting with Mr. Poe. They talked a few minutes about fishing, weather, and tomato plants. I was standing beside Dad when he bent over, gave me a hug, and said, "I love you." I was at the age when you get somewhat embarrassed about being hugged and so forth by your parents. I was an outdoorsman, and true outdoorsmen don't get hugs from their dads before going to conquer the outdoors. When I ran around the front of the truck to get in the cab, I was happy Dad sent me off with a hug, but next time we might have to do the hugging part in the house.

Billy, Mr. Poe's son, slid over next to his dad to give me some room on the bench seat.

"Hey, Billy."

"Hey, Brian," we exchanged, when I got in the truck. We ran together so much we didn't have to catch up with each other's goings on. Mr. Poe and Dad, finally, were just finishing their conversation.

"Have fun, boys," Dad said, as he patted the truck with his palm and walked across the yard to the front porch.

"You boys ready?" asked Mr. Poe.

We both said, "Yes, sir," but were sound asleep within a mile. I opened my eyes a couple of times en route, just long enough to notice the sky changing colors, but dozed off quickly to the sound of country and western music from the radio.

The truck came to a stop about an hour later on the right side of a dirt parking lot at Muddy Creek Marina on the edge of Back Bay, Virginia. Billy and I woke up in the sho' 'nuff country. The kind of country where you feel like you traveled back in time. Weathered skiffs, with antique black or white motors, hung off the sterns, atop rusting trailers along the shore. Under tin-roofed pole barns, crab traps and eel pots, thinly coated in dried algae, were loosely stacked for storage. They were amongst a clutter of outboard motor parts, containers of lubricants, trailer tires and rims, trailer parts, a scattering of tools, an anvil on the end of a very well built wooden workbench, and a double handful of extra-long cane poles, their brightly colored floats making them stand out amongst all the other stuff. Additionally, there were some children's toys they had dropped off here and there when the mood hit them to go do something else. Dirt covered most everything in and around the pole barns. A pattern emerged; the higher something was off the ground the thicker it was coated with dusty spider webbing. If the coat hangers, used to suspend the cane poles from the rafters, would ever give way, the poles would remain in place.

Mr. Poe hopped out of the truck and went to the main store. After scanning around awhile, Billy and I walked toward the store. It was a wooden structure, built on top of a three high cinder block skirt. The majority of the vertical boards that made up the outside building were wide and thick. Nails held thinner boards, where the wider boards abutted, to cover the seam. The boards were grayed, grooved, and hairy in texture from beating back decades of weather. The tin-roof had an obviously new shiny section laid next to a still-good section of the old roof, dulled with blotches of light rust stain. On the other side of the roof, a metal pipe jutted up a few feet higher than the peak of the roof with smoke swirling out the end. The smell of wood burning was in each breath. It was a good smell and meant there was a touch of warmth in the store. It was early spring and there was still a nip in the morning air.

The main wooden door was propped open on the inside. A heavy, wood-framed screen door was shut with a sign, head high, that said, Closed. There were people inside, so Billy and I went on in.

"Sugar, would you be a dear and flip that sign over for me?" asked the lady behind the counter. Billy flipped it over.

"You boys want any snacks?" asked Mr. Poe.

"No, sir, I brought my…. My lunch!" I left it on the front of the boat this morning when I loaded the fishing tackle in the back of the truck. I ran outside to the boat. The lunch was somewhere between where I was standing and my house. I had a washed dollar bill in my pocket.

"Crap, that ain't going to buy much to eat or drink," I ran back to the store. "Mr. Poe, I accidentally left my lunch on the boat and it blew off on the road," I said, in a semi-panicked voice.

He smiled. "Son, don't worry about it, we'll get some extra food here, and Billy and I will share ours."

"I only have a dollar, Mr. Poe."

"Son, I said, don't worry about it. Today we'll eat an outdoorsman lunch…, man food." I wondered what that might be, as I watched him dart around the tiny store, bringing back a little of this and a handful of that to the counter.

"What do you like to drink? You want a six pack of beer?" He laughed and got me to smile.

"Coke's, good for me," I said, as the lady was enjoying the whole show. I went to the counter to see what was for lunch. She rang up two cans of Vienna sausages, two cans of potted meat, two cans of pork and beans, two tins of sardines in spring water, one big bag of pork rinds, three candy bars (Mars, Baby Ruth and Snickers) a six pack of Coke, and two bags of ice.

"Sugar, you need a can opener?" the lady asked.

Mr. Poe said, "No, thanks, I've got a P38 can opener on my key ring I've had since my service days." He made one last run back in the store. We couldn't see him; he was behind a wall where the tackle hung. Billy and I were telling the lady where we came from and how this was our first trip out together, when Mr. Poe dashed back to the counter with a handful of small, fuzzy, all pink jigs.

71

"I got twenty jigs," he told the lady. She opened up a small brown paper bag and he dumped them in without counting. As she was ringing up everything else, he said, "Don't forget about the dollar ramp fee."

"You taking those boys fishing?" she asked.

He said, "Sure am."

"We're going to skip the ramp fee, as long as they catch a fish," she smiled.

"You boys grab two bags of ice from the box outside and put them in the boat cooler and get the tackle and stuff ready," Mr. Poe sent us on a mission. As we were heading out the door, I heard him say we needed five-dozen minnows. It didn't take us long to get the boat ready, Billy knew where everything went. We ran back behind the store to the bait house by the water. Pumps brought water from the canal through a series of hoses and pipes that squirted water into two large tanks. One pipe at the top of the tank carried the overflow back down to the canal. I stood up on a cinder block to look into the tanks. Swarms of small minnows scurried around in the vats.

"Where do you get the minnows?" I asked the store lady, as she was dipping and loosely counting them out into a bucket with a small inner tube partially inflated at the top and lots of tiny holes drilled in it. The bucket floated around in the tank and she dropped the counted minnows in with each dip. She got to a stopping point and told me her husband and son netted them in the canals. *Maybe I can become a professional minnow netter*, I thought.

"There you go, Sugar," she told Mr. Poe.

"I'll pick them up once I get the boat in the water," he said back.

While we were walking back to the truck and boat, I said, "Mr. Poe, we've got more than five-dozen minnows in that bucket."

"Son, they always give you more than you buy, because if some die, you don't have anything to complain about, right?" he informed me.

Mr. Poe checked to make sure the plug was in the boat, before trimming up the motor a couple of inches so he could disengage the lock-up mechanism on the motor. He did a quick visual of things on the boat, then hopped in the truck and pulled in front of the ramp, backing the boat down the ramp. In one smooth motion, the boat was halfway in the water.

"Billy, unclip the wench strap and grab the bow line." Billy did. Mr.

Poe dropped the boat all the way down and hit the brakes. The boat slid back a foot or so. He then, pulled forward and the boat slipped off the back of the trailer a little more. Backing down again and hitting the brakes, forced the boat off the trailer. Billy held the bowline and pulled the boat up against the boat ramp as Mr. Poe drove off to park. Mr. Poe was back in a minute, with quickness in his step, excited about going fishing.

He got in the boat by high stepping onto the bow. He quickly walked halfway back to the helm station on the starboard side of the boat. He lowered the motor all the way down, using the tab switch on the throttle handle, then went to the back and gave the fuel bulb a couple of squeezes. Plopping down in the seat behind the side console, he turned the key, and the motor roared to life with a billow of gray smoke. Mr. Poe idled the motor down, flipped a switch on the console, and peaked in the live well located in the middle of the back deck. I could hear water splashing in.

"Billy, go ahead and get that bucket of minnows, would you?" he requested.

"Hold this line for me," Billy asked. In a minute, Billy was hustling back to the boat with the bucket full of holes, water splattering all over his pants. Mr. Poe was at the bow to get the bucket from Billy. He snatched it away from his son, hurried back to the live well and dumped the fish in.

"Son, next time dump the minnows in the outside bucket that doesn't have any holes, before coming down to the boat; it's a lot drier that way." Billy ran the bucket back to the bait-house. When he returned, "Ya'll get in," Mr. Poe said, in a let's go voice. Billy jumped in and I followed with the bowline in hand.

"Brian, just toss that line at the bottom of the front seat," Mr. Poe told me.

Before, when the boat was on the side of the driveway, I had looked at it, but I was really looking at it now. To me it was a *dream boat*, for it had everything I knew about and some things I didn't. Mounted on the bow was a trolling motor, a foot control letting you run the boat and fish at the same time! That was fantastic to me!

On the raised front deck, there was a pedestal seat. Under that, were two compartments where the anchor and the life preservers were stored with slots for tackle trays. The boat cooler was against the bow platform, giving more walk-around space. Stepping down from the bow, there was an open area before the side console on the right, starboard side. The console had a bunch of switches and gauges and a black and white Hummingbird fish-finder mounted on the top of the console above the steering wheel and behind the small plastic windshield. It was NASA stuff to me, at the time.

The back of the boat had a raised platform where Billy and I sat. The live well was in the front center. Two other compartments were on either side of the rear deck. One was a fish box. A pedestal seat was in the middle of the rear deck in front of the motor. Horizontal rod holders were along the port gunnel, and bolted to the side of the console were vertical rod holders. A radio hung below the steering wheel tucked under the console. Screwed into aluminum deck plates were four freestanding, low-slung pole holders. Pole holders were on either side of the bow and one was on each side of the stern. The rod holders were made out of black, plastic coated, quarter-inch steel rod; the rod holders bent in a fashion to cradle the fishing pole and reel for easy placement and removal. They were an after-market addition Mr. Poe installed but were, apparently, a needed addition. They looked cool to me. I was in a space-aged fishing-machine, waiting for blast-off!

Mr. Poe backed the boat away from the ramp, while turning halfway around to head up the fifty-foot wide canal in front of the boat ramp. An eight-foot wall of cattails sharply defined the arrow straight canal. If you stood up in the boat, you couldn't see over the cattails, even if you were tall. When Billy and I were prepping the boat, I stood in the bed of the truck and looked across the marsh at an endless sea of cattails. There was still quite a bit of brown foliage in the sea, but it was greening up in the warmth of spring. I wondered where the water was.

In the canal, the water was tea stained. It was the natural color of the water, clear, but dark. In the water along the edge of the cattails was a two-foot swath of dark green milfoil that grew in a loose wad. In the summer time, it could grow out across the canal at times, choking it out. Now, in the spring, it was a neatly trimmed hedge in the water with minnows flickering amongst it.

"Ya'll boys ready?" asked Mr. Poe, as he turned around and looked at us. I didn't answer. I didn't know if I was ready or not. He turned back around and twisted his hat backwards. That was enough of a clue for me to snatch my hat off my head and stick it under my butt. Mr. Poe pushed the throttle full forward and the boat went from canoe speed to supersonic in a blink. My hair was straight back, my eyes were wide open, and my knuckles were good and white. The front of the boat wasn't even touching the water. We were chattering smoothly side to side on some small portion of the back of the boat that remained in the water. The engine noise was so loud it absorbed your mind. There was no need to attempt to speak. Breathing required cracking your mouth open, not to take in air, but to exhaust the spent air being injected into your nostrils or vice versa. My lungs inflated like balloons. Wow, what a ride!

Ahead, I could see where two canals intersected. Mr. Poe took the boat off plane, nosed around the corner cautiously, turned to the left, and hit it again. We slowly crossed several large intersections to blast off again. The blasting off part was exciting. It was like a carnival ride but real. Numerous, small, one-way boat trails poked into the cattails. I wondered if they led to secret pockets of fish. We came to an intersection and turned right. We were in a maze of cattails. I was lost. Within two minutes of making that right turn, we were in a left hand curve and suddenly shot out into open water!

Open water you couldn't see the other side of. I looked back to see miles of cattail banks with openings here and there punched in the wall. *How does Mr. Poe know which one to return to?*

The open water had some chop on it; it wasn't smooth like in the canals. Not only could you see the difference, but you could feel the difference. My butt was taking a pattering. Mr. Poe eased back on the throttle and the boat responded by sitting down more in the water. The ride improved, except for a few sprays of water blown back in the boat on Billy and me, especially Billy. Billy didn't say anything, just pushed over to my side, ducked, and covered.

"Boys, we got about another fifteen minute boat ride," Mr. Poe turned to us and said. We nodded in agreement, as if it would have made a difference. He punched it and changed course a hair which made for less water on us. The light chop was more on the stern and less on the quarter. I noticed the cooler that was pushed up against the bow platform had baby-stepped its way back toward the console; and the bowline I had dropped by the front pedestal seat had dumped in the crack between the front platform and cooler.

"Mr. Poe, do you want me to push that cooler back up?" I asked, in a yell.

He said, "Don't worry about it," and I followed instruction and sat back. I learned if things change while under way, it ain't hurting anything, so let it ride. It was safer than getting up in a moving boat. I would find out later that such matters are time dependent. A fifteen-minute ride is totally different from an hour and a half ride offshore, but the principle still applied.

The cattail wall we came out of was slipping off to the far back of the boat at a falling angle. More cattails were barely visible on the horizon in the direction we were going. Strange clumps of stuff appeared off in open water, far ahead between the cattail bank and us. We were, at a good speed, pointed toward the first of many distant clumps. The clumps became squarer as the distance shrank.

"Ahead are some duck blinds we are going to fish around," announced Mr. Poe. A hundred and fifty feet off the first blind, he throttled back to neutral in slow graduation and sat the boat flush in the water. We had entered a quaint town of duck blinds that stood approximately a hundred yards apart. Mr. Poe guided the boat past several of them, going to one particular blind out of the bunch.

The duck blinds were homemade, stilted structures approximately eight feet by eight feet. Usually, the corner posts were store bought four by fours or stouter; the other support posts were mostly made of cut and trimmed young tree trunks. The floor was made of two sheets of plywood laid side by side; hence the eight by eight dimensions. Layered in the opposing direction, on top, were extra sheets of plywood, to give the floor more strength. Most floors were raised a foot or two above the water surface. Some floors were even higher, to accommodate a boat underneath the blind. Bundles of cattails, woven and tied to a chicken wire frame, formed the walls. To cover the gap left to enter the blind was a small, slide-across wall. Roughly sculpted, the top of the cattail walls allowed the hunters to pop up and shoot ducks over the blind. Some blinds were pieces of rural art and workmanship where the builder was obviously committed to the upcoming season. Those blinds had built in seating and gun racks made of adjusted branches that required forethought and time. Other blinds, obviously thrown together just before season opened, looked as wobbly as the thought and effort put into them.

Built well to begin with, and maintained through the years, old duck blinds had stubs, sticks, and trimmings in the water around them from remodeling and upgrade projects made by the hunters who used them. Because of the additional debris in the water, old duck blinds were the best fish sanctuaries, I later found out.

"Billy, get the anchor out of the nose compartment," Mr. Poe said. Billy went rooting through the compartment, pulling out the mushroom anchor and a tangled mass of quarter-inch nylon rope. It took some time for him to undo what had taken time to scramble. Mr. Poe was, let's say, encouraging him to get it done in a hurry. Billy became slightly frustrated but got the line straightened out. In the meantime, Mr. Poe had pulled another mushroom anchor out of one of the back compartments. There was about fifteen feet of line attached to that anchor. On his hands and knees, Mr. Poe tied the free end to the back right cleat.

"Brian, when I tell you to, slip the anchor off the corner of the boat." I was on my knees ready for the command.

Mr. Poe eased the boat on the backside of the blind, in the slick water, out of the light breeze. Fifteen feet from and parallel to the blind, the bow of the boat coasted some ten feet past the back corner of the blind.

"Billy, drop the anchor!" He did from a standing position five feet above the water, making the five-pound anchor a cannonball off the high dive. Kaawoosh! Blobs of water shot above Billy's head, raining down on him, the boat, and the water.

"Son! You're dropping bombs; now every fish knows we're here," said with great inflection in his voice. The rant continued while he had the boat in slow reverse. The stern of the boat went just past the other corner of the blind when Mr. Poe said, "Brian, ease the anchor over."

I placed it in the water after learning what not to do. Mr. Poe put the boat in slow forward briefly, then neutral and turned off the motor. He asked Billy to pick up the slack line from the bow anchor. Just before the back anchor line got tight, Mr. Poe told Billy to hold the line as he went forward and tied it off at the bow cleat. The boat came to rest parallel to, and twenty feet square behind the duck blind, perfect boat position. I began to respect Mr. Poe more after that anchor job for I'd never seen it done like that before. Most people drop anchor and let the boat swing as it may. He, on the other hand, parallel parked the boat.

The laid-back Mr. Poe I knew was transforming into a fishing machine, right in front of us. He was focused.

"Brian, cut that jig off your line and tie on this Pinkie® Jig; don't use a leader," he instructed. I cut off the bulky white rubber-tailed jig with a quarter ounce head I had tied on there the night before. He tossed me a Pinkie® Jig, which was an eighth ounce jig with the body made of marabou feathers, fuzzy, frilly, and bright pink. I don't know where they came up with the name. My main line was an eight-pound test. I decided to tie the jig on with a small loop knot to give it more action. The loop knot is simple to tie. Simply tie an overhand knot six inches from the end of the fishing line. Take the end of your fishing line and push it through the hook eye of the jig and pass it back through the overhand knot. Adjust the size of the loop by pulling on the end of the line. I adjusted my knot to the size of a small pea. Then I made five twists around the main line above the overhand knot, and next, dropped the end back down through the overhand knot and brought it tight. I clipped the tag end close with my fingernail clippers.

While I was doing that, Mr. Poe was looking over my float rig pole.

"Brian, you did everything I told you to do in the rigging, but the tackle is too big. You've got to scale down. These fish can become skittish and not hit bulky tackle. A softer touch will catch more fish. I'll give you some of my stuff to tie together," Mr. Poe instructed me.

"Remember, set the cork at two and half feet; we're fishing water four to five feet deep around the duck blinds," he said, while gathering some things in his hand and laying them beside me. There was a small, inch-and-a-half float that was bright red on one end and white on the other, one small, red-plastic bead, two BB sized split shot, and a #4 Aberdeen hook. I had rigged similar items on my pole, but my tackle was larger. I cut my rig off and put together his tackle. I began by slipping the bead on the line, then the float, red side up, and tied on the hook, using an improved clinch knot. Six inches above the hook and below the float, I pinched on the two split shot. Two and a half feet above the hook, I had tied a piece of thread on my main line the night before. The thread acted as a bobber stop. I had rigged a *slip cork rig;* when cast out the weight pulled the fishing line through the bobber as it sank, the bobber would push the bead up the line until the bead jammed against the knotted piece of thread that could be tied anywhere on the main line to set the depth of the bait. The bobber stop could easily run through the rod tip, rod eyes, and wind on to the spool. The simple rig made casting easy and controlled the depth you were fishing.

While I was re-rigging, Mr. Poe and Billy were setting up their fishing poles. Their gear was pre-rigged, of course, but Mr. Poe had to have everything just right before he would start fishing. When I finished putting the slip cork rig together, they had been waiting on me a couple of minutes. The timing was pretty good.

"Let me explain this to you, boys," Mr. Poe started out. We were fishing for spawning crappie; some folks call them speckled perch; they were using the duck blinds as structures to spawn on. Small minnows are the number one bait for taking these fish, and the local Pinkie® Jig is a close second.

Mr. Poe flipped the live-well lid open and used an aquarium dip net to get the first bait. He had it in his hand as he went to the bow where Billy was sitting in the pedestal chair. After pulling the hook free of the eye brace that secured the hook to the pole, he attempted to run the hook through both lips of the minnow. When the sharp point touched the fish's lips, it flipped out of his hands into the water. Billy and I could tell that didn't make the man happy. He brought the pole with him back to the live well and pinned on the first bait there. The minnow was flipping on the hook as Mr. Poe walked to the front of the boat and tossed the float rig to the left and three feet off the duck blind.

"Billy, you fish that area there," he told his son, handing him the pole.

"The cork is gone," Billy shouted.

"Set the hook, son!" He did, with the force that would drive a spike through a railroad tie. The fish skidded across the water until the line went slack. When Billy got the line tight again, the fish was gone.

"Boys, let me explain something to you..." He told us the nickname for crappie is paper mouth and the way to set the hook is with a quick snap of the wrist keeping the line tight. That was the secret to catching the fish, a light hook set, nothing more.

Mr. Poe came back to the live well where I was with my hook dangling between my thumb and forefinger.

"I can bait my hook," I said.

He smiled and said, "I know you will next time." After putting bait on my hook, he noticed the handle to my spinning rod was on the right side. "Are you left handed?" he asked.

I said, "Yes, sir." He took my bait, cast it three feet off the right corner of the duck blind and handed me the pole.

He went back to bait Billy's hook with minnow in hand.

"You're on your own after this one, son," he told Billy. He put the minnow on the hook and Billy let it fly back where he had gotten the bite. Billy was a natural at casting. When his split shot hit the water it made a quick *pa lip* sound. The weight took a second to pull the bead against the bobber stop. You could tell when it happened because the bobber would list to the weighted side ever so slightly. Billy's bobber didn't last long, if at all, it disappeared below the surface. He set the hook with a flick of his wrist and a scrap fight was on. The pound-sized crappie darted and tugged, boiled the water surface until exhausted laying on its side, sliding atop the water to the boat where Billy raised his rod tip high and slung the fish aboard.

"Good job, son."

"Way to go, Billy," I said still watching my bobber that refused to sink. Mr. Poe put the first crappie in the fish box.

"Get you another minnow, son," Mr. Poe said, while getting his pole rigged with a Pinkie® Jig ready to cast. Billy moved around his dad to the live well and put on bait. Mr. Poe pitched the jig where Billy caught the fish. His line never made it to the bottom before another fish grabbed it. A quick snatch of the wrist, a moment of fish-play, and crappie number two made its way in the fish box. I reeled in to check my bait that was still there in living glory. I pitched it back out a little more left, behind the duck blind. Mr. Poe and Billy reeled in a double. I hung my minnow rod in the stern rod holder and started fan-casting the Pinkie®

Jig. I started left, worked to the right with no luck. In the meantime, both Billy and Mr. Poe were having steady action. I was happy for them, but really wanted to catch a fish of my own.

To the right of the duck blind, about six feet a single twig poked a hole in the water. It was a long cast for me; about as long a cast as I could make. I reared back and launched the Pinkie® Jig. It landed inches to my side of the twig. I watched the line floating on the water at the far end of the cast. It was being pulled under slowly as the jig sank, then it twitched to the left. I quickly reeled up the slack and snapped my wrist. A solid wiggle was on the other end of my line. A brief battle and I had my first ever crappie in hand. The guys congratulated me. Boy, I was happy! The fish was a foot long, silvered background overlaid heavily with black markings, and an upturned mouth.

"Brian, that's a black crappie. There are white crappies here, too; you can tell by the mouth and markings that one is a black crappie." Mr. Poe taught me, and he went on a bit more.

I did listen, but I was ready to cast the Pinkie® Jig toward the twig again. As soon as he stopped talking, my jig was in the air, landing close to my first cast. The same thing happened; I reeled in another black crappie, identical to all, but good as the first. All the while, Mr. Poe and Billy were steadily bringing in fish from their side of the duck blind.

I took a moment to compare the two spots. The common factor between the two locations was that they were in the sun and not in the long shadow of the duck blind. As the sun rose higher in the sky, the shadowed areas got smaller. Twice, outside the shadow, my bobber went down, each time I lost the fish and rig to the bushes below. However, I was trying to work the jig at the same time and the action was such, two poles were unnecessary. Since the jig was just as effective, I put the float rig pole away.

Mr. Poe never used anything but the Pinkie® Jig the entire time. He worked that jig around every post and twig by the duck blind, not once, but a hundred times. He never made a miscast either, whether he was casting overhead, side arm, or flipping it under hand. It was like watching a professional golfer swing the club, without effort, but with incredible accuracy. He caught more fish than Billy and I combined; however, most of the time, he declared them too small and tossed them back.

Nonetheless, his too small were often larger than my keepers were.

"Billy, how many fish have you put in the box?" asked his dad.

"Twenty one," answered Billy.

"Brian, how about you?" he asked.

"Fourteen," I answered. I never had a chance to catch up with Billy since he got the morning bite, but it didn't matter.

"Well, boys, we got all the fish I care to clean," said Mr. Poe.

"Mr. Poe, how many fish did you catch?"

"Brian, years ago I gave up counting my fish. I've caught so many in my lifetime that I realize counting them belittles how significant each one is to me. The next one is just as important as the first ever. One day you'll come to realize the same thing," he testified. "How about doing some bass fishing in the canals on the way in?" he asked. Billy and I were up for that.

"Why don't you boys get some lunch together on the front of the boat while I rig up some bass fishing gear?" he asked us. Billy and I turned the top of the cooler into a picnic table, stacked end to end with the *outdoorsman* food Mr. Poe bought at the marina, along with the candy bars, of course. It didn't take us long to set the food out. Mr. Poe finished up about the same time. We had lunch and talked about the bass that hit Billy's minnow earlier in the day. It made a textbook showing, dancing on the water with gills flared out. It ended when the thin-wire crappie hook partially straightened out. It looked to be a three pounder that added a spike to the morning. Lunch went quick. The processed meats, oils, and spices saturated an appetite that was overwhelmed with a final load of chocolate, and washed down with Coke.

"Let's go," said Mr. Poe, as Billy and I dumped the ice from one of the bags into the cooler and used the bag as a trash bag. We were ready for the next happening.

After pulling the two anchors, Mr. Poe made a high-paced slalom run through the duck blinds en route to a distant, unmarked hole in the cattail wall. In that canal network was a slot to tuck in and fish. I didn't know which direction was the way back. I didn't have a clue in the vastness of Back Bay, but I knew he did, and we were getting there in a hurry.

We shot in the cattail opening, making the right hand curve, slowed down at the intersection, made a left and blasted off again. A few minutes later, he took the boat off plane and idled the boat into a passage of cattails so narrow you could reach out and touch plants on either side. I thought, *this is totally cool beans*. A hundred yards or so into the cattails, the passage opened up into a shallow bay that was a mosaic of tall, emergent vegetation, submerged weeds, and open water pockets. Various water birds took flight when the boat nosed out of the cattails. At the base of the closest clump of tall plants, a water moccasin was sunning itself. When we invaded, it slinked into the water, slithered across the surface toward a thick mat of weeds, and vanished below. I'm thinking, *this can't get any better; I'm freaking Christopher Columbus in the new world!*

Mr. Poe cut the outboard off and trimmed it all the way up. He moved to the bow and lowered the trolling motor. He handed Billy and me our fishing poles and began to explain what to do.

"We're going to be fishing these Johnson® Silver Minnows™ I rigged on your line with a seventeen-pound test leader. They're weedless, cast them out across the weeds, skid them across the thick patches, then let them drop and flutter into the open water pockets. Give them a couple of light jerks and continue. When you feel a hit, set the hook hard, this ain't crappie fishing. You have to pull the fish from the weeds as fast as you can." With that said, he moved to the front pedestal seat, put his right foot on the trolling motor control, began guiding the boat around the bay, and started casting. Billy took the rear pedestal seat. I stood in the middle of the boat. We all were casting.

An explosion occurred off the bow. Mr. Poe reared back on his bait caster and set the hook in a bass that was already airborne. The fish rooted around the weeds like a pig, then would launch again. The battle stalled with Mr. Poe holding an arched rod with the bass dug into a massive gob of weeds. He used the trolling motor to drive the boat over to the mat were the bass was buried up, all the time, taking up line on the reel to keep it tight. When the front of the boat was right next to the clump, he hopped off the seat, went down to his knees, put his hand around the line, and followed that down into the vegetation using his right arm. He was fumbling around for what seemed forever. All at once, he sprang to his feet with a five-pound bass draped in weeds, in a lip-lock between his thumb and forefinger. After clearing the weeds away, he took his time to display the fish to Billy and me. For that one moment, Mr. Poe was alive, in full happiness. You could feel it coming off him. I was inspired as he slipped it in the fish box.

Those Johnson® baits were heavy and one could cast them for distance. In my excitement, I flung mine out so far I could see the bottom of my spool when the bait finally splashed down. It landed at the edge of a cattail bank where there was a bunch of matted out weeds. I had to skid the bait across ten yards of growth before getting to the first open pocket of water. By that time, I was tired of reeling fast and was happy to let the bait flutter into the hole. The flutter lasted a second before the rod came forward in my hands. I set the hook out of instinct. There was no jump, just a boil, before the fish socked into the deep weeds. I couldn't pull him out. Mr. Poe took notice of the whole event.

"Billy, reel yours in!" he said, with the trolling motor already powering over to where my fish had holed up.

"Brian, just keep your line tight, we'll get 'im." The trolling motor made it all the way, except for the last ten feet when the plastic prop was eventually jammed with weeds. He raised the motor up quickly, jerked an oar from one of the compartments and started pushing and poling to where my bass was out of sight. It took a couple of long minutes and a lot of effort from Mr. Poe to get there.

"Brian, work your way up to the front of the boat," commanded Mr. Poe. I did. My line was straight up and down in the weeds. Mr. Poe wrapped his hand around my line and followed it down into the mix. The thick plant mat shuttered when he went arm deep into it. I wanted to see that fish so bad. Could he pull a fish out of the grass a second time? Mr. Poe was struggling in the weeds. He was talking to a fish we couldn't see. Again, he hopped to his feet with a fish draped in weeds.

"How big is it, Mr. Poe?" I asked.

"Give me a minute to unwrap it," he responded, "but it feels like a big one!" He peeled the weeds away and it was huge. Well, huge to me. Mr. Poe went to his console and pulled out a scale. The fish hung the scale down to six pounds, two ounces. It was black-backed and dark green on the side, with a Johnson® Silver Minnow™ dangling from its mouth.

"I can't wait till my dad sees that," I exclaimed.

"Me either," said Mr. Poe, as he put it in the fish box. Billy gave me a high five, and I said, "It's your turn." I stood there, reliving the moment.

"While we're here we might as well fish," said Mr. Poe. He and Billy started casting. I was still in awe.

Nothing happened there, so Mr. Poe pushed us out to water where he could run the trolling motor. I started fishing again. *Bass Master* Poe picked up a two pound or so bass from the front. He asked Billy to come to the front and join him. Every now and then, he gave Billy directions where to cast. On one such occasion, the advice paid off. A four-pound plus bass hit Billy's lure just as it went over the edge of some weeds into an open pocket of water. The fish struck from below, went airborne and landed on top of a thick mat of weeds, where it flopped for ten seconds with Billy tugging on it. Billy pulled the fish back into the pocket. The fish immediately screwed itself into the weed bank. Mr. Poe went to the rescue again. It ended up in the fish box, like the rest.

We fished our way around the entire bay. Mr. Poe was agile with the footwork on the trolling motor, using his foot like a third hand. If I had been running the trolling motor, we'd have spent most of our time pushing out of the weeds. Along the way, each of us caught two or three, one to two pound bass that Mr. Poe told us to toss back. He didn't want to clean a whole bunch of fish he kept reminding us. We also battled four chain pickerel and smaller members of the muskellunge family which tested our angling skills. Those fish strike violent and become more so when they feel the sting of the hook. They made you feel like you were big game fishing from a small boat. Mr. Poe told us they were bony and tossed them back after cautiously dealing with a mouth full of teeth. For catch and release, fishing a chain pickerel is hard to beat. They are exciting.

We ended up at the hole in the cattails where we started. "You boys ready?" Mr. Poe asked us.

"Yes, sir," we said, as we tucked our gear away. He raised the trolling motor and locked it into place with the clip on the motor mount. He went back to the console lowered the motor, and popped it off in a roar. We idled through the gap in the cattails. When we reentered the canal, he turned right and lit off, making the turns necessary to get us back to the marina. The entire ride back I felt like a hero, a conqueror of fish.

Mr. Poe coasted the nose of the boat up to the ramp. The front of the boat lightly struck the concrete.

"Billy, run up to the bait house and grab a five-gallon bucket without holes," said Mr. Poe.

"What can I do, Mr. Poe?" I asked.

"Gather up all the trash and take it to the trashcan for me," he said. I picked up every little bit of trash in the boat and in the cooler, stuffed it in the ice bag and ran it up to the trashcan, passing Billy on the way. When I got back, Mr. Poe was bent over the live well, dipping minnows into the bucket half filled with water. It took him a few minutes to do it. The last minnow was a challenge to capture. When the last bait was in the bucket, he pulled the plug and carried it to the bow, handing it to Billy.

"Run these back to the tanks and dump them," he said. With that, he went back to the console and trimmed up his motor more than halfway. On his way to the front, he picked up the bowline and handed it to me standing on the ramp.

"Hold this line. I'm going to get the truck," he told me.

Tethered to that line, I felt like a quarter horse tied to a fence. I wanted to run around and tell anyone and everyone about our day of fishing. I couldn't wait for someone to ask how we did. I was going to play it cool, as if it happened that way to me every time, but no one was around. We were in the boonies, so I stood there like a cow in a pasture waiting for Mr. Poe to back the wagon up.

Billy came back about the time Mr. Poe pulled around the trailer. Mr. Poe instructed us to push the boat off to the side. We did, and he backed the trailer in the water. He got in the boat. We tossed the bowline in the front when he said so. While Mr. Poe was jockeying the boat on the trailer, Billy told me he told the lady at the store how well we did. Crap! I wanted to be the braggart. Now there was nobody to tell the story to until we got back home.

Mr. Poe drove the boat on the trailer so expertly, I didn't notice the boat was loaded until he was hopping off the bow and clipping the bow strap on. He cranked the boat tight on the trailer.

"Boys, follow me around to the fish cleaning station," Mr. Poe spoke to us, as he got in the truck. He pulled the boat on the other side of the store where the station was.

The fish cleaning station came up from the ground around a single layer of black, molded, solid side up cinder blocks with shoe traffic markings. The structure, four by eight feet, had posts on the corners made of slightly off square four by fours. On the far long side, was an eighteen-inch wide, by eight-foot long section of pressure treated plywood mounted waist high and slanted slightly back away from the station, spanning the uprights. Two by eights on the edges supported it underneath. A two by eight pine board was mounted horizontally behind the wooden surface where the fish were cleaned to prevent slide offs. There was a half-inch gap at the base to let rinse water, fish scales, and miscellaneous scraps to wash out. An eight-foot high, semi-flat tin roof covered the area supported by the uprights and some extra framing. It was plumbed, a garden hose on the right side. The station had seen a lifetime of dead fish, judging by the roughness of its condition and the cut markers on the boards. Metal fish scalers hung from rusted nails on both sides. A hand written placard on a flaking piece of plywood was posted on the near side upright stating, "Dump your guts in the canal."

"Billy, get a five-gallon bucket out of the back of the truck. Brian, jump up in the boat and dig the fish out of the fish box and put them in the five-gallon bucket Billy is going to give you." Mr. Poe got us in gear. We did that in short order. Billy brought the fish to his dad.

"Give Brian the water hose, so he can rinse out the fish box," he told Billy. "Brian, pull the plug in the bottom right hand corner before you start rinsing it out, OK? Billy, pull the plug out of the boat and put it back in over the transom." That didn't take long to accomplish.

"Each of you boys grab a scaler and start shucking the scales off these fish while I dress them out," he kept us hopping. With three of us working, the job was easy. The fish were dressed out and in plastic bags placed in the boat cooler in little more than half an hour. After cleaning the fish, Mr. Poe took his time to clean up the station, washing the boat, rods and reels, and us down. The only bad thing about it was I wouldn't be able to show dad the whole fish I caught. The good thing about it was

I didn't have to bury the fish guts in the garden.

All of us loaded up in the truck once Mr. Poe locked the motor in the *up* position. We were back at my house by four o'clock. Billy and I slept most of the ride back. When the truck stopped on the side of the road by my house, my eyes popped open. I grabbed my fishing tackle and took it into the garage. I poked my head in the door, yelled I was home. Dad came out, as I went back to the boat. Mr. Poe was standing there waiting to give me a couple bags of fish. I said thanks, ran them to the kitchen sink and ran back out. Mr. Poe and Dad were talking at the side of the truck. Billy asked me if I wanted to play basketball at his house. I said I'd be over as soon as I could. Oh, the energy of youth. I stopped to say thank you to Mr. Poe and he said we'd have to do it again. I wanted to ask about next weekend, but I didn't.

I ran back in the house to change shirts and tell Mom the fish were in the sink. In my bedroom, I changed out one T-shirt for another. Mom was in the kitchen putting the fish away.

"I'm going over to Billy's to play basketball," I said.

She said, "Fine, dinner is at six." On the way to the door she asked, "How'd you like your lunch?" I didn't even turn around; I just said, "It was great!"

Chapter 7 - Catfish Ladies

After the summer of my sixteenth year, my world spread out when the Virginia Department of Motor Vehicles issued me a license to fish outside the range of my bicycle. I bought the old family car for a dollar. My four-wheeled freedom was a nineteen seventies something, tan, four-door Plymouth Valiant, with four-fifty-five air conditioning and three speeds on the floor. The interior was monotone, darker, tan vinyl, which worked like hot glue to any exposed skin when temperatures heated up in the late spring through the early fall. If somebody hopped in the car wearing shorts or a tank top, and bare skin missed the beach towel slipcovers, you could smell the bacon frying, but the sizzle sound was a yelp. I customized it myself by adding tan travel racks on top to carry surfboards, coolers, and fishing poles. We called it, *The Tank*. It was everything I needed to get from here to there, but it was far from cool. Some other guys had jazzed up their cars and trucks with fancy tires and rims, throaty exhaust systems, decals, chrome accessories, stereos and such. When I looked, objectively, at the tank parked in the driveway, I realized my squared off four-door family sedan was what it was and painted brown for a reason. It was in good mechanical condition as Dad put it. I saved the fix-it-up money and bought fishing tackle.

There was a lake half surrounded by a city park on one side and houses or woods on the far side, where my dad took me fishing a decade ago. It was close by my house, very much unhidden, but rarely fished. The park didn't get many visitors, probably due to the lack of amenities. I had a gut feeling that the lake had big catfish because few fished it, and there had to be an abundance of mullet and shad. An urge had developed

89

in me to try something different.

One evening, after supper, I gathered six spinning rods together. The rods were an odd mix of light to medium weight spinners and two heavy surf casting poles. They were all set-up with slip sinker rigs and yard long thirty-pound test leaders attached to 2/0 long shank hooks. The only difference was the sinker weight. The two light spinners had quarter-ounce bank sinkers, the two medium spinners had half-ounce egg sinkers, and the two surf casters had two-ounce pyramid sinkers. My idea was to stagger the bait in terms of depth or distance from the bank and find a feeding zone, if there was one.

I told Mom I was going to the lake fishing. She didn't care. Before I left, I pruned six Y sticks, a foot and a half long, from the Crepe Myrtles in the yard for rod props. I stuck them in my creel. The only other items in the creel were a box of 2/0 hooks, a spool of thirty-pound line, a handful of assorted sinkers, a stringer for the fish, a pair of needle nose pliers, and a rag. I had a large pocketknife on me.

After wrapping a beach towel around each of the two bars of the car rack, I laid the fishing poles across with the handles down between the car racks to work as braces and tied them down with twine. The creel, I put in the back seat, along with an empty five-gallon bucket and a lawn chair. The lawn chair was a luxury item a bicycle couldn't accommodate. En route to the lake, I stopped by a grocery store, picking up a tub of chicken livers for less than a buck, a pack of cheap hot dogs for less than a buck, and two cans of store brand, whole kernel corn. I forgot the can opener, but could make do with my knife.

The area I wanted to fish was on the northwest corner of the lake. That area was located in the park where the shore bulged out a bit into the lake but before where the two shorelines joined at an odd angle to form a cove. In the past, I'd frequently noticed some type of bait working the surface there, especially in the evenings.

The road crested the northern rim of the lake. A ten-yard swath of grass separated the road from the lake. There were no guardrails or trees, just an unobstructed view of a 700-acre lake. I pulled The Tank into the grass at the bump in the shore, where the cove began to form. It wasn't as if I was impeding on anything or anybody. I imagine that the very few who saw me pull off the road did wonder what I was doing. They more than likely assumed I had car problems. That was the beauty of the situation, open stealth.

The lawn chair was the first thing out of the car. I popped it open near the edge of the steep bank. Then I pulled out the bucket with the bait in the bottom and the creel on the top. I sat it in the seat of the chair. The poles, I untied from the rack and leaned them against the chair to form a teepee. I drove off to the parking lot about a quarter mile away and walked back. Back at the chair, I started to set up catfish camp.

The first order of business was to jab the Y sticks in the ground in front of the chair about two paces apart. The creel, I stuck under the chair. The tub of chicken livers, I put on the ground, removing the lid. I cut two hotdogs up in two-inch sections and put them on top of the chicken liver lid. Next, I set the poles in the rod holders in an order of heavy, medium, light and heavy, medium, light from left to right. I grabbed three pieces of hot dog, baiting every other pole from left to right and cast them out. After casting them out, I laid them in the crotch of the Y stick and left the bail open. I did the same thing, using the chicken liver. The chicken liver left my hands a mess, so I made my way down to the shore and got a quick hand rinse. I did things the same way Dad taught me.

The bank was a steep, three to four-foot drop to a sliver of sandy shoreline. That worked out well with the poles in the Y sticks stuck in the bank above because a good length of line would swag down before entering the water. It made it easy to determine if it was a bite or just the wind blowing the line. The only problem was that if you got a fish, you had to jump down off the bank to the shore to land the fish. Nevertheless, at sixteen, I would have jumped off a building to land a fish.

While climbing my way back up the bank, I was thinking all I had left to do was open a can of corn and toss out a few handfuls of fish-call, something Dad thought me years ago. However, when I got to the top, I noticed the far left hand pole had a tight line that was heading off to deep water. I ran and snatched it up. When I flipped the bail over, the line came tight in an instant. The hook set itself. The pull was more than I expected. Far more tug than expected. The drag was chirping, grudgingly giving line up. I walked left to keep from entangling with the other lines. It took a couple of minutes before I started to feel I was gaining more line than I was losing.

When the fish was fifteen feet off the shore, I made the big hop from the bank to the shore. I didn't think about it when I did it; I just jumped. I thought about it when trying to keep the line tight in midair. Free fall is not the best time to do serious thinking, unless you're wearing a parachute and even then I'm not sure, unless you're in prayer. It was a *here we go* kind of moment; I managed to come out well on the shoreline still attached to the fish. The fish was coming closer to shore in an ever-tightening zigzag pattern. When it got in a foot of water, I could see it was a big catfish. I worked it a minute longer, to the point I could grab the leader and dragged it up on the thin strip of sand. It flipped and fluttered, and I bobbed and weaved until I managed to get the fish in one hand then the next. The rod and reel landed in the sand. I didn't like that a bit. Finally, I got a good grip on the fish with one hand and picked up the rod and reel. I walked to where the bank jutted up high and tossed fish and the rod and reel up into the grass. I scrambled up the bank as fast as I could.

When I got to the top, I glanced down the line up of poles and saw the middle, lightweight outfit, baited with hot dog was getting a bite. The line would pull out straight then go slack. I used my foot to push the catfish further back from the edge before running down to the pole having the bite. When I got to the pole, I noticed a lot of the line was already off the spool. I flipped the bail over, reeled the line tight, and struck. The fish was spirited on the light tackle. I fumbled down a goat trail to get to the water's edge. In a few minutes, a good two-pound, channel cat was flopping in the sand. I picked up the fish, the pole and made my way back up the bank. I checked the other remaining lines with my eyes. Nothing was going on.

I unhooked the smaller cat with the pole leaning against the lawn chair. Afterwards, I got the stringer out of the creel, clipped the fish on the stringer, and made my way back down to the water. This was turning out to be work. The lawn chair was nothing more than a leaning post. I scanned the shoreline for a sturdy stick I could use to stake down my stringer. A gnarled branch was washed up on the bank to the right; it was a good ways toward the corner of the lake. I hopped and bounded in and around various obstacles along the shore to get it. The tree limb was firm, not rotten and soft. I used my foot and hand to bust it into a three-foot section. I walked back to where the fishing rods were still working. Things were quiet, nothing to run and get at the moment.

I dropped the end of the stringer in the sand and stepped on it. With my pocketknife, I whittled a point on the stick, jabbed it in the sand as far as I could with both hands and then wallowed it deeper by pushing and making tiny circles at the same time. As the branch went deeper, sand washed in the hole, making a solid seal. It didn't take long before it felt very secure. I clipped the end of the stringer over the end of the stake and went back for the big catfish.

The big channel cat was lying in the grass with its mouth opening and closing, as if it was grazing. I took the needle nose pliers from my creel to help remove the hook. First look, it was obvious, the hook was past the mouth, lodged deeply in the stomach. Using the wire-cutting portion on the needle nose, I cut the line close to the mouth. I took the fish, in both hands, down the bank. Each fish I could take was a proverbial feather in my cap; that's why I was taking special care with this catfish and every other one. Anyway, the catfish was alive but not lively. I put the fish next to the bank, as far away from the water as I could. To the chagrin of the small cat on the stringer, I pulled it out of water. I unclipped the second to the last ring, opened and pulled the stringer in the direction of the big cat lying on the bank. Dropping the stringer, I went and got the big cat; it was a solid eight to ten pound fish, good for a lake this size, and clipped it on the stringer. I tossed the two fish back in the lake and made my way back up the bank.

At the top, I noticed the medium weight spinner with the hot dog bait, was getting action. The line would pull, then slack and pull again. I grabbed it and set the hook. It shot off in a furious wiggle. A three-pound catfish made landfall in a few minutes. I unhooked it and put it on the stringer.

This was too fast and too good for other eyes to see the goings on. The old park lake had more to offer than kids feeding ducks did. I had tapped a secret that was in full view of thousands of people. A public fish bomb.

Traffic on the road going by the lake wasn't heavy but was steady. People were getting off work that time of evening; a car or truck passed by every few minutes. One driver, with a good eye, with a loud mouth

93

could spill my beans. I needed to take the operation underground or at least below the line of sight.

The three poles baited with chicken livers, I reeled in, took off the bait and tossed it in the lake, secured the hooks on an eye braces and laid them flat in the grass. The livers weren't working and the action was so good with the hot dogs, I didn't need the additional poles. I folded down the chair and dropped it below the bank. I plucked all six Y sticks out of the bank and tossed them down on the shoreline. The three poles I was baiting with hot dogs, I carried down the goat trail to the shoreline. I brought the five-gallon bucket and creel down the bank as well. I tucked everything out of sight, below the bank.

I re-baited the three poles with hot dogs and set up a Y stick for each after casting out. If memory served me well, the fish were taking the bait some twenty five to thirty feet out. I cast the three rods in a fan pattern with the big surf caster down the middle. I took the left over liver and hand slung it out, inside the pattern, a fish-call. After rinsing my hands, I plopped down on the bucket and waited. I waited less than two minutes and the light spinner took off. It turned out to be a two-pound bullhead catfish. I barely got that fish on the stringer before the surf caster got a run. It was another two-pound bullhead. I didn't need that many poles so I laid the surf caster in the grass with the other three combos. The lightweight spinner I re-baited and cast out. I just propped it up in the Y stick when line ran off the other spinner. The seven-pound channel cat put up a strong fight. The fight was long enough that I was concerned about the other pole getting a bite at the same time. What would I do then? I'm glad it didn't happen that way.

Within a half an hour, four more catfish made their way onto the stringer. I was more than satisfied and happy that my catfish hunch paid off. The left over hot dogs, I diced up and tossed in the lake. I didn't know when I'd be back, but I wanted the catfish to know there might be food in that area from time to time, whether that was more necessary to the fish or me. I didn't care.

The two poles I was using, I laid neatly in the grass with the other four. The lawn chair and bucket with the creel and two cans of corn, I sat beside the folded down chair. The fish, I left on the stringer in the water. On the walk back to the car, I was thinking, *I can't wait for Dad to see this.*

I pulled the car off the road onto the grass. The six rods, I quickly tied to the roof rack. The lawn chair and bucket went in the back seat. I grabbed a beach towel from the back seat, unlocked the trunk, and laid it flat. The fish would survive the ten-minute ride back to the house. I jumped from the bank down to the shore. When I got a good grip on the end of the stringer, the water erupted. It was as if a newly introduced bunch of catfish had come to the group conclusion that their lives were about to drastically change. I tried to lift them all up, keeping them out of the sand, but the stringer of fish was too long; the bottom three fish dragged the sand. Then it dawned on me, by holding the fish up like that I was showing off the secret I was trying to keep. I dropped all the fish down in the sand. I stood up and peeked over the bank. There was a car coming. I squatted back down. The car passed by. I peeked over again. The coast was clear. I dragged the fish across the sand, up the goat trail and through the grass to the open trunk. Thankfully, the grass removed much of the sand from the fish, because I just hoisted the whole stringer of fish onto the beach towel and shut the lid to the sound of an oncoming vehicle. I hopped in and took it to the house.

When I turned onto my street, I could see Mom, Aunt Quida, and Mrs. Henderson sitting on our front porch, having a gathering. I pulled in the driveway like Fred Sanford in a brand new Cadillac. We all said "Hi," to one another. I popped the trunk to air out the fish, before going up on the porch to hug and kiss the ladies.

"So, how'd you do, Brian?" they asked.

"Ya'll come around and see," I said as casual as I could stand it. When they got a witness of those catfish in the trunk, I got an, "Oh my goodness, would you look at that," testimony that made me grow six inches taller on the spot. I was the catfish man. I enjoyed that.

Dad came around to the back of the house, before I cleaned the fish. He admired every catfish, commented on their size, asked about the bait, how I got the hunch to go fishing there and such. He fed my ego. I loved the attention. It took a little less than an hour before I came back around the front of the house with the fish dressed out. The women were still there.

"Honey, supper is on the stove," Mom said.

I was eating when Mom came in the kitchen; her two girlfriends had just gone home.

"We were talking and you're taking us fishing tomorrow at four," Mom told me. She mentioned taking the Henderson's station wagon. She mentioned lawn chairs. She mentioned picnicking. She mentioned calling Mrs. Wheeler, to see if she could come. I mentioned everybody needed a fishing license. She told me to go in the garage and get the picnic supplies off the shelf so she could get some things ready tonight. I went and got the picnic supplies and set out the four good lawn chairs against the house. The whole time, I was thinking my catfish hunch had backfired on me. I was on the brink of the strangest fishing trip of my life.

I had taken friends fishing in the past. However, they had been guys, who basically knew how to fish. The guys didn't require any special attention. But, taking ladies only? The ladies aren't going to bait their own hooks. I knew Mom could cast, but could the others? This was going to be a challenge. What would they think if they went through all the trouble to go fishing and the fish didn't bite? With the guys, we'd blamed it on the moon or anything else but ourselves. These women might think it was because I brought them to the wrong place. *It would be my fault, if we didn't catch fish!* It was the first time, I had felt pressure like that in regards to a fishing trip. I didn't like the feeling.

Three-thirty the next afternoon, I was carrying the last load of stuff across the street to the Henderson's driveway. There was a two-week vacation pile of stuff sitting in the drive to be loaded in the station wagon. There was a five-gallon bucket with two packs of hotdogs, the two cans of corn from yesterday, my fishing creel, and five fishing poles leaning up against the station wagon. The rest of the stuff had nothing to do with fishing, at least in my mind. There were coolers, lawn chairs, and canvas bags filled with things I had no idea about. I wondered how all that stuff was going to fit, yet still have enough room for four ladies, plus me. Actually, the old station wagon was very spacious. Everything fit in the back nicely. Mr. Henderson helped me load it. The amount of stuff the ladies deemed necessary to go fishing for a few hours, amazed me. In the past, I had always brought the least amount of stuff. This trip was starting out different from any other trip I'd ever been on; we had too much stuff.

Mom got behind the wheel. Mrs. Henderson, in her late seventies, rode shotgun. I got in the back. Mr. Henderson was smiling and waving good-bye in the driveway. He had the wood shop and house all to himself for the next several hours; he was happy. Mrs. Wheeler and Aunt Quida lived kitty corner to one another, so the plan was to pick them both up at Aunt Quida's house on the way. When we pulled in, there were two more small coolers with two more bags of stuff to load. Mom dropped the back glass in the station wagon; I squeezed their stuff in back. After a while, all the ladies got in the car. We headed to the lake. Me, in the middle back seat, surrounded by four women engaged in two to three conversions at once. In minutes, my head went numb. There were too many words in the air.

I was brought out of the coma when Mom asked, "Brian, tell me where to pull off." I told her with a tap on the shoulder and a finger point.

Getting out of the car was a release to me. I loved each of those ladies, but I had never been that exposed to an intense hen party. I heard more words in that fifteen-minute car ride than in two normal days of living. Being somewhat quiet was part of my personality, but I didn't know any guys that talked that much. I was overwhelmed, which didn't take much because I was nervous about taking these women fishing.

Everybody grabbed an armload of this or that. It didn't take long to unpack the car. We placed everything on the ground.

"Honey, why don't you go park the car, OK?" Mom asked. I hopped in and did it. It was the longest car I had ever driven. It felt like there was an acre of car hood between the windshield and the front bumper. I managed to park the land yacht, but it took me three tries in an empty parking lot. I was glad nobody was around to watch.

I walked back. The ladies had opened up the lawn chairs, arranging the coolers as end tables. A bag of stuff was under each of their chairs. They set up a luxury catfish camp on their own. It was better than I'd ever done. However, they had set it up so close to the bank, I had no working area. So, I helped getting the chairs, coolers, and bags moved back from the bank, five feet or so. The Y sticks I brought yesterday were still down on the sand below the bank. I jumped down to get them. The ladies set up a picnic, pouring me a cup of sweet tea with ice. I stuck a Y stick in front of each of the ladies, one on the far side for myself. The ladies gave me a handful of cookies while doing so. I laid a fishing pole in each of the Y sticks, cutting up a pack of hotdogs into two-inch sections and making a pile of diced wieners on the ground by the middle Y stick. The ladies gave me some strawberries and freshened up my sweet tea. I baited each hook and cast them out. My watch said it was ten till five.

I could personally vouch that every one of the ladies was an outstanding cook. They offered me every snack they brought, but I told them I was full. In all honesty, my stomach was in knots. *What happens if the catfish don't bite?* I was thinking. I looked at my watch and it was five-thirty. Forty long minutes snailed by me,

"Is Ladybug (Mrs. Henderson) getting a bite?" Mom asked.

"No, ma'am, it's the wind blowing the line," I answered. Fifteen more minutes passed by. I endured one of the longest hours of my life. I reeled in every rod and checked the bait. The bait was fine. I cast them back out. *This is going to be a flop.* My heart was sinking in self-doubt, sitting on that five-gallon bucket, feeling the weight of eyes like the sole white guy at a good soul food joint. *Where are those fish of yesterday?* Somehow, depression was setting in and I was fishing of all things! It was a first for me, to be depressed while fishing. Focused on the fish, I was not paying attention to the ladies. They were talking and laughing, not even aware they were fishing. I could have put the poles away and I'm not sure they would have noticed. However, I was noticing. Nonetheless, they were having fun; the fish didn't matter. They were giving me a lesson I wouldn't appreciate for another decade.

At six fourteen, the line from Ladybugs pole took a mad dash. I was there and set the hook before the ladies knew what was going on.

"You got one, you got one!" I shouted, walking the pole back to her in a chair. "All you have to do is reel." I smiled, so thankful for that fish. All the ladies turned into cheerleaders. They offered encouragement. I explained to her the drag of the line, and why she should not crank the reel against it.

"When the line is going out, stop reeling and let the line run out; then reel when the line isn't going out," I uttered those words, but they were awash in the cheers. I just let it go. There was too much fun going on to need a coach. The ladies walked in a cluster to the edge of the bank.

I dropped down on the shoreline. The catfish was floundering on the surface. As it got closer, the line swung down within arm's reach above my head. I grabbed it from the air and semi-hand lined the fish to the beach, as Ladybug reeled. A two-pound bullhead made the day. Mom threw down my stringer. I clipped the fish on, showing the ladies the fish, before attaching the other end of the stringer to the stake I left in the shore the day before.

After putting the fish in the lake, I looked up to notice another line unwinding into the lake.

"Somebody's got a bite!" I blurted. With that said, Mrs. Wheeler found herself battling a catfish, with three cheerleaders by her side. I stayed down on the shore. They were fun to watch work together.

"Mom!" I pointed to her pole that had line running out. She broke away and got her pole. Mrs. Wheeler's fish was getting close. I got a hand on her line as soon as I could and pulled the fish up on the beach. It looked like a twin of the first fish. I flipped it up on the grass and went to help Mom. They were triplets. We celebrated until a fish hit Aunt Quida's bait, and we were off to the races again. I asked Mom to reel my rod in while Aunt Quida was bringing her fish in. Aunt Quida was the first person I'd ever seen put a dance step to reeling in a fish. It was a kind of Jitterbug step with a lot of wrist rotation. Her fish was about half a pound bigger than the other three fish. With all the commotion, we didn't notice Mom down the bank, by herself. I looked up to see her struggling with a big fish.

"Mom, you got one?" I asked.

"Yeah, and it's a good one," she huffed. All the ladies went to her with moral support. I managed to pin two of the catfish on the stringer before jogging the shore to help Mom.

"Get him, Brian! Get that fish!" yelled Mom. I felt pressure. The fish cruised the surface ten feet from shore. Everybody got a good look at it. It was a big channel cat over ten pounds. I wished I had a net. I hoped the hook was well set. I thought about the knots I tied. It got closer fast. I was mentally prepared to jump in after that fish. It swam by. I saw the hook buried in the mouth. I chased the leader down and pulled the fish as far up the beach as I could, then took it in both hands in a death grip. I flung it up on the bank and clawed my way behind it. There was a collective, "Would you look at that?"

"Dixie, that's the biggest catfish I'd ever seen in my life," Aunt Quida said to Mom. Mom was breathing deep. The struggle and the excitement got her breath. I stood there smiling, watching the women be themselves. A double handful of catfish slime, stinking of lake water and sweat and my mom came over to me, hugged me and kiss me right on the mouth. I felt like Beaver Clever.

"Mom, I didn't see there was a fish on that pole when I asked you to reel it up." I said.

She told me, "I started to reel it in and it was heavy."

"So, why didn't you say something?"

"All I could think about was getting that fish," she said.

"I know what you mean."

Looking up the bank there were four fishing poles scattered in the grass and Mrs. Wheeler's catfish grazing.

"Let's do that some more," blurted Aunt Quida, caught up in the fish catching spirit. The others chimed in agreement. It took ten minutes or more for me to put Mrs. Wheeler's fish on the stringer and start getting the poles back in action.

I tossed Ladybug's and Mrs. Wheeler's bait out, baited Aunt Quida's, and was just about to make the cast when Aunt Quida said, "I want to cast it out myself."

Mom followed up with the same comment. I baited Mom's hook and handed her the pole. She gave it a nice cast out.

"Brian, you're going to have to show me how to do that," said Aunt Quida. I explained it as I went through the motion of casting.

"Let me go over that one more time," I said.

She said, "I got it, it's simple." I gave her the pole with second thoughts. She stepped to the edge of the bank like stepping into a batter's box. In an exaggerated motion, the pole went high above her head dropped way behind her and she heaved the rod forward letting her finger release the line at the ten o'clock position, which was about the time her windbreaker flew over her head and then parachuted into the lake five feet from shore. Comedians live for such laughter. I was pie eyed, but the ladies exploded in laughter, including Aunt Quida herself. Tears were rolling down their cheeks.

100

"Well, don't just stand there, go get her jacket," Mom said, laughing. I reeled in her jacket, unhooked it, rung it out, and hung it on the back of her lawn chair. They were going through the situation the second time when I caught on what happened. As luck would have it, on the back cast the hook had snagged her jacket from underneath her chair. On the forward cast, the jacket came from underneath the chair like a big red rabbit snatched from its hole. The odd thing was the lightweight chair never moved. You couldn't do that trick again for money. The laughter would die down for a moment, until one of the ladies thought about it again and laughter broke out renewed. It was contagious. I was laughing.

"Well, Brian, cast her pole out; we need to save the lawn chairs," Mom told me and started a new uproar.

I cast out her bait, while doing so, I noticed Mrs. Wheeler's line was running off into the lake.

"Mrs. Wheeler! You got a bite," I shouted, the laughter stopped, the cheering started again. Ladybug got a bite and so did Mom a minute afterwards. There were three fish reeling in at the same time. I dropped down on the shoreline. Mom's fish came in first. It was a couple pound bullhead. I tossed it up on the bank. Mrs. Wheeler was struggling with her fish. Ladybug's fish came in next. It was a solid three to four pound channel cat. I tossed it up on the bank. Mrs. Wheeler was still fighting it out, but now with a support team. The fish boiled the water some ten feet off the shore. It was a big catfish. It dug deep, boiled, and splashed water, giving a tremendous fight. Mrs. Wheeler hung in there, encouraged by her girlfriends. When it rolled into the shallows, I was surprised at its size. It was bigger than any of the fish caught yesterday or today. I waded in shin deep and squatted down quietly until the fish swam by. I scooped that fish up in both arms, dashing out of the lake. I didn't stop until high up on the bank with the catfish like a baby in my arms. It was a fifteen-pound plus channel cat that had more, "Oh my, would you look at that," factor than you could haul in a pickup truck. I just stared at it, while the ladies congratulated Mrs. Wheeler.

"Quida! Your line," Mom shouted, breaking up the admiration party.

I laid the big catfish in the grass and went down on the shore to land the next fish. It turned out to be a seven-pound channel catfish. I put that

101

one on the stringer and the big channel cat of Mrs. Wheeler's. I couldn't believe my eyes at that stringer of catfish.

It wasn't over! Each of the ladies had two more rounds of catfish, before nightfall. We ended up with sixteen catfish on the stringer. I doubled up six of the ten clips on the stringer with fish. The last two volleys produced four fish in the eight to ten pound range. The bite came alive as the sun set. We left the fish biting.

While we were cleaning up, I thought back to yesterday and remembered the fish bite hadn't occurred until after six in the evening. The anxiety I put myself through was because I failed to fit together information given me: the location, the bait, and the time of day. Today I had two out of three factors in place at the beginning, but I had to wait for the third factor—time—to line up for the bite. I kept that to myself, but I smiled, knowing I had figured out something new about fishing on my own. You have to pay attention, to both the positive and the negative aspects of any fishing trip, or you might miss a fish-lesson.

Mom and Aunt Quida walked to the parking lot and got the station wagon. Mrs. Wheeler, Ladybug, and I waited with our belongings. Mom pulled the car into the grass. It didn't take long for everybody to load the gear in. We thought we made enough room for the catfish in the back. Mom put down a towel and covered it with a plastic garbage bag. The last thing in the car was to be the fish. I had to go get them from the lake. I didn't realize it until I pulled the stringer from the lake; there was almost a hundred pounds of catfish on the stringer. It was a load. The metal chain dug into my fingers as I dragged the stringer of fish up the goat trail, across the grass. I stopped once to re-grip. Pumped up, at that moment, I believe I could have dragged them all the way to the house. When I got the fish over to the tailgate, there was an, "Oh my", then an, "Oh no" factor. It was a beautiful stringer of fish, but I couldn't neatly get them in the back of the station wagon.

"Brian don't get Mr. Henderson's station wagon all fishy," Mom said.

I was thinking of the impossibility of that statement when Ladybug snapped, "Don't worry about this car; Mac will clean it up tomorrow."

"Brian, you'll have to go over and help Mr. Henderson clean up his car tomorrow," Mom said.

I thought, *I wasn't the one who created this problem since I didn't catch a single fish*, but I kept my tongue in my mouth so my jaw wouldn't get hurt. Back talk wasn't an option, nor tolerated. I smiled and nodded. I heaved the chain of fish on to the towel in three sections. Although I tried to keep the mess to a minimum, there was catfish slime on the tailgate and along the side of the back compartment. I had a job lined up tomorrow.

Mom closed the tailgate, telling me to ride by the window, because I stunk of fish. She also made me sit on a towel. The hero I was in my mind, was getting the family dog treatment after a skunk encounter. I didn't care; I wore the odor like a badge of honor from a battle well fought.

Looking out the car window on the way back home, the ladies voices faded to white noise as I fantasized about a heroic welcome for the fish slayer..., me. It didn't take long to put that notion in check as my mind wandered past the heroic welcome fantasy and on to the reality of the tremendous amount of stuff that would need sorting and put away. Things in the back of the station wagon, wobbling above my head were a constant reminder. The ladies would help pick through it all to get back what they brought. Mr. Henderson would pitch in, as well as Dad. However, when it came to the fish cleaning, I saw myself at the backyard picnic table with a mechanics lamp hung up in the maple tree, doing a solo mosquito dance with a hundred pounds of catfish to clean. I didn't like the way I was anticipating the ending of this fish story—me being a modern day Don Quixote fighting off mosquito dragons with a fillet knife to an audience of fish. My mood changed to solemn. I wasn't going to be angry or disrespectful. I accepted the predicted outcome. I knew my place in the pecking order. However, I was figuring out a nice way not to get myself in this position again.

The ladies came up with a plan en route that would be easier for everybody, we would go back to Ladybug's home, unload everything including the fish, sort and separate out everybody's things, then put Aunt Quida's and Mrs. Wheeler's items back in the station wagon for their return home. It would require some back tracking, but they lived close enough for that to be less of a problem than going through things twice. I went with the flow. It was going to be a long evening for me, regardless. As if, I had an opinion that counted anyway.

Mom backed the station wagon up the Henderson's driveway. I was impressed the way she whipped that urban land yacht up the drive, backwards to the garage door without having to pull forward to re-align. She was a trucker mama and the ladies commented to that effect with laughter. Laughter was a love language amongst those girls. They spoke it to one another all the time.

Mr. Henderson must have been watching for us, because the car hadn't even stopped before the automatic garage door opener was drawing the double door up. I could see him coming through the garage when the door was waist high. He was wearing work boots, khaki work pants that had seen tons of grass clippings and sawdust, a tucked in, relatively new, plaid shirt with the sleeves rolled up to the elbows and a big smile below a grayed crew cut.

I loved him like everybody else, more than I knew how to express. He was real. You could always feel the honesty in his presence. There was nothing fake; there was nothing hidden. I admired the man. He went to Ladybug, first, and gave her a hug and a kiss. He asked how she was and how things went. She said, "Fine," as he went around the car and gave all the ladies a hug and a peck on the cheek. He got to me when I was dropping the tailgate down to get the stuff out. In a bear hug, he mashed me against his chest and asked how I was doing. I didn't get a chance to say anything to him, because he saw over me the pile of catfish still on the stringer in the back of his station wagon and started commenting. Dad had also seen us back in and had stepped across the street to greet us. Mr. Henderson started talking about the fish.

"Oh my, would you look at that," Dad blurted, after coming out of the shadows and around to the light of the open garage where he saw the pile of fish. Dad started carrying on with the ladies about the fishing trip and everybody started talking at once. I hadn't noticed, but Mr. Henderson had gone back in the garage, returning with two large galvanized washtubs.

"We can put the fish in these tubs," he said. It amazed me that he always had the right tool, part, screw or nail, piece of wood or metal, jar or whatever, somewhere in his garage, when you needed it most, and he knew exactly where to find it. I know for a fact, we couldn't have found a washtub at any of the houses around us, yet he had two. He sat one on the drive by the tailgate, so I could roll the catfish out of the back, into the tub. When the fish landed in the tub, they were still squirming. Catfish can live a long time out of water.

Mr. Henderson grabbed a handle on one side and I grabbed the other. Following his lead up to where the driveway met the garage, we sat the tub down. There the catfish shone in the garage lights.

"Brian, go ahead and take those fish off the stringer," Mr. Henderson told me. He went around the corner of the house. I unclipped the fish from the stringer. I was just finishing, when he came around with a garden hose with a nozzle. He excused himself to get through the ladies admiring their catch.

"Ya'll, step back," he said, before turning the water on those fish. Some water splattered out of the tub, most went in. The catfish came alive in the cool water. It took a few minutes before the water covered the fish's backs. Grass that was stuck to the fish slime, floated to the top; dirt stained the water while sand sank to the bottom of the tub.

"Brian, dump the dirty water out," Mr. Henderson asked. I went around to the high end of the tub, tipping the tub up so the water ran down the slope of the driveway. Afterwards he refilled the tub with clean water.

Dad and the ladies were busy taking everything out of the back of the station wagon and sorting through this and that as to what belonged to whom. Individual piles formed for Mrs. Wheeler, Aunt Quida, and Mom. Ladybug's stuff came directly into the garage or house. She put it away. Mom and Dad took Mom's stuff across the street and put it away. Aunt Quida and Mrs. Wheeler put their stuff back in the station wagon then went in Ladybug's house to call their husbands, letting them know they were all right.

While all that was going on, I was helping Mr. Henderson put together a long table out of sawhorses, two by fours, and scrap plywood in the garage. Mom and Dad came back across the street, carrying two large plastic bowls, a handful of sharp knives, and a box of plastic bags. Mrs. Henderson, Aunt Quida, and Mrs. Wheeler came out of the house into the garage. Mrs. Henderson brought a couple of sharp knives. I got happy, realizing I wasn't going to be Don Quixote tonight with the fish.

105

Instead, I had temporarily joined the Amish, but instead of raising a barn, we were going to clean catfish.

Mr. Henderson set up the disassembly line by placing the short edge of the long sawhorse table at the garage opening by the tub of catfish still at the top of the drive and just outside the garage down slope. He put a wooden mallet at that end of the table, three sharp knives, and three pairs of needle nose pliers. An empty galvanized tub was sat on the floor under the middle of that table. Mom's two big plastic bowls sat atop a small rolling shop table Mr. Henderson made for woodworking.

The plan went like this... I would grab a catfish for each of us guys and put them on the table. Mr. Henderson would whack them in the head with the mallet, to stun or kill, before he, Dad, or I would cut the skin around the head, skin the fish, gut and behead it. Guts and heads were to go in the tub below the table, the dressed fish put in the plastic bowls. From there, Mom and Ladybug would dump the skinned and gutted fish into the garage deep utility sink, located by the washing machine and drier, to give them a good scrubbing before carrying it over to Mrs. Wheeler and Aunt Quida. They were setup on a fold out card table, ready for bagging up fish. We had just got started when Mr. Wheeler and Uncle Russ drove up in the driveway. After a quick greeting and a brief, "Wow, would you look at those fish," they were involved in one process or another, helping. It took less than an hour to get the fish cleaned and bagged up. Nobody was in a hurry, judging by the conversions going on about the fishing trip, as well as, other topics. Mrs. Wheeler got special attention for the big fish. I intentionally set it aside for cleaning last. It was the grand finale, the last flash of the cameras.

Mr. Henderson and I took the tub of guts around the back of his house to the garden for deep burial. Dad took the garden hose, washing down everything that had touched fish. Mr. Wheeler and Uncle Russ broke down the make shift fish cleaning tables, while the ladies cleaned up remnants. Apparently, Mrs. Wheeler and Aunt Quida had told Mr. Wheeler and Uncle Russ about the catch over the phone, because they showed up with coolers in Uncle Russ's car. The ladies put their share in the coolers. Mom put Ladybug's fish in her garage freezer. We placed our fish in two paper grocery bags and sat them in Ladybug's freezer for the time being.

I was going to run the fishing rods and tackle across the street to our garage, but Dad had already taken care of that detail. From familiarity, I knew these adult chitchats could go on for a long time, especially once they broke out the leftover snacks and ice tea. I needed a shower, bad. I invaded their conversation, as politely as I could, to say good night. That announcement brought on hugs and kisses. I was the center of attention amongst people I loved so much. I excused myself. Don Quixote strutted into the darkness of night; victorious in his own mind that he had slain the biggest catfish dragon womankind had ever seen, empowered by the love that just wrapped their arms around him. It was a good occasion for all.

"Good night! M' ladies."

Chapter 8 - Head Boat Monkeys

Growing up in Virginia Beach, Virginia, I had seen countless boats of all shapes and sizes by the age of thirteen. Everything between a leaky, riveted Jon boat customized for duck hunting, flounder gigging, bass fishing, and anything else, to a high dollar yacht, factory personalized just to one up the Jones. Ironically, it was a rare occasion when I got to step foot on any boat. I was a bank, beach, or pier fisherman shackled to hard ground with my heart afloat in an area surrounded by water.

The first time Mr. Sebastian, our neighbor across the street, invited me to go with him and his buddies on a head boat, along with his son Tony, it was an invitation for high seas adventure. I asked my parents about it and they casually said it was fine; what they granted me was an idealized notion of a floating freedom ticket to the east, off the beach.

Back then, head boats in Virginia Beach were large drift boats that worked the warmer months, looking for the quickest tug on the line of whatever available bottom fish to a gang of fishermen, at an affordable price. Spot, croaker, and flounder were typical targets. Occasionally, they would bring back something special; a fish that created a crowd on the dock and might make the newspaper. It might be a smoker kingfish, an eighteen-pound-plus blue fish, or something else outside the lines.

On this trip, I was dreaming of a fish outside the lines. Deep-sea fishing for a sea monster was my recurring thought since the invite. I couldn't wait until Saturday morning; my gear was in order Thursday. Being ready that soon wasn't a big deal since my gear was simply the largest spinning reel and rod combo I had, spooled with thirty-pound test with a store bought wire leader and the biggest hook in Dad's tackle box, a 7/0 nickel plated jobber. I knew from the get go that my tackle would never fulfill my grandiose vision, but it was the best brush I had to paint my dream.

Naïve would be an understatement concerning what I actually knew about fishing from a head boat. I had seen them leave and come back, but I had no idea what went on between dockings. When a boat came back in, twenty to forty people would disembark, loaded down with fishing poles, tackle boxes, buckets of miscellaneous stuff, and heavy coolers full of spot, croaker, and some flounder. The boats brought back plenty of fish and the people looked worn out and sunburned for doing it. Some even appeared drunk they were so tired. Most folks would lug their fish coolers over to the fish-cleaning shack where some well-organized black men hustled to weigh them and turn the rough fish into fish dressed for dinner.

Saturday was going to be a big adventure for me. I was looking forward to finally finding out first-hand how a head boat worked, hoping for a shot at a big fish, and of course, getting my picture in the paper. I was dreaming large, going deep-sea fishing. However, the reality check I was about to be given had little to do with what I was thinking, for the most part.

The boat left the dock at seven sharp. It was a forty-minute ride from the house to the dock. The men decided we were to leave Mr. Sebastian's house at five-thirty to give us forty-five minutes to get our things in order at the dock. Not being a morning person, that was an awful call for me. But, I was there, fumbling around in the driveway at five fifteen to help load the food and drink coolers, fish coolers, and fishing gear in the back of a truck. Actually, the men did most everything. I did very little. I was there that early just to be on time. It took less than ten minutes to load our gear up. Not everybody could fit in the truck, so we took Mr. Sebastian's sedan as well. It was Saturday; the traffic was light that early in the morning. We made it to the dock in thirty minutes. I barely had time to doze off before we were there. The two vehicles pulled up front and we rolled out, unloading the gear on the curb. Everybody pitched in to carry the four coolers, two tackle boxes, and two handfuls of fishing rods out to the boathouse for check in. It was a short walk.

As we neared the boathouse, the smell of the ocean covered us. The aroma of saltwater is a wakeup call to fishermen, more stimulating than the smell of fresh coffee in the morning. Salt air is not merely a stimulant, but the very breath of life from the largest organism wrapped around earth. That day, the breath was good, fresh, and light.

At the boathouse/bait house, the men paid for our boarding tickets and bought six-dozen bloodworms, two five-pound boxes of squid, and a big sack of ice for each fish cooler. The ice they put in one cooler and the bait in the other.

From the boathouse, we carried our stuff up the pier to a wide set of stairs that stepped down below the pier and on to a dock where the boat was moored. The men grabbed up the coolers. Tony and I divided the fishing poles and grabbed one tackle box each. We laid the poles over our shoulders to carry them in reverse rifle fashion, the reels behind. We had seen a guy carry a couple fishing poles like that; it looked pretty cool. I imagined us, looking like a couple of soldiers carrying weapons into battle. Carrying the weapons was cool, but toting the ammo boxes, i.e. tackle boxes, was far from cool. There must have been just about the same amount of leads in the bottom of those boxes as flew in both directions at Normandy. My hand was numb, cramped up, and my shoulder stretched out by the time we got the gear to the stairs. We were early, first to arrive, so we stacked the coolers two by two, the tackle boxes next to the coolers, then leaned the poles against the coolers.

It was twenty after six. The man at the boathouse told us there would be somebody coming at 6:30 a.m. to start loading the boat. That meant there was ten minutes exploring time. Down the stairs I went to get my first look at the *magic carpet* that was to take me to my dream fish. On the way down the stairs, I could hear the sea hissing as water rose and fell away from the stationary frameworks under the pier. The sound gave the waters additional life. Standing on the floating dock, I found the bottom of the pier was stifling compared to the sea air above. Hampering the slight wind under the pier, the air became chilled and concentrated in the shade, making it richly aromatic. My nostrils only wanted to inhale. My face instinctively turned east into the fresh sea breeze.

Through the array of pilings, under the pier, a brilliant, orange semi-circle perched itself above the horizon. The one-foot chop on the near and distant water worked like facets on a gemstone to bounce and scatter

110

the warm, rising sunlight. It was bright. I turned away to see the boat awash in warm light. My pupils were pin dots from looking into the sun, unfocused I could see the boat in its majesty. A navy blue hull and mostly white from there up, sharp lines, thick and sturdy. A young man came behind me and hopped onboard.

"Brian! Come on, we have to bring this stuff down to the boat," was a snap back call from somebody above. On the way up the stairs, I met the guys coming down, I skinnied up against the rail to let them pass. Some other folks were making their way down. I got to the top to help Tony with the rods and reels and tackle boxes. Going down the stairs with the tackle boxes wasn't that bad, but I knew getting back up the stairs at the end of the day wasn't going to be easy. We were in a short line to get aboard. Tony and I sat those heavy tackle boxes on the dock every time the line stopped moving. The young man who hopped on the boat was helping people with their belongings and giving directions. We saw Tony's dad coming out of the cabin. They had stored the coolers inside. When Tony and I climbed on board, we told the fellow we were with those guys over there and pointed them out.

"Go ahead," he told us, and we were on.

Mr. Sebastian had us located on the starboard toward the stern. We took up two sets of bench seats on the rail. Tony and I shoved the tackle boxes under the most forward bench seat, since it was more accessible.

"Boys, hand us our poles," one of the fellows said. Everybody except me had similar set ups. Solid fiberglass rods with wooden handles, stainless eyes and tip, with a black 4/0 Penn reel screwed on the reel seat loaded with at least fifty-pound test, curly line coming off the spools. The line looked to be the original stuff spooled on the old reels. My thirty-pound test dream maker was a lightweight next to these beef sticks.

"Let me string some leadered hooks on them before I hand them out," I offered. Pre-rigged, each of the combo's had a standard two-hook bottom rig, like Mr. Sullivan first showed me, but without the hooks to prevent tangling. Tony and I strung the hooks on the rigs, as more people boarded the boat behind us. The top hook we secured down to the base of the second wire arm of the rig so it wouldn't dangle around wildly. The bottom hook we attached to a horizontal bar on the reel. We'd add the sinkers on once we were about ready to fish. Tony and I handed the rods over to the guys as we finished the rigging. The gunnel was ten inches wide, flat on top, and a bit over knee high. Fittings screwed onto the top of the gunnel every three feet had large galvanized pipe stanchions threaded into them. The pipes supported a hand crafted two by six rail which was waist high. Many people before us had carved crude notches on the inside to lean fishing poles against to keep their pole from sliding left or right. Some of the larger, probably older, notches had a small hole drilled in front of the notch and a piece of string threaded through and tied in to further secure the rod from falling over. The guys leaned their poles in the best available notch in front of them, the ones with the strings.

"Brian, where is your fishing pole?" asked Mr. Sebastian.

"It's here, Mr. Sebastian," I showed him.

"Why ain't it rigged up?" he asked.

"Well, I was going to free line some bait off the boat," I told him.

"Before you go and try that, it would be best for you to rig up with a bottom rig and see how this thing works and go get me a beer," he told me. I did what he told me to do, but in the back of my mind, I was going to be free lining live bait sometime during the day.

I didn't notice the captain get aboard. There wasn't an announcement. He must have walked on like anybody else and slipped in the pilothouse. At 6:55 a.m., he fired up the diesel engine. It came to life with a roaring sound that vibrated the deck. Black smoke billowed out the stern, then rolled up in the wind, blew back, smothering the entire boat in the smell of diesel fuel exhaust. I stopped breathing until the air cleared. The engine rumbled on for five warm-up minutes. At 7:00 a.m., two young guys threw the mooring lines off the boat onto the dock, and the boat chugged straight away. I was ecstatic.

"Folks, it is going to be approximately a forty-five minute ride to the fishing grounds," said the voice through the intercom. Water gently slapped against the hull as the big boat eased away. Ten minutes later, we passed a big point of land and headed into wide-open water. The diesel throttled up to a whining roar. The deck shook from the power below. Gobs of black smoke blasted out the back. The smoke hung in the air as the boat heaved away from it. The hull of the boat spanked the

112

water. The exhaust cleared. My *magic carpet* was underway.

Tony and I told his dad we were going to check out the boat.

"Be back before the boat stops so ya'll can cut bait," he said. Everywhere we could walk, we walked. We went through the open cabin, where many people sat on the bench seats fastened to the wall. They were chit chatting, smoking, and/or drinking beer. Coolers and buckets were stuffed under the benches they sat on. I never have liked the smell of cigarettes. The area in the cabin reeked with cigarette smoke, so we quickly went out for open air. On the port side, we discovered the bathroom with a stenciled, Head, on the door. A fellow stumbled out the door as we were approaching. He looked pale, blank eyes looking out to nowhere, seemingly seeing nothing. That was weird to me. We went to the point of the bow and hung out, letting an occasional splash catch us and cool us down. In our walk about, I noticed the deck lacked paint and had some wear on it in high traffic areas. Where feet couldn't tread, the painted deck appeared fresh. Anything above the deck had a thick multi-coat of flat white paint. Up close, you could see where paint chips were painted over and brush strokes were obvious. It was a working boat; paint jobs were necessary, but apparently hurried. It looked good from afar, but far from good. The paint was functional. In years to come, I'd find out first-hand about fighting the rage of corrosion on a boat.

"We'd better go back and get the bait ready," Tony said. We made our way around the starboard bow going to our seats. En route, we saw the same guy who came out of the head, hanging over the rail, throwing up. I couldn't look directly at his action, but felt sorry for him. What bad luck to have a stomach virus on his fishing day. He looked miserable.

We made it back to our station. Tony told his dad we were ready to cut the bait up. Mr. Sebastian seemed satisfied we were back, ready to get the bait together.

He said, looking at the man vomiting over the rail, "You boys ain't going to end up like that poor breakfast tosser you just passed by, are you?"

"No, sir, it was too early for me to have breakfast this morning," I replied. He looked at me and smiled funny.

"Bring the two fish coolers from the cabin and put one behind each bench and bring three beers," he told us. Tony and I went in and grabbed

113

everything requested plus two Cokes for us. While we were getting the stuff together, Tony informed me about seasickness. I had no idea about it and decades later still don't. I guess I'm as stupid now as I was then. Sometimes stupid ain't as bad as it's made out to be.

When we got back, Mr. Sebastian told us to find one of the mates and have him give us two cardboard beer flats to put our bait in. Tony went on that mission. I pulled out a five-pound box of squid from the fish cooler the men had put the bait in. In the second tackle box I looked in there was a short wide-blade bait knife with a wooden handle; it was almost sharp, but sharp enough. A five-gallon bucket that contained peanut oil years ago was pushed up against the outside of the cabin. It was obvious it belonged to the boat. I borrowed it for the bait detail. I flipped it upside down behind the fish cooler that I had sat the box of squid on. It was my seat. The tops of the fish coolers had markings from preparing bait in the past, so it wasn't a big deal to cut bait on top of the coolers. I placed the box of softening, frozen squid on the left hand side of the cooler, opened the lid flat on the cooler, and began to pull the heads off all the squid, putting the tentacled heads on the right hand side of the cooler lid and tossing the bodies back on the box lid. Tony came along halfway through this process with two empty beer flats, one inside the other; he put them face up on the deck and sat a heavy tackle box in the middle to keep the wind from blowing them off. It took him no time to find a spare bucket seat and join me in dismembering the squid. For us, it was a cool thing to do. Tearing apart a dead animal was acceptable in boy world. We decapitated the rest of the squid in a couple of minutes.

"Now what?" Tony asked.

"How about we pull out the other fish cooler, separate the beer flats, and divide the bait between them?" I suggested. It sounded good and we did it. Two hands full of squid heads went in each beer flat at one end. From there, Tony borrowed a knife from one of the guys, his uncle, and we began to slice the squid bodies into half inch by three-inch strips. Half the strips went in one flat and the rest in the other flat on the opposite side from the heads.

The next step in bait preparation was bloodworms. Bloodworms are creepy critters. They are colored brilliant red and the size and shape of a large red wiggler or small night crawler. That's not bad, the creepy thing is, they can flare out a hidden circle of fine sharp hooks from their heads when handled and squirt blood when cut. It is no wonder some squeamish people opt not to use them as bait. However, the hooks have high shock value, but lack strength; if they grab your finger it doesn't hurt; it is just unnerving. In nature, you can find them under previously submerged rocks or dig them up on mud flats at low tide along the mid-Atlantic coast. It is a lot of work and a mess to collect your own worms, so most people simply buy them. They come a dozen per bag and each bag has a gob of wet seaweed to keep the worms moist and happy.

Tony grabbed one bag and I took another. We decided to dissect two dozen worms apiece into two-inch sections in the middle of each beer flat between the squid heads and squid strips. It was a fine idea not to get the cooler lids stained with blood, but afterwards, Tony and I looked like post-op, vascular surgeons. Modern art bloodworm squirts crisscrossing the fronts of our shirts marked us proud fishermen, as well as, gave us Halloween ideas.

With the bait chopped, the rigs were ready once everyone had snapped on a four-ounce pyramid sinker. The stage was set. All we needed was for the boat to come to rest somewhere in Chesapeake Bay.

The diesel motors that had droned on for forty-five minutes throttled back to a low, peaceful rumble. The voice came from above, "Folks, this is Captain *I-can-not-remember-his-name*, we are approaching the fishing grounds. In this area, over the past two weeks, we have had great catches of spot and croaker on incoming tide. The tide has just turned in. Folks, do not start fishing until you hear the ships bell. Oh, report all injuries to the captain. Be sure and tip your mates today. The mates are Andy, the tall redheaded boy who appears lost most of the time and Brent, who has a bad habit of falling off the boat. Folks they try hard, have mercy on them. Good luck."

I was excited. Tony and I put one flat of bait on each bench seat. We put the two fish boxes where everyone could toss fish in easily. All of us baited up with one piece of bloodworm and one squid strip. We lined up on the rail like the rest of the fishermen.

Ding-ding went the bell and down went forty lines. From the fishes' perspective, it must appear like a bait blitzkrieg. It is a wonder a couple fish didn't come floating up with knots on their heads. Imagine the fish

115

milling around a sandy bottom, rooting for a tidbit of this or that, then the area explodes with food. It must not bother them, because hook-ups were immediate. Ten to fourteen-inch spot and croaker rolled over the gunnels all around the boat. Some were double hook-ups, but most were single fish. All six of us had fish in the boat at the same time. Tony and I unhooked our fish, and then went behind the bench to unhook the fish for the other guys. The catching was so fast, they were back in the boat with more fish before Tony and I could get back to fishing. After ten minutes of steady unhooking fish and tossing them in the coolers, we looked at one another with a shared epiphany. Fishing wasn't the primary reason we were invited. The bite trickled off in ten to fifteen minutes. The bell sounded, meaning everybody reel up. The captain pushed the boat back up into the current to set another drift.

"Tony, go get three beers and a Coke and something for you and Brian," said Mr. Sebastian to his son. "Brian, cut up some more bloodworms," he told me. He was right. The bloodworms were the bait ticket. They worked and that is why they cost so much. Ninety-nine percent of the spot came in on lines with the bloodworms; the croaker preferred them as well. I cut up the last two bags of bloodworms, dividing them between the two flats.

"Mr. Sebastian, that is all the bloodworms," I told him. Tony came back with the drinks. I said thanks, and then sucked the bottom out of the can. The big belch came in seconds. It was great. It cleared my head.

The boat slowed down, this time the captain turned the bow the opposite way from the first drift. The bell sounded for lines down. Tony and I were ready. We came to realize that we had limited opportunities to fish. We weren't going to miss any chance. Our bait went in the water, but this time they sank under the boat instead of away from it. Tony got a fish in short order. I got one a moment after. Both of us got single fish, not the doubles we were wanting. We went behind the benches, unhooked the fish, put them in the cooler, stowed our rods neatly, and were stationed up for the onslaught. Three fish came flying over to us. Tony got two; I got one off their hooks. One of the fellows' rods bowed over heavily. He was running off at the mouth about the big one he had on the line. It was easy going at first, but got harder as he gained line. Usually, it's harder at the beginning, then easier as the fish runs out of gas. Not this time. The closer it got to the boat the more it would pull back. We were all excited, yelling. Even the guys on the other side of the boat got into the action and started yelling. One of them had a big one, too. Maybe, we drifted across a school of big blue fish.

"Get 'em from underneath the boat," we yelled. The other guy's fish had run under the boat as well. It was a tug fest on both sides of the boat. Which one would boat the fish first?

"My fish is caught in the propeller," declared the fellow on the other side.

"Mine, too," said our man. The battles turned into a Mexican standoff. Each guy was worried he was going to lose his big fish.

One of the mates, Andy, had been standing nonchalant amidships for several minutes with the grin that told me he wasn't worried about the two fish the guys were fighting. He had something else on his mind. Andy went over to the other side of the boat to help that man once his line was under the boat. I stepped over to eavesdrop thinking, *Andy, you're a little late with the helping hand, dude.*

"Put your thumb on the spool and take the reel out of gear," Andy told the man. If the man hadn't had two hands on his rod at the time, judging by the look on his face, he would have put both hands around Andy's neck.

"We're going to let the fish swim away from the running gear then reel him in, OK? Don't do anything until the fish pulls at least thirty feet of line from your reel," Andy said. The man saw the strategy and complied.

At that very moment, Roger, our man of the hour, said loudly "He's coming from under the boat; I got him!" Andy was there, waiting when Roger reeled up the other man's rig. Andy cut that rig off, told the man to reel in, then went over and tied the guy's rig back on. It obviously wasn't the first time the mate had seen that happen. It was a first for me.

Ding-ding the bell sounded us to reel them up; we were about to move again. While we were underway, Roger was explaining to us he had a big fish on, but the other guy had fouled his line and knocked his fish off. It was funny the same story was being told on the other side of the boat. After that incident, I started looking around the boat more instead of focusing on our private universe. It didn't take long to notice that tangles between two to five people were common. The mates spent most of their time, cutting and rigging after foul ups. Some people would get mad. Some would take it as part of the game.

One guy in particular, on our side toward the bow, seemed always to be in the mess middle. He was popular in an unpopular sense. Most everyone who fished around him came to get to know him, at least briefly. People gravitated away from him. Soon, everyone left him alone. He was either the world's worst fishermen or the smartest guy on the boat. Regardless, he found himself some peace, and a piece from the rest of the crowd. He was happy to be alone, reeling up fish the remainder of the day.

The boat slowed down, the captain turned the bow around so our side would have the bait drift away. Every other time the captain turned the boat in our favor. He was being fair to all. Tony and I anticipated the ring of the bell. One ding and our bait went down. In one minute, both of us had our first doubles. We were excited, taking our fish off the hooks, but didn't get long to talk. We realized quickly that fish for us meant work soon to come. Four rigs swung our way for fish removal and bait replacement. They kept coming our way for the next half hour. This was the best drift of the day. Apparently, the tide was really turning in and carrying the fish with it. My hands had pinpricks and blood drops from handling so many flipping fish. Tony's hands were in the same shape. We were thankful when the bites slowed to a stop. Ding-ding.

The people who waited for the mates to take their fish off were lagging far behind those who would remove their own fish. Our group was ahead of the rest because the men hired two personal de-hookers for the price of a boat ride. I felt a little tricked into it, but was enjoying myself just the same. It was a brand new experience for me; one I had wanted to do for some time.

Every time the boat would move, we'd roll bags of ice on top the fish, keeping them cold top to bottom. Our two coolers were getting full. One more good drift and we'd max out. The captain pushed the boat back in the current from where we just drifted. I could tell because there was a green nun buoy positioned where the bite was the hottest. Ding-ding. Tony and I sunk our bait. Our weights hit the bottom and we reeled up fish. It was on again.

Twenty minutes later, "Dad, the coolers are full," said Tony. All four men turned around, looking in the coolers. There was no surprise; the coolers were full except for a scattering of top ice.

"Tony, empty the food cooler into the drink cooler and we'll start using it. While you're in the drink cooler, bring back three beers and a Coke and something for you and Brian. Brian, just toss these fish in a five-gallon bucket till Tony has the cooler ready, OK?" He resolved the problem without having to miss a fish. By the time Tony returned, the five-gallon bucket had six-gallons of fish. No kidding, it was machinegun fishing. The bite was as fast as it could get. I was the weak link in a five-man fish chain. I was happy when Tony came back. He dumped the fish in the new cooler and joined in.

We did one more drift and that cooler was full before the drift finished. Now, what? The bloodworms were gone. The last part of the second box of chopped up squid was in the bait flats.

"Boys, you can fish now. We'll just give the fish to whoever needs them." I went AWOL with my dream maker spinning rod. First, I asked Mr. Sebastian what time it was.

"It's around one thirty, Brian, why?"

"No reason, just wanted to know, thanks," I said back to him. Actually, I was doing some quick math in my head. The boat would be back at the dock at 3:00 p.m. The ride out took forty-five minutes, so, the way I figured it, I had forty-five minutes of free fishing time.

In the time it took me to cut off the bottom rig and tie on the wire leader with the big hook, the tide went slack high. The boat barely drifted. I waited several precious minutes for one of our gang to reel up a croaker for my bait. That fish didn't have time to notice it was off the hook in his mouth and back on the second hook in his back. While I was waiting for live bait, I noticed two guys had left their positions on the stern. There was now room for me. With the croaker flipping around wildly, I scrambled back to the stern, I flung that croaker at the only target I could see; the green nun buoy were we had loaded up with spot and croaker less than an hour ago. I don't know why I needed a target to cast to. It seemed meaningless after I made the cast. The target must have been a habit from bass fishing. It was my stump in the big pond. The fish splashed down near the buoy. I flipped the reel bail over by hand. While

119

I was doing that, I glanced at my watch. It was five to two. I had, at best, twenty minutes to fish.

"Folks, we're going to be heading back in ten minutes. It is a good time to get your things together for the ride. The ride in will take approximately an hour. Remember to tip your mates. Hopefully, Brent remained on board this trip. Thank you," came the voice from above. *Crap! I've only got ten minutes.* I almost said that out loud. Instead I said, "Hey…, Hey…, HEY…, HEY! I've got one!" My rod was bent in a U. Line was running off the spool. Andy happened to be coming by, collecting tip money. I looked dead at him.

He nonchalantly, and he did everything nonchalantly, said, "Your bait just swam around the buoy, kid."

"Then why is my line way over there where the big, brown fish is?" Was my not-so nonchalant reply. He looked at my line and followed it out with his eyes to see a big, brown fish cruising on the surface off starboard stern.

"Oh, (pick-your-own-word)," he shouted. "Brent! Go tell the captain this kid's got a monster cobia on and to turn to port, now!" There was a non-nonchalant side to Andy. "Don't put too much pressure on him, kid." The boat was turning to the left slowly putting the fish directly astern. The drag slipped with the boat movement.

"Give me the pole, kid."

"Kiss my butt," I told Andy. He reached to grab the pole away from me. I leaned away from him, toward the fish and back kicked him in the knee.

"Hey, you little—"

"Leave the kid alone!" I heard guys tell him.

"He's just going to lose the fish." Andy told the crowd. I looked behind me, but he wasn't grabbing for the rod any more. When the fish moved to the left, I moved with it, left. I'd move to the right when it moved right. A crowd formed around me, but gave way when I needed room. I'd gently pull up with the rod, and then wind down with the reel, making sure there was no slack in the down stroke. As the fish came closer to the boat, I eased the drag back off. I had read there was less elasticity in monofilament line the shorter it was, and it was good to ease off the drag as the fish approached. Thank you *Outdoor Life*.

"Brent, get the gaff!" yelled Andy. It was a long, sturdy handled gaff.

The first time I managed to get the fish close to the boat, it rolled its head to the side to get a good look at the situation and bolted off. *Oh, God don't break off,* I thought. *Oh, God, my arms hurt.* I could hear Mr. Sebastian and our crew yelling their support. I needed it. This was a first for me. I was making it up as it came along, like fishing for carp off the bridge by Aunt Quida's house. However, this fish could eat the biggest of my trophy carp.

I glanced down at my watch; we were past our departure time. Would the captain run the boat in and make me lose my fish?

"Andy, the fish is tiring, have the young man lead the fish to the stern and take him over the back," I heard the voice from above, but it wasn't over the intercom system. The captain was standing on the hard top directly over me, watching the battle. He was in to it himself! That was cool.

It took three more tries, each try taking less time than the previous, for me to lead the fish to the back of the boat.

"It is all you, Andy," said the captain. Andy lurched over the transom with the gaff. He sunk the gaff into the tail section of the fish. The tail rose above the transom slapping the boat. The gaff flew out of Andy's hands, landing in the water, ten feet behind the boat. The fish fell back in the water with fury; my line made a popping sound heard round the boat. It was gone. I stood limp.

"Andy, I want to see you in the wheelhouse, immediately!" barked the captain.

I don't know how many strangers patted me on the back or hugged me and told me I did a great job, but there were a bunch. I ended up over at our benches. The guys gave me the huddle hug, saying nice things to me. Tony told me he was going to find Andy and whip his butt. His uncle heard that and held him back.

Tony and I sat quietly on the fish coolers on the ride in. Several guys came by while we were en route to shake my hand or muss up my hair and tell me I did a good job, saying it was the mate's fault. One guy took the time to sit on a five-gallon bucket, asking me if I knew what a cobia was. I told him I didn't. He explained all he knew about cobia. That was a lot, too.

He said, "Cobia like structure and that fish swam from the nun buoy to take my croaker." They are excellent sport fish and fine table fare. The fish I had on was about five feet long, and weighed between seventy and eighty pounds. I thanked him for the information. It was the information I was going to share with Dad.

Once I looked up to see Brent going along with both tip cans. I overheard one guy ask him if they split the tip money. He said "yes." With that, the guy looked at me and stuck some cash in Brent's pocket and said, "Don't split that."

Brent said, "Don't worry, I won't."

The captain backed the boat against the dock between the outer pilings so smoothly we never felt the boat come to a complete stop. We didn't realize we were tied to the dock until the motors shut down. Everyone got things together, forming a line to disembark. Brent was there helping people off the boat. Our coolers were so loaded with fish, it was decided two trips were necessary to complete the job. Mr. Sebastian had a handful of fishing rods. Tony and I split the remaining rods between us with a tackle box apiece. The three other men had formed a two cooler train. We were inching along in line when a tall, bearded man in a diesel stained shirt, smoking a cigarette stopped beside me. I looked way up at him. He looked homeless.

"I'm the captain," he stated. I stood silent. "I wanted you to know you did a fine job fighting that fish. I've seen a lot of people fight fish. You did an excellent job. I'm sorry the mate lost your fish. It was his fault. He is well aware of that, trust me. It won't make up for your lost fish, but here is a free boarding pass for your next trip, son," he said to me, wasting no words. He shook my hand and walked off. The free pass was his business card with his signature on the back and the word *Freebie*.

"Wow, Brian, you get to go for free next time," Tony blurted.

I said, "Yeah, you want to come, too? The line jumped forward breaking the conversation. We told Brent thanks as we got off the boat and told him we had to return to get our other two coolers.

I was right. The walk back up the steps with the ammo boxes was a lot tougher than the walk down. Somehow, the boxes gained weight though we lost a couple of rigs. The guys toting the fish boxes walked right by the fish-cleaning shack; I figured as much. Luckily, they went back and got the other two coolers while Tony and I organized the back of the truck.

On the ride back to the house, Tony and I relived the cobia from my perspective, his perspective, the captain's perspective, and the mate's perspective.

"That mate is lucky my uncle held me back, because I was going to beat his butt for losing your fish," Tony said at every opportunity. "I bet that captain chewed him a new one in the wheelhouse." Mr. Sebastian had heard enough by then. He turned around and told his son he didn't even know what a wheelhouse was or where it was.

"Do to! The captain told me to get out of his wheelhouse one time I was getting everybody drinks," Tony said, while trying to stop saying it as the words kept rolling out of the mouth he was sticking his foot in.

"You went in the wheelhouse?" snapped his dad.

"It was an accident," Tony replied. They dropped the subject.

At the house, we set up some makeshift, fish cleaning tables with sawhorses and plywood. Tony and I cleaned the fish along with two of the other guys. It didn't take as long as I thought it would. Dad had stepped across the street just after we pulled in the driveway. He smiled, asking Mr. Sebastian if I was worth the fare. Everybody told him about the fishing trip. The cobia was the highlight of the trip, even though it got away. We were still cleaning fish when Dad turned to go home.

"Jimmy, if you want Brian to go again I'll pay for his ticket," Dad told Mr. Sebastian.

I piped up saying, "Next time nobody has to pay for me. I got a free pass from the captain, Dad."

I brought home bags of cleaned fish, but I would have traded them all for that one cobia. My dream came true in a roundabout way. The news of my *one that got away* made a single sentence in the fishing report in next Friday's newspaper. They didn't have my name, but I was the "kid." I walked away from that boat hooked on fishing more than ever before; I didn't think that was possible.

Chapter 9 - A View from the End of My World

I never forgot about the cluster of guys fishing the end of the pier since my first pier trip with Mr. Sullivan. The six to eight men milling around out there with joisting rods or cudgel sticks were fishing for big fish. The thought of those guys fishing for big fish from the end of the pier grabbed my interest. After asking a few loose questions then, later, and here and there, I found out they were competing to battle with kingfish, big bluefish, cobia, or shark. The shark guys were obvious with their reels the size of small hubcaps screwed down to short, thick solid rods.

In general, the guys on the end of the pier were not interested in the spot, croaker, or round heads the majority of the pier crowd was happily fishing for. Well, they were interested in the small fish for bait, but not food. They'd catch a fish on their bait rod when needed or better, when bait was running by the pier, to maintain a small supply of live bait. Bait needed to be always available to be catapulted as far from the end of the pier as humanly possible, using their twelve to fourteen foot poles called heavers.

There was no doubt these guys were serious about their fishing. I could tell by the way they moved about with purpose, where and how they placed their rods against the banister, the extra time they took rigging, the amount of pre-rigged stuff they'd pull out of tackle boxes or organized five-gallon buckets and large, elaborate bait buckets. Furthermore, they had rather unusual items like lanterns and flashlights, four-foot diameter hoop nets, or homemade three pronged rope gaffs, for bringing large fish up on the pier. They also had specialized rods and

124

reels, as well as, niceties like the fold out chase lounge chairs to flop/sleep in while they waited for the big one, and custom built pier carts so well designed, they could roll all that crap to the end in a single trip. It all looked cool to me. At that time, the end of the pier was the furthermost point of my fishing world.

Three times, I went to that last man-made fishing extension in feeble attempts to join the action. Me, my biggest spinning combo and a hodgepodge five-gallon bucket of tackle, trying to fit in amongst an often, odd collection of guys, some of which actually knew what they were doing. I'd catch a small bait-fish, pin it to the largest hook I happened to have in my tackle bucket, toss it out down current without a sinker, and casually lean back against the banister and eavesdrop.

Before I resorted to spying, I tried to get information from regional and national magazines and the only local fishing program that aired from 7:30 to 8:00 p.m. Friday night. However, the media did not cover this type of fishing. Apparently, this local trench fishing didn't have the allure for the masses or tourists, nor the glamour yachts adorned with fishing toys, bringing in prized offshore fish to warrant recognition. You had to want to do it, before you were ready to do it, and then, maybe, get an apprenticeship from somebody already involved if they tolerated you.

I didn't catch a thing on those first outings. Well, once, I had my bait snatched. The line squealed off the spool with the speed and sound of a fire truck balling down the interstate. I heard the siren, but couldn't determine where the sound was coming from. I was busy looking left and right along the banister to see which other fishermen was having a runoff, when some fellow yelled, "Boy, you got one!" I gyrated around, did a quick imitation of Barney Fife in an emergency, only to have my line cut off the moment I touched the pole.

In the midst of my flash of depression some guy said, "You should have had a steel leader, boy." I wrote that quote down on a mental shopping list.

Three times, I took the long walk back off the pier fishless, but I walked away with what I wanted in the first place, an education. The education came because I had a strong enough interest to hang around, even through the dull, fishless hours to gather information in bits and pieces. In school I was told, if you wanted to improve your grades, sit toward the front of the classroom, so, on the pier I positioned myself close to the end, where I could see and hear but didn't interfere. From there, I could observe their fishing equipment, watch the techniques used, eavesdrop, have idle chitchat, or ask questions of the guys that seem to be in the know. Staying the duration, I saw everything from set up to when fish happened. I watched it all, not just the fun part when some guy was working in a fish.

Initially, the hardest part of my education was finding the nerve to ask a question to a complete stranger. I was young and a bit shy. It turned out, most everybody was very helpful once a question fell out of my mouth. It certainly helped that the people I asked first saw me put forth the effort and time before I mentioned my question. The value of their answer was better once they'd seen my sincerity. Often, a simple question opened up a library of information. A lot could come at me in an overwhelming dose. I found out quick, people liked talking about themselves, especially about what they love to do. A simple question could take an hour to answer. Answers were like rivers, each one unique. Some answers were straight, fast, and to the point, while others meandered through the meadows of the mind, taking me fishing to distant places, meeting family and friends along the way. Asking questions became easier, the more I did it. The answers received were quite helpful, but the stories I filtered through to get a piece of information were so entertaining that I'd often ask a question I already knew the answer to just to get the story that came with it.

Some fishermen could naturally tell stories so vivid, the excitement of their adventure transferred down mutual interest so pure, to me, that I discovered myself feeling the lurch of a fishing pole in my hand, fighting their long ago fish. The stories were wonderful, I wish I could remember each one of them; actually, I was interested in living out my own stories to tell. The information I gathered from various folks was more than I expected. While trying to put together all the bits and pieces, I determined fishing for big fish off the end of the pier wasn't as simple as it looked.

So what did I learn? Patience plays off. If you stick a big chunk of fish food on a hook, send it off the end of a pier, and have the patience to wait long enough, something will eventually come along and eat your offering. Many times, crabs would whittle the meat away from the iron, but there were beautiful moments when the dream swims through, providing an epic battle for one, or at times, for more, in front of a select bunch of volunteer peers.

Preparedness is a must for success. Observing the whole experience from start to finish was more satisfying to me than the feature battle. The crowd attracted to the angler fighting the fish was seeing the highlight clip but not the entire game. The essence of the battle was in knowing how much preparation took place before turning on the spotlight. My time on the pier made me aware how much was required not just to get a sparkle in the spotlight, but better yet, to stay there until the fish was won. I came to understand the drive and knowledge necessary to select the correct tackle, to rig wisely, to pick the best technique, and to be prepared, from bait collection to harvesting the prize. I was appreciative of the anglers' accomplishment and their feeling of fulfillment after bringing a quality fish way up on the end of a high pier. It was inspiring.

Teamwork was necessary. It took teamwork to close the deal on a big fish. Although the end of the pier heaped together a random assembly of individuals or small groups homesteading an undesignated but respected section of banister, when anyone of the bunch hooked up a quality fish, a union would spontaneously form. They'd bond as pier pirates working in accord to bring the fish to the planks. Unselfishly, the guys would work around or bring their gear in so the pier was open. The impressive heat of the moment and harmony needed to flop a big fish up on the pier seemed comparable to the choreography of a Broadway production, but the happening was impromptu amongst salted blue-collar men, not fancy dancers with waxed and polished toys. The angler had a support band of men dancing pier music around him and his leading fish in sync, following the impulsive gyrations of the coupling in the spotlight dance. The scene was analogous to what I had watched on TV when a billfish crew performed in metronome synchronicity to land a monster marlin. However, that professional bunch toured together, often aboard a carefully designed battlewagon that moved the dance floor under command of the maestro at the wheel. These guys had recently met, were unrehearsed, had no bandleader, but were fun to watch while doing a great job to give the angler the best chance to land a big fish from a most

127

difficult stage.

Everybody knew it would be far more than a minute waltz. It was never certain how long it would take to land the fish. Minutes would easily roll into the first twenty-minute prelude, then blend to the first hour and then go into the necessary. Excitement can drag time along with it. Time has the ability to hesitate when suspended in a cloud of emotion. Moments intensify toward the end of the dance with the angler trying to trade his partner over to the man with the swinging rope gaff. The transfer had to be solid even though it was happening twenty some feet directly below their feet, awash in a rising and falling sea, next to barnacle encrusted pilings. It had to go perfect. When all went well, the thud of the fish against the planks was a moment of celebration. Everybody was happy, because everybody participated in some way to make it happen.

Bringing the right equipment was essential. Equipment was not referring to tackle, but the other stuff necessary for fishing and a few items that made life more pleasant at the end of a long pier for a long time. Some people brought so much equipment, I thought they were camping, not fishing. The folks that set up tents, fold out tables with chairs, and a Coleman stove jump to mind. On busy weekends, it was front row at an outdoor gear exhibition. Some folks were so involved in setting up camp, cooking, making coffee, and cleaning up, that fishing became an afterthought activity; since they were camped out near the water they may as well fish. At times, it became humorous. The Clampets go a-fishing with laundry drying on the banister, blowing in the sea breeze. Their life defined, "Different strokes for different folks." Nevertheless, I actually got some tips from watching the show. Most of what I learned was things not to bring. On the other hand, a roll-up camping hammock that can roll into a pouch the size of a baseball, strung up in a corner section of the pier, makes a mighty fine way to lull away time between bites and makes for a doable nights rest. A small radio was nice to have around. Can you have a party without music? I remember moonlit, shag dancing on the end with some of the wives or girlfriends that, somehow, were coerced into the pier experience. Sunglasses and sun block are a must, since the only shade is under the pier. In addition, at that time in my life, I wanted to look cool with the shades and having sun block could be an icebreaker for any pretty weekend girl lost on the pier with her family.

"You seem to be getting a sun burn on your back. Here is some sun block. Would you like me to rub that in?" Hey, I still remember the rush of hormones, and any angle was better than the gawky stare and Gomer look that tended to be my Plan A for meeting girls. I recall catching myself in mid-gawk, thinking if I had a banjo in my hands, I'd easily be an extra in "Deliverance." The gimmick never worked like planned, but it was an icebreaker with a smirk.

A couple of small flashlights always came in handy for tying knots at night. Hint: bring two because one will either be broken or borrowed forever. A five-gallon bucket with countless half-inch holes drilled in the bottom and around the sides complete with lid and enough rope to tether the bucket to the pier and have it drifting below. Hint: countless means the seawater drains quickly so you're not hand lining a forty-pound bucket of seawater up on the pier every time you need bait. Hoop net or swinging gaffs are highly recommended items. Some folks would opt not to bring a net or gaff because they were either too cheap to buy one or the other, or too lazy to carry the bulky items to the end. They depended on some other angler to have one and loan it to them when needed. I shuddered at the thought of going through all the trouble of set up and so forth, just to dangle a big fish from the end because nobody else had a gaff or net. I couldn't afford a pretty, stainless steel rope gaff, but creative time in shop class brought forth a medieval death implement, I swung with pride. The gaff fits nicely in your five-gallon bait bucket. In addition, the item that pushes or pulls it all together, the pier-cart. One could tell the guys with mechanical ability and a welder, they constructed elaborate fish wagons that were just short of motorized. They got everyone's attention like the high school boy with the hot rod. I, on the other hand, had a shopping cart someone abandoned in the grocery store parking lot. It even had the one front wheel that wobbled. I wired some short sections of PVC pipe to the basket to convert my shopping cart into a pier cart. The other guys custom built their cart around their gear. A bracketed spot for the food and drink cooler, for the fish box, for the tackle box, for the five-gallon bait bucket and gaff, stainless rod holders and on and on. I brought stuff that would fit in the basket or would make it to the end, hanging off the side. I had the Clampet thing down. It was a wonder people didn't offer me aluminum cans as I went to and fro. Anyway, it wasn't pretty, but it worked.

I determined I wasn't going to be a shark fisherman when I looked into getting the hubcap reel and broomstick rod combo. The pre-owned gear was too expensive for me at the time. Heck, it still is.

The bluefish, kingfish, cobia, and small shark fishermen divided into two camps. Spinning gear verses the conventional, revolving spool reel. When spinning reels went super large in the early seventies there was a boom in surf fishing for the sole reason that spinning reels did not backlash. The old timers had to be skilled to heave a half a pound of lead and big chunk of cut mullet a hundred yards into roaring surf and not develop a backlash a knife was the only solution for. With a big spinning reel attached to a twelve-foot or better surf rod, anyone could quickly learn to toss bait out of sight and not worry about spending the next thirty minutes, picking out a ball of knots. The draw back to the spinning gear was it didn't have the line capacity. The heavier the line you spooled on the spinning reel, the less line capacity you had, because the line was thicker. Furthermore, you'd lose the cast ability of the reel if it were spooled with heavy line; thirty-pound test was about the max line strength. The conventional reel was the way to go, because it had plenty of line capacity and could handle fifty or sixty-pound test without taking away from the cast. However, there were certain situations and techniques that were best suited for large spinning gear.

What to do, what to do? The answer was to have a couple of large spinning outfits and two conventional outfits. It was just a matter of money, but money was the matter I didn't have a lot of. It took time and savings for me to cluster together a mishmash of rods and reels to feel comfortable with my tackle. Granted some of the conventional reels were attached to spinning rods, but most people didn't recognize that, so I went with it. FYI, spinning rods have noticeably larger eyes near the rod handle to compensate for the wide coils of line coming off the spool when cast. The conventional reels I ended up with were Penn 4/0 113Hs. Casting them was not an easy feat. I wanted a reel a step or two down from those, but beggars can't be choosers. An avid desire to pull a huge fish up on a pier, forced me to learn how to cast those demonic reels.

Some of the backlashes I put in the reels, looked like monofilament Afros. Ungodly gobs of line pouring over the reel I had to pick through in public. Moreover, there was always a *Captain Obvious* who would walk up out of the blue, after twenty minutes of frustratingly picking to say, and I quote because it is scratched in my mind, "I see you got a backlash."

I'd smile and say, "Yes, sir." Nonetheless, I did finally learn how to cast a Penn 4/0 and it made me a better fisherman; it taught me patience if nothing else.

The spinning and conventional reels were spooled with twenty and fifty-pound test, respectively. The line selection kept a good balance between strength and cast ability.

Long distance casting was necessary when fishing off the end because you didn't want the first dance with the fresh fish to be literally around pilings covered in sharp barnacles. You had to fight the fish in open water, and then bring it next to the pier, exhausted. The exceptionally long twelve to fourteen-foot, heaver poles gave the leverage necessary to launch bait as far away from the pier as humanly possible. The joisting rods had a function, an idea based on the catapult.

Techniques I saw used ran the gamut from the unusual to the useful. The unusual rigs you could spot from a distance. They had flashy spinner blades, a necklace assortment of multicolored beads, lines with hooks dangling off the left, right, and center and tended to have a sinker so heavy it could be an anchor for a small boat. They were always handcrafted rigs, made by guys who spent more time reading about fishing than actually participating in it. When asked about the rig, the answer was an unfurling backlash of knowledge gleaned from back issues of outdoor and fishing magazines.

"Well, you see, this dandy rig I made here is a blended fluke and striper rig with additional hooks, small and large, that allows you to not only slay the fluke and striper, but pick up bait fish and the occasional shark as well." If it weren't for the small anchor crimped on the end, the volume of garnishing would create enough wind drag to make the Christmas rig uncastable. Nevertheless, you could appreciate the artisans' satisfaction in creating his very own fish trap. The rigs were special, the makers, one of a kind.

I took note of three techniques. First, there was the fish finder rig that soaked the bait just off the bottom. Second, there was the two party balloon float trick that drifted the bait away. Third, there was the imaginative, breakaway production that required two fishing poles. Well, there was also a fourth technique, the simple, free lined live bait.

Fish finder rigs could be store bought, but were easy to make and much cheaper by the dozen. Start by tying a three-way swivel to the end of the main line. An improved clinch knot is a good choice or a Uni Knot, if the main line is forty-pound test or greater. To the second eye of the three-way swivel, tie or loop in a six to twelve inch piece of twenty-pound test monofilament to attach the sinker. Use the least amount of weight needed to hold bottom, not letting the bait roll with the tide. The last eye of the three-way was for the leader. The leader was the important connection. Shark, kingfish, and bluefish, all have substantial dentures that make thick monofilament like licorice sticks; wire was vital to success. Candy (plastic) coated, multi-strand store bought leaders with cheap, breakaway swivels were the flag of a novice and were often too short anyway. Single strand number 5 to 7 wire leaders were a pretty good middle of the road choice, but allowances up or down were often necessary, depending on circumstances. Wire leaders of that size could handle a juvenile shark, but weren't too rigid for finicky kingfish. Bluefish weren't in the wire equation, because those crazy fish wouldn't care if the bait were attached to a tow cable; they'd hit anything like a cocky, rich boy at an upscale singles bar. However, wire required the user to know how to make a quality haywire twist with a barrel wrap to the swivel and the hook. Twisting wire was a hurdle for many, but instructions were given in word and diagram on the back of the package it came in. Practice at home was all it took to get proficient. A three to five foot wire leader was good taking into consideration cast ability. The longer the rigging, the more difficult it was to cast. The hook size depended on bait size. Small bait, four to six inches long, needed a 3/0 to 5/0 hook. Medium bait, eight to ten inches long, needed a 6/0 to 8/0 hook. Large bait, dead or alive, needed a bigger hook or a tandem rig of two hooks wired together. In any case, short shank hooks reduced stress allowing the bait to remain frisky longer. It doesn't take much strain to put a ball and chain on a live baitfish.

The kicker to the fish finder rig was the addition of a small float or cork. Actually a submerged bobber positioned six inches or closer to the hook, between the sinker and hook, which buoyed the bait a tiny bit from the bottom to put the deer in the headlights for the target fish. To save time and have something interesting to do in the evenings prior to the trip, a dozen or more rigs of various designs could be made up before hand and stored in individual plastic bags.

The party balloon rig cheated the Olympian casters because no one can cast a balloon. It wasn't up to the angler to deliver the bait, but natural forces. The balloon required wind and/or current, whichever was in most control at the time, to take the bait away from the pier. The beauty of the rig was that bait depth could be preset and multiple baits could be fished on the leeward side of the pier using different poles, varied by distance away from the pier itself, as well as, depth of bait. It was a chocked slip sinker rig in reverse. Here is the rigging: Thread on the smallest plastic bead (buy cheap variety packs from local craft stores) the main line will pass through, followed by a much larger bead. Behind that, slip the main line through the eye of a small snap swivel, next thread on a one ounce egg sinker and tie the main line to a quality barrel swivel.

It's like making a necklace. Haywire twist: a three-foot or so wire leader on the terminal swivel. Then twist a hook, appropriate to the size of the bait, on the end of the leader. Set the bait depth by firmly tying a coarse section of thread using a series of flat knots on the main line a measured length above the hook. All you have left to do is make a party balloon. The size and shape don't matter much, so have fun with it. Open the snap swivel, punch it through the tag end of the balloon, and close the swivel. Now, put bait on the hook and lower it over the pier on the down current side. The egg sinker will pull the bait down until the small bead jams against the wadded thread. The rig will float away from the pier by the wind or current as far as you let it go.

Sometimes the wind or current doesn't carry your ballooned bait where you want it to be. The breakaway set up will solve this dilemma. Tie a sinker heavy enough to hold the bottom well to the end of the line on your spinning combo and heave it in the direction you want your bait to be. Draw the line tight with the reel. Place a clothespin over the line from your spinning reel so that the line is in the hole of the clothespin where the clothesline would normally be. Keeping the clothespin closed, it is able to slide freely up or down the line. Next, clip the line to your baited pole to the clothespin. The length of line between the pin and the hook is up to you. If the bait is heavy or lively, multiple clothespins may be necessary. Now, put your bait over the side of the pier and play out line as the bait slides down like a backwards ski lift. Two people make the job a lot easier, but one person can do it, if they take their time. When a fish takes the bait, the line will break away from the clothespin. Be sure and have somebody reel in the spinning line or you may have a tangle

So one day I rolled my wobble wheeled cart of crap up the first island of the Chesapeake Bay Bridge Tunnel pier, thinking I was the man with my rock 'n roll shades, surfer sandals, and a small bottle of pineapple scented sun block in the back pocket of my cutoff jeans. Shirt? No way, I was Tom Cruise way before Top Gun hit the theaters. Thinking back, I was just a teenaged boy who loved fishing, armed with an adequate amount of knowledge to almost fool myself into believing I knew what I was about to do. The closer I got to the end; the nervousness was erasing the overconfidence I had at the beginning of the pier.

Two big spinning rods, two conventional 4/0 rods and one bait pole propped up in the short pipes wired to the outside of the basket. A big cooler tilted in the basket for the soon to be fish, but was now carrying some drinks, sandwiches, ice, and a pound box of squid. The five-gallon bait bucket was atop the low end of cooler, in the back of the cart, with the medieval death gaff inside and the camp hammock. My tackle box rode on the rack below the basket. It was a beautiful, sunny day. I was hoping it was going to be my day. The local fishing report was positive; big blue fish were crashing bait along the oceanfront and up inside the Chesapeake Bay.

I actually got the prime corner spot on the end. It was on the right, down current, during the beginning of an incoming tide. I parked the cart on a diagonal in the corner to create some sort of barricade to deter others from crowding. The cooler, I pulled out of the basket and placed it on the outside of the cart away from the banister as more barricade. The first order of business was to catch bait. The bait pole was already set up with a bottom rig as Mr. Sullivan showed me some years ago. I cut up a double handful of squid strips on the cooler lid. Two strips went on the two hooks of the bottom rig. I lowered the rig on the down current side of one of the mammoth concrete pilings supporting the pier. In fifteen minutes, I had an integrated collection of small black sea bass and white croaker in the bait bucket below. It was fun catching the bait; actually, a couple of sea bass and croaker where large enough to go in the cooler for cut bait or food later.

I had noticed on my spying missions, most successful fishermen used multiple poles with appropriate rigging so their bait were positioned in various sections of the water column from top to bottom. With my four rods, I was attempting to do something comparable.

My first shot off the pier was with one of the big spinning outfits rigged with only a two foot section of #5 wire leader, barrel swivel on the front and 6/0 short shank hook on the end, baited with a small croaker pinned at the front of the dorsal fin, it could swim natural in the current. I free lined it off the down current side of the pier. It was the first shot because it was not only the easiest, but gave me an idea of where the balloon rig would end up. I leaned the pole against the rail, opened up the bailer, and placed a four-ounce sinker over top of the line, nearest to where it crossed over the banister. It pinned the line down firmly enough to hold the bait in position, but would pop away when a strike occurred, letting line flow from the reel. That last step was very important, because if the bailer wasn't open or the drag set extremely light, the violent strike would yank my pole over the rail.

I saw that exact incident happen to a fisherman. It rattled him when he saw his prized fishing pole cartwheel over the rail and then arrow down into the ocean. It was the slow motion piece of a movie when something horrible happens and the man is running into the situation yelling, "Nooooooo." His next verbal exchange, to no one in particular, would have surely changed the movie rating from PG to R. Keeping an eye on your fishing poles was essential, even during the boring times, when the movie seemed to be on pause. It was a fireman thing where no one knew when an alarm would sound.

My second shot off the pier was the balloon rig on one of the 4/0 heavers. The pre-rig was set with everything but the balloon. A few puffs of air into a festive pink round party balloon and I was ready to pin on a large sea bass to a 7/0 hook. It was likewise pinned in the front of the dorsal fin so it would swim naturally in the current. I set the depth at ten feet; it was a guess to be in the upper middle part of the water column, where the bottom dwelling sea bass was vulnerable. It took some time to hand feed the line out from the pier. At fifty to sixty yards, I stopped pulling line from the reel. I checked the drag by hand and found it would give line under firm pressure. All 4/0 Penn reels, and most other conventional reels, have a clicker device built in that will hold the spool in place with light pressure, yet the clicker will yield line from the spool when a fish strikes. As line is pulled from the reel, the clicker will emit a ratcheting sound; the pitch is dependent on the speed the line is taken. It is a reel alarm clock set on fish. I engaged it and pulled the lever back so the spool was out of gear. The resistance of the clicker held the balloon in position; my fish alarm was set.

My third shot out was a fish finder rig on a twelve-foot heaver with a 4/0 Penn patience maker. I looped on an eight-ounce pyramid sinker to the second eye of the three-way swivel. The pyramid style sinker held bottom very well and the pointed shape somewhat improved cast distance. I hooked on one of the largest croakers firmly through both lips, so the leverage wouldn't tear away during the heaver cast. A conservative cast sent it straight off the pier. I placed the rod against the banister far left of the corner, disengaged the reel, and put the clicker on. There were a few people around. I was quietly proud that the cast went smoothly.

My last shot was with the biggest spinner on a twelve-foot heaver rigged with a fish finder, made with a short two-foot, #5 wire leader and a terminal, short-shank 5/0 hook. I looped on a four-ounce sinker to the second eye of the three-way swivel. Four ounces was heavy enough just to hold bottom and required little effort to toss out. For bait, I selected the smallest black sea bass. Reason one, the smaller bait was less likely to draw the attention of a fish too large for the reel to handle. Reason two, smaller bait tended to get more action; I love action. I pinned the hook midway between the front and back and just above the anal fin. I chose that hook placement because casting was far gentler on the bait using the spinning rod. The easy cast from the spinning rod didn't exert excessive pressure so the hook wouldn't tear away from the tender tissue above the anal fin. In addition, the puncture wound was blindly irritating to the bait, making it run away, act unnatural, and draw the attention of something I was wanting. Lots of wiggle and wiggle leads to more gobble-gobble, which was why I was there in the first place. I put that rod in the very corner with the bailer open and four-ounce sinker tacking down the line to the banister. It was my hot rod. The anticipation kept me watching it and the rest with it.

It took a real time of forty-five minutes to make camp, collect bait, and set out my four poles. In my time, it was the equivalent of a one-man pit crew when all went well. For some unknown reason, there weren't many people out on the end that day. On my way out to the end, I did notice a strong run of spot and croaker next to the front of the pier had kept most fishermen soaking tidbit bait in the wash waters. Since my arrival, there had been one hardcore *sharker* homesteading the front and center end of the pier, monitoring an enormous hubcap reel assisted with a heaver breakaway spinner. He sat on his cooler of beer, thinking of or, waiting for something meaningful to happen in life. He looked at me a couple of times, but didn't say much more than, "How's it going?" He was hunkered down on his world that day.

Then, there was an ever shifting group of touristy, nomadic, aimless type, half-assed, fisher people that wasted some time in the surrounding area of me and the sharker. They had to meander themselves to where the pier ended. They were having fun amongst themselves, concerned more about their time together than disrupting the fellowship with a fish. I could tell by the laughter and careless regard to fishing. Each group was, at least, entertaining for me, and I hoped for the man on the beer cooler. They'd wander back down the pier after a while but on the opposite side they came from, to get the reverse view of the same water.

The fishing reports I had read appeared to be outright lies after the first fishless hour. I checked my free lined bait three times, the fish finder rigs twice, and the balloon rig once, during the first hour. In each case, I found the little fish lively.

The elapsed blank time made conversion with shark man compulsory. It was not that I didn't want to talk to the man, but I wanted enough activity to make our conversation broken at least. However, at the time, I had the time. We both had the time. One of the wonderful aspects of fishing is the bond; the love of fishing that allows people to come together across age, sex, cultural, socioeconomic, and language barriers. With the exception of a very fine shark fishing set up and kempt hair, Bill, the older man sitting on a cooler of beer shark fishing, looked like a vagabond summering on the end of the pier. We could have joined forces with my shopping cart and walked the streets at night as a father and son bum team. Nevertheless, I remember the adage about a book and its cover.

"The fishing is slow; how long have you been out here?" I asked.

"About three hours," he responded.

"Have you had any runs?" I asked.

"Not a one," he said. He wasn't talkative so my third question was going to be my last. I didn't want to be the bothersome kid that threw him into a tantrum.

"What bait are you using," I hesitantly asked.

"I'm using stingray wings," he said.

"I heard that is good bait," I responded in a lie, which was the first time I had heard of stingray as bait. I was putting that information in my mental filing cabinet, as I was turning back to my corner.

"A lot of people don't know that stingray is the best shark bait. I found it out in 1963 when I was Spanish mackerel fishing off the beach in Jacksonville, Florida, one evening. I was stationed there in the Navy." He went on to tell me the story about two young men who paddled out on a surfboard with the small dead stingrays they had gigged the night before. One of their dads was a charter boat captain and they had borrowed—the father didn't know they borrowed his rods—two of his heavy rods and reels. One would paddle out the bait on the far side of the first sand bar into the trough on the backside, while the other played out line from the reel. They did that with both reels that evening an hour before sunset. The first bait set went to the far left. The second set went to the far right. They sat on a beach towel next to one another with the rods laid flat on the towel between their legs and waited with just the clicker on.

Finished fishing, he was overwhelmingly interested in what they were doing. So, he went and got some beer and sat on the beach above them and watched. The night fell. A half-hour after dark he heard a reel alarm clock. The two young men jumped up. One began rapidly reeling

138

in his rod. He thought to himself, *That huge rod and reel is like driving a finishing nail with a sledgehammer or the fish wasn't big at all.* There was no bend in the rod. The young man was a reeling machine. In a few minutes, something was splattering through the surf, sliding up on the beach. The first young man was just reeling in his bait. He didn't have the fish.

As soon as the bait was out of the water, the second young man picked up his pole and began to walk toward the surf; his friend behind him. In water up to his shins, he pointed the pole into the offshore darkness. In a few seconds, he jerked the pole up and started running up the beach, holding a pole that flexed back toward the water. When he reached the first part of dry sand, he twisted his body around and flopped back in the sand, driving the butt of the rod in the sand between his legs. He had created a gimbaled fighting chair made of beach sand.

Bill said, "The fight went on for over two hours." He said he knew it was over two hours because he had to go get more beer. Line would wind on the reel at times. Line would rip off the reel at times. At times, he saw a large piece of white water, not from a wave, off the beach. Toward the end, he saw and heard splashing and thrashing just off the beach. The animal was big and furious. One time, he saw the bulk figure of a shark in the wash water as a wave receded. The shark wiggled with the water back across the sand into the next wave. At the end, the young man was using wave action to pull the exhausted shark up on the beach.

When the fish was securely in shin deep water, his partner rushed in cautiously, grabbing at the swinging tail. He could hold the tail for only a couple of seconds before the fish would tear it from his hands. At times, the fish threw him from his feet. During those brief moments, he would yank the fish up closer on the beach. It was a battle by the foot. Bill told me he couldn't stand it any longer and rushed into the water to help. The fellow was thankful for the help and just told him to be careful. Twenty more minutes, sloshing around with the shark in the wash water, and the beast was up on the edge of the beach.

"Everybody, including the fish, was exhausted," stated Bill.

"Well, what kind of shark was it?" I asked, so involved in his story I was tired.

"It was a nine-foot sand tiger. The fins were as rigid as plywood, the back was arched and the teeth exposed and ragged; it was as beautiful as it was scary. That first experience got me hooked," he said.

"I hope you catch—" I almost finished, but I heard the thud of a sinker hit the deck of the pier. I turned to see line whipping off the free lined spinner. I ran to it. I picked up the rod and then flipped the bailer over. The line came tight the instant the bailer caught it. The pole was snatched down in an arc. Line buzzed off the reel. The fish ran over top of the other three lines I had out. I raised the rod as high in the air as I could to give more clearance and stutter stepped my way behind them. My fish was zipping its way over to Bill.

"Coming through," I yelled. The fish passed over his shark fishing gear and took me quickly to the far left corner of the pier. Would it stop? Could I stop it? At that moment, it reversed course and came back through the same way it came. It stopped running where it had taken the bait. The fish had exhausted itself. It came to the pier easily after that. Bill swung the gaff into the fish on the first try and hauled it up on the pier. It was a ten-pound bluefish.

I just got it in the cooler when the float rig alarmed off. The line was clicking off the reel at an alarming pace, until I flipped the reel in gear and turned the clicker off. The fifty-pound test with the tighter drag halted the fish quickly. No long spirited runs this time. Instead, I got circled zigzag patterns with some figure eights. The fish dogged down deep most of the fight until the very end when it frothed the water just away from the pier. It was another bluefish. Bill took two swipes with the rope gaff before pulling the fish up. It was a little bigger than the first, eleven or twelve pounds.

After taking a few minutes to talk about the fish and say thanks to Bill for the gaff job, I looked out from the pier to see a massive school of mullet darkening the water surface.

We said, "Look at that" in accord. Several blues darted in on the school, slicing numerous mullet to pieces as they came through. The school showered the surface to get out of the way of the blues, if for nothing more than an extra second of life.

I put the float rig pole in a pier cart rod holder, and then hauled up my bait bucket so fast most of the water was still in it when I brought it over the banister. After ripping the lid from the bucket, I hurriedly pinned a larger croaker on the free liner, flinging it toward the school of mullet. It landed on the edge of the school. Bill was kind enough to lower my bait bucket back down. The rod was still in my hands when line shot off the spool. I flipped the bailer over. The spool sounded like it was going to whirl off the reel or melt down. Line was vanishing. It was unstoppable. The run went in a straight line through the pod of mullet. Mullet jumped out of the way as the fish barreled through. They looked like line dancers kicking out in a domino effect. The line went limp. I reeled in over a hundred and fifty yards of twenty-pound test and a cut section of #5-wire leader.

"That one was a brute," Bill quipped. I looked at him awestruck. I was high on fish dope.

In lieu of tying on a fresh leader, I opted to use the spinner with the fish finder rig. I knew I needed a spinning outfit to make the long cast. I, also, knew the fish were running through quickly, making the extra poles unnecessary, potentially in the way. Bringing in the spinning reel with the fish finder rig would accomplish two things at once. Besides, the only difference between the free line spinner and the fish finder spinner was the presence of a three-way swivel once I cut the sinker off and removed the float. It sounded reasonable to me. So I brought the fish finder rig up on the pier, the bait was still frisky, cut the sinker off and removed the float before launching it back where the blues were still feeding. This time I had time to lean the rod against the banister and put the sinker on the line to hold the bait in place.

From there I tied on another leader to the spinning rod with the cut off leader. The leader was made of heavier #7 wire, obviously necessary. As I was putting the leader together, Bill and I were chatting. I said I had all the bluefish I needed to eat. For my family, bluefish was a fresh fish dinner only, because even carefully trimmed, bluefish fillets don't freeze well. You have to cut away the dark fatty tissue from the skin side to avoid the strong fishy flavor and eat it fresh for the best meal. I also told him I couldn't stop fishing for them. It was too much fun. He chimed in, "I could use one for bait."

"The next one is yours," I said, as I was hauling up the bait bucket to put something on the refreshed free liner.

The largest croaker in the bucket I selected for bait. The larger bait could better handle the extra stress of the heavier leader. I hurled it off the corner and set the rig up on the banister. Stepping back, I watched the ill-fated wads of mullet wander through the water, waiting for the next blitz of bluefish. People think of nature as serene, picturing doe and fawn grazing in a meadow of grass with wildflowers while birds sing. I was watching nature being vicious, as gluttonous bluefish herded terrified schools of mullet from below and leftover chunks were carried off by seagulls from above. What was going on out there wasn't a game.

My revised fish finder rig popped the line from under the sinker. The game was on, again. I was there in a flash to flip the bailer over and have the rod tip snap down under the pressure of a very surprised bluefish. My bait was likely the first food that fish ever grabbed that gave the slightest resistance. It ran like a scared rabbit through the mixture of mullet and bluefish, dragging my line behind it in a fury. I was up on the pier, with the pole held high and arched over in a bow, my right foot propped up on the lower rail, immersed in the moment; I was tethered to my dream. The line quickly and quietly parted, the rod recoiled, and I stumbled back a couple of steps. It was over.

"Why?" I said that with my face. I reeled in a blank line. "Did I tie a bad knot?" There was no curled pigtail at the end of the line indicating a failed knot.

"Brian, I'll tell you what happened," Bill said bringing me back from myself. I turned to get his input. "I watched you as you cut the sinker off that rig, but you left the three way swivel on the leader. The swivel was shiny gold. As your fish pulled that flashy swivel through the school another blue mistakenly took it as food and cut you off clean," Bill opened up my mind. He was right. I didn't know any better.

"Bring me your pole, a two foot section of wire and a hook and I'll show you something," he said in a sympathetic manner. I did as he asked, keeping an eye on the two poles; I still had fishing to do.

He haywire twisted the hook on the end of the wire. I said I knew how to do that.

He said, "Here's what you need to learn," and proceeded to bend back the last three inches of the other end of the leader, over on itself, to form a tight, open-ended loop. Then he took the fishing line, passed it through the loop, and wrapped it seven or eight times around the double strands of wire before passing the line back through the loop the same way it entered. He licked the loose knot before slowly cinching it tight, using his fingers to control the tightening process. He clipped the tag end of line off, using a pair of light wire cutters.

I thought he was going to snip off the tag end of the wire also, but he showed me a trick. He bent the tag end of the wire flat, back over the knot, then he bent the wire again in the middle of the tag end at a ninety-degree angle to form a tiny handle crank. He held the knot in place with his right hand and with his left hand turned the new formed handle two or three times in a full circle. The wire broke off flush to the knot. Bill asked me to run my fingers over the knot to feel if there was a spur from the wire. There wasn't, it was smooth.

"That is called an Albright knot and you'll use it for the rest of your life," he smiled as he said it. I smiled as I thanked him. He was right. It is a knot for a lifetime.

The thud of a sinker hitting the deck of the pier broke me away from the lesson. The corner rod was off to the races. I dashed around my pier cart to flip the bailer over. The rod bowed over. The drag squealed. I was back in the saddle, loving it. The battle took ten or fifteen minutes before Bill impaled the blue on the end of the swinging gaff.

"That one is for you," I said with pride.

We left the blue on the deck while he brought in his gear for fresh bait. Meanwhile, I tossed out fresh bait on both spinners. I, also, retrieved the fish finder rig on the 4/0 Penn that was doing nothing but taking up space.

"Hey, why don't you take the corner spot and just float your bait out on the tide. I've got to leave shortly," I suggested to Bill. He agreed. I moved the pier cart and cooler barrier to give him room in the corner. It took a cluster of three balloons to suspend and motivate his modified bluefish bait away from the pier. He floated it out, stopping it in the vicinity of the ever thinning and dissipating school of mullet and blues.

Bill modified the blue simply by lopping off the tail and scoring the flesh three times on both sides with a knife. It let the juices flow. He said the activity of the mullet and bluefish had to draw the attention of any shark in the area. The scent of mullet chunks, drifting away from feeding frenzies was better than any chumming he could do. "The sharks should

143

be staged underneath those bluefish," he told me with confidence. I noticed he had set his float rig so the bait suspended ten or twelve feet below the surface. I take note of things.

The tide was changing. The school of mullet was breaking up. Every now and then, a bluefish would hit the surface, taking a stray mullet out of the food chain. Bill sat on his bottomless cooler of beer in the corner of the pier, waiting for his moment in the limelight. My time was drawing to a close. I let the two spinning outfits continue to fish as I straightened up my clutter of gear. I asked Bill if he wanted my extra bait. He said no thank you. Some other guys, who recently came out to the end, ready to do battle with their joisting rods, said they'd take it after I asked. It only took a couple of minutes for me to reel in the two spinners, toss the bait over, and stick the two poles in the rod holders on my pier cart. Shaking Bill's hand, I told him how much I appreciated his help and teaching me a new knot.

"It's called the Albright, right?"

He said, "That's right."

"I'll see you out here again someday," I said to him, rolling my wobble wheel, fishing cart back down the pier.

I was feeling not heroic, but satisfied with the way my day went. I had been patient. I had prepared myself well. The teamwork was great and informative. Moreover, my equipment held up, for the most part. The fishing was fantastic; I had two fine blues in the cooler. My dad would be proud of me and my mom would be glad to cook the fish. Everything was good as I watched the front wheel wobble from plank to plank. However, there was one question in my mind, *What happens if a woman wanders to the end of the pier when Bill is there?* He drinks beer without regard; he pees off the end of the pier with regularity. I guess she'll have to pull a Dixieland and look away, look away.

Chapter 10 - The Ranger Station

I didn't discover it. My best friend, George, found it during one of his wintertime, cabin fever, ambles in the country. He introduced me to the abandoned ranger station, on the shores of Bay Back in Virginia Beach, Virginia, in the late spring when I was sixteen.

"I was riding around in the country and I ended up here," he told me, as we pulled up in his small Dodge truck a half-hour after day break one Saturday morning.

"It's an old ranger station," he told me again. He had described it one day when we were at school. He told me, "We should fish it." Today was the first day we'd had a chance to do so.

What I saw, when I got out of the truck, was pretty much what he described. An abandoned clapboard house pinched between the last foot of paved road and the bay. There wasn't much property about the house. On the right side, there was a concrete area large enough for two vehicles. We parked there, in front of the faded *No Parking* sign. Judging by the surroundings, the sign had long ago lost its meaning. The concrete parking area was an extension of slab from the house. Pop up arrangements of assorted weeds grew in all the cracks and seams of the broken concrete. In the vicinity of the house, a clutter of oddball stuff was laying here and there. Things such as a few pieces of rusted out machinery, a broken push mower, pushed as far as it would ever go again, and cinder blocks were here and there. Leftover large timbers and logs, positioned as they were once stacked, had since been pushed or floated to the ground where they laid, and artistic formations of pipes that used to be plumbing. Amongst the mix was a fallen over toilet that

145

stood out to me; it gave me a sense of hopelessness for some reason. On the backside, relative to the water, of any large object were large wads or mats of decomposing, aquatic vegetation, mainly milfoil that apparently washed over the small, man-made rock embankment during past storms and were trapped behind when the waters receded. The natural aroma from the blocked vegetation was fresh, like good compost. It gave clues to why the house was finally abandoned, frequent flooding.

George and I had to explore the house more before we went fishing. The house itself was weathered anywhere you looked and well weather-beaten on the waterside. High-water markers were evident on exterior boards. Surprisingly, the windows were still intact. One window had the tattered remains of a curtain. On the side, by the parking area, a locked sliding glass door allowed a view of most of the interior. Inside, there were some rusted folding chairs propped up against cheap, wood, paneled walls, a military surplus, gray desk and matching swivel chair, the last decomposing, the mice nested remains of a sofa, an end table that was about to topple over, and two lamps, one of which had a shade. The kitchen area was in shambles. Some wrinkled wildlife posters still hung on the walls. To the right of the sliding glass doors, toward the bay, was the main entrance door. Posted to the left of the door was a placard giving the hours of operation, stamped with the fish and game commission insignia.

George and I poked around the house some more. On the ground, there were loads of mice droppings near the house. When we walked to the far end, where most of the big timbers were scattered, a black snake slithered away, over and under some clutter, finally through a hole in some boards and down on to the rock bank. Mud dauber kingdoms were under any and every over hang. Gnatcatchers were nesting in all available spaces under the roof. The house/office had been vacant for a while; the critters were well established. It was a critter shelter run in reverse.

On the other side of George's truck we found a narrow concrete boat ramp mostly buried in mud, flocculated rotten vegetation, chunks of floating wood, and a bit of trash. It was unusable. On the opposite side of that was a long boat dock that jutted from shore some fifty to sixty yards. The main dock was in surprisingly good shape; we didn't feel nervous to walk on it. It was solid, supported underneath by twelve-inch diameter, creosote treated, pine pilings that were more than likely slated for use as telephone poles but ended up as government surplus and became the dock. The same pilings supported a bulkhead three feet to the right of the main dock.

The bulkhead was a submerged stockade fence made of thick oak boards back braced by the pilings spaced six feet apart. The top of the bulkhead was a foot and a half to two feet above the waterline, trimmed with two by fours on the backside of the oak boards. It was mostly intact, still doing its job, though time battering was evident. On the left side of the main dock, twenty some finger docks stood, for mooring small boats. Two or three of the finger docks, those closest to shore, were still in one piece. All that remained of the rest of the finger docks were the four by four posts that had supported them. Some remains of the old finger docks littered the slips with debris.

Out toward the end of the dock, forty yards or so to the left, was a ramshackle building, at best guess, an old boathouse, standing in open water. It was approximately thirty feet wide, twenty-five feet deep and twenty feet high off the water at the peak of the rusted tin roof. It was open on the end, facing the bay. A dilapidated, submerged, picket fence of a bulkhead surrounded the structure six feet away except on the open end. It looked like something that would attract fish, but we needed a boat to get over to it; or so we thought.

George and I were at the end of the paved road, a place where Mother Nature was slowly, but obviously, erasing the hand of man. There was an eeriness, but at the same time, it had the forgotten look of a place that might hold a few fish like largemouth bass, bluegill, crappie, and some catfish. We were there to find out if there were fish around. We were there to find out if George had found a fish bomb.

Uncertain as to what to expect, my creel was bulging with every lure I thought might work and a bunch of extras… just in case. I brought two medium action spinning outfits spooled with eight-pound test line. George brought the same things I did.

"What do you think will work?" I asked George.

"Well, there is a lot of sunken stuff in the water around the dock, so something weedless should work best," he replied, as he lowered the tailgate. The tailgate was our rigging station. I leaned my two poles against one side of his truck and he leaned his on the other. We started rummaging through our tackle. We both Texas rigged eight-inch Mann's Jelly Worms, a technique where the hook point is embedded back in the worm to make it weedless. His worm was black with a red fire tail. My worm was plain grape jelly. He rigged his other rod with a floater diver four-inch Rapala. I went with a silver bladed, white Snagless Sally®. The Snagless Sally® was my old stand by bass catcher, my *confidence bait*.

It didn't take but a few minutes for us to tie on lures. Then we briskly race-walked each other up to the dock. We both were excited. It was a picture perfect spring morning. The air was crisp. The morning sun still had scattered cotton ball clouds colored light pink. The air temperature was going to rise to the high seventies, maybe low eighties. The wind was a mere breath out of the southwest. We were about to fish a place we had never fished before. We were both excited.

"George, the water looks dirty," I said as we went up the dock. It was turbid, the color of coffee with just a splash of milk.

"I know," he said. It wasn't as if we weren't going to fish because the water looked off colored. Nevertheless, we didn't like the color.

About thirty feet out on the dock, George stopped and put down his creel. I followed suit.

"How deep is it here?" I asked. George jabbed the tip of his fishing pole down into the water. He stopped just before the reel was to get wet.

"It's that deep?" I questioned.

"I don't think so," George replied. "The bottom is muddy, real soft mud." George described it.

I let my Snagless Sally® flutter straight down from the edge of the dock. When it stopped pulling line from the spool, I reeled the line tight to where the tip of the rod was at the waterline and lifted up. It was about two and half feet deep according to the line.

The bottom was soft pudding mud. We both had a concerned look knowing that mud bottom wasn't the preferred bottom for bass, crappie, and bluegill. The bulkhead on the opposite side had worked so well at calming the water behind it, over the years sediments had accumulated.

"Maybe the debris, posts, and pilings will hold fish," George said,

148

trying to give some hope. I wasn't that optimistic.

I was less optimistic fifteen minutes later after George and I had quickly fan cast the Rapala and Snagless Sally® everywhere around the dock without a strike. We regrouped back where we had dropped our creels.

"I don't know, George, we've worked the entire dock and came back empty," I said.

"Let's try the rubber worms," George suggested.

"Let's first take off the bullet sinkers to keep the bait out of the mud," I inputted.

George flipped his unweighted worm next to a lone, large pine piling. He let it sink and twitched it once. His pole jerked over double and then there was the report of a .22 rifle; his line snapped in a boil of water by the piling.

He turned to me and said, "They like worms." When he said that, my worm was mid-air aimed at a row of four by four pilings. I saw what had just happened. My cast wasn't perfect, so I adjusted my position on the dock to make the worm work back close to the posts. On the second post a tap, tap signaled up my line. I dropped the tip of the rod toward the water while speed reeling until the line came tight and set the hook. A frisky one-pound bass vaulted out of the water. It splashed about a bit before I lifted it from of the water by raising the rod up. We admired the scrappy fish.

I said, "They like worms," and tossed it back. From there, George and I leap frogged around each other, casting to each of the pilings and posts on the left side. We leap frogged all the way to the end. The action wasn't a fish on every cast, but more than steady. We managed to put six two to three pound bass on the stringer. We tied off that stringer to the dock near our creels. Between us, we caught at least a dozen throw back bass. The real story was the ones that got away. We hung some large bass, but the eight-pound test line and complimenting drag settings were too light to keep them from running around whatever was under the water, breaking us off. George did manage to land a five plus pounder toward the end of the dock. That event was a mix of skill and luck. By the time we fished all the way to the end, we came to the absolute conclusion that we needed to upgrade our tackle, if we wished to land the big ones.

Fan casting over the bulkhead to open waters on our way back down the dock, we didn't get a strike. We fished back where we left our creels. The bass were around the structure of the dock. I pulled up the stringer of seven bass. George's fish was by far the trophy. George was one happy, young man. He wasn't only happy he had caught the largest fish, but because he had stumbled on this forgotten place, seen the potential beyond the ruins, played a hunch, and found a fish bomb. I was happy to share the moment with him, my best friend.

George went back to tossing the worm around the posts and pilings on the left side of the dock. I thought I'd try something different. In my creel was a spool of twenty-pound line I used to make catfish leaders. I made up some crazy knot to connect my main line, the eight-pound test, to the twenty-pound test line and reeled on fifteen feet, top loading my spool. Then I slipped on an eighth ounce bullet sinker and tied back on my worm hook. A grape Jelly Worm went back on the hook. My thought was twofold. First, the heavier line was necessary to pull the bass off the pilings. Second, slowly working the worm vertically along both sides of the bulkhead and in the area between the bulkhead and the dock might produce some fish if footsteps hadn't scared them off.

I started dipping the worm on the outside of the bulkhead, using the space between the pine pilings as the distance I'd work before backtracking along the inside. Eighteen feet from where I started on the outside bulkhead, my rod curved down with force. I couldn't fight a fish that strong, standing on the dock with my pole poked out over the bulkhead. Without hesitation I took a big step of faith and perched myself on the top of a piling, like a pelican. I was hollering, "I got a good one," to get George's attention. I was also hollering because I realized what I had done and thought about falling in the water. The bass squirmed to and fro along the bulkhead. It would boil the water, but wouldn't leap from it. The twenty-pound test was working, but now what? A minute or so more tussle and a gorgeous four-pound bass lay on its side, two feet below my feet. I reeled down to where there was four feet of line from the rod tip to the fish and lifted the rod up and back, counting on the strength of the line and forgiving pole flex to lift the fish from the water safely. It worked! The fish rose from the water in one smooth motion and swung back to me for a lip lock. There I stood a pelican on a post, with a fine bass between my thumb and forefinger, feeling like the center of attention to the world. A world made up solely of my friend George. Now for the big step back to the dock.

"Should I lead with my left or right foot?" Even though I'm left handed, I stepped off the piling, leading with my right foot. I stayed dry! I held the fish up for George to see before going down the dock to clip it on the stringer. I thought I was the coolest person in the world at the moment, no kidding. Actually, I was the coolest guy in the world, because nobody was taking a survey at that moment.

I got back to fishing the bulkhead quickly. I pulled two more bass off the bulkhead before getting to the end. One fish was uncontrollable. It walked off, giving me back a bent hook. I saved that one in my creel to show Dad. By fishing the bulkhead area and having to jump back and forth a few times, I became comfortable, hopping from the dock to the bulkhead. I gained confidence through several successful leaps of faith.

George and I met up at the end. He had landed a couple more bass along the left hand side of the dock, while I worm dipped the bulkhead. We had enough bass. The fishery was incredible. If we had the fish that got away, our stringer would be legendary, at least to us.

"George, this place is unbelievable!" I told him as we were walking back to our creels. I could tell by the way he was talking and acting, he was also pleased; he wasn't cocky, that was never him, but he was happy, very happy.

"Do you think there are any crappies holding on the structures?" I asked George.

"There is only one way to find out," he said, smiling.

I questioned, "Pinkie® Jigs?"

He nodded. We cut the Snagless Sally® and Rapala off our extra poles, tying on Pinkie® Jigs. George worked the left side of the dock. I jigged around the bulkhead, the same way I worked the worm. George hadn't been working the jig around many pilings when he got the first hit. It cork screwed up from the bottom and went airborne when George raised his pole up. It was an overstuffed bluegill, the size and shape of a dinner plate. The markings were beautiful. Deep blues, purples, and blacks blending above an orange tinted belly, it flashed in the sun like

151

the gem of a fish it was.

He caught another big bluegill, and I released a yearling bass before we found ourselves halfway up the dock where the water was three and a half to four feet deep. Right beside one of the pilings that supported the bulkhead, my jig got heavy. I set the hook; a slab sized crappie wallowed out of the water. Two more came from the same area. George caught three on the left hand side by flicking the Pinkie® Jig under the dock. Then, the bite quit there. We continued to bounce our jigs on up the dock. On the outside of the bulkhead, I set the hook on a big bass that came immediately up out of the water, shook its head wildly, slung the jig back at me, and escaped. I got a good look at that fish; it was bigger than the one George had on the stringer. This place was becoming more and more amazing. You didn't know when a fish bomb was going to explode, but you knew it was coming soon enough; we were walking over a minefield.

On the very end of the dock, we found a nest of crappie. They were concentrated around the pilings. We picked up at least fifteen fish. The action was so hot, I ran down the dock to pull an extra stringer from my creel to use on the end. The fight of a crappie is no epic battle; it is a brief tantrum, but there is something special, knowing you're going to catch a fish every time. It is fun for kids of all ages.

"We've got more than enough fish," I said to George. He agreed and added, he didn't want to clean all the ones we had now.

"Do you want to throw some back," I asked.

He grinned, "I've got to show these fish to my parents."

I understood. The fish would not be lost to freezer burn; both our families enjoyed eating fish, especially fresh.

We gathered our things, the two fine stringers of fish, and walked down the dock toward his truck in some sort of outdoorsmen afterglow. The tackle, we laid out neat in the truck-bed. The fish went in a large, plastic garbage bag, placed toward the truck cab to keep them from drying out in the soon to be wind. Actually, we were ill prepared for such a catch; normally, we didn't bring back that many fish. However, that issue wouldn't happen again at the old ranger station. On the ride back we beamed about each fish, especially about the jumbo bluegill and bass that got away. We knew we needed stouter tackle to handle the fish we left behind. We wondered about the big ones that we hadn't yet had a chance to tangle with. It wasn't long into the conversation that we let our minds wander a bit, "We may have walked over a state record largemouth bass!" We broached a lot in questions. What about that ramshackle building, across from the dock? If the building didn't fall down on us, was there possibly a record bass using that old boathouse as home? How are we going to fish it effectively?

George decided it would be easier to first swing by his house to show off the fish and take pictures, then take me home and do the fish cleaning after taking more pictures. We followed that plan. Everyone we showed the fish to had the same response. Saturday heroes we were, thanks to George. When George pulled off to go home, we had next Saturday scheduled. It was just a matter of getting our tackle together, but this time, we'd be better prepared.

At school, he and I talked on and on about the past and upcoming trip. Some of the guys we told of our fishing trip asked where the ranger station was. We gave them directions. Our directions would require them to buy a freshwater fishing license somewhere in North Carolina.

Both of us concluded we needed bait-casting outfits. The reels could handle up to twenty-pound test and the rods were stiff for pulling fish away from structures.

I took my savings and bought the reel, a Shimano reel of some model I can't remember. I also bought a stiff, six-foot rod to go with it. I spooled it with seventeen-pound test Stren. It was a sleek looking outfit. I took it backyard practice casting. In the backyard, I learned to pick out bird nests of various catastrophic levels. When things didn't feel right, I programmed myself to mash my thumb against the spool to muffle the line explosion billowing up from the spool. It tested my patience; I had moments wanting to make that sleek, satanic Shimano into a short-term hammer. When I was about to lose my mind, I'd lay it calmly down on the picnic table and walk away. I'd come back when I was ready. Once, it meant the reel stayed on the picnic table overnight. I did learn how to cast the bait caster. It wasn't the reel; it was my problem. It took far more than the week I had planned to become proficient, but by the time Saturday rolled around, I could cast well enough to use it, if I slowed down and didn't force the cast.

A second idea George and I came up with wasn't something new. It

153

was the old-fashioned Calcutta pole. They sold them for bream fishing at all the mom and pop bait shops on the way to the ranger station. They came in eight to fourteen foot lengths. We figured on buying a couple of sturdy long ones, coiling thirty-pound test line around them from the base to the tip, and making the working line the length of the pole. With the long poles, we could dabble the worms all around the pilings, work the entire area, and simply yank a fish from the water before it had a chance to run around things and breakaway.

A third idea was live bait, minnows for crappie fishing. That idea was a no-brainer. All we had to do was bring a minnow bucket and an extra spinning rod rigged with a small cork, split shot, and a thin long shank hook for each of us. The spinning outfit with a Pinkie® Jig was to become a standard for fishing crappie and occasional whopper-sized bluegill.

The first trip to the ranger station, we brought two poles each. The second trip we were already up to four poles each. It wasn't going to get less on subsequent trips.

Saturday morning found George and I, once again, alone at the end of the road, parked in front of the "No Parking" sign at the old ranger station. Our rods and reels were pre-rigged. The bait casters had a single worm hook. A Pinkie® Jig adorned one spinning rod. The other spinning rod had a cork, sinker, and hook for the minnows. The only thing we had to do, besides race up the dock, was spiral some thirty-pound test monofilament onto the two twelve-foot Calcutta poles we bought at the bait store and tie on a worm hook. That took five minutes or less to complete, and we were rushing our way up the dock, toting four poles and a creel each. I grabbed the minnow bucket. We were ready to fish. We had been ready to fish for days. We had been fishing there in our minds for the past six days.

In the same spot we dropped off our creels last Saturday, we dropped them off that day. The first thing in the water was the perforated portion of the galvanized minnow bucket. George tied it off to the dock, using an extra stringer. The next step was to rig a fresh, grape plastic worm on the big Calcutta poles and start dabbling around the pilings. George took the left side boat slips; I took the right side, working the bulkhead and adjacent side of the dock.

"George, we have to slow down. We're so excited we're fishing too fast," I said.

He agreed and we cut our pace by more than half. A minute after we slowed down, I heard a loud, hard, cracking sound, the sound of swirling water, and a word from George that he normally doesn't say. I turned to see George scrambling to hand line a mad, confused fish. We were side by side. I reached over, grabbed the butt of George's pole, and lifted it up and toward me. Fishing line slipped through his hands, as far up as I could push the rod. When I could give him no more line, he started hand lining as fast as he could. In seconds, a big large-mouth bass was flopping on the dock, and we were using our feet to keep it there. George put a lip lock on it using his thumb and forefinger. He lifted it up. It was between four and five pounds. It was a solid fish, which was apparent. It broke off the first two foot of his Calcutta pole. The tip section was dangling by the thirty-pound test we spiraled around it.

"I guess your pole is stiff enough now," I said with a smirk.

I hadn't worked my bait another three feet before a yearling bass jumped on my worm. It was easy to snatch it from the water. That fish wasn't aware it had been out of water before I tossed it back. George was back in action with his sawed-off Calcutta pole by then.

Five feet up from where the yearling hit, but on the outside of the bulkhead, my Calcutta pole jerked down hard, breaking the tip. I couldn't see on the other side, but there was an enormous commotion. Sprays of water were coming back across the bulkhead, something slammed against one of the oak boards solidly. I had to make a quick step up the dock to be in front of the next bulkhead piling. I stepped over on the piling, raising the Calcutta pole high.

Glancing down, I saw the bass tail walk away from the bulkhead, flaring its gills to and fro as it went. It slung the worm off the hook. For a moment, I thought it had thrown the hook as well, but the pull on the pole shot me back to the battle at hand. It was huge. The biggest bass I had ever hung. It pulled the pole down in my hands. Normally, pulling the pole down is good; it takes stress off the line. However, in this scenario, the tip had broken away from the Calcutta pole. The line I'd coiled around to transfer pressure along the pole, was now uncoiling from the pole itself, creating a burst of slack. I brought the pole back up in the air and started rotating the pole in my hands, in an effort to turn, no pun intended, the stick into some sort of makeshift, slow retrieve reel. It wasn't working. My fishing line was now at least three feet longer than the pole, and rolling the line on the pole while I held it upright was making the line crawl down the pole, making the effective part of the pole shorter as the working line got longer. Things were going from bad to worse. I was perched on a piling, holding on to a stick, tethered to the biggest bass of my life; my heart was pounding while my other heart was hoping. Life wasn't going to pause because I was more confused than the bass I was trying to take; I needed to think quickly and go with it.

With no thought, I stepped my left foot out from the piling along the top of bulkhead trimmed with two by fours. The next motions were an adlib set of gymnastic complexities I would have bet against myself pulling off, even at sixteen. I squatted down while taking my right hand behind my back and swinging my right leg out in front of the bulkhead. The right leg held momentary balance, as my butt fell to the piling, braced by my right hand. When my butt touched the piling, I realized I wasn't going in the water. In the next second, my left leg swung behind the bulkhead and my right leg fell in front. I was straddling the piling. It wasn't comfortable. Somehow, I managed to keep the line tight during the process; well, the fish still had the hook, anyway.

After running back and forth along the outside of the bulkhead, slamming itself into one of the boards, and doing an aerial dance, the bass was mostly spent by the time I found myself straddling the underwater fence. With my left hand, I raised the pole as high as I could, waving it back toward the dock while I leaned forward till my chest touched the top of the bulkhead with my face on the outside. My feet grabbed, whatever monkey grip they could, to support my body. The bass slid toward me, still looking confused. I was confused. My thumb went in its gapping mouth. I pinched. I threw the pole over in the direction of the dock with my left hand. Then, taking my left hand to push myself up and away from the top of the bulkhead, I brought the bass with me. Triumph! I had the fish. Now what? My two feet were dangling in the water on either side of the bulkhead. My right hand clenched the biggest bass of my life, and after all the excitement, I realized I had shifted to where I was no longer straddling the piling, but the top of the bulkhead. It wasn't uncomfortable; it hurt. Until then, I hadn't realized I was in that much pain. Using my left hand, I pushed my butt back on the piling; there it was better, but the pain lingered.

By the time all that happened, George had already abandoned whatever he was doing. He was standing across from me, on the dock, waiting to help. I felt like throwing up. My eyes were watering.

"Give me the fish," George yelled to get my attention.

He was leaning out over the dock with his right hand outstretched. I had to transfer the biggest bass of my life from my right to my left hand then to George's and, over the water. It was going to wiggle. We were going to drop it exactly where the fish wanted to be, back in the water. I stared at the fish, as if it were to be my last look. One would have thought we were handling explosives by the caution we used, but the caution paid off; George had the fish safely on the dock. Now, could I get safely there myself? There was one stutter step incidence complete with a moment of flailing arms, but I made it back to the dock. Funny thing, the pain went away instantly.

"Here's your fish," George said.

"No, you hold it so I can look at it," I replied.

It was something off the cover of every outdoor magazine, one time, or another. The bass was mallard green on the side, turning blacker up toward the dorsal fin. The white sowbelly protruded, explaining why they call big bass *hawgs* in the south. I couldn't wait to show my dad. I made a fist, putting it inside the fish's mouth. After I put her on the stringer, I was done bass fishing for the day; nothing could possibly top that.

"George, I'm going to dunk some minnows for crappie out on the end, do you want to join me?" I asked.

He wanted to catch a monster bass too, but decided it would be fun to watch the corks dance. George fished around in his creel for a spare stinger, we both grabbed our poles rigged with the corks; I carried the minnow bucket to the end. The two-dozen minnows we bought didn't last long. We managed to take a dozen fat crappies and two couple pound bass. There is something special in watching a cork. It never gets old. At any moment, the brightly colored Styrofoam cigar disappears; signaling you that your wish was granted.

While we were fishing, we kept gazing over to the run down boathouse across the way.

"I wonder how we could fish that?" I asked.

George stuck the tip of his pole over the end of the dock. About four feet below the water, the tip hit hard sand bottom, and the pole flexed a bit when it touched.

"We could wade over there," he said, in a questioning voice.

My first thought was snakes, but I didn't say it aloud because it wasn't manly.

"Check the bottom again," I asked, to give me time to do some quick thinking. I was thinking about water moccasins. I was thinking of submerged timbers and rusty nails. I was thinking of stepping in pudding mud and being sucked down under the water. I thought, *Over there, somewhere in or around that dilapidated boathouse, lived a bass larger than the one I had on the stringer.* I no longer thought about the snakes, rusty nails, or mud.

"Let's do it," I said.

George and I took the stringer of crappie and the two bass we caught at the end of the dock back down to where the second stringer was hanging. We transferred one stringer of fish onto the other giving us one empty stringer to go on our wading expedition. Our next step was to rummage through our creels and find a small handful of tackle; we thought would do the trick. Everything we brought had to fit in a shirt pocket. It took a couple of go throughs before we thinned tackle out enough to fit in our shirt pockets. We over stuffed both of our shirt pockets, to say the least. If we had two shirt pockets, we would have looked like women. I packed in a wad of various plastic worms, an assortment of bullet sinkers, some lose worm hooks (which was dicey), a Snagless Sally® of course, and a Hula Popper I hung in the brim of my ball cap. George brought mostly the same type of tackle. We grabbed our bait casters. As I touched the rod and reel, I flashed back to the worst backlash, I'd encountered backyard, practice casting. The thought made me hesitate about my choice of weapon, but the bait caster had the line strength necessary to pull a good fish away from the submerged timber. It was the only real choice I had. The quarter-ounce bullet sinker, pre-rigged, was enough weight, along with the plastic worm, to make casting easier, if I didn't hype-up, taking it easy with my new toy. I thought that as George and I walked toward the end of the dock.

At the end of the dock was the last stay of excuses for our mission. We stood there silent, looking out across the water at the distant boathouse. It seemed as if the boathouse had moved another quarter mile from where it originally stood, maybe more. I pulled a purple Culprit eight-inch, swim-tail worm from my pocket, rigged it Texas style, hooking it to the bottom rear, eye brace. Then, I laid the rod, butt end out, on one of the outside posts. I knelt down and crawled to position my body so as to slide, somewhat supported, into the chocolate water. I felt the cool water saturate my high top Chuck Taylor, last year's basketball sneaker, on my right foot. The water went on cooling up my right leg then my left sneaker as it went in the water. My body swung down in the water like a pendulum, but stopped swinging when vertical. I relaxed my arms and let my body go down into the water until my toes felt the sand. There was a touch of security in that sand. The water level was between my naval and my chest. I swung my right foot around under the water, feeling for anything like a blind man with a cane. It was all sand around me.

"Are you coming in or what?" I asked George, kind of cocky to get him in the water quickly and to calm my nerves.

"I'm coming if you'd get out of the way," he said. He eased down into the water like I had. "Kind of chilly ain't it?" he asked.

I agreed; glad I wasn't the only fool in the water.

We made our plan of attack while standing there. We were to wade together to the closest corner of the picket fence bulkhead; then he was to fish his way around toward the shore on the backside while I went into the interior. We'd meet back at the furthermost corner and come back across together. It sounded good. At least, the wading over together part was brilliant.

Our first twenty some steps, we appeared to be learning to walk again, baby steps. We went one foot in front of the other cautiously feeling through our sneakers to determine if the ground we were walking on was firm enough to support us. We were talking to one another about the deep, soft mud at the beginning of the dock. What happens if we both walk into a section of sucking mud bottom? I was going to raise my rod

159

tip up above me so somebody might eventually find us. That was stupid thinking, but a game plan that eased me forward another step. As we waded away from the end to the boat channel, the bottom became increasingly soft. I could feel the ooze fluffing up above my Chucks toward my shins. The flocculated bottom triggered the hairs on my legs to send me a message that bugs were crawling upwards. The flocculent came up between our shin and knees midway between the dock and the boathouse. George was feeling the same thing on his legs and on his mind as I was.

"What do you think?" George asked.

"If worse comes to worse, we draw up our feet and backstroke," I said. We soft shoed ourselves the forty more feet to the corner of the bulkhead as planned. The mud bottom actually thinned out, ankle deep, and we felt comfortable with that.

"OK, George, you fish your way around the backside and I'll go inside. We'll meet back there," I said, using my fishing pole as a pointer to the far outside corner of the picket corral surrounding the boathouse.

"Go slow, there's no rush, yell if you need anything," George said, as he made his first cast parallel to the pickets in front of him. I threw the same cast but on the inside. The thirty-foot casts were blank and we diverged.

On his third cast, George brought in a scrappy pound and a half bass, he put it on the stringer we intended to share.

He held it up and said, "They're here."

From then on, I couldn't tell what George was up to or what he encountered. He waded on down the picket bulkhead while I waded to the left-most corner of the boathouse. Before I got in there, I made several tuning casts. My past performance with the bait-casting reel gave me reason for concern. I wanted to know I was ready to make the perfect, or an acceptable cast down the left hand outside of the boathouse when positioned. Ten feet in front of and slightly outside of the corner post of the boathouse, I let the worm fly. The worm splashed ten feet in front of the backside, less than two feet away. I stepped to my right to make the worm crawl closer along the outside perimeter. Slowly raising the rod tip then dropping it down and collecting line as it went slack, I worked the worm back, trying to keep it visible to the fish above the muddy bottom. After three casts, I moved two steps in to the right, to view and think about how I should best approach the interior of the boathouse.

From where I was standing, the boathouse was a vast cave with a rusty tin roof. In the very back, in the shade, was a feeble six-foot dock jutting toward me, dividing the boathouse in half. Along the back wall, both left and right of the dock and all along the sidewalls was a narrow wharf supported underneath with four by four pilings. Those structures George and I couldn't see from where we waded. The extra structures in the water could hold bass. I pitched three casts in the middle, while I was still thinking and adjusting to what I just discovered. The expedition was becoming more interesting. I wanted to make the least amount of disturbances (casts) into the inner sanctuary, yet get the most coverage. I still had confidence in the worm. It was snag free, non-intrusive, and had proven itself on the dock walks. Besides, I didn't want to change anything, because I was casting well. I came up with a simple plan to work the worm, as best I could, parallel along the walls and docks ahead of me and hit the stick outs with a few extra casts. The biggest part of the plan was to stay calm and work slowly. Doing that would decrease my likelihood of backlashing and increase the worm's time in the strike zone. I sucked in a deep breath, exhaled slowly while my little voice coached, *relax*.

The left side of the boathouse I was standing in front of was awash in sunlight. I could see every piling that supported the boardwalk on the left side and on toward the middle. It made casting and working the worm easier. I'd watch the tick mark where fishing line entered the water and knew where the worm was working. I addressed every piling on the left side of the building with my worm without one hit. However, I was pleased with my casting. One cast developed a minor fuzzy bird's nest, but I quickly picked it out, no problem. Nonetheless, I wasn't too happy about the fish cooperation. I heard George yell out to me a couple times, he had one on. Thankfully, he was the one carrying the stringer. I was happy for him. Still, I was an absorbed fishing spelunker in a world of my own.

I decided to move to my right some, wading forward to where I was just inside the boathouse. Instinctively, I looked up to see if those old rafters would sustain the roof for another half hour. The boards were weather beaten, appearing as if cemented together by a thick coating of mud dauber nest. Above the mud dauber nests, on top of the joists, were countless Gnat Catcher nests. When I entered the boathouse, the bird colony alerted with peeps, then shrill bird yakking. Many of the birds took flight. Some of the birds unloaded their bowels as they flew by. They missed me, until the second wave flew. One of those got me on my right forearm. I was lucky to get away with just that. I rinsed my arm in the water. Smiling to myself, I thought, *I could be dunking my head in the water.* No I wouldn't, I had a ball cap on. Nevertheless, George would get a kick out of seeing me with a bird-splattered hat.

Three more steps into the boathouse, my right foot bumped into something solid. It was wooden; I could tell through my sneaker. Using my foot like a blind man's cane, I went left then right, up, and down. The outside of the object curved slightly. It was approximately two-feet high and hollow in the inside. I had literally stumbled on to a sunken wooden rowboat. It was good future information. I was sure I spooked off any fish using it for cover. I stepped back one pace, steadied myself, and sent a cast down the left hand side of the middle dock. It was a good cast, yet nothing happened. At an angle, I cast over to the right side of the same dock. The right side was in the shade of the far wall. The high wall cast a sharp angular shadow, the edge of which was a moving light to a dark dividing line governed by the suns movement. When I'd worked a worm to the front post of the dock, it stopped solidly where the dark went to light. It felt like it snagged into a submerged timber. I reeled down to jerk the worm off the log.

When I snatched, the log bolted away to the far, deep, dark, right corner of the boathouse. It left a trail of wash water behind it. The fish was large, very large. It had to be, pulling line off a tightened down drag. I had set the drag super firm, recognizing beforehand, any fish had to be muscled away from the structure to win it. A forgiving drag would mean losing fish. This fish took the line off a grudging reel; it pulled my arms down a bit as it drove back. The power was far more than expected; and far more than I had ever encountered. The fish paused just before a cluster of pilings in the right corner. I pulled back as it burst forward. It was a do or die moment; the line went slack without the pop of a busted line.

I reeled in the line. I could feel a touch of weight on the other end as I reeled it back in. The worm was gone, but the bullet sinker and the worm hook were still there. Once reeled in, the worm hook was bent out, not straight, but it had lost the curve of a hook. Disappointed, I thought about all the work needed to get to that one moment and then to have the hook fail. Thinking back, spending the money on the new rod and reel, spending time to practice casting, going through the trouble to position myself well, then feeling cheated, because I had bought cheap hooks to save less than fifty cents. I was really disappointed in myself. There, standing up to my shins in oozing mud, under a falling down boathouse, I learned that you can be frugal with many things in life, but tackle wasn't one of them. I would have given all my savings just to see the fish that wrecked that hook.

"I lost a monster!" I yelled out to George.

"Yeah, I heard what you said and I'm going to tell your mom," he joked back.

George caught four good bass on his venture. I caught a couple, but only put one on the stringer; I was too lazy to wade the first one over to George. He and I met up where we said we would. While wading back to the dock, I told him about the one that got away. I even showed him the bent hook.

He looked at it and said, "That fish must have an iron jaw."

Over the next two years, George and I fished the old ranger station many times. Each time, we were just as excited as the first. We got so into it; we bought waders and belly boats. Belly boats were seat covers that zipped around inner tubes. He and I would float, rather than wade. Our toys made fishing more fun. By getting in the water, we found every piece of debris around the dock, as well as, the boathouse. Over time, storms helped add debris, and especially in winter, tore away sections of the dock and boathouse. Through that time, fishing remained fabulous. The old ranger station gave up many fish to remember. However, it never gave me the one I wanted most, *Old Iron Jaw*. I hung that fish a total of six times, same spot, during those years. The last five times, the line broke, but the hooks never bent. Some fish.

Chapter 11 - The Walk

Sandbridge is the southernmost beach community in Virginia Beach, Virginia. As the name implies, it is merely a bridge of sand, less than a mile wide, which separates the Atlantic Ocean from the marshlands of Back Bay. Historically, during strong winter nor'easters or summer hurricanes, the ocean violence would at some random beach place rip all the way through a small section or more of the sand barrier. The freshwater of Back Bay would be stormed-over with a quick and massive flood of raw saltwater. Afterwards, in short order, the ocean retreated, backfilling the bridge-breach with sand, re-establishing the sand bridge.

That natural periodic flush of saltwater into Back Bay made it a unique balanced environment, rich with crabs, fish, wildlife, and especially, waterfowl. The violent winds and seas from the storms were, actually, the breath of life in the otherwise stagnant, shallow waters of the bay. Due to the storms, Back Bay was a sportsman's paradise year round but bloomed in plumage fall through winter, during the migration of ducks and geese.

In the mid to late nineteen seventies, beach houses were scattered along the dunes of Sandbridge. During the summer, people would drive through farmlands leading to undeveloped beaches that stretched from Southern Virginia past the North Carolina state line. At the south end of Sandbridge road, a sign read, "Back Bay National Wildlife Refuge." At the sign, there was a literal line in the sand, separating the bare sand/beach community from the raw, natural, thriving dune community of plants and animals.

164

The beachfront and backdrop plant communities rooted down the dunes. Sea grapes sprawled down on the beach. Sea oats flagged the tops of the high dunes. Wind sculpted live oaks were anchored down behind the dunes. That shifted onto various mild thickets of clump grasses, shrubs, persimmon trees, and a rim of pines on high, freshwater wetted dunes, before fading into the marshland of Back Bay. It spread out beyond one's eyesight into a sprawling, shallow-water open bay, ecologically balanced with aquatic plants that helped support a sprawling food chain. A freshwater watershed fed from the run-off of woodlands, farmlands, and some creeks. Back Bay was an environmental wonderment, a one of a kind natural phenomenon

Behind the refuge sign resided an Audubon list of: birds, small rodents, rabbits, raccoons, opossums, fox, deer, hogs, hawks, American eagles, more varieties of snakes than you could shake a stick at, and wild horses. When the weather was warm, biting flies and mosquitoes were tiny deterrents to would-be-visitors who happened to find the entrance at the end of the road and decide to look around. The mile or so drive from the entrance to the visitors' parking lot was quaint, but that was as far as most folks got at times when mosquitoes and/or biting flies were thick as air. Once the pale faces exited their vehicles, exposed themselves to nature, nature would yell, "FOOD"! The onslaught would send them flailing and dancing back to their vehicles, breathless with a faint bit of blood drained for their nature encounter and polka dots of bug bites to remind them never to return.

"We ought to go hiking down at Back Bay National Wildlife Refuge this weekend and look for wildlife," George suggested.

To me, hiking was some naturalist term for wandering around aimless in the wild, looking for something to do while trickle-donating blood to bugs, thorns, scrapes, blisters, and whatever else, until finding your way back, ending in a feeling of, *Why did I do that?* "Hiking?" I asked.

"Yes, the Canadian geese may be in," he said, looking kind of excited about it.

"But, we see those in the corn fields on our way fishing," I snapped back.

"I know, but there can be thousands of them on the refuge and we might see other things like bobcats and cougars," he said, getting more excited. Respecting him, I agreed to go just to put one chip in his IOU box.

We went there in mid-fall; it was still warm during the day, but cool to chilly at night. There was no a rush to get there. We pulled into the empty visitor parking area about ten o'clock with our knapsacks stacked between us on the bench seat of George's truck. The knapsacks contained a jug of water, two apples, a sandwich, binoculars, and a can of bug spray. When the truck stopped, two yellow flies pinged off the windshield, so we applied bug spray still seated in the truck. It took seconds before he and I rolled out of that truck, hacking and coughing like Cheech and Chong. The bugs buzzed but did not bite.

In front of the parked truck was a mobile home used as an office for refuge staff. On the bayside was a short wide dock. George and I walked over to the dock; small bream were milling around the pilings. Walking back toward the office, we stopped at a kiosk which posted a map of the refuge, complete with a "You Are Here" arrow. There were info sheets on commonly observed animals and a warning notice picturing poisonous snakes found on the refuge. The words pit viper popped up everywhere on the page.

"George, I saw a cotton-mouth water moccasin, one of those pit vipers mentioned at the kiosk, over by the dock; apparently they're thick around here," I mentioned.

"That was a black snake and don't be a girl," he replied.

I smiled; I wasn't up for the hiking thing. He was all eager about.

"Did you read the notice about what to do if we hike up on a bear?" I asked.

He said, "Yes."

I said, "You know I can out run you."

He smiled, "We're going on a hike."

A short road leading due east was the beach access for government vehicles only. We crested the top of the road, walking down to where the asphalt gave way to sand. To the south was an endless empty beach. We hiked down the beach for about a mile or so. On the high tide mark, we found shells, garbage from foreign ships, and the remains of fish, birds, and other sea life. Whalebones were cool and the occasional shark tooth was a hot ticket. I put a few blackened shark teeth in my pocket. A sign on the beach directed us to a boardwalk that wound its way across the back dune environment.

When we got to a wide observation area, perched atop the highest dune, George stated, "Stop!"

I did. George rarely used an authoritative voice.

"Look over there in the scrub of live oaks."

I jerked my head around to see an albino, white-tailed deer browsing. It was the first one I'd ever seen. We didn't get to watch her long; the onshore winds delivered our scent. When our smell arrived, her ears stood straight up, and her head turned directly toward us. We were statues. She couldn't make us out, but knew we were there. She bounced briefly over some clump grasses, disappearing into a live oak thicket. This hiking thing was turning out to be pretty cool after all.

The boardwalk ended, or started depending on how you look at it, at a gravel road, laid on top of a slightly elevated ridge scraped up from the land beside the road. I wondered why they went through the trouble of building the road up. George and I continued south on the gravel road. To our left was the dune environment. To our right we saw a tract of waterlogged land so thickly filled with cattails we could barely see over the top. At regular intervals, a gated culvert was set under the road. Where some of the culverts went under the road, a small pool of water would develop on either side. We learned to sneak up on those areas to get a glimpse of muskrats, turtles, snakes, or whatever, before they caught sight of us. Every now and then, we'd jump a rabbit. Most of the time, it darted directly off the road into the marsh. But every once in a while, the rabbit would bolt up the road, giving us time to watch. George saw a fox sprint across the roadway up in front of us. I missed seeing it.

About every couple of miles or so, we'd come to a crossroad. From the intersection, you could see that the cattails were growing in paddocks surrounded by embanked roadways. Five miles or more back into the refuge, one of the cattail paddocks had been recently burned and roughly disced. Thinking aloud, I asked George why they had burned this area and turned the soil. He told me the refuge principally managed the area for waterfowl, and he guessed they were going to let new growth develop, before flooding, to create a large food plot for waterfowl. When he said that, it all came together for me; the raised roadways, gated culverts, and paddocks were for the migratory waterfowl. I felt somewhat inattentive. I also felt tired of walking.

"Let's go back," I suggested.

He agreed but said, "Let's take the road over there." He pointed across the burned paddock to the parallel road on the far side. "I want to see something different on the way back," George said.

"Why don't we go back to the crossroad a mile back," I asked.

"Oh, come on," he said, while going down the embankment.

I followed, thinking that it wasn't the best idea, but thankful I was wearing high-top construction boots. The clods of dirt we saw from the road didn't seem like much, until we walked across them. It was like walking on the moon. We stumbled and staggered halfway across the field before we stopped for a breather. We could see the road from where we stood. It was trimmed with a swath of bushes; we'd have to crawl through those to get to the road. I couldn't wait to get to that road. As we approached, some forty yards ahead, the trim turned out to be a very wide swath of green bushes; but there was no turning back. I wondered why the bushes had not burned in the recent fire. When we got closer, I found out why. The bushes were protected from the fire by a fifteen to twenty-foot canal of stained water.

"Now what...?" I asked George.

Propped up, a hundred yards to the south, was a twelve-inch pipe, three feet high on pilings, spanning the canal.

"There's a bridge," George announced.

I looked at it, envisioning one or both of us doing an Olympic, flailing belly flop into the canal, followed by a chaffing walk back to the truck. Nevertheless, I wasn't about to walk back across the field.

"Let's do it," I said.

A few snakes slipped into the water as we made our way to the pipe bridge; it was only getting better or worse, depending on the next.... Before, we got to the foot of the bridge, one snake didn't head for the safety of the water. It coiled up, hissed, and laid back its mouth one hundred and eighty degrees to show the pure, white, cotton interior.

"That's one of those black snakes, right?" I pointed out to George.

"No, that's a cottonmouth, you know one of those pit vipers

mentioned on the notice where we parked," he said without expression.

He was going to throw a dirt clod at it, but I said, "That's only going to piss it off."

"You're right," and he dropped the dirt clod.

The pipe bridge sloped down to a huge valve. It was easy to climb up. I hoped it wasn't just as easy to fall off. We both kicked a piling to knock the slick mud from the bottoms of our boots. I went first. It wasn't as tricky as I thought it would be. Aquatic vegetation rimmed the canal a foot or so from the bank. Here and there, a gob of vegetation would mat out on the surface, in the middle. When I walked the pipe to where I was over the water, two boils of water occurred in the vegetation next to shore and made a wake for the middle of the canal.

"There are fish here," I yelled back.

"I saw them," George replied.

I went on across to the road. George was right behind me. He made it across safely, but no fish boiled the water as he came across.

"Those boils were made by some fairly large fish," I pointed out.

"Let's snatch up some grasshoppers and toss them in the canal," George came back with.

We literally beat the bushes to come up with a half dozen grasshoppers. He had three and I had likewise. We balanced ourselves out on the pipe, halfway across the canal. After giving the grasshoppers a slight squeeze in our palms to wound them so they couldn't fly, we were ready to toss them. Our backs to the wind, George gave the first one the toss. It landed close to the middle of the canal. It twitched on the surface, sending out tiny ripples to both canal shores. It twitched long enough to where George and I looked at one another. When we turned our heads away, we heard the slurp. Looking back, we saw a swirl where the grasshopper used to be. I let go two grasshoppers in the same area. They hit the water, twitched a couple of seconds and were engulfed. George let go a single grasshopper. It landed off center toward his side of the bank. The fish must have seen it coming, because I don't believe the hopper actually had time to get damp before the fish ate it.

"That was a bass," I barked.

"Yeah, and a good one," George said.

He said that as I tossed in my last hopper. It twitched on the surface for ten to fifteen seconds and was then boiled away.

We tight roped our way back to the road, took a hit of water from our water jugs, and hiked north, chattering about what just took place. The canal followed the road all the way back to the parking lot.

A little more than a half a mile from the parking lot, there was a fork in the main road that lead two ways into the refuge. One road diverged toward the dunes. We looked back to see the boardwalk over the dunes we had been on. In addition, the road we hiked back on trailed back along the bayside. We knew the road we had to follow next weekend.

When we got back in the truck, I said, "George, you found another fish bomb!"

The next Saturday morning, George parked his truck in the same parking space, but this time we were four hours earlier and toting fishing poles. We left binoculars behind in lieu of tackle in our knapsacks. The game was on. Both of us had medium-light spinning rods. They could best cast the small popping bugs and top water lures we brought. We also brought small floater/diver Rapalas, small Snagless Sally's®, spinner bait, and the bass killingest lure ever invented, the plastic worm.

We humped it back into the refuge past the pipe bridge in good time. Well, we stopped twice to test the waters in wide places. In each of those places, fat bream, scrappy pound to two-pound bass, and chain pickerel hammered whatever we jiggled on the water's surface. We thought about putting a few of those fish on a stringer, but didn't. There was no need to carry the fish deeper into the refuge only to backtrack them out. During our hike, we saw several small groups of doe grazing. We froze when George saw a buck nibbling around the base of a persimmon tree. When the buck raised its head and turned to us, it was awesome looking, gorgeous, demanding that we stare. We stared as long as he allowed; one leap and he was gone.

"That was at least an eight pointer," George whispered excitedly.

"It was beautiful," I replied.

In a clearing, we stopped to watch a sow and her piglets root the ground. Those animals can tear up ground like an earthmover. When we moved, she grunted and her piglets fell in line behind her, forming a ham train into the marsh. We saw a marsh hawk with fresh kill, some muskrats, an otter, and some other wildlife. It was a beautiful experience just getting to where we were going to fish. We had hiked at a quick pace to the first intersection, a mile beyond the pipe bridge.

"This is far enough," we agreed.

The intersection was new to us, and the best looking fishing location we'd seen; that was saying something. The crossroad coming from the east had an adjacent canal on its northern side that joined the canal we had been following. Where the two canals met, it formed a large, open pool. A three-foot culvert under the cross road allowed the main canal to pass underneath it and continue south.

A marginal elevation change, from the north to the south end of the culvert, gave the water current once it went under the road. The canal had been widening for the last quarter mile of our hike before the intersection. Along this section of the canal, the bank sloped gently on both sides. What that meant was slight adjustments in the water level caused great changes in the area the water covered. This was evident in the vegetation. Typical vegetation that grew along the bank couldn't establish well because the area was often flooded, while aquatic plants didn't colonize because the area was often dry. Plant growth was sparse, the slope was easy, and we could fish next to the water, not above it from the road. If there was ever a picture that showed what a fishy place looked like, this was the place to take that photo.

It was about eight o'clock in the morning. The sun had fully lit the sky some twenty minutes ago. The morning crispness was melting into a warm autumn day. What clouds there were, were high wisps. You couldn't look down the canal to the east because the sunburst, off the mirrored water surface, blinded you. George and I dropped our knapsacks on the crossroad over top of the culvert.

"What do you want to do first?" I asked.

"Let's hit that running water on the backside of the culvert."

George was using a small floater/diver Rapala minnow, green with black tiger stripes and a yellow belly. I went with a light blue Pop-R with a white belly. I love the way that lure spritzes water from the concave face when twitched; besides, I thought, *something that mimics a frog might be a good choice in a marsh environment.* From the top of the crossroad, directly above the culvert, we flicked our lures in the tannic stained waters below. The fishable area wasn't of much size. One guy

171

could have hit all the good spots in less than ten minutes, but George and I liked fishing together, sometimes. For us it didn't matter whose lure was hit, we both got a kick out of it either way. Most of the time, I was watching his lure and he was watching mine anyway. He tossed his Rapala just past a point of floating weeds. I landed mine along the bank. The casts were short of distance, the area was small, so we had to play the lures, twitching, pausing, and Jell-O jiggling to keep them long enough in prime locations. George did the twitch and pause routine, while I Jell-O jiggled the Pop-R.

Simultaneously, our bait got smacked. I jerked out a fat bluegill. It was almost solid black from living in stained water. It was a little bit bigger than my hand, a fish worth keeping. Georges' fish danced around the pool, darting to every hidey-hole; it was frisky, even pulling a chirp of drag once. When it finally settled down, George lifted it up from the water. It was a full-grown warmouth perch with a set of red eyes. I'd never seen one quite that large before. We took a moment to admire the fish before putting it on the stringer with my bluegill. I hung the stringer up on the opposite side of the road, so that the fish were in water running through the culvert.

When I came back, George was already fishing. He was working his bait along the right bank. I tossed my bait down the middle. I was watching his lure when a V wake dashed from underneath some weeds and exploded on it. Caught up in the excitement, he jerked back hard to set the hook. It was a swing and a miss. The lure flew up and out of the water. I ducked to let it pass by.

"What the heck was that?" I asked.

"I don't know, but it wanted that Rapala," George gasped. "Sorry about the fly by," he said.

When the water calmed down, I resumed Jell-O jiggling my Pop-R. The lure was halfway in when a fish came from behind, slurping the tasseled rear hook. I paused until the lure was almost submerged, and then set the hook on another big warmouth. I put that fish on the stringer.

"George, I'm going to start fishing over here," I yelled back to him.

He stayed and fished that piece of water for another ten minutes, before determining the fish had wised up and the show was over.

On the other side of the road, standing on a mound of wet sand, there was an eager pool of water waiting in front of me. The east canal was shining to my right, the north canal to my left, meandering back to where we needed to return; I was poised to make a cast into still water vibrating with fish, that few if any had ever sampled. Charged with life, I was fully alive. I tingled. If someone would have promised me heaven then and there, I would have said, "I don't want to go backwards." Some moments in life are precious gifts; we're blessed if we take time to notice when they're happening. The beautiful hike that got me to this place, where I stood, prepared me to have the presence of mind to drop my rod tip in the water's edge, taking time to admire my surroundings, what was happening and to be thankful for my friend, George. The joy of life cannot be bought. The man inside has to be happy.

I flung the Pop-R up the eastern canal, toward the far bank that was rung with a foot wide of matted-out milfoil. The Pop-R plopped down in the middle of the canal. Wind had carried the cast a bit off course. I worked the errant cast back, just like I intended it to land where it did. Three foot from splash down, a pound size bass hurled itself on the hook and line danced its way to me. It had attitude, the fish was fun, but it needed to grow up. I cartwheel released the fish into the middle of the pool. The fish was healthy enough to enjoy the only Disney World® ride it would ever know. The second cast I made, I adjusted for the wind, and the Pop-R landed a foot or less from the edge of matted vegetation. I was trying not to be self-congratulatory; no one else saw what happened. But, it was cool to watch the lure sail over the marsh, and then get blown back to where it needed to be with the help of the wind in a roll pattern, and landing better than I expected. The cast delivered satisfaction all its own. I worked the bait back without a touch. It didn't matter.

George came over the bank on the opposite side of the culvert.

"Take that side of the canal," I said to him as he was making his way to the water.

He was now in charge of the east canal. I focused my attention down the main, north canal.

The canal was widest where I was standing, but slowly necked down the further it went north. The sun was getting high in the sky, pushing noon. My confidence in the top water action waned after too many ignored well-placed casts. The light level had changed. I cut the Pop-R off, tied on a worm hook, no Bullet Weight®. I weedless rigged a dark, purple, Culprit curly tail worm. The worm color chosen most resembled the snakes we'd seen. By using the weed-less worm, I could cast recklessly, throwing in the cattails beyond the canal and snake it back. There is liberty in recklessness. As it turned out, the plastic worm was a ticket to bassville. Regardless of where it landed, I could present it like a rich drunk staggering through a Vegas casino, knowing that sweet target wasn't going to make it through without a fleecing. I'd snake the worm over and around anything and everything in the canal, and bass couldn't stand it. Sometimes they'd come through the weeds to grab it. That semi-educated choice of lure made me consider, largemouth bass may eat baby snakes. The idea had merit, since there were an awful lot of snakes around the canal. Later on, their stomach contents confirmed it. Bass eat snakes.

George was having great delight fishing the east canal. Still using the Rapala, he was catching a number of chain pickerel, a small southern cousin of the northern pike. Some people call them jacks. Pickerel are elongated—twelve to twenty-four inches long with yellow and green markings that resemble a chain—hence the name. The mouth protrudes while flattening out with a full set of teeth; a fact they are aware of because they are fearless with attitude. Being aggressive and acrobatic, they are more than average-fun to catch; however, most folks disdain having one strike because they are considered poor table fare due to the many hair bones.

George wouldn't have cared if they were pure poison to eat; catching them was cool. He would twitch, vibrate, and jerk the bait, making it imitate a wounded fish. Pickerel would rocket over in V wake to take it out of the food chain with explosive violence. That fish may come completely out of the water, during the strike. It was fun to watch George twitch and vibrate with the pickerel.

Actually, it was too much fun just to watch; I wanted some jack action, too. Using the Rapala, George was not just catching jacks, but warmouth, bream, and bass, as well. The plastic worm was only catching bass for me. Well, bream and warmouth would peck at the worm but wouldn't get the point. The reckless worm was great, but I needed more fun. I wanted the full spectrum of fun from the canal. Without a second thought, I cut the worm off and tied on a Rapala similar to George's bait. The Rapala dangled two treble hooks, which meant, in no uncertain terms, casting could no longer be reckless, if I cared to keep the lure.

I fished the Rapala in the waters I had run the worm through, but that water was spent. The Rapala drew no attention. The fish had become distrustful. It was time for a move.

George and I had started fishing where the two canals joined up. Then we fished away from one another to the point of barely being within yelling range with the help of arm motions. I thought it was about time to start fishing together again, especially since I wasn't getting any bites, so I yelled to get his attention and motioned with my arms to come on over. My canal was the one leading back. George must have been thinking and/or encountering the same thing, because when he saw me motion, he immediately stopped fishing, except for a couple of last casts, and started my way. We met on the east road where we started fishing over the culvert. There we collected back our creels. I went down and got the stringer that had a half dozen or so bluegill, bass, and one pickerel on it. George must have put the pickerel on the stringer for us to test fry. While getting the stringer, I thought about having to drag those fish all the miles back to the truck. It being our first trip on the refuge, we needed to bring back proof of success.

We started our walk back. Wherever there was a clearing in the brush or clear water to cast into, we'd stop and toss our Rapalas in to sample. The anticipation something might happen was the best part of walking up to a new spot. Most of the time one of us would pull a fish out of the water and through the brush up to the road. If the fish was small or we didn't want it, we'd send it back to the canal in a dizzying aerial display. If the fish were large enough, we'd clip it on the stringer, adding to our collection.

It didn't take a mile before our collection was running heavy in hand. I found a stick, on the opposite side of the road, five feet long about two inches in diameter to attach the stringer to one end. Using that I could more easily carry our fish with it over my shoulder. It helped, but there were still many steps in miles. Toting fish became a burden we alternated on. After a short while, we decided we had enough fish to carry home. From then on, all the fish went back in the canal.

The Rapala was the lure of choice for catching the most variety of fish, but at some spots in particular, you needed to squeeze the lure into a tight opening. You had to measure the cast well to keep your lure from hanging up. At times, a reckless worm would be a better choice, but when cast well, the Rapala floated above the submerged weeds and could be worked slowly enough that fish would come from a distance to take it.

Some of the open water pockets were so small we could only Jell-O jiggle the lure in the pool middle, it was either hit or we had to snatch it out. Flying the lure over the brush, not only to retrieve it, but also to keep it, we called that *the snatch*. Nonetheless, it was unnerving to watch and wait for a V wake to come from fifteen feet away to smack the lure, or see a wad of vegetation shift from the thrust of a fish coming out to take your plug. You had to wait and let it happen. Numerous times, waiting to let it happen was an impossible task. At the first sign of water moving around the plug, we'd snatch it away. The lure would fly up off the water and sail directly toward us. An ill-prepared snatch was a dangerous move. We had several close calls where George or I almost snagged the other or ourselves. The close calls taught us patience to set the hook. We learned to relax. We relaxed to the point it didn't matter if we caught the fish at all. The explosion on the lure was excitement enough.

The pleasure of fishing is more than the catching part. Through the excitement of what may come next, we found more value in the live fish at the moment, than the dead ones at the end of the day. Simple truths develop from experiences like those that we were having. Over time, simple truths grow in our minds to form ethics and standards that we carry for a lifetime, but not on a stringer. My vivid memory of this can attest to that because this experience happened over thirty years ago.

As unbelievable as it sounds, several times fish would take the bait the moment it hit the water. You'd never see the fish take it behind the splash-curtain. When that happened, the fish was always of size. The fight was tough; the fish had time to root into weeds before we could respond. If the fish buried up too deep in the weeds, whoever had it needed to push through the brush to the water's edge and get a better angle to horse the fish out.

When the vanishing act happened, we didn't go through the bushes like an elephant either. We'd seen more water moccasins along the canal than any other place on earth. Going into the bush meant looking real close at the ground around you and carefully picking your next step. Then doing it repeatedly until you were next to the water. It took time to move forward, feeling safe. We kept in mind, water moccasins, unlike most other snakes, stand their ground and give no warning, maybe a hiss, if you're lucky. The snake demanded respect for their coiled up piece of earth. An accidental misstep would be horrible. You lose regardless if the snake dies.

Once I came back up on the road when I saw a cottonmouth the size of a small fire hose between the fish and me. It knew of me before I saw it; when I noticed it, it smiled cottony white and I backed off. I was happy I didn't leave anything on the ground or in my pants. George could tell what was below the road when I bounded up, blurting broken English and a word or two my mom would slap me for saying. I managed to pull that fish out, but from way up on the road.

Why didn't we get a stick or rock to chase the snake off? Some would ask. Twice we pitched rocks from the road at cottonmouths; that move encouraged the snake toward us. The second rock thrown really encouraged them toward us. The cottonmouths were too aggressive to scare off. The snakes proved they could move two young men up the road in a hurry.

Once the sun warmed up the low marshlands on the skirts between Back Bay and the Atlantic, all sorts of snakes came out. It was prime habitat for snakes in general, and the water moccasins that helped make up the population. Snakes were a part of the hike. Accept it or don't go traipsing. In hindsight, keeping such a close eye out for snakes helped us see wildlife we would have missed otherwise.

It took approximately two hours to hop fish the canal all the way back to the truck. Wherever we could, we'd dip our catch in the water to keep them as a live as possible. At one dipping spot, we inadvertently fished out a cottonmouth that found one of the smaller bluegill irresistible. The snake had the fish's tail in its mouth. Because the fish was on the stringer, the snake attempted swallowing it backwards. The dorsal fins prevented the snake from getting all the fish down. George was as surprised as the snake when he raised the stringer and brought the snake out with the fish.

"Brian, look at this!" George yelled over to me.

He had the stick held over the water with fish and snake hanging down from it. It looked cool. The snake wouldn't or couldn't let go of the fish, even with George shaking the stick. It got to the point, we were wondering what to do next, and then the snake fell back in the water, thankfully. Completely irritated, it inflated itself with air, floated high on the water like Styrofoam™ and swam toward us. We left. No time to be a hero.

When we needed a breather, we stopped speed hiking. The fish the snake had was dead on the stringer. I unclipped it from the stringer. George and I examined the fish closely, as if we were medical examiners. It had chew marks on it, but little else, no fang holes. I tossed it in the brush next to the bank. A hawk, osprey, raccoon, opossum, fox, or something else would later deal with the fish. It wasn't a waste for sure.

When we got back to the truck, we put the fish in the cooler we carried in the truck bed. The fish cooler was standard equipment in the truck after the goof at the ranger station some time ago. The rest of our stuff went in the truck bed in a semi-organized pile. It was almost three o'clock. We had been hiking and fishing for about eight hours. There weren't any major muscle aches between us. We were too young for that. However, we were tired. The kind of satisfying weariness you get after an activity you really enjoyed doing.

"George, I'm tired, but there are more fish, and snakes, in there than you can shake a pole at," I said slumped in the passenger seat.

He agreed and it spun into a conversation of hike high points. Then he mentioned we could ride bikes in.

"The sign says "No Motorized Vehicles," but bikes are fine," he informed me.

His idea meant the hour and change hike would be a twenty-minute bike ride on a flat gravel road. That also meant we could explore more of the refuge, particularly the waterfowl canal system.

The next trip, we came with bikes in the bed of George's truck. The bikes opened up the refuge. Twice we found ourselves on the North Carolina state line. We'd roll around inside the refuge, taking whatever gravel, dirt, or sand road that struck our fancy. We observed wildlife from afar and startled much when turning a bend in the road. All the time, we were searching for a secret, wet spot to fish. Looking for the unknown is a driving force, or in our case, a peddling force. In our explorations, we found the major canal system was basically, what we saw on our first day. The system changed to a network of drainage ditches the deeper we explored. The habitat beyond the managed areas, where the water was not controlled, were low live oak hammocks, shifting to pinelands wherever the sand humped up in mounds of various expanses.

The bikes let us see where our imaginations had wondered, giving us peace of mind that the spots we fished were indeed the best places to wet a line. The effort was worth the learning experience. If we had been wildlife photographers, the photos would be photographic standards. We didn't carry a camera. Mental snapshots were all we took; the gallery of which travels in vivid stories that are brought to life every now and then since. Such is life. Such was life.

George and I would fish the refuge many times over the next four years. We saw things changing with each passing year. The farmlands leading to Sandbridge produced more houses than soybeans, corn, or wheat. The dunes sprouted stilted houses the prices of which made the grains of sand golden. A few paces before the Back Bay National Wildlife Refuge sign there was now a booth staffed by someone in ranger garb that charged money to enter. In addition, a gate posted hours of entry and the time one must depart. Times were a changing; so were our lives. George went to work; I went away. We've stayed in contact, always will. George is my best friend, and I wished he lived next door to me, wherever I wander. Hopefully, everybody has a George.

After college, I joined the Peace Corps for a two-year stint stationed in Honduras. Coming home was something I always looked forward to, but during my time in the country, I had fallen in love with many of the people that made up the villages where I worked and lived. Strangely, leaving wasn't as easy as I thought it would be.

When I arrived back at Norfolk airport that Saturday evening in December, it was after dark and the temperature below zero. It was bone cold, something I was unaccustomed to feeling. Family and friends greeted me with blankets and appropriate clothing. I was numb from the cold and in culture shock.

It was the experience I was still feeling the day after returning home, sitting on a steel, fold-out chair in the middle of a large room somewhere amongst the labyrinth of Sunday school classes at London Bridge Baptist Church in Virginia Beach, Virginia. My father was a deacon and had early obligations Sunday. The logistics fell that I was the first person in the Single Adults class my dad told me how to get to.

I was adjusting to a big change in my life when she came in the room carrying doughnuts, coffee makings, and a hint of perfume, the aroma of which blended well with her chemistry. It wasn't the cheap kind filling the room with an odor to escape, rather a fine scent you look to find the source of.

"Hi, I'm Gina, you must be Brian?" she said, looking very pretty and graceful.

"Hola, I mean Hi, I'm Brian." I was still thinking in Spanglish.

She was chatting about the snacks while preparing the snack table with blurts of this and that the way conversation strolls, ending with "So, how'd you like it in… Honduras, right?" She smiled, saying it.

I noticed she had a full set of white teeth before answering, "Good." She bounced around the room setting up for others to arrive, maintaining an unbalanced conversation with me. She bubbled with life. Her hair was straight with a long, semi-curl or bends to it, shoulder length, lightly frosted, but not overdone. She had it pinned up on the sides with fancy barrettes so her ears were seen, showing some stylish earrings. The back of her hair mixed and merged with the sides, then hung down with sections curled under while others rolled out in whimsical fashion that reminded me of an orderly disorder of ruffled feathers from a beautiful bird, the type of which I'd just been introduced. In the front, a few sprigs of hair arched down, drawing attention to a beautiful pair of brown, cow eyes. When she blinked, a hair or two would flex with her eyelid. The flex of those few moving hairs gave more expression to her face, a beautiful face that beamed, life is grand. A look I hadn't seen in a long time.

I can't remember a thing about the dress she was wearing, but I remember becoming slightly embarrassed when I noticed how her lumps and bumps flattered the dress so well. Whichever way she walked looked nice. Those thoughts, I was running through my head in Spanish, so she couldn't read my mind, but my eyes read in the universal language. I found myself, looking down at the floor a lot, so my eyes wouldn't give my thoughts away.

After Sunday school she asked, "Do you play racquetball?"

"I never have," I answered.

"Would you like to play sometime?"

"Sure," was the start of our first unofficial date.

One week day night, we found ourselves bundled up in athletic gear inside an outdoor racquetball court at a city park. She explained the rules to me. We warmed up and then played several games. She played well. Tenacious and uninhibited, she played with heart and soul. Ball marks on my thighs, butt, and back, reminded me of her style the next day. At some time, I had to confess I'd played college tennis for many years, so a ball and racquet weren't alien tools to me. She showed me a game I came to enjoy thoroughly. We played it often that winter.

In the springtime, my thoughts naturally turned to fishing. Between college and the Peace Corps, it had been years since I'd been home long enough to fish. In reflection, I remembered fishing with George from ponds to piers and docks to dunes. I gave him a call and asked about fishing in the Back Bay National Wildlife Refuge. He told me things had changed down there.

"How?"

The price of admission had gone up on the weekends. During the summer, a trolley carried visitors along the hiking roads for a fee, and they banned fishing, except off the beach.

Urban sprawl had pushed the public to the refuge gate. In an effort to control the masses, in one of the last remains of a fragile environment, admission fees went up. I imagine for a two-fold reason. Reason number one, was probably to collect additional revenue for cleanup and repairs after public misuse. The second reason was probably to discourage entry to the small portion of the public that caused the majority of the cleanup and repairs. If admission costs were more than a six-pack of beer, then the partiers would rather have the six-pack and go trash somewhere else.

In the back of my mind, I understood why they banned fishing. It is easier to stop it than regulate it, whatever *it* might be, in this case fishing. If they allowed the public to fish, there wouldn't be a fish left behind

181

worth catching. Heavy traffic would crush the vegetation and brush along the embankments, like a herd of cattle had been through there offering no soil erosion protection. In addition, in mashing down the weeds some people were bound to get snake bit, stung by insects, or attacked by wild flowers, bringing on a lawsuit against the government. I am sure Joe Q Public could find a lawyer willing to file suit against the United States government for being negligent of not removing the poisonous snakes from the snakes' environment in the wildlife refuge, Add to that, the expense of hiring extra wildlife officers to protect the animals from the people and the people from themselves. It is no wonder they posted the "No Fishing" signs.

"George, we have fishing poles we can break down and fit in our knapsacks, and we're just going to catch and release anyway," I offered him the mission.

He accepted it. The next weekend we rode our bikes into the refuge with the rods in our knapsacks. Along the way, we saw wildlife in flight, trotting through, and slithering away. We fished and it was like old times. Bass, pickerel, warmouth, and bream smacked our Rapalas and such. We tossed them back one after another, until the game warden rolled up on us from around a road bend and saw us fishing. He told us we couldn't fish there and gave us a verbal warning. We told him of fishing there a decade ago before the population squeeze. At the end, we thanked him for not giving us a ticket. He smiled, told us the area is mainly patrolled on the weekends, and drove off. He grew up in Virginia Beach during the simple times as well.

George and I peddled back to his truck. We didn't go directly home, but decided to ride around, looking at how things had changed, a mini flashback tour. It was an enlightening trip. While we were doing that, I was thinking how I'd like to introduce Gina to an area I thought so much of as a younger man. She had already told me how she would like to go fishing after it warmed up. She told me she loved wildlife, hiking, and the outdoors in general. She had shown me some of her equipment that proved her interest. Caving, surfing, fishing, hiking, and other gear told me she wasn't acting interested; she had been interested for some time. That pretty young woman that sashayed around the Sunday school room with elegance the first time we met could shake off the finery and get

182

dirty in the outdoors. An attribute I admired.

A walk in the refuge, during the week, was something I wanted to do with Gina. I thought about using the bikes, but thought better of it. Where was I rushing? I wanted to walk and talk with her while keeping an open, anticipating eye; ready to point out something wonderful she may have missed without my expert observation skills. I wanted to be her super-man and guide for a day. It was my dream to show her all the best I'd seen in the past. Wildlife like hawks hunting the marshlands, hogs with a load of piglets rooting, deer perched up on hind legs browsing, rabbits nibbling and then darting, otters teaching their young to catch fish, and whatever else came in sight whilst bringing her to an out of the way, exciting place to fish. I wanted to reveal to her what gave me satisfaction and see how she responded. We talked and made another date. I was excited about it from that moment.

When the date was set, I started planning the day. I started with the fishing tackle. That was the easy part for me. The lures were nothing, but past proven ones. The tackle consisted of break down rods with small spinning reels that would cast the Rapalas, Pop-Rs, plastic worms and such into the canal with least effort. Next were the drinks, which were bottled liquid weights in my knapsack. I choose water, apple juice, and a surprise. For food, I decided on a few bananas and apples, and some bologna and cheese sandwiches, because I like them. It wasn't much on romantic cuisine, but a test menu without the hardcore beanie weenies and sardines in hot sauce.

The forecast told of lows near forty, followed by highs in the fifties, with strong winds, overcast skies with a good chance of rain in the evening and then temperatures were supposed to plummet. A cold front was coming. The weather in March is predictably unpredictable. The blue bird spring day I was hoping for was going to be a blustery cold front in March. I was wondering if this was going to be the first time I'd wander into the refuge and not catch a fish. The cold front could cause a bad case of lockjaw. Would there be any wildlife milling around to see? I called, asking her if she still wanted to go through with our hike or change our plans to something else. She wanted to go see the wildlife. I hoped it would happen. The only good thing about the weather I could think of at the moment was, I didn't need to spook her with the watch for snakes spiel. It was going to be too cold for Mr. No-shoulders.

I picked her up at her home mid Wednesday morning. We got a late start to avoid the morning chill. On the way to pick her up, I took notice of the low gray clouds clipping overhead. I wasn't sure there'd be much day warming. I wasn't even sure we'd make it all the way down to the south beach before the bottom fell out. Things looked dicey. The weather was disheartening to me. What happens if we hiked four or five miles back into the refuge and the sky opened up with freezing rain? I had extra rain gear, but rain sure would put a damper on our hike.

She was ready when I pulled in the drive. She skipped and bounded down the short walk, I noticed she was dressed in appropriate, layered clothing. Somehow, the layers of cloths didn't mask her femininity; I took note of that, too. I hope turtleneck sweaters never go out of style; there is something about a woman in a turtleneck. It certainly took my mind off the weather.

We pulled in the visitors' parking lot, the only ones there. The heat of the cabin vanished the moment we opened up the truck doors. A Toyota 4X4 cools or heats up quick, but doesn't have a large volume cabin. The wind was pumping from the northeast.

"You sure you want to go?" I asked.

"We're here," she replied.

"Are you cold?" I asked.

She said, "No."

I knew once we hiked in behind the live oaks that the wind wouldn't be so bad.

"Look! That sign says 'No Fishing'," she pointed out to my chagrin.

I was hoping she'd miss that sign, but not a chance. She lived with eyes wide open.

"That sign only applies to tourists," I quipped.

"You're paying for my fine," she said.

"Get your knapsack and come on," I teased.

Her knapsack had a sectional fishing pole and a plastic tray of lures. Mine had a fishing pole, all the food and drinks, with a surprise thermos of hot chocolate.

We started walking the gravel road into the refuge under warning skies. When we got out of the open area, to the protection of the live oak hammock, the wind wasn't as much an issue; it warmed up without the wind-chill. As we walked along, the exercise warmed us. The big heavy coats we shed and hung on the straps of our knapsacks. The overcast sky was a blessing in terms of seeing wildlife. Rabbits were nibbling on grass growing in the road middle and sides. If we saw them before they saw us, we'd stop to watch awhile, then proceed to watch them dart until they found their favorite escape corridor into the marsh. Deer were actively browsing on the grass and brush along the road. We saw three or four does at times.

"Stop!" I'd say under my breath when I saw deer. "Don't move a muscle," I'd whisper.

If we didn't move, the deer couldn't see us until the swirling winds brought our scent to their nose. We knew when that happened, because their ears drew to attention and they swung their heads around directly toward us. The deer moments were intense, until the deer bounced off. They were beautiful. Engrossed in seeing the deer, Gina was beautiful. I was caught up in her seeing them.

One hawk challenged the winds like Charles Lindbergh, soaring low over the marsh, looking for the first available small animal to take away. It would hunt just above the cattails, then rise, letting the wind blow it back to a new starting point. It was an aerial display the Blue Angles wished they could pull off. We were watching God fly a complicated kite; a kite that could roll over and over and not twist his strings. The bird freely demonstrated command without effort. To witness the flight was a privilege in and of itself. Gina and I stood, watching the hawk's splendor, until its starting point was blown back to a fleeting speck in the sky.

We were coming up to a spot on the right side, it was a peek-a-boo opening in the cattails, allowing a clear, yet hidden view of a uprooted cattail field wild hogs were feeding in last Saturday when George and I were here. With the soil moist and sky overcast, I was reasonably sure the hogs would be there, plowing up the cattail roots with their babies mucking around behind. It was an opportunity to pull off the safari guide routine.

"Let's take a break, OK?" I suggested.

As she was telling me how much she was enjoying our walk, words

I loved hearing, I slipped out the thermos of hot chocolate and poured us a big steaming cup. Her eyes lit up when she saw what I had. I knew I'd scored points for doing the hot chocolate thing. She said thank you with a kiss; one of those good kisses, far better than Hershey ever made.

"Come here, I want you to see something," I said.

We walked a few paces up the road; I pointed through a gap in the cattails. Out in the field were a dozen or more hogs of various sizes. One was a large boar, in the far distance most were smaller females, two watching over three or four piglets.

"They are so cute," Gina whispered. The mother was busy, tearing up the ground with her snout, eating whatever rolled up. The piglets sprung around playing and eating. "They are adorable," Gina whispered.

We stood there watching for some time.

"Watch this," I whispered. I clapped my hands and every hog out there raised its head. The second clap sent them bolting into the marsh. The piglets single filed behind their mother.

"You're mean," Gina admonished.

"Yeah, but wasn't it fun to watch them queue up and scuttle away," I said.

Another half-mile up the road was where I wanted to start fishing. It was a nice open area, a place I'd caught many fish. When I could see it coming up in the short distance, I began telling how George and I fished the area. She listened intently; it made me feel a bit uncomfortable, like speaking in public, for some odd reason. Was I coming off like a know-it-all, or was she really that interested in how to work a plastic worm? I assembled her fishing pole, standing in front of the wide pool of water. I rigged it with a weedless, plastic worm, grape of course. She started casting, while I assembled my rod. I wasn't sure how well she could cast, but that first shot told me she was fine. On her second cast, a bass boiled up on the worm and she jerked it away, sending the worm into the bushes. She was so apologetic, but I was laughing while she was saying how sorry she was.

"Let the fish eat the worm. If it takes it away, I've got more to give you," I told her. "Remember don't snatch until you feel the fish," were the foretelling words I told her.

I had just enough time to tie on a floating Rapala before she caught her first bass. The fish danced around while she mixed sounds and words telling me how much she enjoyed it. I hadn't made my first cast, as she pulled another bass through the bushes. She had the scrappy one pounder dangling in the air by the fishing line. I came over, seizing the moment to give her a quick hug and a kiss on the cheek.

I reached for the fish, she said, "I got it."

She lipped that bass, snapping the hook free without a problem. She then tossed the fish back into the canal under handed; next, she straightened the hook back in the worm. I was impressed. She didn't need my help in the least. I felt somewhat jilted.

"If you need me, I'll be back there fishing," I said.

"OK," she said, and moved a few paces up the road and started fishing again.

I was mop up fishing behind her. She was a hundred or so feet ahead of me, working the worm. I was lagging behind, twitching the Rapala. Both of us were pulling in a fish every now and then. She was catching bass with the plastic worm. The Rapala was taking pickerel, warmouth, bream, as well as, bass. Whenever I'd catch something different, I'd take it to show her; otherwise, I'd just hold it up in the air, before tossing it back. She'd let out a little scream every time she hung a bass. I'd stopped fishing to watch her reel in each fish. A few times, I stopped fishing just to watch her; she was beautiful. The hair that fell from underneath her knit hat would blow around in the wind, but she was never overly concerned about it. Immersed in the enjoyment at hand, she was a kid in a very large toy store. Twice, I hustled toward her, because she had been caught up in what she was doing and wandered out of my comfort zone.

One unforgettable memory that occurred while I was hustling to catch up to her, I stopped in front of an open piece of water; it called me. I cast and the wind caught my Rapala, banking it off course, but it landed well beside a gob of floating weeds. I jiggled the lure to put off a ring of vibrating water. Looking right, I watched her. I jiggled the lure again and watched her. She was fine in many ways. I couldn't keep my eyes from her. She captivated me more than the prospect of a fish. I turned to see my lure, lifeless in the water. One twitch, the water exploded. I set the hook hard, but to nothing. The lure sailed from the water, over the bushes. I saw it coming. It was like watching something move under a disco light; the lure would blend into the background, then I'd catch another glimpse. In the last glimpse, there was nothing to do, but let it hit me square in the mouth. The rear treble hook embedded dead center inside my lower lip. Thank goodness, Gina was up the road and couldn't see me, standing there with a lure hanging out of my mouth like a fish. I turned away from her, so she couldn't see what I was doing.

The hook went in the tender tissue past the barb. At first, I was gently trying to ease the hook from my lip. Everything I did hurt. Minutes passed by. With each minute, the swelling became worse. The swelling was forcing the tissue further up the hook shank. I could taste blood in my mouth. This was embarrassing. Forgetting the pain, I yanked on the hook, fumbling around in my mouth with a pair of rusted pliers. The tissue was elastic. I felt like I was trying to pull my lip over my head. The pain was getting more intense. My eyes began to water. *Oh, great, now I'm a crybaby with a lure hung in my mouth.* I got my pocketknife, wiped the blade off with my shirt, and tried to nick and whittle my inner lip away from the hook. Closing my eyes, I tried to imagine where the knife blade was in relation to the embedded hook, and then tried to make the most effective incision. Nothing I did worked. All I was doing was making a bad situation worse. I began to drool. The reality of knowing I was going to need her help, hurt more than anything going on in my mouth. I was embarrassed, humiliated. The great safari guide stood there watery eyed, bleeding, and drooling. Why couldn't this happen when George was with me, not Gina! If George were here, he'd call me an idiot, cut the lure out; we'd laugh and move on. I was out of options. I cut the fishing line from the lure, took a deep breath, and walked toward her. She was happily fishing, not knowing what she was about to have to do.

I walked up to her with my head hanging down.

"Hey, this is great, how are you doing," she asked.

I raised my head, "Could be better," I slurred.

"Oh, my God! What happened?" she blurted.

"I didn't wait until I felt the fish," I slurped with a mild smirk.

"Let me see, let me see." Her eyes said it before she did, "The hook is buried. You're going to have to go see a doctor"

"No doctor, we can do it," I said. Nervously, she gently tugged at the embedded hook. By this time, there was no pulling it out.

"Take this," I said, handing her the knife.

"No way, I'm not doing it!" she stated.

"You have to do it," I said.

"You're going to a doctor, I'm not cutting you!" she said again.

"Just try it; it can't hurt any more than it already does. Besides, I'll be in pain for at least two hours before I can see a doctor," I explained.

"OK, OK, I'll try," she said taking the knife. With that, she rolled back my lip and starting picking at my flesh with the knifepoint, prattling on and on. Her picking with the knife, not trying to hurt me, was killing me.

"Stop," I said. "You're going to have to cut the flesh on the backside of the hook by running the blade of the knife along the hook and cutting the meat away."

She didn't like the way that sounded. I didn't like the way that sounded.

"OK, OK," she said breathing heavily. She rolled the lip back again, laid the blade against the hook, I closed my eyes, ready, and she said, "I can't do it."

In pain, bleeding, drooling, angry, humiliated, embarrassed, and becoming more impatient, I calmly said, "Simply lay the blade against the back of the hook and drag it all the way across. The blade is cutting me, not you, you understand?"

She did it. It stung, feeling the flesh peel away with the stroke of the knife. The hook still wouldn't come out.

"Do it one more time," I asked.

"You're going to have to see a doctor," she replied.

"Just one more time, please."

"You're bleeding," she informed me.

"One more time, please."

She drew the blade along the hook a second time, and the hook popped out. We were both relieved.

"Thank you," I mumbled, stuffing a bandanna in my lip.

"How did it happen?" she asked, started a long volley. Unable to speak well, I stood there in silence, witnessing a stark difference between how men and women handle things.

"Oh, my goodness, you can't talk; I'm sorry, I think we need to get back and let a doctor look at that. Here's your knife back; does it hurt? Of course it hurts, you poor thing—"

I raised my hand and she stopped talking. "Thank you again, you did a great job. I'm going to go catch that fish, then we can head back, OK?" I stammered through the words.

I tried, but I never caught the fish. We ended up putting the fishing gear in our knapsacks, having a leisurely walk back to the truck. She did most of the talking. I got over my embarrassment along the way. The walking actually helped flush away the swelling. A mile or so from the truck, the sky thickened up and started to change from shades of gray, to dark gray with hints of black. We had to turn the leisurely walk to a brisk pace. A cold light rain started falling when we turned the corner and saw the truck. We were too close to stop and cover up in rain gear; it was better to step up the pace. We managed to get the doors closed before big globules of water splattered against the windshield.

"Our timing was great!" she said. "I enjoyed the walk."

I replied. "So did I."

She walked into my heart that day. We've been doing the walk of life for over twenty years now, through good times and bad.

Chapter 12 - The Skiff

Leaning on the concrete rail halfway across the Number Four Channel Bridge, I peered out across a vast, saltwater estuary. Cedar trees randomly dotted the tops of high, oyster shell mounds as far as I could see. Landward, to my right, looking northwest, a ragged wall of various oaks mixed before some tall pines. I noticed two pines which had been much taller than the rest. Struck dead by lightning, there was a zipper scar running down the length of their statues to ground. There were no houses or developments to delineate where the marsh ended sharply and land began. Plants simply got taller as it got drier or less salty. Grasses stratified by proximity to water, Spartinas on the water's edge with Black Needle Rush behind. Those plants were the mascara drawn around each tributary, whether it was too wide to throw a rock across, or so small it was only there during high tide. The grasses were two to three feet high, stretching to the horizon, masking most of the cuts and meanderings of the tributaries that fed them. Occasional thinning in the glades allowed the setting sun to splash off the water above the foliage, making broken silver ribbons in the natural labyrinth. It was nature art. I was falling in love with this, new to me, region. Well after I drove away, the mind photos intrigued me. Even the odor of it brought back old memories of marshes in Virginia Beach, yet with a new, seductive twist. The same perfume, but atomized on a different woman. I was attracted. My mind wandered with the waters that poured beneath the bridge I had stood on. What else lies out there? It has to be good.

That adventure started one afternoon, following a brief map reading. I needed to know where the closest point of saltwater was next to me. A week ago, I'd moved to Gainesville to start graduate school at the University of Florida. I was planning and investigating an escape route from the institution where I placed my mind, to a place where my heart beat, saltwater. At the time, I wasn't fully aware of what graduate school would impose, but I was aware I'd need a break from it from time to time, to keep my heart in rhythm. Cedar Keys was the crows' flight to saltwater from Gainesville, due west.

The next Saturday morning, I was pulling my truck to the side, midway across the bridge, so I could off load a collection of fishing tackle and associated necessities before driving off to park the truck and walk back across the bridge. I had premeditated the drop to minimize the time it took for me to dump a select pile of crap and least hamper traffic, if there was any. There wasn't any traffic. Everything went smoothly. The truck I pulled off the side of the road in a wide spot of grass, at the end of the bridge. I hopped out, locked up, and began speed walking back to the deposit I left in the middle of the bridge. The bridge was much less than a quarter mile long. I was in a hurry to see what might happen that day. As I went along, the black night sky peeled back from above in dark oranges in front of me. Clouds began to take shape, silhouetted in orange and darkish yellows. At the moment, it was quiet, except for the soft pat of the sole of my boots on the roadway. I walked while watching the atmosphere dramatically change to the east from whence I came. The transition was something I wish I could push myself to watch every day.

The first thing I did when I got to my crap pile was push play on the boom box and set it atop the concrete guardrail. Jimmy Buffet started a long, uninterrupted concert in the middle of the Number Four Bridge in Cedar Keys, Florida, at daybreak, to my heart's content. I was wasting away in looking forward to what will happen-ville.

I had dropped off a forty-eight-quart cooler of iced down drinks with sandwiches on top and a five-gallon bucket with a six-foot cast net inside. I had one over-stuffed, soft tackle bag that contained four slide in plastic trays of tackle with a jumble of pockets filled with some necessary items, but mostly stuffed with things that caught my attention at countless tackle shops here and everywhere. Add to that, three medium-weight spinning combinations loaded with fresh twelve-pound main line, and the boom box with my favorite Jimmy Buffett cassette preloaded. I

192

also had a forty-eight-quart bait cooler bottom lined with a broken up eight-pound bag of ice with a thick overlay of wet newspaper, and five dozen live shrimp laying on top of the papers in cold shock, but alive, the way I bought them en route to the bridge.

The bridge didn't have a protected walkway, but the pavement was extra wide, so there was safe room for outside traffic. I kept my stuff well inside the yellow stripe. First thing was to arrange fish camp in the middle of the bridge. The five-gallon bucket with the cast net I pushed against the concrete guardrail. The bait cooler I did the same thing so the lid opened toward me. The drink and food cooler I placed to the right of the bait cooler, but just away from the railing, so I could sit on it and not be too close to traffic. That cooler opened toward traffic. One pole, with an all-white, plastic, four-inch grub tied directly to the main line, I leaned against the rail over the five-gallon bucket. It was my ready rod. I felt a leader was necessary, but decided against it to improve the jig action without the stiffer line. The first active fishing rod was rigged with a concave, popping cork pinched against the main line, eighteen inches above a 1/0 bronzed, short shank bait hook with a couple of small, split shot between the two items. The other pole was the same way but without the cork so it fished the bottom. I could add weight if needed.

I was thinking, the night before, my rigging may prove weak, but I was willing to lose fish to find out what swam beneath the bridge, rather than spook the bite away due to heavy rigging. My rigging was a gamble I was willing to take. "Better to have loved and lost than…."

I selected the largest shrimp in the bait cooler for the cork rig. The hook slipped behind the back of the collar halfway before I wiggled the point through the shell. For my own satisfaction, I lowered the bait directly below so only the shrimp dipped in the warm water. I wanted to know how that chilled down lethargic shrimp was going to react to the warm Gulf waters. Within seconds, it was back, flipping about the surface as natural as one could expect with a hook in its shirt. The water was flowing away from my side of the bridge. The tide was high an hour before sunrise and was turning out, going by the tide chart information given in the newspaper, the "Gainesville Sun" locally known as the "Mullet Wrapper." Casting wasn't necessary, I simply lowered the cork down and let the current float the popping shrimp away some fifty feet.

193

While I was letting the cork out, I was looking around on the pavement and found a golf ball sized rock. When I let out enough line, I set the rock on top of the line on the concrete guardrail to keep any more line from pulling off the spool. The catfish trick Dad showed me so many years ago. The cork settled in the current.

On the bottom rig, I pinned the shrimp on the hook, slightly offset from the middle of the tail vein in front of the rear flipper, so the shrimp would behave erratic. I tossed it out to the right of the cork rig in darker water that appeared deeper. While doing so, I took closer notice of power cables that swaged down in front of me from a series of telephone poles set twenty feet away from the bridge. Countless fishing miscasts wrapped the cables. Old sun dried shrimp, pinfish, and lures hung in view like dead pirates at entries of Caribbean seaports some hundreds of years ago as hazard warnings. I wasn't the first pilgrim on this two-banked pier.

It didn't take that long to make camp and get the bait in the water. Ten or fifteen minutes after walking back, I sat on the drink cooler, watching my two poles. During that time two or three trucks towing boats passed by on their way to the public boat ramp in town. I wished I could have hitched a ride with them instead of holding ground.

While I was getting my show started, I wasn't paying that much attention to anything else, but the matters at hand; I had noticed a tiny bite now and then on my calves, forearms, and neck. For that matter, any exposed skin, even the backs of my hands. It felt like the slight prick of a mosquito, just before she had a chance to go for it. I thought I was swathing back a light batch of saltwater mosquitoes. The biting attempts were annoying, but not painful. However, when I sat on the cooler, the annoying little pricks began to escalate to the point I looked for what was biting. There was no hum of mosquitoes or visible mosquitoes in the air. It felt like my skin was crawling. The treatment was working its way up the legs of my short pants. With both hands, I'd rub down one leg, then the next.

Sun light finally rose well enough above the horizon to let me clearly see the backs of my burning hands. The back of my hands, my forearms, legs, neck, and any other exposed flesh looked like it had been heavily peppered. The pepper flakes would move a wee bit. I looked into the sky

194

and there was a thick cloud of pepper all around. While looking up, one of the flakes got in my left eye. This had gone way too far for me. Those unidentified tiny bugs were feeding on me and driving me crazy. An old can of Deep Woods® Off was in my truck, under the driver's seat. I reeled the two lines in so the bait dangled a foot above the water line, then ran, not speed walked, back to the truck, wondering the whole time if there was enough bug spray in that can to handle what was going on in my world at the moment. Moreover, if so, would it work in the first place? I didn't know the bugs consuming me, but I was under siege, being eaten alive.

I fumbled with the keys. I could feel them crawling around in my hair now. I had to scratch everything before opening the truck door. I danced around on the side of the road as if I was taking a shower in scalding water. The door opened. I jammed my left arm under the driver's side seat. In my haste, my head pin balled between the dash and the steering wheel. The pain was welcome relief from the onslaught of bugs. The can was a quarter full and rusty. I mashed the atomizer button desperately. No spray! Oh, God, help me, the juice merely drizzled from the nozzle. I held the can level to the ground and let the insecticide run in my left hand until a small pool formed in my palm. Tossing the can on the bench seat, I rubbed both hands together and started running my hands through my hair, on my face, and around the neck. I applied the second application to my forearms and shirt. I needed two more applications to cover my legs. The bug spray ran out but gave me one complete body coat and the bites stopped. Thank God.

How in this world could the coastal Indians handle living with these tiny teeth with wings? They had to have had a natural secret or a medicine man that kept them doped up. Whatever the case, the Indians that lived here before the white man had to be a tough breed.

I looked at myself in the side mirror of the truck. Tiny black flakes were all over my face, I dared not wipe them off for fear of removing the repellant. Life lesson number 1024-A: do not go to a marsh/estuary in Florida, or anywhere else for that matter, without bug repellant handy! When the sun got higher in the sky, around nine o'clock, the bugs disappeared until a little more than an hour before sunset. Dawn and dusk were apparently their feeding periods. I had naively placed myself in their neighborhood during the feeding period. They found me good eats.

Later I asked around with some questions. I tried to describe the bug that was so small I couldn't see it or describe it very well. My questions resulted in laughter, which heightened as I told of my encounter. The bugs bugged me into making new friends. I found out they called them *no-see-ums,* for obvious reason; the insect is a sand gnat. The sand gnat is a tiny creature by itself, but when the entire clan rises from the earth to feed, the impact is overwhelming. The clan drapes over you in an intense, black pepper, hellish cloud wrapper, during twilight hours.

I hadn't noticed it during my battle with the sand gnats, but it was the first thing I noticed once I got my act back together. One of my fishing poles was missing; the one with the cork on it. Nobody could have stolen it. I would certainly have seen that happen, or so I thought. Walking down to where the other one was leaning against the rail, I heard screeching from beneath the bridge. Peering over, three sea gulls were dipping and diving to pick off the half dried out shrimp from my remaining fishing pole; the one without the bobber.

Putting one and one together, I figured one gull snitched shrimp and in so doing snatched the pole over the railing. When I looked out just beyond the bridge, I could see my bobber floating in the tide. Putting one and one together had merit. I reeled up the other pole to keep from losing that one as well. I had been lucky; the pole that went over had a tattletale bobber. I cut the single hook off the pole I just reeled in and replaced it with the largest treble hook I had in my tackle conglomeration. The treble hook was as large as a half a dollar with rust spots, but that didn't matter. The rig was weighted well enough to cast underhanded out and across from where I perceived the rod to be laying on the bottom. I got lucky on the first cast. The treble hook snagged the line between two eyes, then was lead up the line to where it latched into one of the eyes. The rod and reel slowly rose from the water. I was thinking the whole time how lucky I was and how much money I saved by not having to buy another rod and reel, as if losing one would make a difference in the ever-building collection I had in the first place.

The morning was off to a rather strange start with me fighting the bugs and the birds in lieu of the fish I'd hoped for. Fortunately, after bringing in the lost rod, things got back in order. Over the course of the day, saltwater catfish and skates, a smaller relation to the stingray, kept the action steady. There were two periods, when the tide was moving strong, that I had a flurry of speckled sea trout action. The trout averaged about sixteen inches. A couple of trout I caught on the jig but most came in on shrimp under the cork. Two or three redfish hit the shrimp on the bottom. One was two feet or so, but all had to be released, because at that time, redfish were closed year round in an effort to rebuild the stock. The blackened redfish craze had led to over fishing. Nonetheless, the redfish were a hard pulling fish and fun to catch. All in all, the day had enough activity to manage away boredom, yet had periods of inactivity that allowed one to relax and enjoy the day. I brought back a few fish on a day well spent. Toward the end, Jimmy Buffett got a little tired. The batteries petered out. The last time around, he sounded real wasted in "Margaritaville."

At the last of the day, I did it; I wrapped one rig around the cable aside the bridge. After being cautious all-day and snickering at those before me who fouled up on such an obvious hang up, I cast a shrimp to the wind, spinning that little booger multiple times around the cable. What was worse? A line of vehicles, leaving town at that very moment, saw me. One blew their horn. I wrote it off as my small piece of graffiti on a wall well scribbled on.

I've spent numerous other days on that bridge since the first. Each day went pretty much like the first. Plenty of catfish and skates with a mix of trout and redfish were the predictable. An occasional sheepshead, black drum, Spanish mackerel, or a load of silver perch made things more interesting. Sometimes, I could cast net mullet from the bridge. In so doing, I found out where the snags were on the bottom. Dolphin would cruise through from time to time. When they did, the bite would stop. It didn't matter. They were beautiful to watch and didn't hang around long.

The best days on the bridge were when Gina, my soon to be wife, would come down from Virginia Beach for a weekend visit. She and I would make a day of fishing together on the bridge. She loved to fish, and I loved to watch her fish, or do anything else for that matter. She and I would talk about everything, make future plans, and let ourselves dream together like young lovers will.

"Once I make my first million what would you like to do?" I'd ask.

197

She'd take me on several wanted travels about the globe, and then she'd tell me she'd buy me a boat. I'd get caught up in the moments of travel, envisioning where she wanted to go visit, then dropping in some fantasy romance along the way and end up spending most of my thoughtful moments, designing the boat she said she was going to buy me as her afterthought. Actually, I spent more time thinking about the boat than she imagined. She isn't a stupid woman and knew most of those pensive quiet moments weren't being reflective of travels, but in a boat to come. She was right, as usual, but she under-guesstimated my longing for a vessel of any sort. Those were fond times. I remember her holding my hand all the way to and all the way back from fishing, often we'd even shift gears, hand in hand. I was falling more and more in love, I could tell by the way it hurt more each time she left. Our weekends seemed to last but mere moments. When she left, I was empty, counting down the weeks and what spare money I had to contribute until her next visit. I wouldn't wash my clothes that held the smell of her perfume until the odor vanished after being in my pillowcase. Love makes one do silly things.

Every time I found myself on that bridge, I longed to be out on the waters I saw in the distance. The salary I was getting wasn't going to float a boat. However, within the first year of my moving away to school, Gina and I tied the knot and she moved to Florida. She found a good job at a printing and design house. We were happy newlyweds in a single bedroom apartment. That is all fine and good, but what does that have to do with fishing? Well, it wasn't but a couple of months later that she and I found ourselves in a boating, family way. A small fourteen and a half footer with a thirty-five-horse tiller kicker that was new to us, but not to use. She needed more attention than we expected when we first got her home. Her trailer bearings needed changing frequently at inopportune places such as on the side of the road in swathes of sand spurs or next to fire ant mounds. She needed fiberglass diapers applied on the inside and in a few necessary spots; she also had to be flipped over to keep her bottom in good shape. We powdered her with navy blue paint on the outside and white inside. Scrap plywood collected at night with new indoor/outdoor carpet made for a nice new deck. We dressed her up with plenty of rod holders made from pieces of PVC irrigation pipe someone had thrown away in storage. The boat was the pride of her mom and dad, giving us both times to look forward to. However, she was Daddy's little girl.

The first time we trailered our bassinet to Cedar Keys, I had an odd collection of feelings. It was akin to bringing your baby to the mall the first time and feeling, somewhere in the vastness of the mall, something bad was going to happen to her. I wasn't overly familiar with how the boat would handle. I had a fear of doing something or multiple things stupid, such as knocking the lower unit off on a rock, or misreading the tide and ending up stranded in the night. I wanted to fish, but didn't have a clue as to where to go. The natural coastline went for as far as one could see and it all looked fishy. Grass flats went further south or north than gas would carry you. Oyster bars and creeks, winding into nowhere, carved into the landscape a labyrinth overlaid amongst labyrinths. Being lost and stuck was a real possibility. I needed to explore, if for no more of a reason than the overwhelming feeling of being free from land. All that pent-up energy needed release like a bomb. *Nevertheless, where do I go first? Do I head up and find the waters I'd seen from the bridge? Do I work around the islands? Do I set up a drift on the grass flats and trout fish? Do I run into the estuary and hunt redfish on the oyster bars? Do I start left or right?*

We ended up pop fishing. We'd see something interesting over there, pop over, and fish a bit. Soon enough, something else would attract our attention and we'd pop over and fish. It was haphazard, didn't work to catch a bunch of fish, but it was pure fun.

Being on the water and making my own decisions was a freedom I had never experienced. Released under my own recognizance, from a prison bank I wasn't aware I had been living in, until my wife gave me a weekend pass. I remember feeling the anticipation of what may come next on our own adventure. That feeling blew life into living. Salt air blowing through our hair, occasional splashes from odd waves, misting or even soaking us, having dolphin swim and play with the boat, watching fish move around in the grass flats, turtles popping up, and birds working the water; it was like being in my own private Disney World®. During all our newness, I tried to remember every detail such as where we caught fish, where deeper holes were, the location of oyster bars around the islands, sightings of baitfish, and importantly, how the channel markers numbered in all three channels, going out and coming in. There was a lot on my mind, too much to be absolutely carefree, but I loved every minute of it. Every day we had on the water went by so quickly. If I could have put change in a sun-meter to keep it in the sky, there would have been weeks without nightfall. We were caught up in the excitement of saltwater fishing from our new-to-us boat. Actually, I was more caught up in it than Gina was. She did love it and was happy that I was happy.

Our little skiff opened up a whole new world to me. The skiff was the key that finally opened my landlocked door to saltwater fishing. I was no longer confined to land or structures attached to land like piers or bridges. I was no longer restricted to someone else's time frame or game plan as a guest or customer aboard their boat. My spirit was free in the currents that previously ran by or under me. I did what pleased me. It did take time on the water to learn the spirit of the skiff, to learn what I could get away with and what water conditions weren't worth the risk. Behaving conservatively in a boat was a product of growing up in Virginia Beach, Virginia, seeing first-hand the strength of storms and reading in the newspaper of the boating disasters and the fatalities left in their wake. Gained through time, experience and long-term exposure is absolutely necessary to learn the lay of the water. Furthermore, replication reinforces memory. I don't care how smart one is, seeing or doing something more than twice is necessary. Especially important issues that might at first seem mundane such as, putting the plug in the boat before launching, become routine with time. The weight of an important matter sinks through the now and wow, and begins to network with other important issues to the point one develops a sound routine, whether consciously or subconsciously, or as often as not, a mixture of both. I found that applied to the mechanical movements as well as the biological ones. Through repeated exposure, I was able to watch the same assorted environments I'd seen before, but during various stages of the tide. Each time I went out, whether with Gina or with friends, I gained more knowledge. I began to connect the pieces of how the tide impacted the fishing and the influence of season. A puzzle was coming together in my head. When that began to click, it felt good. It was an informal self-paced study in which I was genuinely interested. I'd pay attention to an assortment of aspects, even those that seemed to have no significance at the time. I was gaining more and more insight each time I went. I remember running the boat out of an estuary on my way back to the ramp with a friend seated in front of me on a forty-eight-quart cooler, and having, what felt like, all edge pieces of a puzzle snap together. It was an epiphany. The puzzle was coming together after a long period of time. Before, most pieces had merely cluttered a prominent tabletop in my mind. I was thankful I started seeing the forest for the trees. I was also thankful that Gina was supportive of my time on the water, knowing my addiction to fishing.

The influence of the tide was most apparent to me in the saltwater marshes. During extreme low tides, water was basically gone except for main channels and a sparse few cuts that were deeper than most. At low water, the marsh was a montage of fresh, naturally sculpted islands, the shapes of which were as unique as the spots on a leopard. Some of the islands were tiny, no more than a pace in width any direction. Some of the islands were large, more than fifty yards at the two furthermost points. Some of the islands were low, made up of oysters caked in black, oozy sediment. The low oyster islands or bars weren't always small. Some of the oyster bars sprawled around, or even between, multiple other islands that were more elevated. Most of the low oyster bars were never seen other than during extremely low tides. The high or elevated islands varied in size, just like the low island/bars. The higher islands would be better described as mounds rather than calling them islands. Some of the larger and higher ones had scrub cedar trees growing on top. The high spots looked snow-capped in sun bleached oysters shells. The tree-line was a wide swath of Spartina grass close to the water's edge. On the high mounds, it was common to find an odd collection of stuff washed in during exceptional high tides. Drift wood, Styrofoam® balls used to mark crab traps, tattered sections of rope, large mats of rotting vegetation, life preservers, and anything else that might have blown off a passing boat. They were also different; you were likely to see individual lime rocks the size of golf balls to coffee tables or slabs of lime rock all covered with oysters. In certain areas around the high islands, there were fields of lime rocks the size and shape of bowling balls all covered with oysters. It was tricky to walk through those areas, because the oyster balls would roll beneath your feet. When you fell, you bled.

Getting back into the marsh, during low water was difficult at best, even in an airboat. Again, the water was basically gone except for main channels and a sparse few cuts that were deeper than most. The deeper cuts would drain the marsh waters into the main channels. In my situation, we'd use the main channels as far as possible, before tilting the motor and idling as far as the boat would take us. When there wasn't enough water to float the boat, after tossing out the anchor so the boat wouldn't float away during the incoming tide, we'd wet hike up on the mounds.

The obvious question is…? Why would I take a boat, run it into super, skinny water, and walk to dry land on a fish trip? Answer one; because it was fun to do. It was a marine Easter egg hunt from finding something interesting that floated in on the tides to finding crabs for bait under those oyster rocks. The crabs under the oyster rocks were an important piece of the puzzle. I had learned, redfish came into the bars with the tide to feed on the shrimp and crabs hidden amongst the oyster covered rocks. Redfish were, and remain, a favorite fish to catch. They fight hard, you use light tackle, and wade fishing for them heightens the excitement of the catch. I went for bait and booty.

Answer two; I was using the extreme low water periods to survey the lay of the land, like a hunter scouting the woods prior to opening deer season. Only in my case, sixty to eighty percent of the land would be covered up with water when I came back to hunt for redfish. A sturdy pair of boots to hike around, a keen eye for high, prominent landmarks and the pocket trick, a hand held global positioning system (GPS) helped me determine were the fish might be when the seawaters returned to rebury the treasure. I went to find the feeding stations, the submerged oyster bars, so in the future I spent most of my fishing time in likely places. I also found out where the deeper cuts were, which helped lead me through the labyrinths. Whether it was a method or the madness of fishing, the time afoot did pay off.

Guaranteed Bar, named it myself, was one of the prizes I found on one of my low water treks. It was located on the leading edge of the marsh open to the Gulf of Mexico to the west. When the tide was halfway or better in, all that marked Guaranteed Bar was a thin band of Spartina grass on the southwest side and a cluster of the same grass on the northern lump. Guaranteed Bar was actually two small bars laying south to north separated by a twenty-yard long, ten-foot wide sand bar between them. From due west, the sand bottom got shallower and shallower as you approached. That was a good deterrent for most fishermen who happened into that semi-remote area. They would steer clear of the shallow, sand bottom usually seen in yellow. I would idle in from the west, over the yellow bottom, during the latter part of the incoming tide using the Spartina grass to the south and north to lead me in like a goal post. At all but the highest tides, the boat would slowly skid to a stop some ten to fifteen yards away from the sand spit that divided the bar. The anchor would be set, not thrown, overboard and thirty feet of line played out. From there, we advanced the landing on foot with each angler-marine armed with a single fishing pole and a fanny pack of extra bait.

In all honesty, for some of those who had never wade fished before, the idea of getting out of the boat and wading in knee to waist high water, did add a level of anxiety/excitement to the fishing trip. A few refused to get out, saying, "I'd rather fish from the boat." They were like new a parachutist whose first landing was in the plane that brought them up. It was all fun and games until someone said, "It's time to go," and they decided they weren't jumping out of a perfectly good airplane. To each their own, but I knew what awaited me, and I couldn't wait to jump.

The canvas creel I'd grown up carrying had to be replaced with nylon fanny packs that were more durable to saltwater with plastic zippers and Velcro® flaps. The largest pouch in the fanny pack was loaded with a couple of handfuls of live shrimp and zipped closed. The other smaller pockets carried an extra popping cork or two. Velcro® closed so they wouldn't float away in waters above waist high. Another pocket had a pinch of split shot and three or four 1/0 bronzed hooks that were considered disposable, because they would corrode before the next adventure, and the last pouch had an assortment of quarter ounce jig heads and fish-proven jig bodies to catch trout and redfish.

The jig body I liked the best was a three-inch, gold metal flake by

Cottee. When worked right, it snapped up from the bottom with the color and action of a live shrimp. Silver metal flake was a great choice in clear water.

The rigging for wade fishing had to be simple and easily changed, from fishing with live shrimp to jig fishing, by tying a single knot. The basic rig began by tying an eighteen-inch section of twenty to thirty-pound test leader to the main line, using a double Uni Knot. If you were going to jig fish, tie on a jig head to the end of the leader with an improved clinch knot. To fish live shrimp, tie on a 1/0 hook to the end of the leader, pinch on a piece or two of split shot six inches above the hook, and peg a popping cork just above the leader connection.

Popping corks come weighted and un-weighted. The weighted popping corks did add distance to your cast, which can be important when wade fishing. To switch back to jig fishing, simply cut the hook off and tie on a jig head, then pinch off the split shot(s) and un-peg the popping cork from the line. The whole switch takes less than two minutes standing in waist deep water, holding the rod and reel under one armpit.

I took loads of people wade fishing in our little skiff. Some days there'd be four people packed in the skiff with all the gear. Those days wade fishing proved the best way to go, because during transit was the only time we had to crowd into the boat. The rest of the time our confinement consisted of as far as you cared to walk, or more precisely, as far as you cared to walk back. However, my favorite situation was just Gina and I. Sounds cliché, but I loved to wade fish with my wife, because she loved it so much. She is actually a very good fisherwoman who can take care of herself. She didn't need my help, but I'd keep close by so we could wade and talk. I could point out a place I wanted to plop a shrimp to and she would smile and tell me she was going to fish there as well and she'd begin to point out all the hot spots around us.

"Baby, where do you want me to fish?" I'd ask.

She'd reply, "Behind me, of course," and I'd laugh.

I was her net man and fish toter.

At Guaranteed Bar, we developed a tag team routine. We'd start at the southern part. Wading in, she and I would put a few casts on the southwest rounded corner. There, a six to twelve inch high step of oysters had developed over some lime rock. There was grass growing around the area so you knew where it was even when the water was off colored. The fishing there was hit or miss, mostly miss, but every now and then a horse redfish would deflate your cork and it was off to the races. There was a time or two when we didn't make it past the southern part before we had all the redfish we could keep. The limit was now one per person in the slot of eighteen to twenty-seven inches. When that occurred the net job got hairy as I'd have one fish in the net, trying to dip the second without losing the first. I got a hug and a kiss if I did it right. There are perks to fishing with your wife. Of course, if things didn't go that well, we had a cooling off period. It was funny that it was always my fish, if one got away. If we caught a limit of fish there, or anywhere for that matter, we'd continue to catch and release fish. After all, we fished because we loved it; the take home part was a bonus.

From the southwest point she and I would split up somewhat. The bar wasn't big enough for us to get too far from one another. She would continue to fish around the outside edge, which turned more easterly as she fished along. I would wade to the backside of the sandbar where the yellow sand dropped off abruptly from shin deep to over your waist. I'd adjust my cork so the shrimp hung down two, to two and a half feet below. I didn't want to hang the bottom, but I wanted the shrimp close to the bottom where the redfish feed. You could tell exactly where the drop off was by the color change, a line from yellow to dark brown. The back of the sandbar was crescent shaped, headed east, and turned northeast. I could cast my shrimp so it presented along the break and cast out into the half moon bay. Every time I fished the back of the sand bar, I caught redfish, most of which were in the upper part of the slot limit. Many redfish were caught, casting ahead on the deeper side of the break. One particular spot out in the half moon bay constantly produced redfish, for some reason I could never explain. Once I waded out to the spot, belly deep, and felt the bottom with my feet to find out what made that spot special. I discovered nothing different. I had to be happy simply knowing where to cast, not why.

I remember the anticipation I felt, fishing the backside of Guaranteed Bar. I knew I was going to catch a fine redfish, but not when it was going to happen, yet, knowing soon. Each cast I made was the one. Every cast was measured out, taking into account the effect of the wind during the cast and the effect of the tide once the cork splashed down. Working the edge of the drop off, I'd cast so the cork landed two feet up on the yellow sand bottom. The incoming tide would catch the cork and float it naturally over the drop. The cork added greatly to the excitement. I'd watch it intently, waiting for the moment it would be yanked underwater. With a snap of my wrist, the rod would whip upright, tighten the line, and pop the cork. *Bulug* was the sound the cork made on the surface. The cork sound mimicked the noise of a fish feeding on the surface. The cork was a foot or so past the drop off. I'd let it rest a few seconds, envisioning the live shrimp below it, snapping around, trying to free itself from its bent metal harness and escaping from a very dangerous swimming area, at least if you were a shrimp. *Bulug, bulug*…. I produced a two-beat, fish-call. I'd let it rest, allowing the tide to carry on. The cork was four feet out from the drop and nothing. Triple *bulugs* brought the cork within a foot of the drop and closer to me. The bait was zig-zagging its way back to me over the drop off. I give it one more *bulug* to keep it tight to the drop twenty feet from me. The six-inch shrimp panicked, fought the tide and the weight of the split shot to start dancing and clicking on the surface. The dead weight of the shot soon exhausts the shrimp. The tattle-tail twitches of the cork told me the shrimp was still fighting on its way down. This moment was what I'd prepared for, got up early to see happen, drove an hour on land and a half hour over water to get here to do. I was fixated. I blinked, something I hadn't done since the cork landed on the water. Opening my eyes back up I needed a second to readjust. I can't find the cork. My eyes dart around trying to find it amongst the light choppy waves it could be behind. There it is… *bulug*. It lurched forward, making noise and tiny bubbles from the concave top of the cork. It's gone! The shrimp dances no more, my turn. Dropping the rod tip and reeling at the same time, all as fast as I could get it done, I stopped when I felt the tight line and instinctively jerked the rod tip up to bury the steel. The sting of that hook was the shock of electricity to the bull's balls; off to the rodeo saltwater cowboy, time to ride the bull redfish named Sir Drag-a-lot. The squeal of the reel drag alerts Gina that I'm having a good time.

"Get him, honey," I think I hear her say.

I look over to make sure she is looking at her cowboy. She was and

I played it off coolly. *Kiss ya in eight seconds, babe.* I'm letting my imagination run amok like the fish. The fish squalls off into the half moon bay, taking line with it. Standing like a statue in knee-deep water, the butt of the pole held straight up and the tip of the pole angled down toward the water in the direction of the fish, there was nothing for me to do except watch the ten-pound test line disappear from a spool, spinning so fast it looked like a blur. I was going to run out of string. The reel spool was getting skinnier. It was getting too skinny! This ride was going into overtime. Send in the clowns, I was stuck to the bull. Wait a minute; I was the clown, too.

In I went. Plowing into the water, I gave chase and collected line as I went. The water was waist deep. The water was slowing me down. Some more line creeps off the spool. I went deeper. I was up to my chest. The fish stopped taking line and arced back to the left, west, toward the sand spit that separates Guaranteed Bar into two parts. I was walking and reeling, keeping the line tight all the time. The cork-handled dip net I clipped to my belt with elastic rope was floating up behind me, occasionally bumping and spooking me. *Keep cool, keep cool, and don't lose focus.* The redfish made it to the drop off, turned left, and hugged the deep-water edge. I followed slowly, gaining line.

The water was down to my waist now, getting shallower. It was easier to move. I was the one giving chase now. I moved along, getting closer to the drop off. As soon as I could, I stepped up on the sand bar. Wading there was certainly easier. The fish burst back into the bay, but not that far. It was getting tired. Standing where I started, I slowly begin to pump and wind the fish toward me. The fight was coming to a close with one more, short dart back toward the bay; a left to right swinging pattern narrowing back to me. The fish was persuaded to swim over the drop off up on the sand bar, with a gentle, yet steady pull from my fishing pole. Before I did that, I loosened up the drag just a bit, in case I got excited and/or heavy handed. She came up on the bar like a full, golden log of deli lunchmeat with a black olive stuck to the back end. She was tired, but hadn't rolled over on her side.

I reeled in all but four feet of line. With the rod in my left hand, the dip net in my right, I squatted down while raising the rod up and back, swinging the fish into the out stretched dip net sunk in the water. It worked perfectly. I stood up with the net, exuding happy beams all around me. Gina came over to get a better look at the fish.

"Wow, what a fish," she exclaimed.

"Did you see the whole fight?" I asked, while hugging her lightly.

"Yeah," she said.

"Did you see when I went in the—"

"Yeah, didn't miss that."

"Remember when it went—"

"Honey, I saw the whole thing"

"When I was dipping the—"

"I got it, I got it all," she exclaimed. "How big is the fish?" she asked, with inflection that hinted she thought the fish was over the twenty-seven inch slot limit.

A permanent mark I had previously made on my fishing pole from the butt of the pole up twenty-seven inches was for just such an occasion. With the fish still safely in the net, I took the hook out, stabbed it into the cork handle of the rod, and tightened up the string.

"Honey, hold this rod level so I can measure the fish," I asked.

She balanced her pole under her arm and held mine horizontal. With the fish still in the net, I held it flat as possible. The entire fish tail flopped over the twenty-seven inch mark on my pole. The redfish was too big. I got down on one knee on the flooded sand bar, easing the fish out of the net. Gently holding it, I pushed it to and fro to force good water through its gills. The fish swam off under its own power, lazily gliding over the shallow sand bottom, appearing somewhat disoriented. It stopped for a second, collected itself, and shot out over the drop off with purpose.

"So, how big do you think the fish was?" Gina asked again.

"It was between three and three and half feet long," I answered.

"It was beautiful," she added.

"It was," I agreed, then said, "I want you to get one bigger," and smiled.

"Maybe there is another one where you caught that one," she said.

I told her I wouldn't think so since I had stumbled around out there chasing down my fish. She agreed.

I had noticed where she was fishing before coming to see my fish. She was standing up current of a submerged oyster bar that branched due south off Guaranteed Bar. The oyster bar jutted out an addition ten feet past my longest casting range. The outline of the oyster bar was marked in the tide with rippled waters that poured over the bar. I knew from wading there before that the water was two, maybe three feet in depth at most and then dropped off another foot or so on the backside. I set both our corks at eighteen inches and picked out the biggest shrimp for her hook. The shrimp was select, large enough to serve at any restaurant. That shrimp would have ended up in my pot, if the fish didn't cooperate. As we walked over to the spot, I was describing the location to her. I didn't know if she was paying attention or merely humoring me, but her cast was perfect, slightly up current of the bar. The tide got hold of it, brushing it into the feeding zone. She popped the cork, just before it floated over the bar. The shrimp sprang from the water, clicking wildly. A V wake charged her shrimp from six feet further out on the bar. I couldn't believe it. I counted on her catching a redfish on Guaranteed Bar, but not on her next cast. The dorsal fin and most of the head came out of the water to suck down the shrimp in a violent boil. I was awe struck, silenced. Gina lowered her pole down quickly and started reeling until her line became taut. She set the hook. The pole snatched over, and the reel screamed.

She whispered, "I've got 'im."

I was a pillar of salt. The fish swung back behind the bar into the deeper water. It was running with the help of the current. The spool on her reel was whirling around in a blur, emitting a high-pitched sound like a blender on frappe.

"You're going to have to follow this one," I said to her.

She said, "I ain't getting in that deep water like you did."

"Follow the sand bar around then," I pushed her gently.

The last of the sand bar arced around to the northeast, the direction the redfish was heading.

"He's going to get off, he's going to get off," she said in a low, sad, fixing to get mad voice.

"Just keep the line tight and walk him down," I said in assurance.

An assurance I wasn't so sure of myself. The redfish ran down until it broke into a stronger current that was visibly ripping by the tip of the sand bar. The line she had gained or maintained was lost in a burst of speed in the current. If it kept running in the current and she still wasn't willing to go in, the fish would spool her in the next minute or so.

"I'll go with you if you want to go," I said.

She said, "I ain't going in the deep water."

I didn't push it any further. For some unknown reason, the redfish broke out of the current, to the left, circling into half moon bay. It was swimming at a diagonal toward us, left. We started moving back along the drop off in the direction we had come from, but on the opposite side. Gina was winding on line as we paced ourselves back.

"I'm going to get this fish," she blurted.

I was glad to hear her confidence. The fish stopped running at the bar, did an about face, swam toward the middle of the bay, this time not racing, but with bulldog strength and determination. Line grudged off her reel slowing, but thankfully, it wasn't screaming out like before. When the fish stopped, we did likewise. The fish ended up directly in front of us, rubbing the bottom to shake the hook. The run so far had been spirited, but considering most of the flight was with a tail wind current, the fish was far from burnt out. This fight was going to be a dogged event; the outcome could swing either way. Gina had never been one to give in. The redfish decided to take the fight to the bottom where there lived multitudes of sharp-shelled oysters. The constant rubbing against a single or many shells could cut the line, breaking our hearts. The fish never ran more. It chose to hold ground until that became too uncomfortable. Then, it would move a foot or two back toward us from side to side.

Gina kept the pressure on the fish. The rod tip held high to keep as much line, as possible, off the bottom, out of the oysters. Winding down, followed by a measured pull up with the rod, was her method of operation. It was tedious, but working. It was working, like using a fishing pole to drag a small anvil across the bottom. Her arms and shoulders were getting weary. I could see it in her face and hear it in her breath.

"Don't give up, Bunky,"—her nickname—I'd tell her.

"I'm going to get this fish," she kept repeating.

Every time she'd raise the pole to force the fish closer, I was thinking, *Oh, Lord don't let that line break.* It was getting closer and

210

closer. It was nearing the point I needed to be net ready. Then, I thought, *Oh, Lord, don't let me screw this up, I have to ride home with her.* The story of how I let her fish get away would be wildfire spread to everyone I knew, and many I didn't but would soon meet. I stepped out over the drop off, directly five feet in front of her, grabbed the dip net in my right hand, held my rod horizontal with my left hand, and squatted down in the water, while extending the net in front of me toward the bottom. I extended my rod flat in front of me, which laid her line across the top of it in the notch created between the cork handle and the rod itself.

"What are you doing?" she yelped.

"Trust me," I replied.

I was using it to force the fish up in front of me, while not allowing it to swim blindly around my feet, tripping me up and breaking it off. With the fish in front of me, I could easily see it and come from underneath with the net. The still squat in deeper water was to maintain a low profile in an effort not to spook the fish with my presence and avoid the natural, startled response when the fish found itself moving from the perceived safety of deeper water to the vulnerability of shallow water. My move had reason; I didn't have time to explain. I just hoped it would work as it had in the past. Furthermore, I was concerned about how much abuse the line had taken and how well the hook had set. I was thinking in the negative, worst case scenario, but preparing as well, hoping for the best.

"Just keep doing what you've been doing, Bunk," I said in a low, calm voice, turning toward her, and she did.

The moment of truth was coming up from the dark water soon. I watched the angle of the line rolling over the fishing pole I had extended for support. The angle was quickly becoming less obtuse. The fish was near. I was frozen in place. Would it sense me? A glimmer of bronze appeared two to three feet below the surface, five feet out from me. It was large and wallowing up. I eased my rod closer to my neck. Gina had instinctively slowed down, that signaled we had a connected effort. The redfish rose in the water three feet from me. I could see the entire fish when the sunlight caught the fish broadside against the dark water beneath. It was gorgeous, a living, golden log. It was definitely oversized. Two feet away and the net was coming up from the bottom

211

for capture. When I saw the net rim under the water, I used my pole to raise and guide the fish into the net it had yet to see coming. When the head and majority of the body was in the net basket, I stood up quickly to flop in the rest. With rod in hand, I grabbed the outer rim of the net for support. My reel dipped in the saltwater in doing so, but I didn't care. There was a massive redfish in the net, a trophy fish.

Gina had pulled it off in more ways than one. I was so happy for her. Waddling up from the drop off with the redfish, tail jutting high above the net rim, I couldn't wait to congratulate her with a wet hug. Gina stood there exhausted, surreal in the moment.

"You did it, Bunk!" I literally yelled to nobody around but her. That broke a smile on her. "Look at your fish," I said, as if necessary.

She couldn't keep her eyes off it.

"So... what do you think?" I asked.

"It is beautiful, two dots on this side and how many on the other?" she asked.

"One."

She went off on a chatter of happy, ending with, "It's too big to keep, ain't it?"

"Yeah, we got to let it go."

While I was getting the hook out, she petted, talked to, and even thanked the fish. It sounds a bit crazy, but she gets attached to animals quickly, testimony to our collection of unique people who walk on four legs around the house. I let it go in good shape like the first redfish.

"Now, what you got to say, Bunk?" I asked.

"My fish was bigger than yours and I didn't have to get wet," she smiled.

Women are smarter than men are, proved to me yet again, this time wet.

Over the years, our little skiff took us and most of our friends on mini-adventures into the Gulf of Mexico. The fishing trips cemented friendships evidenced by the fond memories rekindled each time someone tells the story of one adventure or another. It really doesn't matter whether the story is about a pristine day, soaking up sunshine or a semi-misfortunate event such as someone caught in a pop up storm, spending some of the day being soaked in rain; the outcome is still smiles and laughter. Oddly enough, few of the memories or stories are about a particular fish. The fish, which we were after, are strangely absent from the stories as a whole.

Which makes me think, often times, we miss the true point of a fishing trip. I, too, am guilty of fixating so intensely on the fish I'm after that everything, as well as everybody else around me, becomes nothing more than background noise. Fixating on a fish can be one of the best elements of fishing. It takes you away from problems or troubles that await you once the trip is over. However, being myopic the entire time can also diminish the value of the trip. Whether becoming oblivious to the beauty of the environment you're stirring in or ignoring the people you are with, you risk losing the interactions, which are most important, the part of the trip that lasts the test of time. The fish are soon forgotten. That isn't to say there is no time for honing in on a fish, during the day. Closing down ones world every now and then to a single focal point, for example a redfish tail popping up, requiring a long cast to an oyster bar, is healthy. Nevertheless, step back and take in the big picture. The joy is in the journey.

For me, the little skiff was one of the best fishing instructors I've ever spent time with. There was a constant *show and tell* lesson going on, whether one noticed or not. I took the time to pay attention on how to work with the water, not against it, became familiar with movements and characteristics of various species of fish and how best to apply the tackle to catch them. Through it all, I learned some of the ins and outs of targeting trout, redfish, black drum, Spanish mackerel, sharks, and cobia. Those are more stories to share later.

Since the skiff, I've bought other boats. Each new boat has been progressively larger, but none has been enjoyed more or, it seems, has caught as many fish. In the future, I may find myself on a fine yacht, pursuing billfish in exotic waters, but my heart will still float in that collection of fiberglass patches that formed my first boat.

Chapter 13 - Black Drum Beat

It wasn't going to be much longer before high tide, judging by the water height on the Spartina stems and shrinking oyster mounds. I was thigh deep in saltwater, a good ways back in the estuary, boot-scooting the edges of oyster bars in pursuit of redfish and trout. I was fishing my confidence bait, a gold metal flake plastic jig. Back there, you could not judge the incoming tide by water rushing in, but by the slow sinking of hard ground and plants surrounding it. Things quietly disappeared below water line.

The skiff delivered Dale and I deep into the estuary, back where you needed familiarity and experience to fish the sweet spots effectively before the tide retreated enough to leave you dry before the next return. There was less fishing pressure and more solitude far back in the tributary maze. Dale was a friend who enjoyed wade fishing as much as I did, and still do. We separately waded in quiet serenity, feeling a part of the natural ebb and flow of life around us. Wade fishing with no-noise, no conversation, and no other boats, only the occasional sound of a gull; there was simply the comfort of quietness. Quiet is a beautiful commodity, forsaken so often in the rush of life that we become uncomfortable or fearful when it occurs. I was embracing it, not wanting so much to make a sound or ripple. I was focusing on the jig tapping against the rocks, shells, sand, and even the mud bottom. Bouncing the jig along, I would feel it by laying my left forefinger against the rod blank ahead of the cork handle. While doing so, I'd plan my next cast. It was peaceful, mechanical, and rhythmic. It was broken only when the jig would occasionally hang up in a cluster of oysters or, best, when a fish struck the shrimp-imitating jig.

The fishing had been good that day. It wasn't hand over fist reeling them in, but that wasn't the point in the first place. I had four good trout and one large keeper redfish. The action was steady enough to keep my anticipation peaked. It was a good day overall. I was happy to be there, having a good time with my buddy Dale when we joined back up at the skiff.

I was fishing a long, ragged-edged oyster strip, most of which was under water. Though the bar was nearly all submerged in the tide, Spartina grass framed the outline. I would simply follow the border of grass and cast to the edge ahead of me. At the time, I had almost worked my way to a major point that jutted off the main bar. That point had produced many a fine fish. I was doing a fair job, managing my composure, not rushing to the point and ignoring the flooded bank that led to it. The point dropped back around into a cove that continued the main oyster bar. A ten-yard cut of water that was chest deep or better, came out from the point. There, one could see the moving tide. The flow of water by the point was what made the point so productive. On the other side of the cut, was a low, somewhat irregular shaped oval of an oyster bar that was three to four casts long and two casts wide at widest. I had fished there many times before, often enough I gave it the name Beulah for some unknown reason.

Consumed more and more in the moment, I was wading to the point, one-scuttle step at a time. When could I finally cast the jig so it splashed down partly up current in the cut and bounce past the point? I knew there was a hook up waiting. I could feel it like it happened so many times before. It was a winning lotto ticket, but I didn't know the prize. *Would it be a bronzed redfish or an outsized trout? On the other hand, would I get let down with a small trout prize that picked off my jig before a larger fish had a chance.* I eased along getting into position for the perfect cast, to the perfect spot, for the perfect fish. When I finally got into position, I took a few seconds to settle down and look over the situation.

A few tiny pieces of grass floating on the surface let me know there was a mild flow of water moving past the point. In the past, I'd walked the point, during low tide, observing a thin oyster bar protruding five feet or so beyond the last stick of Spartina grass. On the backside, the oyster rake wing was a six-inch step off where the water would eddy but wouldn't be evident on the surface. Good fish waited for shrimp or minnows, to be carried along in the current, becoming momentarily disoriented in the soft backwash. It was an ambush point most good fishermen, from a drifting boat, would cast to. Yet unaware of how good it really was, because they could only present quick bait before the current carried them away to their next casting opportunity. Their cast had to be perfect to tap the secret. Wading is good, because you can hang around as long as it takes to make the cast you feel necessary, yet not be held down to a clumsy anchor, if you thought one particular spot, amongst tens of thousands, was worth the effort of putting out an anchor in the first place.

From where I was standing, everything looked in order. All I needed to do was to throw a decent cast and not be stuck on the bottom. Not being hung on the bottom had me concerned, since I approached the point in stealth mode. Was the gold, metal flake jig the best lure for the job, considering the quality of the spot and the obvious probability to screw up with a hang up? No, it wasn't worth the risk! It would only take a minute to switch things around and re-rig the jig for a live shrimp I had in my fanny pack. I cut the jig off the eighteen-inch section of twenty-pound leader tied to my main line; I tied on a short shank 2/0 bait hook. A three-inch weight, coned shaped popping cork with a concaved orange top, sold everywhere in Florida, I slipped on, approximately a foot and half above the hook.

The fanny pack I spun around my waist so it was facing forward, unzipped the large compartment where I had loaded in a healthy handful of shrimp. I ran my hand through it with fingers spread to select the best live shrimp available. All but the tiniest shrimp had cashed in to shrimp heaven, but their bodies were still in good condition. I picked out the king of the dead shrimp and pushed the hook from the collar toward the tail so it hung in the water as natural as possible. It wasn't the best it could be, but a five-inch dead shrimp was the best I had to offer and certainly beat having the jig hang up in an untidy heap of oysters. I cast the weighted popping cork with shrimp well up current, into the cut, letting the water flow semi-direct its course, while making slight adjustments to assure the bait would float over the top of the oyster bar and wash into the sequestered eddy. My cast was long, as intended. The cast gave me time and workable space to best present the bait by the point.

I watched the cork intently as it drifted lackadaisical in the weakening part of the last incoming tide. The cork was under natural forces, not subject to my will that wanted it in the strike zone now. I was focused on the reddish-orange band at the top of the popping cork ever so slowly floating with the tide, and adjusted by me to tumble over the oyster trick fault I figured a prize fish was waiting on; the fish I had been working to catch. As the float neared target, I noticed out of the corner of my eye, from somewhere near Beulah Bar, a large flicker. I glanced and it was no longer there, but a faint, concentric ripple tattle-tailed. I wasn't just seeing things. A light snap of my wrist caused the popping cork to put out an understated glug as a polite announcement that something was coming. It wasn't an alarm to spook the fish, but more like a doorbell letting the fish know something was being delivered. Three more feet and the cork would be in the center of the fish's universe. It disappeared with force below the stained tidewater. It happened sooner than I had expected.

I reeled in the little bit of slack line and jerked the rod straight overhead. The rod tip bowed down deeply. This was a good fish. It ran through a small section of the tidal flow, then into the basin of still water in front of me to my right. The reel gave a slip of drag, not much. The fish didn't bolt away from me, but rather forcibly swam at an angle. It was strong, yet not with the moves of a redfish. It didn't behave like a trout either; it didn't thrash the surface, trying to shake the hook. The fish only pulled strong, determined. I was making slow progress by reeling it closer while doing a slow wade toward it. What was this fish? In the very back of my mind, I was thinking a gaff topsail cat or skate had engulfed my bait, taking me on a letdown ride. Twenty feet from me, a large, golden hued fish briefly wallowed on the surface then went down to fight some more. In that split second, I loosely identified it as a trout but not the normal, run of the mill size. It was huge. It was possibly the largest trout I'd ever hung. In this part of the Gulf, any trout over five pounds is considered a gator trout. This fish was in the gator family, if indeed a trout, as I suspected. My nerves were starting to take me over. *Settle*

217

down, settle down! My little voice kept telling me. I was working the fish in easier and easier.

It wallowed to the surface again. It was without a doubt a gator trout! *Easy, easy,* I whispered in my little internal voice. But, was I playing too easy, prolonging the fight to give the fish more time to escape. *I don't know, I don't know; I'm just doing the best job I can, trying not to screw up.* If I lost this fish, I'd be devastated. I'd have to tell Dale about the fish, but it would sound just like any other fish story of the one that got away. He would put on his best, I believe you face, yet feel cornered, like by a used car salesman. *Anyway, don't think about it.* Give and take, inch by inch turning into yards gained; the fish and I were coming together.

Waist deep in murky water from me kicking up sediment, the fish was four feet or so in front of me down in the water. I reeled down on the line some, stopped, took my right hand, and loosened the drag a quarter turn to have some forgiveness, just in case one of us had a conniption when we finally saw one another face to face. I grabbed for the dip net behind me. The elastic cord caught on something on the fanny pack. Of all times to foul up! I began a quick jiggle and yank on the cord. Mercifully, it unwrapped, maybe due to my floundering, or divine will. Once in hand, I extended it deep in the water in front of me, while carefully lifting the rod high. The fish was coming up. I could see a glimmer of gold a foot below the surface. I slowly swung the net around so it was below the fish and continued lifting the fish up in the water column. Just before the fish reached the surface, I raised the net from below and it slumped down into it. Oh my, what a trout! It was thirty inches long if it was an inch!

Apparently, it had lived in the estuary for so long the tannins in the water tanned the skin a golden hue. Nonetheless, the multitude of black spots that covered her sides stood out boldly from the golden canvas, lacquered in the wetness of good saltwater. My trophy was golden and I appreciated her as much as real gold. Standing in the tide wash, alone, I admired her in my net. The eye, yellowed with a black pupil, pronounced her face. It led to a gapping, yellow trimmed mouth with twin fangs hanging from the top. She was an apex predator in the estuary I had trod through. She was the best I'd ever caught. I thought about letting her go, but wanted others to admire my trophy. Yet, when her eggs spilled out as I cleaned her, my pride was tinged with guilt. I would have felt better about myself, if I had done what I thought about first and put those prize genetics back in the water, instead of a trash can. Anyway, live and learn; I've found tossing quality fish back into the gene pool gets easier the more I do it. It actually feels good to put something back rather than taking it all.

I waded directly back to the boat with her in my net. I couldn't take my eyes off her. I stumbled twice, not watching where I was going. She was absolutely beautiful. Once I got back in the skiff, I placed her in the fish cooler. She dwarfed all the other trout in the cooler, the redfish as well. I got a drink, called out to Dale, who was working his way back to the boat. When he got back in, and situated, I flipped the cooler lid open for him to put in his two trout and a redfish. He stopped when he saw my fish.

"It's the biggest trout I've ever caught," I said, then continued on with my tale.

For the rest of the day, on the ride back to the boat ramp and on the ride back home, the thought of what flickered over at Beulah Bar kept recycling in my mind in mix with the gator trout. It couldn't have been a tailing redfish. In the glimpse, I recalled it was too large. It couldn't have been a dolphin or a shark because they both would have produced wake. Perhaps a manatee? The water was too shallow. Did I actually see something? I was sure of it. Next weekend I planned to be at Beulah Bar right before high tide to fish for the answer.

High tide was a 2:53 p.m. Saturday afternoon. I had piddled around solo that morning and early afternoon doing the usual hunt and peck, ending up with some trout and one redfish in the fish cooler. At 2:00 p.m., I anchored the skiff up current on the long side of Beulah Bar. I set out two poles with shrimp and a cork, just because I needed something to do, while waiting for something to happen, if it was going to happen at all. Scanning left to right, from one end of the bar to the next, I was watching the same slow motion tennis match my dad and I watched while catfishing some twenty-odd years ago. This time I wasn't following fishing lines, but looking for a flicker. Within fifteen minutes, I was bored. In another ten minutes, I was thinking how this was a total waste of time. I probably didn't see anything last weekend. Hanging my head down, I was thinking of what I would like to do before getting back to the ramp. I'll catch a couple of jumbo pinfish and toss them at channel markers for cobia. That sounded great to me. It sure beat sitting alone in a boat, waiting for a big uncertainty. That was my end of the day plan.

That plan changed in a flicker of my eye. I happened to be looking directly across the northern part of Beulah Bar, at the point where I had caught the gator trout. A tail fin, at least a foot wide, materialized from the water and waved at me! I was stunned, briefly. It didn't take me long to lob cast a large shrimp over to where the fish exposed itself. The nervous cast was off, putting the bait behind the fish some ten feet. I reeled in and re-launched. In my excitement, I slung the shrimp off the hook. In the time it took me to reel in the empty hook and sort through the shrimp bag for another large shrimp, the tail waved at me again. It was a shot of adrenaline; something I was already over dosed with.

I cast. The cast was too perfect. It landed directly on top of where the tail was just at. Splash down set off a big rocket V wake toward the cut of water between Beulah Bar and the point. The V wake wasn't slender like those put out by mullet, abundant in the area. This V wake was broad, as if a fair sized piglet had been startled and ran submerged across the bottom at sixty miles per hour. The sad thing was other large V wakes followed suit toward the cut. I was unaware there was a sounder of piscatorial pigs within casting distance of my boat. What were the big fish that rooted up on the oyster bars during high tide? I was stunned, again.

The tide had gone slack; I sat in the boat, wondering about the situation. Did I spook all the fish off with one errant cast? From what I saw, the ten-pound test trout gear I had was going to prove too light, especially considering the size of the fish and the roughness of the environment. Was shrimp the right bait? What were they looking for amongst the oyster balls? I remembered flipping over the oyster balls during low water and finding tiny shrimp and an abundance of crabs of various sizes and types. Maybe a bait crab was the ticket?

As I sat there in thought, I noticed more huge tails popping up in the backside of Beulah. I took several minutes to watch the tails. There were at least eight huge fish in the shallow cove, grazing randomly around. At times, a fish would get excited, thrashing its tail in an effort to roll the oyster balls around the bottom. While watching, I sewed on a fresh section of forty-pound leader, picked out an appropriate sized hook, hand selected large shrimp from the bait cooler, and snapped on my fanny pack. I, also, re-tied my leather, ankle high, construction boots tight, and rolled my socks down so no sand or shells would get inside to drive me crazy during my wade. Silently as possible, I slipped over board, stalking my way over the oyster balls that tumbled under my feet, through the sparse Spartina grass toward the far side to get one good cast in. The cast had to be perfect like the Pop-R cast through the willow branches when I was a young boy bass fishing with Dad. In order to pull it off, I had to figure which way the fish was facing so to place bait at the feeding end. That part was easy, tail fins point toward the head. *Of course, the fish could pivot around on its head at any moment,* I thought. That was my mind making things far more complicated than necessary, as usual. Anyway, loosely considering the head position that could change while the bait was in flight, my objective was to cast past the head, then skid it on the surface, and stop to let the bait sink directly in front of the feeding fish.

Waist deep, I warmed the water once before getting close. It was nervous relief. I checked the drag. It was firm. I selected a shrimp from the select shrimp in my fanny pack. It was the biggest of the bunch, kicking wildly after reviving in the warm saltwater. My hook, piercing through the horn on the shrimp, hadn't harmed it in the least. Creeping closer, I dipped the jumbo dancing shrimp in the water to keep it alive. I inched along, until I got the feeling, I was close enough to make an accurate cast in most directions. I stopped in a crouch, waiting for the tails up signal to place my cast. Within a minute, a huge tail breached the surface twenty feet in front of me and lazily flagged the air. The fish faced to my right. The shrimp was so large, I figured I didn't need the extra weight of the popping cork, nor did I want the extra noise of it after the cast. I unpinned it from my line and put in my shirt pocket. I flicked the shrimp airborne like the popping bugs through willow branches in my pond of yester year. The shrimp plopped down five feet ahead of the fish. Hand flipping the bailer on the spinning reel, I quickly skid the bait toward the tailing fish, letting it come to rest within a foot or closer. The water was two feet deep, maybe a few inches deeper. The shrimp floated down, either in a daze after taking its first ever flight, or it could have sank naturally, enjoying its new, perceived freedom. Whatever the case, it didn't last long, because in the brief time it took to get to the bottom, it found itself in harm's way. I could tell by the wild swimming motions I felt, telegraphed up the fishing line. The fish washed to its left.

The line went dead. No more swimming action. The line was limp, stationary. Did the shrimp breakaway? Did the fish suck the shrimp off the hook? What happened? I raised my rod tip to feel the other end of the line. When I did, the hook point pricked flesh, and that flesh charged away, snatching my arms down and making the reel drag squeal. I had not prepared for this. Mentally, I wasn't ready to ride this bull; my tackle was far too light. Line was rolling off my spool so fast and with such force; all I could think to do was follow the pig to which I had hooked onto.

Wading toward the fish gives the wrong picture of what was occurring in my world at the time. I was trying to speed walk to the fish just to keep from running out of fishing line. Staggering over the rolling oyster balls, my movements became more exaggerated, exponentially so in each passing second. I fell. Using my left arm, I tried to cushion my fall, but I was going down hard, uncontrolled. I felt oyster shells slicing into my left palm, then cutting into my forearm, then my left calf and knee, then my ribs on my left side and finally the left side of my head. My God, it hurt. But, I could still feel the surge on the rod I was holding straight up in my right hand. *I've still got 'im*, I thought. About that time, the line was down to the end knot. The rod jerked down a bit, there was a snap, and the last of the line went through the rod guides. The fish was gone. I was on the oysters, bleeding.

Water floated me up off most of the oyster shells. I peeled my left hand and calf off the rest. It hurt, but getting back up didn't hurt as bad as I thought it should. I was bleeding liberally from every cut and scratch. Hobbling back to the boat, I picked shell from the palm of my hand. My hand and knee took the brunt of deep cuts. In the boat, I took off my shirt and rinsed the cuts with bottled water, while fumbling to get my medical kit from a stern compartment. I had a clean rag on the boat to pat down the cuts and see how bad the worst of them was. None was overly deep, except for a gash on my palm. Clutching a paper towel, I kept pressure on that cut. I soaked a roll of gauze in hydrogen peroxide and wiped down all the wounds. That magic solution bubbled out a lot of shell and grit. The next step wasn't as pleasant. I soaked a roll of gauze in rubbing alcohol and did the same thing. It was a John Wayne move, I knew would pay off in the end. I poured a good slosh of rubbing alcohol in my right-cupped hand and simply rinsed whole areas in one single painful swipe rather than endure the sting one cut at a time. It hurt so bad, it had to be doing some good. My hand and knee required some antibacterial ointment and bandaging, so I took care of that before organizing my toys and taking myself home. The fish certainly won the battle that day, but I was coming back, in seven days to be exact. In the days between, the soreness of those cuts made me need that fish more and more. Every time I looked in a mirror was a reminder of my return date.

Seven days later, I anchored up in the same place, a half-hour before high tide. This time I had taken into consideration what happened last time and was better prepared. I brought a large, spinning rod/reel combination I used for light surfcasting. It was loaded with fresh thirty-pound test main line, end tagged with an eighteen-inch section of fifty-pound leader. At the end of the leader, I carefully tied a Mustad 9174 short shank, 6/0 bait hook. The hook pointed up on a whetstone. The drag was smooth, the spool had plenty of line, and I could cast it as well as a trout rod with a touch more weight. There would be no more run offs. The fish would know I was there during the struggle.

During low tide, I spent an hour, flipping over oyster rocks, picking up bait crabs the size of half dollars or somewhat larger. I brought cheap, leather construction gloves for this detail to protect the healing cuts and prevent any more. Pain is a quick teacher; I knew because my parents weren't shy to apply that treatment to my butt when required. The gloves were considered disposable, yet they lasted more than three months on the boat. They made handling things fearless. Each crab I'd claim for bait, I'd crush the top pincher between my thumb and forefinger, so it was defenseless in the live well. I only wanted to deal with their weapons once. Of the twelve crabs I'd collected, eight were small blue, the others stone. Later, I found out all were illegal to harvest or use as bait. Anyway, they weren't in short supply under the oyster balls. I also culled a dozen jumbo, live shrimp from the marina, amongst the three dozen more intended for trout and red fish in before time. This battle, I was ready for. In this battle, I wasn't going to fall and bleed. I was prepared to win. Gina, my wife and good luck charm, was with me. Actually, that day, she might have been mercy fishing. She was more concerned about me falling down again, as opposed to watching me pursue the big one.

I was so excited about tangling with another big fish, I slipped overboard and was standing waist deep ready before seeing fish tails. I was confident they would show up for the fight. However, I did feel silly, standing there stagnant, waiting on fish to show up. Normally, I got out of the boat and went directly in pursuit of fish. In this case, it was nice to take a moment and chat with my better half.

Whatever we were talking about was instantly forgotten when she said, "Oh, oh, a tail popped up over there!"

My head spun around. The tail popped up in the same cove I fell in last week.

"Wish me luck," I said.

She bent over and kissed me, telling me she was camera ready. My first thought about the camera was, jinx. Before I started out, I double-checked the few items I needed. The crabs and jumbo shrimp I felt crawling around in my fanny pack. I remembered putting two extra hooks, one popping cork, and a six-foot section of fifty-pound leader material in the small pouches. On the back of my leg, I felt the mesh of the dip net clipped to the fanny pack. It was a go.

Slowly, I waded through the oyster balls and patches of Spartina in a semi-crouch. As I was going along, I noticed a few more tails popping up in the shallow cove. There was a sounder of wild pigs ahead. It was my personal *Bay of Pigs*, more important to me at the moment, than the JFK historical event decades ago. I got to a point I needed to bait up. Should I deliver a jumbo shrimp or live crab? After giving it two weeks of off and on thought, I was convinced the fish came up on the oyster balls in search of the abundant crabs that hide beneath. I went with a small, biscuit-sized blue crab hooked in the corner of the shell, rather than the jumbo shrimp used before. It took some finagling to work the hook through the hard shell, but the liveliness of the crab indicated it was no worse for the wear. In addition, the crab was of good weight for long casting.

I began to inch closer and closer until my little voice said, *enough*. From there, I could make the toss to most of the tails seen. At the time, there were two tails popped up in the distance, not one in casting range. Did I spook the fish off? I squatted down in the water so my butt submerged. I was still. Peering over the Spartina, across the cove like a hunter overlooking a field from a duck blind, I waited for tails to reappear. A couple minutes later, several tails popped up within casting distance. The closest was fifteen feet straight ahead. I tossed the crab past the fish, using the long rod to guide the crab back so it dropped down in front of the fish. The fish rolled to the right. The line went dead. The fish tails were gone. I relived last weekend. I waited until I couldn't stand it any longer. Holding the rod flat to the water, I reeled up the line until almost all of the slack was out. Then, I slowly lifted the rod tip. It was heavy and firm. I didn't wait for the fish, I struck. The rod tip bowed down hard. Whatever happened between the crab and the fish, my hook ended up stuck in a clump of oysters. Rather than wade over to get the hook back and chance spooking fish, I chose to break it off after a bit of hard jiggling proved useless. As I tied on a fresh, leadered hook, more tails popped up in the cove.

Gina was behind me, I was loud whispering to tell her what had just happened. I waved her off. I didn't feel comfortable, speaking over water. I didn't want abstraction by so little as conversation. However, I enjoyed and wanted to be alone, within the comfort of her presence.

A new leader, new hook, new crab, and a new shot at one of those big fish were ahead. I picked out a fish that was in close casting range and fired a shot over its head, slid the crab back, and let it drop. Nothing appeared to happen. The fish did not roll on the bait. I thought the crab had scurried under an oyster ball, fearing for its life. Now, I'm stuck. Watching where my line entered the water, I was thinking, *what's my next step?*

Then, the line twitched. It began inching toward the left. It stopped, and then resumed inching to the left. It began a lazy swim to the left. I flipped my bailer open to play out line. It was now time; the time I had been waiting for. I got my feet situated so both of them were firmly grounded, flipped the bailer over, did a quick drag check, let the line run out as far as my extended arms would allow and set the hook hard enough to drive it through brick. The water exploded. The pig I had and all the other pigs in the cove, blistered out toward deeper water. I was in a controlled walk behind my fish, holding my rod high to reduce the chance of cut off. Gina was in the background being my personal cheerleader. *Oh God, let this dream come true,* I was thinking. The fish had bolted out of the cove, to deeper water, four to six feet deep; there the bottom was composed of mud/sand. I was happy the fish was fighting in the open, not in the cove with the oyster-strewn mess. The give of the reel drag gave me enough time to safely make my way outside the cove, wading waist deep in the soft bottom. The fish pulled away to my right. I followed, gaining line when I could, giving it away when demanded.

This fish was strong; I felt it in my arms already. It was pulling me to the south side of Beulah Bar. Into what little remained of the moving tidewaters. That didn't concern me; I followed, keeping steady firm pressure. I was relaxed, realizing the fight was happening in open water and not in oyster rocks. When I could, I'd hustle step to gain some line back on the spool. Somehow, the fish knew when I'd gain and immediately burst off in a run taking line away. The battle was a series of give and takes. We ended up on the south side of Beulah. From there, the fish turned west. Seventy-five yards west was the cut in the long outside oyster bar the tide came and went through. West of there was Texas. If the fish had it in him, he could pull through the cut, too deep for me to follow. The fish would swim to freedom.

However, the surges had become less long and less strong. I didn't think the fish had enough freedom spirit. However, if he did, he could have it because my arms, legs, shoulders, and back were burning tired. He dropped into the trough and was cut headed. I stood, rod held high, making the fish fight the pole flex, as well as the reel drag. The pole bowed down hard. The drag moaned off inches of line. It was a standoff boxing round. My arms felt all three punishing minutes before the fish broke out of the trough, to the right, up on the shallower, muddy bottom. I waded toward him, reeling as I went. He was on the surface, thrashing water. His huge body and tail were causing as much commotion as he could muster. His spirit had broken, his body worn out.

When I got over to him, I realized my net was far too small.

226

Thankfully, the last part of the fight was ending in an embrace. The fish had fought us back near where we anchored the boat. Now, the fish was lying on its side doing little more than emitting a loud gonging sound from deep within, not only heard but also felt. The fish was a black drum, the size of which I'd never seen before. I'd caught many small black drums when red fishing, but they were one to three pounds. This fish had to be fifty pounds. The mouth, eyes, fins, scales, everything was freakishly outsized, compared to the fish I'd seen. Gina was calling out to me, but I kept looking at this magnificent fish lying on its side docile as a lamb spent. It was beautiful, but in an odd sense, like a woman who attracts you, yet doesn't have the typical features that normally draw your attention. The fish had barbels—fleshy tentacles—under its mouth. The coloration was gray and black. If fish played football, the physique would put it on the offensive or defensive line.

Clinching the cork handle section of my rod in my teeth, I slid my arms under the submissive monster and picked it up out of the water, carrying it like a baby calf the sixty feet or so over to the boat and Gina. While en route Gina was blurting out all manner of questions. I couldn't respond to her because my rod was in mouth. That didn't stop her from prattling on. To me, it sounded like cheers from the sideline. At the boat, she took the rod from my mouth.

"Wow, what a fish!" we both started with. I flopped it in the bottom of the boat. The fish drummed hard enough to vibrate the deck.

"Listen to that," I said.

"Is that the fish?" she asked.

"That's why they call them drum," I explained.

The sound was resonating off the deck loudly; I couldn't imagine how loud it would sound amplified underwater. One distressed fish could send a message to all fish over quite a distance. I pulled myself over the gunnel into the boat, stood up, and admired the fish again. That's when I felt the gravity of my tiredness. I sat down and asked Gina to get me a bottle of cold water.

"What are we going to do with it?" she asked, handing me the water.

"That's the biggest fish I've ever caught!" I said excitedly. She told me she took pictures during the whole ordeal. She made me pose one more time with the fish in the boat. I didn't mind that a bit.

227

"So, what are we going to do with it?" she asked, again. I wanted to show that monster off to everybody I knew and anybody I didn't.

"Well, if we package it right, we'll have plenty of fish to eat for a long time," I said. I was still in college and that much meat would be a good thing. Regardless of the meat, that was more of an excuse to keep the fish than anything else. "We're going to keep it," I said.

Then she asked, "Where are we going to put it?"

It was a good question, because we didn't have a cooler large enough. We ended up taking out the few trout we had in the forty-eight-quart cooler, then fit the drum in head first, as best as possible. The trout went back in whatever space unfilled and covered in ice. As an afterthought, I took my T-shirt off, wet it in saltwater and draped it over the body and tail that hung out of the cooler. Away we went, back to the boat ramp. I remember I couldn't wait for other fishermen to ask how my day went. Gina didn't have to ask why I was taking so long to ready the boat and gear for the ride home. The extra time allowed folks at the ramp and park to observe the big tail hanging out of our cooler. I sat it on top of the rear bench seat and uncovered it, as I went through the motions. People stopped by quickly, once the first person asked to see the fish. I climbed up on the trailer, into the back of the boat, pulled the fish out to display for that individual and anybody else within eyesight. I didn't give anybody all the details, but most got a healthy dose of half-truth. Standing up on my rolling stage, showing off that big black drum was the closest I'd ever felt to being a medal winning American Olympian.

I looked over at Gina. She smiled, sending me three messages. One, she was happy, I was happy. Two, the ham-bone routine was getting a little over the top. And three, she was ready to get out of the biting sand gnats, go home, and get a shower. I received the first message clearly. After another half hour of fish talk to other fishermen, I received the last two messages in a whisper with an arm pinch that left a small bruise.

The ride back to our apartment was approximately an hour. During that time, I tried not to talk anymore about the fish. Nevertheless, every now and then I couldn't help myself; something more would bubble out. Whenever I'd finish my ramble, Gina would ask how long it was before we got back home. I picked up the subtle, verbal hints after my third ramble and told her I couldn't help myself. She smiled; every guy knows *that* smile.

I backed the boat across the small parking lot of the eight-unit apartment complex in the last light of dusk. Gina had to get out and guide me for the final zigzag to park the boat behind the dumpster. It was the only place I could park, without messing up the parking routine for everyone else. After unhitching the truck from the boat, I swung the truck around in front of our door in the wall, got out, lowered the tailgate, and placed a scrap of plywood on top, making it my fish cleaning station. I did all that quickly, not because I was in a rush to clean fish, but I wanted to be casually ready when someone came by, to flop that huge drum out and garner one more bit of attention before the fish became a frozen, forgotten slab in the back of our freezer. The trout and red fish, I cleaned thoroughly, meaning slowly, waiting for a moment to shine in front of anyone who just happened to be taking trash out. No one came out. I ran out of fish and daylight. After getting a lantern propped up on a cooler in the bed of the truck for light, I lifted the drum up on the cleaning board. I still couldn't get over how large it was.

The fillet knife I had seemed inadequate for the job. I thought, *It's just a fish that is going to require a few more cuts to fillet.* After initial cuts, I filleted it through feeling fingers under the slab, governing a sharp knife. In cautious time, I cut the fillet away, except the small flap of skin at the tail. I flipped over the massive slab. I was shocked. The flesh looked like someone wove it together in spaghetti! Lots of spaghetti! The fish was infested with parasitic worms. My stomach rolled and my mouth watered at the sight. I had not prepared for what I saw. I placed the whole fish back in the cooler and hauled it off to the nearby woods.

"Where did you go?" Gina asked after returning. I told her part of the story, but at first mention of the worms she stopped me from going further. Large black drum are known to carry parasitic worms, and the infestation can be severe, especially if the fish is caught in warm waters. I wish I'd known that fact earlier. I would have still fished for the black drum, but I wouldn't have killed it.

Since then I have enjoyed fishing for and catching summer time black drum in the oyster bars at high tide. Some of the fish have been larger than the first, caught on lighter tackle. Although the thrill has remained just as intense as it started, it is no longer a hunt for the kill; it's just a wrestling match where both of us survive the end. A good fish doesn't have to die to make a great story.

Chapter 14 – Part I - Patchwork Trout

On my last outing, I discovered a beautiful grass flat. That's good sounding fishermen's lingo, but it is likened to a Japanese tourist coming to Florida the first time and discovering Disney World®! I had cut across a new, to me, section of water and noticed a beautiful grass flat, zipping under the hull. It was my first visit across; I was far from Christopher Columbus or better yet, the Indians that met him as he discovered their land. Nonetheless, it felt great seeing something new.

The flat surrounded Deadman's Key; a small key, smaller than many large putting greens, that was fully vegetated, including a few palm trees. There were also oyster covered lime rocks here and there, protecting the key, similar to sand traps guarding a golf course green. Deadman's Key is no more than two feet above the waterline at high tide and is prone to be washed over during storm events, especially when winds came from the west. Centered, loosely, between Seahorse Key to the south and North Key, which are less than a mile apart. The grass flat encircling Deadman's Key and flanked by Sea Horse and North Key was a thick, luxurious mat sparsely pockmarked with sand holes. The sand holes were two to four feet deeper than the lawn around them. They were easy to spot; the sand bottom reflected a golden hue through the water. For the most part, the edges of the sand holes dropped off abruptly, cutting a sharp contrast between the grass and sand environments. Looking across the flat from the bow of the boat, there was a canvas of dark green below the gin clear water with an irregular patchwork of golden ponds. It looked like a speckled trout factory. It was....

On my next outing, at daybreak, I was alone in our fourteen and a

231

half-foot fiberglass skiff, powered by a thirty-five horse Johnson tiller kicker. With just me in the boat, the thirty-five horses were released. I gripped the tiller slightly tighter than usual, without the extra weight of others and their belongings, the horses were friskier, and the tighter grip on the rein made me feel more secure. The boat skipped through the swagger of channel markers en route to my new trout area. Sweet salt air blew forcibly into my nostrils. It smelled, tasted, and felt great! There is something edgy about being on a vast piece of water by one's self. I felt alive!

Swinging around the easterly side of Sea Horse Key, I slowed to a quick idle before killing the motor. The boat slid forward toward the first part of the grass flat. I opened up the fish box/bait cooler, taking out a small squid from a one-pound box. I sliced it like Mr. Sullivan showed me long ago, but the strips were much smaller, about half inch by quarter inch. They were squid tidbits for catching small pinfish, trout bait. After cutting the bait, I took the only rod I'd placed in the gunnel rod holders. It was an ultra-light, spinning reel combo I knew I'd need right off the bat. I had pre-rigged it the evening before with a hair bream hook and a BB sized split shot; it was set-up for bait fishing. I dipped an empty five-gallon bucket over board, scooping up three gallons of saltwater. In ten minutes, there were a dozen three to four inch pinfish darting around the bucket.

A quick snatch of the cord popped the motor over with a brief stream of bluish smoke. I had added some extra two-cycle oil to the six-gallon fuel tank, thinking it was better to have a little too much rather than a little too little. A click into forward with a twist of the tiller handle and the boat was on plane without a hole shot. I directed it to the left of Deadman's Key where a mosaic of sand holes awaited my arrival. In less than two minutes, I was off the throttle, letting the boat come to rest a tenth of a mile before the sand holes started. Standing up I could see them plainly. The outgoing tide would carry me the rest of the way, in due time.

I was one man with an eight-rod selection, pre-rigged the night before and laid out in front of me. I arranged the rods so the butt ends rested on the food cooler at mid-ship and a goodly portion of the rod tips were supported on the bow-casting platform overtop of a wet towel. The wet towel wouldn't blow off easily, maintained rod positions and cushioned bow bounce. The reels hung down free in the gap between the cooler and bow.

I had to pick the first rod to use. The first point of business was to impale one fresh caught pinfish on a 4/0 short shank bait holder hook tied to the end of a twenty-pound test leader with a popping cork pinched on the line, fifteen inches above, no weight. The rod was limber at the tip, stout at the butt, bait caster with an Ambassador 5000 reel loaded with twelve-pound test. I cast that out the stern as far as it would fly, adjusted the star drag so it would give line with a strong tug, and set the clicker on as an alarm. I placed that pole in the windward, stern rod holder fashioned out of PVC pipe and two aluminum pipe brackets. It was a dead man's stick, I was fishing, even when I wasn't casting. The pinfish's struggles made the cork dimple the water. That little fellow was sending off all the wrong signals, if it wanted to stay alive for long. He was a drunken sailor, in a bad neighborhood, on payday.

What did I want to do next? That was my big predicament; a predicament I enjoyed having. Should I throw the tried-and-true, gold, metal-flaked jig? Work a floater/diver plug like a wounded fish? Use the extra popping cork rig with a live shrimp? Wobble a Johnson® gold spoon through the grass and sand? How about working a fresh cut shiner tail with a quarter-ounce jig head? Or, my favorite plug forever, a simple, light blue backed, white bodied, orange-drop bellied Pop-R with the silvery flashed white tassel on the rear treble hook? Wouldn't it be nice if everyone had predicaments so frivolous?

The water was placid. The morning was just starting. The air still had some Florida chill to it. It was top water time. I picked up the Penn 4300SS spinning reel, loaded with eight-pound test and an eighteen-inch section of fifteen-pound leader tied to the Pop-R, and sailed it toward the closest sand hole. It was a very long cast, landing just inside the middle of the sand hole. The outgoing tide was drifting the boat toward the bait, but at a slow pace. Prompt judgment told me I had plenty of time for several casts before drifting across the first sand hole edge.

The lure landed. I let the splash down ripples dissipate before the first glug from the lures concave face. Out in the sand hole, I worked the Pop-R in an understated pop, pop, pop, then pause routine. A big pinfish

233

came up and pulled at the tassels on the rear hook while the bait was in the pool. I gave a subdued tug on the pole. That pulled the plug away from the enamored pinfish long enough for a juvenile to slurp the bait. I jerked pre-maturely, sailing the bait toward the boat. I reeled it in quickly and cast again toward the right-hand side of the sand hole. The lure landed ten feet past the line on the sandy side. Without letting it rest, I worked it continually back to the boat in a series of small sprits and spurts. That method would certainly draw attention, yet the constant motion would ward off the pecks of the pinfish. I paused it at the edge of the grass and sand.

A V wake came from the right-hand side and crushed the bait in an explosion of water. I set the hook spastically. Caught up in the excitement of the moment, the moment I had prepared for, waited for, and planned on, I behaved like the most uncoordinated kid on any ball team, who through some odd series of events, found himself with the ball in the last seconds of the big game. Glad I was the only one out there, because instead of being the smooth, polished, professional angler as seen on TV, I jerked around as if receiving electro-shock therapy. I laughed at myself after managing to reel the fish in. The fish was a sixteen-inch trout that took the entire bait in its mouth, including the pair of treble hooks. It was a mess extracting the bait. I would have let the fish go, but the damage was too severe; I had to keep him.

Two casts and one fish isn't a bad way to start the morning off. Furthermore, it didn't take many casts to determine the edge was an ambush point for trout. Either the trout were laying below the drop off in the sand, waiting for shrimp or baitfish to wash out of the grass or trout were in the grass, waiting for something to take a short cut across the desolate sand tract. In either case, the life expectancy of a food source in the transition zone seemed to be short.

I wanted to test the edge theory out from another point of view, but I needed to hustle up because the boat was only ten feet away from drifting over the edge. Grabbing the spinning rod with the gold metal-flaked jig, I made a hurried cast parallel to the edge on the sandy side as the boat slowly drifted into the sand hole. Bouncing the jig along for a mere ten feet, I got a hit. I set the hook in a smooth motion this time. It was a lack luster fight; I figured it was a small trout, which for some reason, didn't thrash the surface. Instead, I had nailed a fourteen-inch flounder, one of my favorite fish to eat. It went in the fish box with a dream of a broiled dinner tomorrow.

The edge theory seemed to be a good working pattern that day, especially, after peppering the middle of the sand hole with the Pop-R, gold jig, and a floater/diver Rapala with no response. The deal was complete when the live pinfish drifted behind the boat under a cork, crossed the edge, and became the final meal for an eighteen-inch trout. The rod bent over and the clicker chirped off startling me; I had been engrossed in fishing the lures. While turning to see what that noise was, it dawned on me I had forgotten about the dead man pole. I quickly reeled in the jig and dropped the rod in the bottom of the boat in a rush back to the fishing rod working a good fish solo. The trout thrashed the surface as I got to the pole. It darted and ran, splashed and did a brief tail walk. I was doing pretty much the same thing, trying to play the fish while fumbling for the landing net stashed toward the bow. When the fish was close enough, I had the rod in one hand and the net in the other. I slid the fish across the surface into the waiting net. I took time to admire the fish, while getting it out of the tangled net. She was a pure, white canvas on the belly that was almost completely covered with shiny, black blotches the higher up on the back you looked. The yellow in the eyes perfectly matched the yellow in the mouth. She had one large fang tooth. A beautiful fish, it is no wonder why so many people fish for them, they look wholesome.

I noticed the boat was drifting within casting range of the opposite edge. After putting the trout in the fish box, I hooked another pinfish under the cork and sailed it off the stern. The Pop-R was too irresistible not to cast. The explosive strike of a fish taking top water bait is a fine moment in any anglers' life. The Pop-R landed six feet on the far grassy side of the edge. Slow popping and working the bait until it was on the edge, I stopped the action. Twitch and twitch, nothing. Again, twitch and twitch, nothing. One more time with the same result, I reeled the bait in and started fan casting the edge from left to right. The next three casts were as blank as the first. Was the magic over?

The fifth cast carried fifteen feet into the grass flat. On the very first pop a fish boiled from underneath, sucking the plug down. Truthfully, I wasn't ready. I was focusing on getting the strike on the sand/grass line. This strike was premature, to me. The jerk on my line caused a reflex jerk back. It was on. The fish barreled in back and forth arcs over the grass. One time, it sloshed at the top. I could tell it was a large trout. While fighting the fish, I inched myself closer to where the net was in the boat. Then the line went dead; it was still taunt, but dead. The fish buried itself deep in the thick grass some twenty feet directly in front of the boat drift.

Whatever I was going to do would have to work the first time, because if it didn't, the boat would drift over top of the fish then the fight would get too awkward for me to win. Should I plunge the net down in the grass to try to roust the fish out? Should I wind the line in tight so the rod tip touched the plug then hope for the best? Did I have the ability and time to ease the anchor over board and wait this fish out? Too much thinking in too little time, the boat was at the fish so, as a last resort, I wound the line to where the rods tip touched the plug. The fish darted out of the grass. Thankfully, the drag chirped up some line. If the drag were set a hair tighter, the line would have popped. The fish dashed around the back of the boat. Why the line didn't ride against the prop and cut off is a mystery, but thankfully, it didn't. On the windward side now, the fight continued. Again, I inched myself around the boat to get close enough to the net. Planned position or unplanned, the fish net will always be where it is least available. The fish wallowed at the surface. I reached for the net. Using the rod and net like extensions of my arms, I raised the rod up and toward the boat while dipping the net down and away from the boat. The trout and the net came together in a loud splash of water. The trout was the mirror beauty of the last trout except, I was looking in one of those trick mirrors that make things larger and this fish had two fangs. She was twenty-three inches long. Her belly was turgid and bloated full of eggs. When the clicker sounded on the dead man pole off the stern, I unceremoniously tossed her back in the Gulf. My hands were so slimy from touching the big trout I had to wipe them on the back of my pants before grabbing the pole. The boat was over the grass flat now. Looking out, trying to locate where the line was running off to, I concluded something caught the pinfish as it drifted to the edge of the grass. The trout that took the bait was a scrappy seventeen incher; I put it in the fish box.

The first drift across the first sand hole had produced four keeper trout and one flounder. Looking around there were at least seven sand holes ahead of me, some of which were large enough that two, maybe three drifts were necessary to fish the entire hole. My confidence was running high. In addition, I had learned something new, which in the world of fishing, is more important than fish caught on any given day. However, should I anchor on the up current side of an edge to fish the edge thoroughly, as far as I could cast? Would that enhance the catch? I would do that another day. Today, I was doing just fine, floating in and out of the holes. I had a bird in the hand, why change what was working. Besides, I was having fun.

In the next two hours, I limited out on trout, picked up two additional flounder, and caught and released a small red fish. In that same time, the tide had bottomed out. It drew down much lower than expected. I had forgotten about last night's full moon. The tides on the full moon are more extreme. I found myself somewhat stranded in the deeper sand holes. Just before the tide would be fully out, I kicked the motor up and idled into the largest of the sand holes around. There, I would stay until the tide let me back out. Perhaps, I could pick up a couple more flounder during my stay. However, I didn't like being stuck. Fishing from the boat, to me, had become a series of orchestrated movements. However, judging by how far Deadman's Key jutted above the water line, my orchestra was going to be a one-man oompah band for quite some time. I didn't bother to put the anchor out; I let the boat pinball around in the sand hole, directed by the wind or current, which ever was strongest at the moment.

In an effort to kill time, for the most part, I pitched out two live pinfish under corks. One, I tossed out the back and the other off the bow. I sat on the fish box in the middle of the boat, casting the gold metal-flaked jig into the middle of the sand hole with all the enthusiasm of a caged lion in a traveling circus. Maybe an oddball flounder would strike the jig if I accidentally bounce it across its head. I looked at my watch, determining I'd most likely get out of the pit after the first couple of hours of incoming tide.

I was thinking of taking a nap after the sixth cast of nothingness.

The seventh cast I went for the fun of distance. It went past the middle of the pool and sank to the bottom. In no rush, I worked it back to the boat, wondering if the next cast would be further. Bang! A fish pounced violently on the jig. I set the hook, not as bad as the first trout. A small trout danced in the middle of the pool. It threw the jig back at me. It got my attention. I was back in fishing mode. Flinging the jig as far as I did the last time in the same general direction, I worked it back and got another hit. This time I played the fish back to the boat. In one smooth motion, I flipped it in. It was fifteen inches and change. Of keeper size, over fifteen inches, but I had already caught my seven fish limit. The fish went back in the drink no worse for the wear.

I got to thinking, *If I had more weight, I could cast further and that might make things more active, more fun.* So, I cut off a two-foot-six-inch section of twenty-pound test from a spool of line and tied one-quarter ounce jig head to one end, then slid a tiny, barrel swivel on the line followed by tying another quarter-ounce jig head to the other end. After trimming off the tag ends, I pinched the barrel swivel between my thumb and forefinger and pulled the jig heads until they hung evenly. Then I pulled on one jig head until it hung down a foot more than the other did. I finished by tying an over-hand knot behind the barrel swivel so the two jig heads remained a foot apart on the tandem jig rig. I tied the main line to the free end of the barrel swivel. My choice for the jig bodies? What else, a gold metal flake on both jig heads, positioned so the flattened tails rode perpendicular to the eye on the jig head. In that position, the flat part of the tail would flip the back of the jig up as the weighed jig head fell through the water. It would better mimic the snapping action of a shrimp.

The first cast sailed well past where the single jig splashed down. Now, I could reach the far edge of the sand hole. The tandem rig sank quickly. I flicked my wrist to activate the two jigs into impersonating twin shrimp trying to make their way across a wide-open playing field. On the tenth flick of my wrist, a fish picked off one jig. I felt it when the second trout hit the second jig being fished by the action of the first trout. Twin trout bounced around the boat deck. The trout were identical to the first trout I released five minutes ago. I released those two as quickly as they allowed. Those three trout couldn't have been more than an eighth

238

of an inch different in length. The trout that followed came out of the same mold. Schooling trout run in groups of similar, if not exact, size. If you're in a school of sixteen-inch fish, you will continue to catch sixteen-inch fish until they quit biting or you decide to leave. The same thing if the fish are eighteen inches long. However, larger trout, greater than twenty inches, seem to be more solitary in nature.

I must have caught thirty trout out of that school before the bite stopped. Maybe I caught every last one of them and ran out of fish to catch, I didn't know. I did know it sure helped while away a dead low tide. In addition, I surmised when the tide dropped that hard, the fish had no other place to go except those deeper sand holes. Stranded in a sand hole for a couple of hours, this was good information to know, if you could stand the solitude that long. However, it was not that bad when the fish were biting strong. During that time, two more flounder managed their way into the fish box as a fine dinner bonus. I caught those fish, bouncing the jigs along the sandy edge of the hole the boat had drifted against. One flounder I saw burst from its camouflage of sand to take the jig only ten feet from the boat. Flounder appear to be docile creatures, but they are killer snipers in the battle for food.

Chapter 14: Part II - The Patchwork Expands

Within a year, Gina and I bought a used nineteen-foot center console. I thought I was captaining the *Queen Elizabeth II*. I got to drive the boat standing up or seated on a cushioned, flip-back cooler bench seat. The boat had simple gauges on the console which I thought were cool. I mounted a cheap, black and white sonar on the top of the dash and the plastic mount for my hand held GPS. I plugged it into the main battery system. It also had a VHF radio hanging inside the opening at the bottom of the console below the steering wheel. That simple boat was a yacht to me. I felt so important behind the wheel I almost bought the hat with the spaghetti strands on the bill to match how I felt; but I'm glad I didn't go that far overboard. It was nothing more than a step up boat. One of more to come, but it was an important step to make. It opened up more water to explore. Pandora's Box of fishing boats was starting to open wider in my life, to the chagrin of the love of my life, Gina.

I'd heard of deep grass beds seven miles or so off the end of Cedar Key's main channel. Sea Horse Reef was the name of the place I had heard and read about again and again. The reef was famous for producing loads of Spanish mackerel, some kingfish, and trout during the heat of summer. The *Iron man*, a steel tower seen from several miles away or less, depending on weather, marked the south end. In the summer time, visibility of the tower was more a factor of humidity than anything else. Humidity is the thick blanket of air-water that shrouds the view during the dog days of summer when fog isn't the proper term.

When air and water temperatures exceed ninety, the trout bite wanes on the shallow water, grass flats. It was a summer pattern. Yet, the trout bite continued in the relative coolness of the deeper, grass beds. The, new

240

to us, nineteen-footer opened up that slice of the trout pie. The boat could quickly make the trip to Sea Horse Reef in the slick seas of a summer morning. Additionally, it could safely make it back in the two to three-foot hard chop conditions that occurred just before afternoon thunderstorms, so common in Florida that they are as much a part of the state as the alligator, the orange, and yes, now, the Mouse.

The first trip out to Sea Horse Reef was awash. Weather conditions from previous days had the water churned. The water quality was poor and the bottom was only visible through the eye of my cheap sonar. Grass beds displayed on the screen as a thick, frilly bottom and the intermittent sand holes showed as thin marks. Except for buzzing around the Ironman and noticing the jump in elevation of the sandbar named Sea Horse Reef, the trip was not much more than a Lewis and Clark run through.

The fish weren't biting, more than likely due to the particulate sand and grit suspended in the water. They had to have been suffering without eyelids and with their gills irritated by filtering gritty water. It would be like us breathing glassy, volcanic ash while dinning. Would you eat when enveloped in an irritating plume? Fish feel the same way we do, at times.

The next trip to Sea Horse Reef was beautifully the opposite. Weather was calm the days before. Pop up storms, but nothing severe. The water quality was pure with the clarity of gin. The water clarity made the sandy reef stand out from a distance. The reef appeared to be a guesstimated two-mile, submerged, golden sand bar bent slightly in boomerang form. Coming up to the reef, the water depth was twenty feet or so, but within a half mile, the depth began a slow climb. When the depth was fourteen feet, vast billows of deep, lush grass were showing on the sonar. I stopped the boat. When the wake died away, Gina and I looked overboard, seeing the grass beds below and the sand holes that separated them. It was a marine aquarium. We saw the fish swimming back and forth across the sandy bottom. I had discovered Sea Horse Reef! It looked so fishy, I was struggling to figure out how to start fishing. It was another fine predicament.

The gold metal flake jig on a slightly heavier 3/8th ounce jig head was my go to bait. I handed Gina the first outfit.

She said, "I don't like that," in a matter of fact tone.

"But Bunky, the deeper water makes the extra weight necessary to keep the jig down where the trout are," I reasoned back.

"Give me the rod with the pink jig head and let me pick out my jig color," she said.

"The jig head is too small, it's only a quarter-ounce, and you'll need the extra weight," I pled. I got *the look*; I gave her the pole she wanted. In the front of my man mind, I was thinking, *I'll just show her, she's so wrong.* That was especially so when she picked out a lime-green jig body with a bright orange fire tail. The pink head, lime-green body with a baboon butt was laughable. She caught me looking; I smiled sardonically. She returned with *the look*. We were starting with a throw-down, a jig-off from a nineteen-foot boat.

I whipped out the first cast. It sailed away with impressive distance. That jig would cover a lot of ground before getting back to the boat. I was sure it would never make it back without a fish attached. Gina put out a good cast in an opposing direction. When I was sure my jig had hit the bottom, I reeled up the slack. The jig felt unusually heavy. Slowly, I raised my rod tip. I felt resistance. A fish took the lure on the fall. I set the hook. There was a pull back then a release. The additional weight told me I had one on, but it was coming straight at the boat. The fish must be swimming at me. With my pole bent, I casually turned toward Gina just to make sure she was aware of what was going on. She ignored me. So what, I had the first fish on the first cast. In short order, something surfaced just away from the boat. To my chagrin, it was a large wad of green grass. Gina didn't ignore my catch, but became more excited when the jig she was doodling back to the boat got whacked hard and line spurted from her reel. A ladyfish, poor mans' tarpon, vaulted from the surface, flinging the jig from itself.

She turned to me to speak. I was semi-ready to field what had to be a smart comment.

"I'm catching fish and you're catching grass."

"Hey, it was only a lady fish; they'll hit anything in front of them. I'm telling you, keeping the bait down in the grass will produce more trout. The bait will be in the strike zone longer." I rallied back.

I pitched out again. I sped up my retrieve to keep the jig out of the deep grass; I reeled in grass that bit my jig. It happened time and time again, until I became frustrated. Compounding my frustration was Gina, catching ladyfish, blue fish, Spanish mackerel, sea bass, and one under-sized trout. The last straw came while unhooking her latest ladyfish; it unloaded the contents of its bowels all over my shirt. In diarrhea consistency, under pressure from my hand around her, the fish signed the front of my shirt in from the shoulder down. Considering the volume, this was a well-fed fish before it took the jig; ladyfish are gluttonous. Gina's semi-hidden laughter forced me to reconsider the heavier jig head. It was good in theory, but bad on pride. There is no greater wrath than a woman scorned, but there should be an adage about her lack of humility when upstaging her man. She went back to fishing; I went to tying on a quarter-ounce jig head.

During her delight in my pride adjustment, we had drifted toward the reef with the outgoing tide. We were now in twelve-feet of water and it wouldn't be long until the boat would be atop the submerged desert sand bar. I took what time we had left in this drift to make four shiner-tails out of two four-inch pinfish. A shiner-tail can be lethal bait. It can be worked quickly like a jig, additionally it has the natural look, scent, and flavor of pinfish. I imagine a shiner-tail delivering the smell of fried chicken to a congregation of Baptists after Sunday morning service, staple food, irresistible. Furthermore, shiner-tails have favorable buoyancy that keeps them from sinking quickly into the grass like regular plastic jig bodies of comparable size.

To make a shiner-tail, I took a sharp fillet knife and cut from the front of the dorsal fin to the middle of the tail, with the fish laid on its side. Both the top and bottom cuts are useable by lightly hooking them once on the jig head in the forward part. The piece of bait should flip and swing loosely to best imitate the real deal it was originally, but you can fish more aggressively with it, like a jig. The shiner-tail was my secret bait on the next drift.

When we drifted over Sea Horse Reef, I eased us, at an angle, to the thickest grass beds in fourteen to fifteen feet of water. The second drift would mimic the first, but be off track so as not to retrace steps, but find new. I like to fish fresh waters. During the move, Gina couldn't help but regale me with her success and the lack of mine "with the heavy jig head in the grass zone," she taunted. It was all in fun, but she made a strong point. I was wrong, but with the shiner-tail on the lighter weight head....

On her first cast, before the jig had a chance to get good and damp, a Spanish mackerel picked off her jig on the fall, ripping line from her spool. A spirited fight, using both sides of the boat, ended with me slipping the net under her prize. The fish weighed approximately three pounds. In the fish box it went, along with the other Spanish she had caught and two fair sized sea bass.

I was off my game plan. A bit rattled or distracted, or both, by my wife's fish catching. However, I had to keep in mind; we came out in search for trout in deep grass beds. So far, my first technique proved ineffective. Instead of keeping my bait in the strike zone, the heavier jig head buried my bait in the structure that supposedly held the fish. In the meantime, *Little Mrs. Can't-do-wrong* was gleefully catching fish right beside me, using an oddity lure that should be on display at Ripley's Believe It or Not. Now, she isn't catching the fish we sought after, but she could care less. She was a kid at a bream pond immersed in the joy of fishing and I was the dad, too busy taking fish off the loved ones' hook to have time to bass fish. Good dads always take the time to unhook fish, even with the kid's constant reminders, telling them they aren't catching fish. It is just part of the deal.

I cast out the shiner-tail on a string of hope. Hope that it was indeed the magic bait. Hope that I had time enough to find out, one way or the other, before *Little Mrs. Can't-do-wrong* picks up another fish. The ladyfish, Spanish mackerel, and bluefish were buzzing like bees in a field of wildflowers. I was on a timer. At any time, one of the swarm would sting her jig. It happened as I was thinking about it. Her rod snatched down. It was off to the races, again. I reeled mine in quickly to give her a hand when something whacked my jig, jerked the rod down, and cut away. A moment later, a fish cut away her line, as well. It was only a matter of time before the dentures of a Spanish or bluefish would clip the mono leader. Both fish sport sets of razor teeth.

"They got us both Bunk," I said, the two of us holding our rods with the line ends blowing in the light breeze.

"It's going to take an extra minute for me to rig yours up. I'm tying in a short section of light wire to avoid cut offs," I told her.

Her smile said she was happy regardless. Her smile had a pinch of gloat left in it, but added a loud whisper of, "I love you." She recognized

244

I wasn't very interested in catching Spanish mackerel, bluefish, or the ladyfish that poop on me when I handle them. We had caught many of those fish in times past. She was happy I was stopping what I was doing to pay attention to her, whether taking off her fish or fixing her tackle.

She revealed that when she said, "Toss me a rag and I can take my own fish off and let you fish."

I smiled, "I love you back," and tossed her a rag.

Trimming off the tag end, I doubled eight inches of her ten-pound test line using a King Sling knot. From my tackle bag, I pulled a plastic zip-top bag with a twenty-five foot coil of number one, single-strand, wire leader and nipped off an eighteen-inch section. Using a Haywire Twist, I attached a pink jig head to one end of the wire and twisted off the tag wire flush. The last step was to use an Albright Knot to unite the doubled main line to the wire leader. She ended up with a pink jig head with a twelve-inch section of light wire leader. The wire would prevent most cut-offs, unless a big king mackerel hit her bait. I handed her the new rig, a lime-green jig body with a fire tail.

"Catch a big one, Bunky," I said.

On my rig, I went back to the twenty-pound test mono leader, using a double Uni Knot to connect the mainline to the leader. The extra flexibility of the mono leader was more important to me than cut-off prevention. Using the bottom part of the shiner-tail, the part with the head, I hooked it through the lips and sent it out and down. Gina had another bluefish in the boat before my bait had sunk. She was handling things quite well on her own. I felt the grass brush against the jig through the line. My jigging pace had to be such that the bait maintained itself just atop the grass bed where the trout were most likely hiding in ambush. If I slowed down, the jig would ball up in grass. If I sped up, the jig would be working open water, exposed to something other than a trout. It was a delicate balance to keep, requiring an experienced feel not taught in books or magazines, but through failures on the tight rope or line in real situations. In theory, it should work. Theory had let me down not many minutes ago, however.

Many casts later, drifting ever closer to Sea Horse Reef in thirteen feet of water, my efforts were unrewarded. I was fishless, except for one short sea bass I picked up over a sandy spot.

245

We washed across the reef. Gina had picked up more sea bass and two Spanish mackerel during that drift. Sounding like sour grapes, I mentioned we should start throwing back Spanish mackerel. Gina was in wholehearted agreement. She and I enjoy eating Spanish, but only fresh. Five good fish were more than plenty for our next meal, plus give away fillets. On the other hand, sea bass are excellent table fare that freeze well.

I steered the boat off on a zig that positioned the boat so it would float over the crotch in the boomerang bend of Sea Horse Reef. The bottom was big fluffy grass, as before, with intermittent sand blotches. It seemed to be the same as the first two drifts and three similar drifts not mentioned. Pinfish pecks and Spanish mackerel or blue fish, had finished off the original shiner-tails. I cut out four more tails, still believing in my theory. My theory was still unproven; yet I hadn't given up on it, even in the face of Gina's fish catching right in front of me.

My hope was still afloat, but not abounding when I made the first cast on the new drift. If the same nothing happened on this drift, as the previous two, I was going to make a change, possibly resorting to catching Spanish, ladyfish, or whatever; letting the trout fixation go. Three casts later, with nothing, watching Gina reel in another sea bass, I went to thinking. *What to do next? Do I keep trying to figure out how to catch trout, if they are actually there in deep grass? On the other hand, do I submit and enjoy the fish actually biting?*

Thump, was what I felt pulse up the line to my index finger. It was a solid thump, not the familiar bump of a sea bass taking the bait. I was surprised. In reflex, I set the hook. There was resistance, but I was alert enough not to say anything without first feeling the resistance a moment more. Was it the resistance of my jig hung up in a glob of grass? Not unless grass learned to wallow around near the bottom, trying to re-root itself. I started pulling up firmly, using the rod and winding down quickly with the reel to move the fish up while keeping the line taunt; no slack means no long line release. The fight in the fish was good, but not overly strong. It was coming up as long as I kept the pressure on. Briefly, it thrashed the surface twelve feet from the boat. The flash of yellow in its mouth signaled it was the trout I had been hoping for. It splashed around for a short time, ending up sliding the last few feet on its side toward the boat where I slipped my net under it. Before doing anything else, I grabbed my marker jug and tossed it behind the boat.

"Wow, Honey, that's a nice trout."

I had to agree with my lady. The trout was eighteen inches long and as fat around as its skin would stretch. The stomach was hard, full of food. As I removed my jig, I noticed the tail of a small pinfish pushed out its throat. My shiner-tail was still attached-to the jig head, so it had to be another pinfish it ate before taking my offering. The fish gave up a clue before I put it on ice.

That one piece of information let me know one thing, I ran with it. The trout were feeding on pinfish; that was definite. However, judging by the small size of the pinfish tail, they may prefer smaller offerings. Torn up, the shiner-tail I had caught the fish on needed replacement, but instead of merely hooking up a shiner-tail I had previously cut, I took a knife and trimmed back the body section to make it smaller. The shiner-tail I cut out was approximately two and a half inches long. It looked a bit odd, cut so small, but I had an idea.

I cut the jig off, leader and all. To the main line, I tied on a 1/0 short shank hook and cut the line eighteen inches above the hook, effectively making a leadered hook out of the main line. Then I slid on the main line, a quarter-ounce bullet sinker, followed by a small plastic bead. Next, I tied the main line to the leadered hook, using a double Uni Knot. In bass circles, I had made a Carolina rig, popular for fishing plastic worms, but instead of a worm, I used a shiner-tail with the hook exposed. In theory, yes another wondrous theory of mine, the bullet sinker would be rather snag-free due to shape, while the smaller hook would allow the bait to move more naturally. I envisioned the shiner-tail twitching around just above the grass, like a small wounded pinfish. What trout could resist that?

By the time I had tied together another theory on my line, we had drifted a good ways from the marker jug. I had tossed it out physically to mark the area where I caught the trout. An old, yellow jug on forty feet of twine, anchored by three eight-ounce bank sinkers, marks the catch location well on a featureless sea. I told Gina, I'd like to make another drift by the jug, and she reeled in her line. As the boat swung around toward the marker jug, I wondered if changing the lure right after

I'd caught a fish was such a smart idea. I reminded myself, I could always switch back. Hunches aren't bad things to follow. Hunches teach something, bad or good, whichever way you choose to look at it. After all, you can follow them as long as you like or quit any time. I was going to follow my hunch the distance of one drift.

I eased the boat past the marker jug. Watching the trail of water on the leeward side of the jug, helped me set the boat so it would drift within casting range of the jug. One hundred feet up current, I cut the motor off. Gina had her jig air borne as soon as the motor was off. She was ready for more action. I tossed my Carolina rigged shiner-tail toward the jug and let it sink. The water was fifteen feet deep. I silently counted out twelve Mississippi's, and then started lightly twitching the bait. I imagined the small tail darting and dipping seductively above the grass bed. My imagination couldn't have been too far off, because it thumped hard. A familiar wallow, it ended with another eighteen-inch trout in the fish box. The shiner-tail was in fair shape, so all I did was secure the hook back in the bait and cast. The result was quickly the same. The trout came from the same cookie cutter. The third cast, I had to cast back toward the jug. Our drift had put it behind us. Thump, another cookie cutter trout. The fourth cast went blank. I let the drift continue until we were almost atop Sea Horse Reef.

"Do you want to trout fish, Bunky?" I asked.

"Sure, now that you've figured it out," was her reply.

Women are smarter than men are. She let me go through the ordeal of finding the pattern, while enjoying the action. Of course, she knew the joy was in the journey for me. The figuring things out part was just as much fun for me as catching. She handed me her pole. I set that one to the side, grabbing another similar pole. The wire leadered jig I had taken time to rig, she might need back later. I handed her a new pole, rigged just like mine, with a fresh trimmed shiner-tail.

"Let's swing back through where you caught the fish," she said.

She wasn't up on the bow not paying attention; she knew exactly where and how I'd caught those trout. I did as she suggested.

The only thing I did different on that drift was to tie a five-gallon bucket to a ten-foot section of dock line and tether that to the mid-ship cleat on the windward side. A five-gallon bucket dragging behind the boat was a poor man's windsock, slowing the drift down considerably. It added time to cast around the marker jug. The bucket sure beat me dealing with the anchor.

The extra drift time paid off in trout. She and I boxed five trout on the first drift. On the second drift, we caught just as many; all but one we tossed back. Thirteen trout were more than enough for us, no need to be greedy. We did drift around more, finding two more areas that held trout in deep grass. I marked those on my GPS for future reference. However, during future trips back, those particular areas proved there was nothing extra special about one day's trout spots. Trout hang out here or over there, in the same general area, on different days like teenagers changing hangouts from time to time. Trout numbers are reference points only.

The second trip to Sea Horse Reef was special to me. I finally was able to see, first hand, what I'd heard so much about. Importantly, I learned a new area for hot weather trout fishing and figured out a new, to me, trout trick, Carolina rigged shiner-tails; Gina and I had fun doing it. It was a shared adventure and memory.

While we were out there, on such a fine day, I had to buzz by the *Iron man*. I idled up near and then cut the motor off; letting the current float the boat close by. Baitfish dimpled the surface near the structure. As we drifted closer, we saw silver clouds of fish swarming around the four barnacle encrusted tower legs. We could see all the way to the bottom. Under the tower, in the shade, lay several three to five feet pieces of something. We thought they must be a part of the superstructure or junk that came off the tower.

"What are those?" Gina asked, pointing at what resembled logs.

"They must be braces for the legs of the tower," I guessed.

"But they swim," she announced.

Upon closer inspection, they were cobia lollygagging under the tower. That started an obsession. However, that is another story, Chapter 16 and a lifetime hunt.

Chapter 15 - Spanish as a Second Chance

The weather was beautiful, well needed, after a prolonged *harshish* winter. It is difficult to use the word harsh in terms of Florida winter, when the Weather Channel telecasts true harsh conditions north. We should be grateful for a period of natural air-conditioning, a time to don the cool weather fashions or outfits long stuffed in the back of our closets. People mostly complain of weather for the sake of conversation. For example, if it is gorgeous, we complain because we're stuck at work.

Harshish translated by fishermen here, is a relative term; the weather stayed cooler/colder longer than normal, with extra rain, and the early spring bite was less than expected. With that said, it was early spring when Ken Langford, my supervisor, and I went fishing. We had enjoyed the light chill of the morning and were really enjoying the warming trend through lunch. The sea conditions were a roll two-foot or less that was dying off as the day progressed. What we mostly enjoyed was each other's company. He has a wit that cracks its way through an endless storehouse of stories. He is genuinely fun to be with. The only thing I did for the conversation was pop in every now and then to keep things rolling.

We had spent the morning searching the shallow grass flats for trout.

Local fishing reports indicated the trout were biting there. We ran around the flats, over here, over there, crisscrossing from his hot spots to my hot spots as if there was a fire under our butts, only to put two, less than stellar trout, in the cooler. We were burning, looking for any trout action. It wasn't happening.

We decided to take a nine-mile haul from where we were at to Sea

250

Horse Reef, just to see if the action was any better, at least, get a change of scenery. For the first two hours fishing Sea Horse Reef, we tried everything in our tackle boxes to fool two small trout. It was a sad day of catching, but a great day of fishing. We laughed at everything, including, ourselves.

I sat down and had a drink. "Is your arm hurting like mine?" I asked Ken.

"It feels like a wet noodle, I bet we've made over four million casts today," he responded.

"That's only a million casts per trout," I said.

"If we were paid by the cast, we'd be rich, but by the pound we'd never make it," he commented.

"Thank goodness, we're not being paid at all, because a job like this would get boring by the second day," I said.

"Yeah, and we're the good trout fishermen, just think how the rest of the guys are doing...." he regaled and we laughed.

"Yeah, we're known far and wide as the ultimate super-stars in the trout fishing world, with respect to today's tremendous catch, and now time for a commercial break," I came back, acting like a TV fishing personality.

It was close to four o'clock in the afternoon. The Gulf of Mexico was calm as a backyard pool, still. Even the tide was low, slack. The water had no energy; the tide needed to recharge the battery. At the moment, fishing was fruitless, so nonchalantly, we jabbered on about this or that. We both knew it was better to be here than at home, cutting grass or scratching something off a honey-do list. We gossiped about everything, whiling the time, and then I noticed, beyond Ken, dimples on the surface. More dimples were occurring and approaching. One gob of dimples started raining around the boat.

"Baitfish! I've been watching the schools behind you," we said together.

Apparently, the schools of bait had been developing behind me, as I was watching them develop behind Ken. Although the conditions had remained slick calm, the tide had turned in and shoals of baitfish had surfaced on, at least, a three-mile area around the reef. The baitfish formed up in pods. Some pods were much smaller than the area inside

251

the key of a basketball court while larger pods were the size of the court itself. The sea had come alive, surrounding us. Things were about to happen; things were about to come unglued!

The sound of the bait pod by the boat was like rain pattering water. If you just listened to the sound, it would be soothing and calming, however, as a fisherman, the sight of a gazillion baitfish surfacing on acres of water had the opposite effect. I could tell by the way my hands were shaking, trying to put together a light (#1) wire leader with a terminal, small, black snap swivel on the end of my main line. I was preparing for an invasion of Spanish mackerel by tying in the trace wire leader, but I was behaving like a drug addict prepping for some long overdue fix. My hands were shaking; I felt my blood pressure go up and my palms were moist. I was addicted to fishing. I needed this fix, so did Ken. We were fish addicts.

My level of excitement went into overdrive when some of the bait pods started getting bombed from below. A school of Spanish mackerel would single out one bait pod and knife through it. Baitfish would blow out of the water in waves, trying to escape the teeth. The calming rain sound from an unmolested pod would abruptly change to a sound of torrential down pour when the pod was under attack. The mass thrashing was loud enough to draw your attention for half a mile. I was glad baitfish didn't have voices, because if so, their screams would be something even Stephen King couldn't describe. High-pitched voices of the damned you couldn't get out of your head in a lifetime of therapy. I imagined a Spanish mackerel simply opening up its jaws, bursting into the meat wad, taking a chunk of this fish, a nip of another, the bottom half of the next, until it passed through the pod or ended up in mid-air. Whatever parts it cut away in passage, were injected down its gullet to the stomach, without chewing.

Sea gulls joined in the melee, bombing the hapless fish from above, either picking-off live bait in flight or snatching bloody remains being boiled up to the surface. There was a fish explosion going on around us. Twice, baitfish or Spanish actually bounced off the hull.

I was so excited, I screwed up, tying a knot twice; knots I could tie in my sleep. During that time, I looked over at Ken a couple of times, to see how he was handling the situation. He was calmer than I, but far from being the old bull calmly walking down the hill to mount all the cows in the herd below. Immersed in the Fountain of Youth, both of us went charging into the Spaniards as young bulls. Fishing, at times, can give squirts from the fountain of youth.

I snapped on an all chrome Bomber plug, five inches long. I guessed it to be about the size of the bait. Ken had twisted on a chartreuse Floreo jig that had some extra colors to clown it up. We were ready, at last. Of course by that time, the schools of fish that were around us had moved out of casting range. No problem, I fired up the boat and idled toward the closest exploding pod, cut the motor off, and let the boats momentum ease us into the muddle. We cast into the action to join the killing. However, we were trying to kill the killers. It is great to be at the top of the food chain; it sure beats the alternative, being baitfish.

Ken launched in first. I watched the jig in flight. The jig never got damp. It was as if Ken tossed the jig into the fish's mouth. Zing went his reel drag.

"Do you need some help," I asked.

Thankfully, he said, "No." I didn't ask again. My chrome Bomber plopped down in the middle of a current scrum. I let it float there for no other reason than to see what might happen. I couldn't stand it still long, I twitched the lure, and it was devoured. Zing went my drag.

I yelled, "I need help," just to get a rise out of Ken.

He said something I won't mention, but it was the expected answer.

The fight of a Spanish mackerel is distinctive. The take is always full speed, so the initial jolt doesn't indicate the fish size. The reel drag will squeal off some line. The longer the reel squeals, the larger the Spanish, in general. The fight is a quick paced, relatively short battle of reel squeals and speedy line retrieval with some violent boat side antics. After that, the angler is charged with a gauged, cautious, aggressive fish grab at a vicious, convulsive fish. It usually ends with a slippery fish chase on deck, all the while, keeping a close eye on where the teeth and hooks are flying from one split second to the next. Fish blood goes everywhere, on you, on the gunnel, deck, console, and anybody standing close. You're trying not to mix it with yours. Once you finally get the fish unhooked and in the fish box, the fish expires quickly. No drawn out death scene from Spanish mackerel, it gives everything during battle. Get a wet rag and clean up immediately or you'll pay for not doing so once the blood dries.

If you didn't bother with a wire leader, you may feel zero; you just reel in blank line at the cost of a two to six dollar lure. Think of how much time you saved by not rigging in a wire leader. No cleanup is necessary. Lazy will cost dollars in terms of fine lures and the like. Luck ain't cheap in the long run; consider how pizzazz is funded in Vegas. It is not on luck!

The action was as fast as one could get bait in the water. The slowdown was due to us trying to deal with trouncing fish in the boat. We had no choice but to slow down, because one mistake in regard to the teeth or hooks would be bloody painful.

Once I had four Spanish in the box, I told Ken those were all the fish I cared to keep. He asked if he could have the rest of my limit of fifteen. He loved eating smoked Spanish mackerel. That was fine with me. Besides, many Spanish tend to incur serious damages during the fight and hook removal; some of the fish caught wouldn't survive if released anyway. The action was so fast and furious that I gave him the hopelessly damaged fish, tossing back the ones in good shape.

When I say the fishing was hot, we would cast into the action and speed reel back, trying not to catch a fish. It never happened. You can't out reel a Spanish mackerel; actually speeding bait excites them more. At times, the Spanish would leave a pod, the bite would end, but all we did was move over to the closest pod under attack and resume play.

In approximately an hour and a half, thirty Spanish were in the box, not counting the small ones I released, or the ones I released because they were in good shape. The fish kept were between a pound and a half and three pounds. Ken caught one over five pounds. That one was the trophy. We couldn't keep up with all the blood, so after all was done, we took five-gallon buckets of seawater and sloshed the blood off just about everything. The boat still looked like a massacre happened aboard.

"How's your arm feel now?" I asked Ken.

"It hurts good," he said. "Look at this," Ken stated, swinging his jig back to me.

The paint was missing off the jig head; the nylon hairs, machine cut to size, now had the hair-do of a balding punk rocker. After looking at his lure, I looked closely at my chrome Bomber. Most of the chrome had been scraped or peeled away, leaving behind an off-white, scratched plastic blank. The two treble hooks were mangled, tines twisted out, in or over into what might resemble a hook. The lure had one red eye left. I showed it off to Ken with pride. After he looked it over, I clipped it off and put it back in one of my plastic tackle trays. That lure wasn't ever going fishing again, but instead would hang on a wall over top the TV to remind me of when fishing was good, real good.

The ride in went too fast. We didn't have enough time to brag on ourselves. We did come up with some ideas for the next time, which according to us, yet without the wives approval, would be the upcoming weekend, Friday, if we could get the day off. Next time, we'd be slinging top-water plugs with the treble hooks replaced by a single rear hook with the barb bent down. That would be fun fishing, save some fish from excessive damage, aid in fish removal, and most importantly, meant a shopping spree to the Tackle Box in Gainesville, Florida, to pick out a handful of special plugs. Though, we both knew a special plug wasn't necessary during a feeding frenzy like what we just enjoyed. In frenzy, a hook run through a straw has proven to work as well as anything to fulfill Spanish fancy. Call it a Spanish fly, if you need.

Spanish mackerel is the most easily dressed fish in the world. Without scales and a rice paper skin, one can simply slice off a fillet from one side, then the other and put the slabs in a plastic freezer bag. Cutting the fish like that does leave the rib bones and pin bones along the lateral line. Ken was planning to smoke all his fish fresh. It is easy to work around the bones after smoking the fish, so we went with the speed cut. If you plan to prepare the fish otherwise, it is wise to take the extra time to cut out the ribs and pin bones before cooking. Regardless of cooking method, Spanish is best served fresh. It does not freeze well. Freezing makes the meat mushy. Therefore, stockpiling frozen mackerel fillets doesn't play out well for good future meals. In the case of Spanish mackerel, it is better to stay within the limit of how many you plan to eat fresh, rather than the regulation limit of how many you can keep.

Spanish mackerel fishing in the Big Bend area of Florida, an area south and north around where the Suwannee River spills into the Gulf, is a spring/fall phenomenon. Spanish are pelagic. Large schools of relatively smaller fish run up the coast in the spring, dogwoods in bloom, followed by schools of well-fed fish running south in the fall just prior to the second real cold front.

Sea Horse Reef is famous for outstanding Spanish mackerel fishing. That deep sandbar of a reef posted eight miles or so off Cedar Keys is a mackerel factory in the spring and fall, if conditions are good. Some of the best mackerel fishing I've ever experienced has been on Sea Horse Reef. I mean Spanish mackerel fishing couldn't get any better than what I've seen out there, unless you've been elsewhere and fish literally jumped in the boat. Actually, one Spanish did free-fall in our boat while chasing bait so…

I've never fished much south of Sea Horse Reef for Spanish, but north of the Reef the Spanish mackerel fishing can be just as fantastic. Spotty Bottom, approximately nine miles off Suwannee, and Nine Mile Bank, off Steinhatchee come to mind. That covers an area of over forty nautical miles. Spanish mackerel assault the western coast for over a hundred miles. Remember, the horde is moving south to north in the spring and north to south in the fall, always pursuing bait. At some time, the wave will be passing by a small town on the west coast. For those with a boat on a trailer, seaworthy in two to three foot seas voyaging twelve miles out or less, you can simply follow the local fishing reports and know from which coastal town to best launch. Traveling on the road is most often easier and less expensive than traveling across water.

Since learning about the seasons and movements of Spanish mackerel and experiencing how much fun it is to catch them on light tackle, I'll incorporate a chance at Spanish fishing in my game plan any day when season and conditions are right. Especially so, if the evening seas are turning calm, I'll plan to be amongst the bait and Spanish for a second chance at some great action to end the day.

There have been times when I was so anxious to fish for Spanish that I, and those with me, arrived early. The players were still warming up, swimming lose. It wasn't time for them to get in formation and let the game begin. I found trolling a productive way to bide time until the baitfish dimple the field. Spoons, jigs, flashy plugs, or whatever looks good to you, on two or more light poles, is similar to trolling the mascot around for the Spanish to beat up on pre-game. Sometimes the pre-game show can be so good there is, no need to stick around for the game.

Chapter 16 - Cobia on the Mark

I had developed a bad case of *cobia phobia.* A self-inflicted irrational fear of not catching every cobia a fishing day had to offer. The symptoms kept getting stronger and stronger, the more time I spent on the Gulf.

I couldn't think about fishing without visualizing log-size cobia laying down current of a channel marker or seeing one swim up behind a trout being caught or glancing off the stern, while anchored, to find a cobia mesmerized by the shiny stainless prop.

I found myself manipulating conversations toward the subject of fishing just to testify about my latest and greatest sighting. Or about the big one that took my bait only to run through a cluster of pilings cutting my line on the barnacles, or embellishing about a small cobia I managed to get in the boat then release after it trashed everything it came in contact with.

It was hard to justify money spent on specialized rods, reels, and tackle, just to have the opportunity of tickling the fancy of a fish, which I might encounter-if lucky. I had a jewelry box of store bought and handmade items waiting for my dream girl. It was like dating a fickle rich girl with expensive tastes and buying her costly trinkets to hold her interest or sway her mood.

My approach to fishing had even changed. In lieu of jigging and popping my way through the day trout and red fish fishing, I was working my way around hitting one cobia haunt after another. I only pitched a jig at trout if the opportunity was handy or I needed big bait. I'd even found

258

myself anchored for hours in deep holes with four rods baited waiting for one cobia hook-up. Friends that were used to fishing with me using the touch and go trout fishing strategy, found the catfishing style for cobia boring. I didn't care; I'd fish alone.

Every channel marker, in the maze of three channels that lead into Cedar Keys, held a cobia. The deep holes in the sloughs had cobia searching the bottom for crab, eel, and fish. Cuts between the bars and the islands had cobia lingering around waiting for food to wash by. I saw more cobia than Custard saw Indians, but most of mine only existed in my head. Cobia phobia was an addictive condition, taking over the mind and wallet with the only intervention being a wife with a legitimate reason to restrict time or money for the habit. Even then....

In time, I had droned on and on about cobia fishing to those who cared to listen and those I'd trapped into it. Then it happened. After a battery of stories about a school of big cobia cruising through a hole and picking up multiple bait at once, cobia shooting out from underneath channel markers to pick-off free-lined pinfish, stubborn logs visiting the boat then sinking away and riveting stories of successful and unsuccessful gaff shots; I heard, "we'd like to do that."

"Do what?" I asked.

"Go cobia fishing with you, silly," announced Big John Grimes. "We're going to trailer our boat down from Georgia next weekend and rent a condo in Cedar Keys. Why don't you and Gina come down, we'll grill steaks, ya'll spend the night and we'll all go cobia fishing on Saturday in my boat?" said Big John with his attractive wife, Judy, smiling in agreement behind him.

"Well, Gina probably won't be able to come because I know she is working on a deadline," I said.

"That's OK, you come," Judy replied in a most hospitable southern voice.

"The weather may not turn out," I countered.

"We'll play it by ear; at least we'll have a good meal together," John shot back.

"Cobia fishing can be slow, sometimes boring; it's more like hunting for fish rather than fishing," I tried to escape with.

"If we don't catch a fish, we'll have a fine floating picnic," Judy said closing the dialogue door.

It wasn't that I didn't want to go cobia fishing. It wasn't that I didn't enjoy hanging out with Big John and Judy. Their boat was better than the one I had. Both of them were experienced fishermen, meaning I wouldn't be baby-sitting; Judy was actually a better fisherman than John was and he would readily agree. The fact was I was having a phobia about having to back up those crazy stories I'd been telling. The stories I told were true, slightly exaggerated in spots, but true nonetheless. Now, I had performance pressure and I was baulking at it. *What happens if nothing happens?* That question unzipped a list of what ifs that I didn't have answers to. I was feeling pressure from the get-go even though they said up front, not to worry about it. I was worrying about it.

The Friday meal went great, even though Gina did have to stay behind to work. A Fred Flintstone steak with a baked potato one could carve a canoe out of served up on a palette of good laughter and talk of the fish of yesterdays and tomorrow. The NOAA forecast was perfect, light southerly breeze with seas two feet or less; just like that, Friday had turned out to be. We expected no change in the weather unless there was to be an improvement on perfection. The boat and tackle were all dressed up and ready to play. Even though Big John and Judy tried again and again to take it off me, I felt pressure. I wanted, well, needed, Saturday to come out well.

Saturday morning we were some of the first to launch from the municipal boat ramp. Everything went smooth. We were underway. They were excited about it. I was excited too, but seasoned with nerves. I decided to go with one, of many, game plans I had thought of the night before. It was simple, direct and didn't require much backtracking. It also maximized the number of spots we could fish for cobia. Each location would be where I had caught cobia before. Thinking about things in that manner, eased my mind. There was nothing else to do, but go fishing. I relaxed into the natural flow.

One thing I didn't have to worry about was the weather. It was perfect as predicted. It was the latter part of June, a time of year when there is just a hint of coolness in the morning air. We appreciated that cool hint, because by early afternoon there was a strong sensation of heat, a heat that would turn into a steady broil for the next three months.

The first order of business was to collect a tank full of live bait. Big John's twenty-one-foot Hydra-Sport had a large excellent live well with super flow raw water. I took the boat over a grass flat that was en route to the first area I wanted to shoot for cobia. The grass flat was a mosaic of grass and sand holes. It looked pretty as a painting. I had pre-rigged three trout poles with number ten Aberdeen hooks and two small shots of lead. In the fish box was a quart size zip-top baggy with pre-cut, half by quarter inch, squid strips. I had done everything possible to make things easier on me during the fishing day.

We baited up and cast out as far as we could on the windward side of the drift; that kept the lines tight as we drifted over the flat. The pinfish bite was instant. All we had to do was toss back fish less than four inches long. Along with the ubiquitous pinfish, we brought in spot-tailed pinfish, hand-sized pigfish, whiting, and an assortment of other juvenile fish. The fish collection went by in a hurry. Besides, if we ran out of live bait, we'd be close enough to a grass flat to dart in and collect some more during the day. So far so good, the pressure was light.

High tide was at eleven o'clock. I knew where I wanted to be at high tide; I planned to fish my way there. At the time, I had three hours to kill.

I took the boat around the landside of North Key to the back of North Channel where it turned hard westward. There on the north side of the channel was a multi-pronged green channel marker that stood just off a deeper pool in the channel. I wanted to anchor up current, adjust for wind, so the boat came to rest just outside the channel within a long cast of the marker. Before I did anything, I had to trick the anchor just in case what I wanted to happen, happened.

The anchor had to position the boat correctly in order to fish the area most effectively. However, I didn't want it to be a burden if we hung a big fish and had to give chase. There is no time to hand pull an anchor when a big fish is spooling a reel. It happens too quickly. A breakaway anchor system was the solution to a hoped for problem.

"How much anchor line do you have, Big John?" I asked.

"I don't know, but plenty."

In his anchor locker was a light Danfort with three feet of chain coated in white plastic, sold every day at Walmart to first time boaters. The first thirty foot of anchor line was laid in smooth. The rest of it was a bulky wad. I pulled all the line out of the hold.

"What are you doing?" Big John asked.

"Help me and I'll show you," I replied.

We untangled the mess in short order. I measured the line off in five-foot shots by arms spread. There was approximately one hundred-feet of line. Considering the deepest I planned on anchoring was twenty-feet and a three-to-one scope was adequate, I measured off the first sixty feet and tied it at the measure to the bow cleat, using a weathered figure eight knot. The sixty-foot of line going to the anchor, I coiled neatly on the starboard side of the bow and laid the anchor chain softly on top of it. The remaining line, I coiled neatly on the port side of the bow and tied a spare life vest to the end then flipped it all over so the rope coils held down the life vest.

"What in the world are you doing, Brian?" Judy asked.

"If and when we hook into a big one, we can quickly untie the anchor from the bow, toss the extra line overboard, and give chase. Afterwards, we can come back and collect our anchor back," I explained.

"Did you hear that, John, we're going to catch a big fish," Judy quipped.

I was hoping she was right; we were prepared if she was anyway.

I swung wide by the channel marker to see if there was a cobia parked against the pilings, none of us saw a fish. Just as importantly, I wanted to look at the tale tail of water that washed through the pilings. Reading the tail water would give me an up-current direction. I kept in mind this was near a bend in the channel and water can behave oddly when it changes course. I took into consideration the wind, and how it might alter the boat in the current. Then I eyed a spot up current of the marker and idled to that spot.

"Big John, I'm going to need your help, can you toss the hook when I ask?"

He said sure and started baby stepping toward the nose of the boat. John didn't get the label big without reason.

"No need to wobble on the bow, just stand back from the bow casting platform and slip the anchor off the side, that way I can see and you're safe," I told him.

At first Big John had a look like he wasn't used to receiving orders on his own boat, but it changed quickly when he realized he had just learned to do something easier, correctly, and safely.

Under most all circumstances, it is not good to try to balance on the bow of boat. The bow is always the most unstable place. Up there, if a mishap happens, while the boat was underway, there can be two hits. First, the person hitting the water and second, the prop hitting the person. A quick unbalanced second can prove lethal, serious, or at the very least, make a bad day. Safety is issue number one, always. When you're on the water, emergency help can be a long time away regardless of how far out you go, if you can get help at all. A VHF radio on a boat is just as important as fuel. Think about it; it is true.

The anchoring went pretty well. It wasn't perfect, but doable. A good cast would reach the channel marker on both sides; the marker could direct float or free-lined bait. We could place three bottom baits in the deeper hole in the channel. The boat was in a good enough position; it wasn't worth pulling the anchor and resetting. I was learning, at the time that it was worth the effort to re-anchor the boat and present the bait in the right spot, rather than fish from a poorly anchored boat, and soak bait. Laziness never pays off. Even if adjusting the anchor position did nothing but add confidence, it is worth the effort. Confidence is always the best bait a fisherman can serve.

I was anxious, but said, "OK, let's take our time and do it right the first time."

That comment was more for me than them.

"What can we do to help?" Judy asked. Her nature was to be helpful.

"I think it will be easier if ya'll let me set it up the first time. I'll explain things as I go. Ya'll pay attention, next time we work as a team," I replied.

For cobia fishing with free-lined bait, float bait, or lures, I liked the large Penn 8500 spinning reels for cast ability. The deep spool held plenty of thirty-pound test line. For free lining or tossing lures, I simply tied on a three-foot section of fifty-pound leader then the hook or lure.

The float rig was a little more complicated because I wanted to preset the bait depth. It was nothing more than a saltwater modified slip-float rig Mr. Poe had shown me how to rig for crappie fishing. The rig starts with a plastic bead followed by a sleeved sinker snap. A sleeved sinker snap is part of a fish finder rig sold in packs of five or so at any saltwater, tackle shop, cheap. After the sleeve, thread on a half to one-ounce egg sinker and tie on a good quality barrel swivel. To the other end of the swivel tie on a three-foot leader of fifty-pound test mono and end with a hook that best fits the bait size. In this case, a 6/0 9174 Mustad was appropriate. Next, roughly measure out from the hook up the line to how deep you want the bait presented and snuggly tie on a few short sections of coarse thread as a bobber stop. Now, the fun part, blow up a balloon to the size of softball and pin it to the snap part of the sleeve. Always have a bag of balloons in your tackle box because they have many applications. The balloon will ride against the sinker when casting. Once cast, the main line will pass through the sleeve until the bead jams against the knots of thread, presenting the bait at the desired depth. It is a slick rig with a lot of uses. Thankfully, I had every pole pre-rigged.

For fishing bottom bait, I had Penn 4/0 reels attached to medium heavy Ugly Stiks®. The reels were loaded with sixty-pound test and rigged with a two-ounce egg sinker that would slip up the main line. A Uni Knot tied the main line to the three foot plus eighty-pound leader. At the end of the leader was a 6/0 9174 Mustad hook; I honed. It was a slip sinker rig commonly used for freshwater catfishing or offshore grouper fishing, but it worked well for cobia fishing. The outfit was somewhat over kill, but I used the combo for inshore shark fishing and, at times, I needed the extra beef to pull or direct a fish away from an obstruction. Not intended for casting, was he drawback of this reel. It took time and patience to learn how to cast a 4/0 reel. I had to go through the same learning curve with it as with my first push-button and the original bait caster. Me, a sinker tied to the end of the line and some wide-open space; I learned to cast and pick out unforgettable birds nest, again in the backyard.

I selected a medium sized pinfish for the first bottom bait. I lob cast the bait toward the middle of the pool. There was a little bit of over run on the top of the spool, but it rolled out easily. The rod was set in the second gunnel rod holder from the stern, port side. Once the bait was maintaining its bottom position, I checked the drag. The spool gave line smoothly with a firm pull. I pushed the reel clicker button forward and took the reel out of gear. When a fish hit, it could take line freely, but the alarm would go off letting us know. The second bottom bait was a fresh dead ten-inch mullet cut along the spine from the back of the head down and out the tail. I lob cast it up current of the live bait thinking the scent trail from it would give attention to both bait at once. That rod was set up in the mid-ship rod holder on port side and set up the same way as the first.

I set up a float rig to present a large pinfish ten feet deep. On the bow platform, I cast it slightly up current on the port side then walked the rod to the back of the boat and set it in the stern rod holder. The float bait would drift over top of the bottom bait without being tangled. The port side was set and ready.

On the starboard side I did the exact same thing except I placed the pole with the bottom bait in the mid ship rod holder. From the way things were moving, it might take ten minutes for the float bait to approach the channel marker.

In the meantime, I free lined a large pinfish off the starboard stern. The cast landed six feet up current of the marker. It was a nice cast.

I handed the rod to Judy, "When you feel a jerk, jerk back," I said.

All the poles were fishing. For the next ten minutes, we waited. I had to reel in the starboard float bait and re-cast it to prevent it from tangling in the free lined bait. I went ahead and re-cast the free liner as well. The cast was on the other side of the channel marker, as if that would make a big difference. We waited another ten long minutes. I reeled in the free lined bait, took the bait off the hook, and had it ready in case we saw a cobia around the boat. I left out the four other poles.

Big John needed some fishing practice and asked about using the trout poles for piddle jigging around the boat while we waited. I set him and Judy up with some jigs.

"Like I said, cobia fishing can get boring at times," I mentioned. "We're going to give it ten more minutes, then move on," I said, while John and Judy bounced their jigs in the channel.

Judy hollered, "I got one, I got one!"

Her trout pole was dancing. It was a strong fish, chirped a little drag off the spool. When the fish was near, she flipped it in the boat. The fish was a prize, a foot long blue runner, one of the best bait you can have for any big game fish. They resemble blue fish at first glance, but are thicker in the shoulders, have a forked tail, and lack the teeth.

"Boy, he hit hard," Judy, exclaimed.

"They put up a strong fight from start to finish and are the best bait," I told Judy.

She seemed slightly disappointed it wasn't a fish we would eat, but happy it had fought and would be great bait. Blue runners usually school and I was hoping there would be a few more to add to the live well. Big John was having a blast. He enjoyed reeling in the spastic runner. They picked up a total of five runners quickly before the school passed on.

"Let's go," I said.

Big John was ready for a change of scenery. We all helped in reeling in the four poles, took off the bait, and put them back in the live well.

"Just leave the rods in their holders, it's going to be a short ride," I said.

I idled the boat forward as Big John collected the anchor line. The water was only thirteen feet deep, so raising anchor wasn't too much of a detail.

We eased out of the channel a third of a mile, moving to a single red channel marker planted close to a shallow grass flat to the south. The channel marker was a wooden post as opposed to a steel I-beam.

From experience, I caught more cobia next to wooden channel markers. I had pulled several fish from this channel marker, in the past. The anchoring went well since I noticed how the boat laid out, according to the compass on the previous spot. We set out the same spread, but this time the bottom poles were on the starboard side where the channel ran. The free-lined bait went toward the channel marker. I didn't use the runners. There was a better spot to use them, next stop. Twenty empty minutes later Big John was pulling the anchor.

"The cobia must not be biting," proclaimed Big John.

"Remember, it is more like a hunt than a fishing trip," I said.

I was feeling some pressure with the burning of daylight and the lack of fish. The sun was getting higher in the sky. The cobia bite is better when the light level is low, such as dawn and dusk. The only thing to do was keep moving and fishing in the hope of bumping into our quarry. The next location was a multi-pronged wooden marker at the end of North Channel. It was a fairly consistent cobia producer. Of course, I'd been there many times when nothing happened. We were moving that way to find out, yea or nay.

I idled by a big marker numbered three, at the end of the channel. There was a scattering of baitfish around the posts. They glittered in the water. I didn't see any sign of cobia there. I was hoping to see a log in the shadows. I would have paid to see a cobia lying against the marker. In the pit of my stomach, I felt this was going to be strike three. If we don't get a hit here, Big John might get impatient and want to fall back to trout fishing. I didn't want to resort to trout fishing, but I would understand. For those who have never experienced a cobia before, the quest for them may feel like a snipe hunt. At first, you're all excited about it, and then you realize you're playing the fool in the middle of nowhere.

The boat rested on the rope sixty feet directly in front of the channel marker. I had noticed on the last stop that the bottom bait were being rolled around by the current, ending up directly behind the boat instead of off to the side as I wanted. Spreading the bait further apart covers more area, which can translate into extra action. At least that's how the theory goes. I needed to change the weight and style of the sinker, so I trimmed out the two-ounce egg sinkers, replaced them with four-ounce bank sinkers. The extra weight and teardrop shape kept the bait where we cast them, where we wanted the bait to be. Before I started changing out the sinkers, I asked Big John and Judy to cast two float rigs out on either side of the boat. They could be working the marker during my down time. This was the teamwork I talked about on the first set up.

"Just put those big, spinning rods in the stern rod holders until I get the bottom rigs ready," I said.

It only took a few minutes to ready the poles. I lobbed the first bottom rig thirty feet off the channel side of the marker. I did the same thing again, but cast further out, each baited with a fresh pinfish.

It was time for the ace bait on a free-line outfit. As I was sloshing around in the tank, trying to net one of those super-charged blue runners, the first bottom pole yanked down hard. The clicker chirped. Line grudgingly rolled off the spool. I had left the reel in gear mistakenly. Big John grabbed the rod, "Judy get over here!"

She was there in a blink. The lady was into fishing. Big John waited until she had a firm grip then released the rod to her. During that time, I put the free-line rod up in one of the T-top rod holders and reeled in the other bottom rig and the float rig on the starboard side.

"Big John, reel in the other float line," I said firmly.

I didn't want this fish to get off because we failed to clear lines it might entangle in. While we were clearing the lines, I was watching Judy and her fish. Her line rode up in the water column. That was a good sign it was a cobia and not a shark. Thankfully, the fish was swimming away from the marker, which was one less thing to worry about. Judy was gaining line, slowly. The drag wasn't giving up line. After I unhooked and tossed the bait back in the live well, I stood behind Judy, my eye following her line out to the fish. Sure enough, there was a cobia arching on the surface away from the boat. The fish wasn't that large. However, the cobia tagging along below it was much bigger. I questioned whether or not the fish on the hook was large enough to keep. I didn't get the gaff. Cobias have to be thirty-three inches from the nose to the fork of the tail. This fish might go thirty-three, twelve to fourteen pounds. There is a tremendous difference between it and one twice that size. A forty plus pounder is a struggle on most all tackle while the occasional hundred pound class fish can break the will of the fishermen.

In this case, the fight was strong, but the tackle was overpowering to the small cobia. Judy had a warm-up fish, but I didn't tell her that. She was enjoying the fight and winning. Big John was giving Judy some tips on fighting the fish, however, she was doing just fine by herself. She kept the line tight, never any slack, and didn't try to horse the fish to the boat. I was beginning to learn that women are often better cobia fishermen than men. The ladies allow the rod and reel to whip the fish, not their muscle. Men will wrestle the hook right out of the fish's mouth or out power the line strength.

At the boat, the fish that had tagged along briefly was gone. The cobia we had thrashed, splashed, and, eventually, crashed, in the boat. I had a wet towel ready to toss over its head. The towel calmed the fish down, giving me a brief opportunity to get hold of it. Cobias have a series of seven to nine dorsal spines behind the head that can rake blood if mishandled. I never forgot that after my first cobia encounter. Her fish may have been thirty-three inches, but no more. The fish never stood still for a good clean measure. Realizing the growth potential of this cub cobia, I said, "Too short," and tossed it back. According to the wild aerial display on release, the fish was unharmed, only given something to remember, if it can remember.

"We didn't get a picture of the fish!" Judy brought to our attention. I explained that sometimes you get a good photo of the angler with a short cobia; however, there are times when the fish will beat itself or exhaust itself to death while people fumble for a snapshot. That fish was on the wild side, so I got it back in the water as fast as possible. Judy liked the idea of keeping the fish alive to fight another day rather than risk killing it for a picture. She identified herself as a fisherman not a simple-minded fish-killer.

During all the activity, my mind kept recalling the fish that had followed Judy's fish. The fish was hot, wanting to bite.

"There are other fish here that are in a playful mood and larger than the one we just boated," I mentioned.

"I saw the big one behind her fish," Big John said, then elaborated.

"Let's keep it temporarily simple," I suggested. "We're just going to use the two float rigs with blue runners!" It was a cat and mouse deal to net two runners out of a live well full of pinfish, but persistence paid-off. Big John lobbed a float rig off the port side of the boat. I cast a blue runner within ten feet on the left side of the channel marker. After splash down, my bait bounced the balloon around for a few seconds then darted away with purpose from the marker. We could see the runner at the surface, dragging the balloon behind it. Darting to and fro like an open field runner with the football. The runner was in a panic for good reason. A V wake brushed the balloon to the side, a boil erupted on the surface, and the balloon lost buoyancy. Big John already had the rod.

"Keep the rod flat, when you feel the surge of the fish, set the hook once and hold on. Do not try and horse the fish to the boat!" I coached quickly.

I had just enough time to blurt out the last word when his rod lunged forward. He set the hook. Well over three-hundred pounds of force drove the hook into the attention of that fish. It responded quickly and powerfully. The fish turned toward the safety of the channel marker. It swam with speed and power. A stream of water sprayed off the line where it entered the water.

"Hold the pole up at the one o'clock position," I yelled to Big John as I was clearing the other float rig.

I knew the fish was going to split the pilings and cut the line. Big John was turning the reel handle furiously, but it was going against the drag, creating twists in the line at a rate of 3.5 twists per turn.

"Hey, Big John, if you ain't gaining line, you're creating line twists," I warned. I figured it was too late. The real life video showed the fish missile approaching the door to explosive freedom. At the last second, the fish glanced to its right and went around the front of the channel marker. It was an unbelievable near miss.

"Big John, you're living right or something. That fish should have been the one that got away. Now let's get down to the business of putting it in the boat," I said in relief.

Then the fish turned, went down and toward the marker again. It was another shot at the freedom target. But below the surface, the fish turned left, arced toward the starboard side of the boat, and started to come to the surface. Fifty feet off the starboard side, the fish was making its way toward the bow, eyeballing us the entire time. Big John followed the fish along the rail. I swung around the port side and untied the anchor line from the bow cleat. The fish swam over the anchor as Big John passed behind me. I released the anchor line, tossing it off starboard. The fish pulled Big John back down port side.

"Judy fire up the motor," I said.

The motor fired as if she was there waiting to do it. I slipped behind the wheel, clicked the boat in forward, idling in the direction of the channel mouth toward the open Gulf where conducting the fight would be without line hazard. The fish was, roughly speaking, four feet. We could have managed without tossing off the anchor, but the stunt did give us some breathing room and added a level of excitement. The fish lapped Big John around the boat once more before I could use the motor to keep the fight to stern.

Then, Big John, politely, gave his wife the pole.

"You take this fish, I'm tired of it," was his excuse to pass the pole to his beloved.

He actually got more enjoyment watching her catch a fish than catching one himself. I'd seen many guys be so caught up in fishing they

270

ignored their wife. It was nice to see the opposite occur.

Judy was more than ready to close the deal on the fish. With confidence, she was reeling down smoothly and pulling up gently, working the fish to the boat. I was doing my part as well. Every time the fish would make a move toward the bow, I hip-checked it by swinging the stern to the fish. Big John had involved himself as Judy's personal coaching cheerleader. He was so zealous I kept getting strange visions of him with pom-poms, wearing a short skirt and tight sweater lettered Judy U. I was glad I was too busy to be the guy that had to hold him up to the fans. The fantasy view most guys think of when wondering about being the male cheerleader during the lift routine would be a life stuttering sight, if it was indeed possible to support Big John as he did a one leg kick out and yelled, "Go Judy."

The fish sounded, gave a series of strong headshakes, and then came back up on portside, closer to the boat than before going down. Judy was doing an excellent job of working the fish. The fish was tiring but had yet to get within its scare distance of the boat. I hoped Judy didn't think it was going to be over when the fish was next to the boat. That's just when things get interesting, a pivotal battle moment.

The cobia started a parade of ever-closing swim-bys. It reminded me of the big carp I caught at the lake with Dad some thirty years ago. Judy was getting excited, thinking about bringing this battle to a close.

"It's coming, it's coming closer!" Judy said, with a lot of happy and a pinch of desperation in her voice. "What are you doing!" she blurted, confusingly at me.

"I'm easing your drag back," I told her, after withdrawing my hand from her reel drag, out of biting range.

"Why?" she asked with intensity.

"You're going to need some more forgiveness in your shocks because the road is about to get bumpy," I said.

I told her when the fish encounters the boat it is going to draw on whatever reserve energy it has to escape.

"Cobia hate boats," I told her and Big John.

As predicted, just out of gaffing range, the cobia rolled to its right, saw the boat, and shot off, squealing the drag as it went. Judy instinctively squatted down and grabbed the rod with both hands above

271

the reel, keeping it up as best she could. She did so speaking in tongues; the only word I understood was, "Jesus."

"Big John, step back, you looking overboard puts too much ugly in the water and it's scaring the fish," I said in jest to lighten the moment.

He gave me a quick bear hug, called me a name. Judy worked the fish back in and it happened again. Moreover, it happened once more. Each time it happened, the battle back lessened.

"When are you going to get the gaff, Brian?" Judy questioned, in a yell.

"I have it in my hand," I said, and showed her.

"You haven't been paying much attention to what's going on in this boat, Dumpling," Big John joked.

"I've been a little bit busy," she retorted.

"Take it easy, it's about over," I encouraged Judy.

"I can't wait to get this stupid fish," she panted.

The movements of the fish were getting predictable; a swing to the right, followed by a left swing, ever inching closer. The energy reserve was depleting. I asked Big John to move up on the rail about amidships, while I positioned myself to Judy's left in the cockpit area. The fish was rolled over well on its left side, moving right to left down the boat. I held the gaff in the water, motionless and away from the boat, waiting for the fish to move to Judy. It did. I drove the point of the gaff in from below the head then continued in the same motion to heave the fish aboard. The fish hit the deck and drew on its last stash of energy, thrashing and twisting wildly. I held on to the gaff, keeping the head up off the deck, while allowing the gaff handle to rotate in hand. It seemed like a long time, but it only lasted a minute.

"Flip the bail open, give out some line," I told Judy, while focused on the fish.

I didn't know it at the time, but Big John had taken the rod. He did as I asked. When the fish was through thrashing, I clipped the leader line at the mouth with a pair of side cutters.

"Big John, open the fish box lid," I instructed.

The fish box was built into the back edge of the bow-casting platform. I took the fish around on the starboard, lifted it up enough so it would flop in the box, and shucked it off the gaff. Big John shut the lid.

We could hear the fish briefly, slapping around on the bags of ice. I looked up. Judy was there. She hugged me. She gave me a kiss on the cheek. I had a smile with ends that met at the back of my head.

"Let's do it again," she said.

Big John used the gaff to snag the anchor rope tied to the life vest. After he caught the rope, I swung around the helm station, grabbed a piece of the rope, and started hand pulling the boat up the anchor line. I picked up—guessing—forty feet of line and stopped and tied it off to the bow cleat. The boat was forty feet from the channel marker. The time was ten o'clock, an hour before high tide. I gave us ten to fifteen minutes to do something before I wanted to move to my next hit. At high tide, I wanted us to be somewhere special.

I wasn't planning to fish there much longer. We had caught two cobia off that marker already. I didn't think there was much chance of taking another fish. However, I was willing to wager one more runner. It was a gamble, because blue runners don't work as well after running as bait the first time. They spend themselves and become lethargic. For the quick fix on a float rig, I netted an average pinfish, hooked it, and tossed it to the right-hand side of the marker. While fishing in the tank for a blue runner, I netted half a dozen sluggish pinfish, previously used. One by one, I pitched them at the marker as live chum. To a bottom rig, I hooked the runner in the anal fin and lobbed it to the left base of the marker. A hook in the anal fin works like an irritating hemorrhoid, making the bait itch and crazy wiggle to ease the behind. If there were an extra cobia on the mark, it would be hard pressed not to take a stir-crazed runner.

"Hold this one in your hands, Big John," I directed.

He took the rod as I went on. "It is so close to the marker, you're not going to have much response time. Set the hook hard, keep the rod at the one o'clock position, and reel as if you lost your mind. Either you lose in the first three seconds or you got a hot fight on your hands," I warned.

I turned to close the bait tank lid. Big John grunted. I turned back to see his pole doubled over. His line was already off the starboard side, the drag giving line.

"Judy, reel yours in," I yelled, as politely as I could. "Cut your drag back half a turn, Big John," I yelled, while turning the motor over.

Big John turned the star drag counter clockwise and line came off the spool more freely.

"I want that fish to swim away from the marker," I announced, while untying the anchor line from the bow. By the time I got back to the helm station, the boat had drifted back to within a boats length of the channel marker. I popped it in forward, gave it a fast boost to starboard, then brought the throttle back to idle. We were in a slow chase. Big John had kept the line tight the whole time, getting a few pumps in when the fish allowed. Sixty feet from the marker, I kicked the boat around, stern toward the fish and put the engine in neutral. I was letting the fish work against the drag on the reel, the drag of the boat, and the last bit of the incoming tide. Big John's fish was on the surface. It appeared to be the twin of the last fish, however, unlike the previous girl, this sister was pitted against a stiff boat rod, heavier line, and an angler more than twice the size. The battle was waning quickly. I just hoped the fish was running out of steam. We didn't need a green cobia trashing the boat.

"Keep doing what you're doing, Big John, it's working great!" I encouraged.

Before getting the gaff, I opened the fish box in preparation. Judy took the opportunity to take another gander at her prize. Big John's fish looked whipped. The last ten feet was pretty much pulling it to the boat. I stood to John's left along the gunnel to have an unobstructed path to the fish box. There was no rush on the gaff shot. I placed the point under the chin and yanked the fish in the boat. It gave a slight struggle, during three steps to the fish box, but was on ice before it realized what all had happened. Things went smoothly.

Big John picked me up from behind in a bear hug and said, "I love this stuff."

Things were pretty cool. I smiled at Judy.

She said, "Let's do it again."

Big John caught the rope tied to the life vest and started hand lining. I idled up the rope. When he had twenty feet of rope collected, I asked him to put a wrap on the cleat before collecting the rest.

Judy asked, "Why are we leaving?"

"We have an engagement at high tide. Don't tell me you didn't get the email?" I answered, humorously.

"We were catching fish here you know," she reminded me. The two fish in the box took a lot of pressure off me; otherwise, I might have stayed there and played one more hand.

"The next spot is even *gooder*," I smiled.

She gave me a partial look, meaning you had better be right because I liked what was going on back there.

Our next location was offshore marker #12—set out by the Coast Guard to guide barge traffic as best I could figure and find out. There wasn't a lot of barge traffic in the area, and what there was usually took the short cut across the open Gulf. They used the offshore markers, during foul weather when the short cut wasn't a wise choice.

Marker #12 was a multi-steel legged structure set in a no man's land of sand bottom. It being the only thing around for miles, fish flocked to it. Large wads of baitfish swarmed around it during the warm months. During the chill of winter, sheepshead used it as a spawning structure. The water around the marker was approximately twenty feet deep, tide dependent. During high tide, when the current was slack, I wanted to see loose clouds of baitfish in and around the marker accented with milling cobia logs. That was my high hope. We scooted across unruffled water for twelve minutes before the marker came into view. Four more minutes, we were idling within sight seeing range. Before we got too close, we saw gulls diving near the marker, a positive sign to every fisherman. As we neared, sporadic small blasts of baitfish scattered the surface, another positive sign for every fisherman. A small flotilla of pelicans drifted about the channel marker. I broke out in cobia phobia.

We were still off #12 well enough not to disturb the rhythm going on there. I put the boat in neutral, cut the engine off, and turned the wheel to starboard, using the lower unit as a rudder to veer off course a bit before coasting to a stop.

"What are you doing, Brian?" Judy asked, fully aware we needed to get closer to the action.

"I need a moment to prep the tackle," I smiled, trying to hide the nerves I couldn't disguise.

Mentally, I pushed rewind and started taking inventory. The gulls were working the baitfish that the fish below were pushing up. The pelicans on the water weren't drifting in the same direction; they weren't moving at all unless they were paddling, so the tide was slack. If the tide was slack or close to it, anchoring wasn't an important detail to start fishing; it would be better to fish from a free-floating boat rather than one pegged down. Continuing along that train of thought, it wouldn't be a good idea to have many, if any, extra poles fishing from the boat adrift. Sometimes, extra effort can lead to headaches if the fishing turns out to be the way you hoped it to be. If necessary, we would anchor to put out additional bait. For the moment, we'd just use what we could handle.

A free-lined bait and a float bait were definite. A ready lure that we could easily and quickly cast to a cobia we happened to notice would be a wise third setup. So, I cut the float rig off one of the big spinners, retied a three-foot section of fifty-pound leader, and tied on a single 8/0 hook.

"Another free-liner?" Big John asked.

"No, it's going to be a trick bait," I replied, while sorting through some of the tackle trays I'd brought.

I picked out an eighteen-inch black plastic worm. It was an oddity I'd found at some inland tackle store stocked for bass fishermen. I'm not a shopper, but I do visit local fishing museums with great gift shops.

The worm, at its thickest point, four inches behind the head, was as round as a felt pen. The tail was pencil thick. It weighed enough to cast well on its own, however, the mass of the worm was such that the sink rate was slow, natural, and the undulations made while doing so were natural, as well as, alluring. I slipped the hook in skin deep at the thickest part, ran it down three quarters of an inch and out the same side, never going through the whole worm. The worm dangled, balanced on the hook.

"What in the world is that thing, a snake?" Judy blurted.

I laughed because it looked like a snake.

"No, it's a super-sized plastic worm, we're going to trick a cobia into thinking it's an eel, one of their favorite meals," I said, smiling.

Before doing anything more, I ran the lines and leaders through my thumb and forefinger to feel for damage. They all felt slick and looked in good condition. A scrape across the thumbnail told me the hooks were sharp. Preventative maintenance always leads to better fish, not stories of them.

We were close enough to the mark to go ahead and hook-up the live bait. I adjusted the float-rig to put the bait four feet down, and then I hooked the largest fresh pinfish in front of the dorsal fin. I handed the pole to Judy, asking her to dip the bait overboard.

I quipped, "Never have live bait out of the water unless you're holding your breath." Judy asked the question I was digging for.

"Why?"

"Well, when you run out of air, you know it's time to dip the fish in the water to let it breath. Fish breathe water, we want them frisky when they're working for us," I ended, smiling.

It took a minute to net one of the last two runners for the free-line. I took the bait net out of the tank, hooked the fish in the dorsal, and then dropped the bait back in the tank. Blue runners are far too active to try to keep in the water next to the boat. They might tear away from the hook or wrap around something. It's best to keep them contained until needed and always remove the bait net before doing so to avoid spending critical time, picking the hook out of the net. Knocking the net off the runner, during a cobia opportunity, can lead to a loss of religious fortitude, not to mention, opportunity only knocks once. I'd found that out the hard way a couple of times and learned from it.

We were as ready as ever, time to play fishing. We were thirty to forty yards off the Marker #12 when I turned the motor over. A slight adjustment pointed us directly toward the marker. I idled us forward for fifteen yards, killed the motor, cut the wheel a touch to starboard, and let momentum glide us quietly to the right of Marker #12, within casting distance.

"Big John, lob cast your runner at least twenty feet to the right of the marker; it will keep the bait from running around the legs," I instructed. "Judy, do you want me to cast your float line out?" I asked.

"I can do it," she said. She could too; I'd seen her do it.

"Put the float rig on the left-hand side of the marker fairly close," I coached.

They both did a great job. We were forty feet off Marker #12 with the bait in good position. Now, I could peer into the water, aided by polarized sunglasses, to see if any fish were home. The first thing I saw was a zip of silver through a loose bait school. It was a flash of light I wouldn't have been surprised to hear a sonic boom behind.

277

"Spanish are working on the bait," I reported.

Focusing on the back legs of the marker, I saw what I want to see every time I looked at a channel marker. There was one large log, tended by two healthy logs, lying just underneath and behind her. There was one large female cobia with two male bodyguards, parked in the shade. Seeing that started a feverous body shake of cobia-phobia.

"There are three big cobia under the channel marker, one is a *Bahama Mamma*," I said, trying to be casual about it. However, I sounded as excited as a young boy telling his friends about killing his first deer. Where was our live bait? Big John's runner had run as far away from the Marker #12 as the string would stretch. Judy's pinfish had sought refuge amongst a school of baitfish off the mark on the opposite side.

"Oh, my God! Look at those fish!" Judy saw the fish and my mind snapped to a decision. It was time for the snake bait."

"Ya'll leave you're bait where they're at, I'm going to pitch this fake eel toward the marker," I followed behind what Judy said.

If it worked, I hadn't decided whom to hand the rod off to. Actually, I hadn't thought that far in advance. I was focused on making the perfect cast and watching the outcome.

I released the worm hung tight on one of the lower eye braces. A hand tug on the line between the reel and the first eye of the pole let me feel the stiffness of the drag. It was fairly tight. It needed to be to persuade the fish not to run back under Marker #12 if one came out to take the bait. I wound the lure back up to where it hung ten inches from the rod tip. In a fluid motion, I overhead cast to the mark, cupping my hand by the spool, allowing the uncoiling line to slap my palm. As I expected, my nerves were sending the worm too far. If let fly unrestricted, the worm would hang high and dry in Marker #12 above the water.

I mashed my palm against the spool, stopping more line from uncoiling. When the line that was away was about tight, I bowed the rod tip down toward the lure, softening the break, reducing the recoil. My motions were a developed instinct from a million casts. The worm came down so close ahead of Marker #12, the splash sound could have come from a pelican relieving itself from the top platform. We watched the lure slowly sink and undulate in front of the three fish. The worm captured their attention. I let it float down to their staging level. I could feel the *it* about to happen. The worm looked in the right zone, to me. I twitched it once. The midsection of the worm popped forward, and then the head and tail surged forward in a swimming action. One of the males moved ahead of the big female. I twitched the bait again. It darted for the bait, stopping just shy of bumping the worm. I machine gun twitched the worm forward, making it look like it was trying to escape in hapless efforts. The cobia shot out, inhaling the worm. I dropped the rod tip down, took up what little slack there was, and drove the hook into the fish with a strong upward sweep of the pole.

The sting of the hook ignited the fish, it rocketed straight ahead, away from the marker on a dead run. The reel drag screamed, though set firm. The fish was as big, if not a bit bigger, than the two we had in the boat already. The rod tip yanked down in recurring surges, but I maintained the butt section at the one o'clock position, which made the fish fight the drag, as well as, the pole flex. I followed the fish, actually, it was dragging me to the bow, dipping under Big John's line, and then standing ground on the deck behind the bow platform.

"Who wants this fish?" I asked loudly. I was letting them make the decision, instead of making the call.

"You do," Judy called back.

"Yeah, it's about time we watch you in action, we're sick of working so hard," Big John joked.

I thought about the adage of things working well when nobody is around, but if there is an audience of at least one, you'll make a mistake. That pressure I let go, thinking I'm going to let myself be myself and accept whatever outcome. I freed myself to the fight; there was nothing else going on anywhere but a rod, a reel, that fish, and I. I was thinking, anticipating, and feeling through a pinhole the size of the line that connected me to the fish. That block-out of the outside world is one of the most wonderful moments in fishing. You're swept away from everything but the moment. It is cleansing. It is soulful.

The fish had taken the worm on the portside and shot toward the bow. It was now somewhere off the starboard bow about two o'clock. Noon is considered straight off the bow. It was going down and out.

There was no tide and little wind, so the boat movement toward the fish meant the fish had us in a slow tow away from the marker. Realizing the fish was pulling us to open water was a relief. There was some background noise, but I couldn't make it out. The fish came up, cruising the surface toward the port side. I crossed over to the port bow.

"Ya'll clean up the deck and put the rods in the T-top holders or the rocket launchers," I blurted.

There was some background noise. There was no loss or gain of line; the fish just changed direction to starboard. I followed suit. The fish angled back toward the boat in an arc. I gathered line, keeping it tight.

"Big John, pop the motor over," I said, like a drill instructor yelling, give me twenty.

I smelled the two-cycle oil. There was more undecipherable background noise. We were a good ways from the marker, on the portside.

"Let's maintain the fish on the starboard for a while; I want to keep the fight toward the starboard bow," I requested.

Big John had turned the wheel hard starboard. When the fish was making way toward the stern, he pushed the throttle forward, almost taking me down.

"Just idle, just idle, nothing drastic!" I popped off, feeling instantly sorry for being so abrupt but not wanting to lose concentration to say that aloud.

Big John didn't take it personal; he fished for the same moment I was in. The fish and I ended up on the starboard stern.

"Backup," I yelled.

He did. The reverse movement put the fish and I back at a two to three o'clock position. Twenty yards off the gunnel, the fish surfaced, shook its big flat head violently and dove toward the boat.

"Kick it around, kick it around!" I yelled.

I bent my knees, ready for some boat acceleration. I reeled to keep the line tight, but the fish was heading fast under the boat.

"Give it some gas!" I yelled.

Big John hit it. The boat whipped around before the fish could make it down under. The fishing line angled toward the motor prop, but the quick turn pushed it back away before the ultimate shame of cutting your own fish off.

The adrenaline rush was wearing thin; I could feel the tightness in my forearms and lower back. The ache felt good to me. When the fish surfaced near the boat some ten yards out, I knew the fish was also tired. It began the slow left to right movements, getting ever closer to the boat.

"Kill the motor and get the gaff!" I shouted. The background noises became voices.

"Where do you want me?" asked Big John, with gaff in hand.

"To my right toward the cockpit," I replied.

"Is Judy OK?" I asked.

I heard her say, "I'm over here behind the center console."

"John don't go for the first opportunity, wait for a clean shot toward the head, and bring the fish in the boat in one motion," I said, calmly. "Put the gaff in the water with the hook facing out and wait for the shot," I said, again with a calm voice.

Big John was poised like a Cocker Spaniel on a covey of quail. The fish swung by the boat several times.

"Easy Big John," I said low. "On the next pass take him," I said.

The next pass the fish would head toward the stern.

The moment of truce came rather quietly in the water. Big John gaffed just behind the head, pulling the cobia aboard in one fluid adrenaline filled motion. It was a fine gaff shot. However, when the fish hit the deck, it exploded the last bit of life it had. It bounced off the gaff, aggressively flopping its way into the cockpit. Judy had wisely swung herself around to the bow. Big John showed agility I didn't know he had, sidestepping, while backing away from the fish. He was a rather large river dancer with a big fish between his legs. While he was dancing, I had ripped three long pulls of line off the reel, loosened the drag, and set the rod in the mid-ship rod holder. I'm quick too, when I have to be. Grabbing the line first, I followed the fish back to the cockpit, pulling the line tight, directing the head forward before it made way to the transom.

"Get a towel," I said, back in drill instructor mode.

Judy threw me a towel and I managed, after several attempts, to drape it over the head. When that happened, the fish settled down, considerably, thankfully.

I took side cutters and clipped the leader. There was no need to fool with hook removal. Straddling the fish, keeping care not to get involved with the dorsal spines, I sighed in relief, savoring the moment. It was over; we had won. Team effort paid off. The fish was a solid forty pounder. Not a submarine beach cruiser found elsewhere, but a quality fish for our neck of the world, especially considering we're taking them around structures.

"You ready?" I asked Big John.

He said "Yes."

I bear-hugged the fish to the fish box, he had the lid flipped open, waiting. Back in the cockpit, we all had stupid grins on our faces. We fell into a group hug. Actually, Judy and I were caught up in the span of John's arms.

Muffled in John's chest, I said, "My shirt is slimy."

"I don't care," was the response I heard back.

"Sorry for being snappy," I muffled; again, the same response.

Judy said, "We understand."

It was a fishing family moment.

"There is a big mamma still waiting," I said after the hug.

John followed up with "She's all yours," to Judy.

I hoped what we wanted to happen, would.

Three good cobia were in the box. Any pressure I felt earlier was gone for good.

Through the chitchat, I was contemplative about how best to take that big female cobia from Marker #12. She was at least fifty pounds, conservatively. Actually, she was sixty pounds by my eye. The tide had started moving out. In the outflow, she had held the same position. Any bait placed up current would be served to her. Do I anchor up current and set multiples of bait? I didn't think so, because the anchor itself would be a difficulty and the extra rods would be a hassle. Furthermore, once freed from the anchor, the outgoing tide would wash the boat in the direction of Marker #12 and that would be compounded with taking up the additional rods in the meantime, if *it* happened. It was bad, considering the boat would be moving in the same direction the fish should and more than likely would move. She didn't get that big by making foolish choices.

The first shot had to be the best shot. My mind relaxed on the *KISS* method; *Keep It Simple Stupid*. One stout rod, appropriately rigged with our best bait, might do the trick better than any elaborate game plan on my part. I selected the Penn 4/0 with the smoothest drag, set the drag on medium firm, and cut the rigging off. The mainline was sixty-pound test; I used a double Uni Knot to add three feet of one hundred-pound test. Three feet of leader should be enough to take the abrasion of the gill plates and dorsal spines; it was a best guess in the shaky heat of the moment. At the end of the leader, I tied on an 8/0 9174 Mustad bait hook. I took a moment to scrape it across a hook stone Big John had had in his tackle box for a while, judging by its condition and its location in a dark corner. Anyway, the hook point became shiny, showing new metal; it grabbed my thumbnail as a sharpness test. After cleaning up the rig, I slid the main line in the side slit of a large, un-weighted, inverted, popping cork. My thoughts were, *It was better the bait and the fish fight the resistance of the concave cork top in the water, than the angler.* The upside down cork was pinned four feet above the hook. That depth should put the bait in the danger zone.

The bait was the last, unspoiled blue runner. Netting that single, spastic baitfish out of the big bait well seemed worse than nailing a cockroach in a cluttered pantry. It took time and effort, but I finally got my mark. I held it against my chest and pinned the hook one nick forward of the dorsal fin then placed it gently back in the tank sans the bait net. It swam around wildly, unknowingly primed for the deadly business ahead.

I explained my plan to Big John and Judy. I was going to run the boat some ten yards up current of the marker, portside, headed directly into the current. When it was good, I'd put the boat in neutral, swing around to the cockpit, pitching the bait ten feet or so in front of the marker and free line off, allowing the current to sweep the bait toward the post so as not to pull the bait away with the forward momentum of the boat. We would have to adjust the bait position, using the reel according to the movement of the current and boat. The runner would pull the cork under, but we should be able to keep up with the bait by watching for it or the bright red cork stripe in the clear water. It would require a sense of feel to distinguish between the pull of the wild runner, reacting naturally as prey, and the actual take of the fish, if things worked out the way I intended. It was cat-and-mouse on monofilament. I'd be on the pole for the initial hit and first minute of the hook-up then pass the rod off to Judy and get behind the helm. We had uncluttered the boat in expectancy.

"Let me have room to move from the wheel to the baited rod and make the cast," I requested. "Judy get a fighting belt on," I said, wanting everybody to be ready, if it happened.

I didn't want to hear, "We should have done…." They were almost as excited as I was to see if this plan would actually work.

I idled well behind the marker in a large circle, turning the boat for the pass-by. When we were close, everybody stared at the base of the marker, looking for Big Mamma. She was still there with her now, single escort male. The turn of the tide had pushed much of the baitfish behind the marker and the two cobias. I noticed the baitfish were further down in the water column. The lack of bird activity indicated such without actually seeing it. The plan seemed plausible.

The hyperactivity of a blue runner makes it excellent bait. The spastic, erratic motions trigger a kill instinct from any predator. We had the best bait going to set Big Mamma off. If my cast was good, we might get a fight.

Fifteen yards up current of Marker #12, I made the cast. It fell slightly left center of the marker. There was no loose line on the spool, well-cast, good job for me. The momentum of the boat was taking us right of the marker, so I mashed my thumb loosely, still playing out some line as needed, dragging the struggling bait briefly at times. I free-lined the spool, letting the current take most of the control when the bait was in a straight line, up current of the marker. The runner took the cork under, but the bright red stripe on the inverted cork was still visible, most of the time. It was being washed toward the marker as intended.

Six feet in front of the marker, the runner apparently revived from the trauma of being tossed in the air, the splash down impact, and the unnatural feel of the cork pinned above it. It oriented itself enough to detect the two cobias it was floating toward. The blue runner reacted naturally, realizing its vulnerability. There was food in the water and it was it. Life could be over quickly; it had to run to live. Why are blue

284

runners excellent bait? The fresh response is always impulsive, seductive, an exaggerated Latin dance move that draws attention. I felt the thoughts of the baitfish, feeling the Moribund Code through the line. That blue runner was about to be whacked, hopefully by Big Mamma. It ran away from Marker #12 to the right, glancing into the current. Through brief glimpses of the red cork stripe and the movement of the mainline in the water, the runner was going with the out-going tide while breaking left and right in an open field swim, eluding the defense, or better stated, the offense, because there wasn't a ball involved with what was going on out there. The blue runner was bolting around for life, hampered by a bright red-striped cork dragging above.

I was happy the bait was moving away from the structure. I had to bump the boat in idle toward starboard to absorb slack line. The boat was idling away from the runner and the mainline was washing astern. Regardless of the boat movement, the chase appeared off port. Dart left and dive then abruptly swing right and up. We were witnessing a dogfight with one life in the balance. I killed the motor.

We had drifted right, parallel to Marker #12, slowly flowing to sea. Our bow pushed westerly, pointing the direction of the tide, stern behind to the east. The chase was happening twenty feet from the marker, inline between us in the boat and Marker #12. I was playing out line, giving the runner slack to keep the dance instinctive without a string attached. Thankfully, the two involved kept boogieing themselves away from the obstruction.

I was trying to keep myself calm, involved in the game, but on the sideline. However, I sensed my hands tremble, my legs twitch, and my heart was keeping the erratic beat of the dance going on off port. I was Barney Fife trying to get his bullet from his shirt pocket, again.

The blue runner started skittering the surface, smartly heading west with the tide, cork in tow. A V wake closed in on the runner's final efforts. The surface exploded with a large fish tail seen above. It had to be Big Mamma! Mamma gets what Mamma wants. I flipped the reel in gear.

I had just touched the reel handle to begin collecting line when the rod was snatched dead down. I jerked up, ringing a bell, letting Big Mamma know round two had started. She had warmed up, I had not. I gripped the pole, one hand above the reel and one below. I looked down to see line roll off the reel spool almost freely. She foamed a twelve-square-foot section of smooth surface water, then embarked on a straight trek back to Marker #12. She had a fifty to sixty-foot swim to get there. If she could do it, it would be over. She didn't get to be Big Mamma by being stupid. This, most likely, wasn't her first rodeo. I turned the star-drag on the Penn 4/0 a quarter turn clockwise to increase the resistance to her effort. It didn't make a perceivable difference in the line coming off the spool. I turned the dial up another quarter turn and felt more power from the fish, meaning the drag was effectively working against the fish. Line stopped rolling off the spool; it was now, grudgingly going out by the yard. Was that enough to break her spirit? She was less than twenty-five feet from her mark, Marker #12.

"Captain B, I'm ready," announced Judy.

"Give me a minute," I shot back. This was no time to transfer a fishing pole; this was pivotal.

She broke the surface, thrashing in confused anger. She was somewhat tired from chasing the runner down and now this struggle. She sounded swimming with the current, seeking a spell of relief. It was a sign to me. The boat again began free drifting into the open Gulf, away from all.

"Judy, come here," I called.

The game stalled, a great time to substitute players for our side.

"Make sure the belt is tight on your hips," I told her.

Big John snatched on the Velcro belt, smoothed the two strips together, causing Judy to exhale audibly.

"That's a little tight," I said.

Judy blew out, "Yeah."

He zipped the two strips apart; gave an inch or two then laid them back together.

Judy said, "That is better."

She turned to me; I put the butt of the rod in the cup of the belt. Judy put her left hand above the reel and her right on the handle. She knew the drill.

I passed by Big John, both of us sucking our guts in, to the helm station. I popped the motor over. Judy knew to keep the line tight at all times, no need to say anything unnecessary.

"I'm going to stay the fight amidships on portside," I stated, kicking the boat one thrust to port then letting the motor purr in neutral.

For the most part, if noise remains monotonous it won't spook the fish.

Big Mamma was lugging southwest trying to turn back east to the safety of Marker #12, but all of us, including her, were well away. She was moving on instinct, in trauma. I knew her battle plan would change once her navigation cleared. The fight was going to become less strategic, more aggressive. The fight in the dog was about to be exposed. Big Mamma was a big dog to begin with. Was Judy ready?

"Judy, things are going to change quickly," I warned.

Judy was standing portside amidships, just maintaining a taut line. The fish was twenty to twenty-five yards straight out, low in the water and, basically, pulling a drifting boat.

The drag was set as hard I cared to make it. The drag had forgiveness, but was stiff. It would need tweaking back once the fight came close to the boat; I knew roughly that a half turn counter-clockwise would be in order. I told Big John about it.

In view of the way things were going, I said, "We're going to have to up the ante a bit."

The fight was safe, in open water, more pressure could be applied. "We need to force the fish to burn juice," I said.

The slow speed chase was allowing the fish rest, which wasn't a winning tactic for us. Big Mamma needed a tad more forced exhaustion. However, it would have been unwise to produce additional pressure by simple-mindedly screwing down the drag. That could prove a mistaken move in the near future.

"Judy, reel down, without creating slack line, then gently pull back up," I told her.

This was going to apply more pressure to the fish, Judy likewise. Judy started applying more pressure, forcing the fish to pull harder. Every now and then, some line would slip off the drag, but she was gaining two for every one yard she lost. Big Mamma turned, swimming with the current. I'd prefer her swim against the current as that would tire her out faster, but you don't always get what you want. I reversed the boat until the line was at the ten o'clock position, thinking that pulling the boat behind it would break Mamma's will sooner. I let the battle continue like that for five minutes. Judy was expressing some fatigue.

"Big John, get her a bottle of water," I requested on Judy's behalf. She appreciated the attention as much as the water.

I got nervous, fearing the line might ride alongside the fish, leading to a cut off on the gill plate. I idled the boat forward and out, so the line was at the nine o'clock position. Judy collected a couple yards of line with that maneuver. The line started rising up in the water column.

"Big John, cut the drag back a quarter turn," I called.

He did it quickly. The fish came to the surface and wallowed. My stomach rolled, fearing the line might pop. A moment of slack during the headshake could be all she needed to throw the hook. It did not happen.

Judy's arms, shoulders, and lower back started cramping.

"John, rub your wife," I snapped.

Big John smiled like a schoolboy.

"John, I'm not cramping there," Judy cracked.

"Oh, this rub down is for you," John retorted.

The laugh cut the tension.

The fish surged, rolling some line off the spool.

"Crap, I worked so hard for that," Judy snapped.

The fish turned, went to the bottom, and started swimming toward the boat. Judy reeled quickly and smoothly, keeping the line taught.

"When you get a chance, turn the drag back another quarter turn," I said as calmly as a man having a nervous breakdown could.

I idled the boat in an arc to the left in an effort to keep the action off the port and not near the motor or under the boat.

The fish did a cruise-by approximately eight yards from the gunnel. She was big, twenty pounds more than any other fish in the fish box.

"Judy, it's getting close." I shot her some confidence.

I didn't want to say ten more minutes, because, at the moment, ten minutes would seem like a long, long, time for Judy. Big Mamma was starting a series of left and right cruise-bys. Twice, the fish glanced at the boat and darted away, taking some drag to the chagrin of Judy.

"Will this fish ever give up?" Judy exclaimed.

"Do you want Big John to take the rod?" I asked.

288

"NO! This is my fish," Judy growled.

"Judy has a hard time expressing herself doesn't she John," I popped off.

The fish was zigzagging five yards off the gunnel, getting closer and closer. The time was nigh. I idled the boat down current of the fish, so the tide would keep the boat from floating over the fish. The fish appeared exhausted, its swimming motions sluggish.

"Take the drag back one more quarter turn," I asked, putting some forgiveness in the line in case the fish lurched.

A couple more weak zigzags and the fish would be within gaff range.

"We're about to end this thing, Judy," I said calmly.

She said, "What's this *we* stuff?"

John and I laughed. I needed the laugh, because I was nervous, real nervous. If I failed to gaff this fish, it escaping, Judy would whip me with her fishing pole. Actually, our collective disappointment would be worse than the make-believe whipping.

In an instinctive moment, I stuck the gaff under Big Mamma's chin, snatched up with both arms, stepping back. Half the fish came over the gunnel then she began to thrash. Without a thought, I let gravity finish the job; I leaned back, pulled, and fell on my butt. The fish went thud on the cockpit deck. I tried to hold the gaff firm in the fish as both of us flopped and rolled on the deck, but it didn't take long for the fish to come off the gaff. I managed to slide the gaff safely forward along the starboard side while using my feet to kick the fish away from me. The fish was too exhausted to bounce off the deck, meaning it wasn't able to leap out of the boat. However, traumatized, it was behaving wildly as any creature would after such an ordeal, with nine sharp dorsal spines sticking straight up ready to rake anyone's flesh. I grabbed the T-shirt off my back, got to my knees, and tried to toss it over the fish's head. Lack of sight can be calming. The fish threw it off five times before, now, bloody and slimy, the shirt stuck across the head with a little help from my hands. There came a semblance of order from what had been like a greased pig wrestle. I held on for five more minutes after the final bell.

"John, if you would, open the fish box and take out any bags of ice you can easily reach," I asked finally, getting myself together.

John did that in short order. Five, or so, minutes later, the fish was docile but not dead. I got better situated on my feet and pushed the fish along the starboard walkway toward the bow and fish box. With one hand on the tail and one in the mouth, I rolled the fish up and into the fish box. John tossed two twenty-pound bags of ice on top of it and I shut the lid, latched it closed, and sat on top of it. I looked over at Judy. Each of us had a wraparound smile.

"Can I get one of those?" I asked, pointing at Judy's cold drink.

"You sure can," Big John said, going into the drink box.

I took a long drink, belched, and smiled.

"Come here, you two," John announced.

He gave us a patented Big John bear hug, which was the two of us smothered in his chest and under his shoulders. It felt good, like closure.

"I'm done," Judy declared.

I looked at Big John.

"Let's go home," he said.

I agreed. It took twenty minutes to put the boat back in order, part of which was getting my T-shirt out of the fish box and washing it around in soap and seawater. The shirt came out sopping wet, but better than when it went in the bucket. The wet T felt good on my skin, smelling rather botanical, with the few remaining suds.

Before we turned in, I took a few minutes to roll over two partial twenty pound bags of ice from the bottom of the fish box, on top of the fish, busting the bags, scattering the ice evenly with the other two, mostly whole, twenty pound bags John had thrown on top. I took the watery bag of ice from the drink cooler and put it in the fish box along with much of the ice-cold water. The four fish were bathing in ice and water. Cold is a dead fish's best deal, a most excellent deal that comes later across a dinner plate from the grill.

That was an incredible day! One particular day that would keep me fishing for cobia for a lifetime, a memory that punctuated our lives. Thanks, Big John and Judy.

Chapter 17 - The Fox is Pushed into the Henhouse

I came in from work one Thursday evening while Gina, my wife, was in another room.

I shouted to her, "I'm going fishing with Larry this Saturday, do you want to come?"

She shouted back, "No, you're not."

Her blunt response set me back. I was on the verge of being ticked off, but held back, waiting to hear her explain, "Why not?" Maybe I had overlooked a wedding, birthday event, or some other annoyance that was to keep me off the water. Gina's steps were coming in from the hallway.

"Why not?" I greeted her with.

"If you're going to take people fishing every weekend, you might as well get paid for it," she shot back.

"Paid to fish?" I was all ears.

"I signed you up for Sea School to get your captain license," she told me.

"I don't want to go to school," I said emphatically.

Recently released from graduate school, yes, with the fancy paper. I was over the schooling part of life. Educated beyond my intelligence, I spent weekends fishing some of that stuff out of my mind to remain somewhat normal.

"I already signed you up and sent in the check, so you're going to Sea School!" Gina told me. "And, no, I can't get the money back," she answered my question before I had a chance to ask.

I thrashed around like a child not getting their way. When I was through, she was steadfast, standing there with her arms crossed, staring me down.

Realizing, through years of married experience, this was a no-win situation, I asked, "What do I have to do?"

She informed me, I was to go to class all day both Saturday and Sunday, then every evening next week and all day the following Saturday.

Then she said, "You take the Coast Guard test on Sunday."

"No, not a test," I bellowed.

"You'll do fine," she assured me, but she wasn't the one going to take the test.

What happens if I failed the test after paying the money?

I showed up five minutes ahead of time in the hotel conference center with my new notebook, fresh pointy pencils, one blue pen, a set of parallel rules, and a divider. I felt like a geeky, older high school senior showing up on the first day with a Dukes of Hazard lunchbox and the house key strung around my neck. I sat at a back table, with a look that said, my wife made me do this.

It didn't take long for us guys to get to know one another. We shared the common bond of fishing and boating. The classes were interesting and informative. The instructor was extremely nice and well versed with decades of experience. He wanted everyone in the class to pass the upcoming test and reiterated subject matter that was sure to be on the test. The bull sessions with the guys during breaks were nothing more than a volley of fishing stories lightly mixed with some of the latest issues brought up in class. I hated to admit to Gina, but I was actually enjoying the experience. Yet, there was a tremendous amount of memorization and the time allowed to cover the material seemed inadequate. Everyone was worried about the test. Four days into the course, I had started making flash cards as memory aids. When the last class ended Saturday night, everyone filed out quietly. The next evening was the big test, a three-part test that included: Rules of the Road, Safety, and Navigation. The navigation section used a real chart and required charting tools and a calculator. The allotted time for the test was four hours. That meant there were to be a lot of questions, many opportunities to go wrong.

Saturday night was a long one for me. Reviewing my notes

repeatedly, flashing cards to the point it seemed like a movie, and rolling out some of my charts to get a handle on everything, trying to avoid embarrassing myself.

Sunday evening came too soon. All the guys were somber. Our test stations were set up before we arrived. Captain Mike, our instructor, proctored the exam. He explained, we were to finish section one, turn it in, then section two and the last part of the exam, charting. He said, "Take your time, check your answers, and begin." Begin was the sound of a fighter's bell.

Three hours later most everyone was finished waiting in the corridor to hear our names called. He had handed out three or four different versions of the exam to avoid cheating, so we couldn't compare answers amongst one another, and not being able to talk about the questions, added to the tension. One by one, he called us in to give our result. All we guys passed the exam, except one. He had an option to take a make-up exam later. Some of us celebrated on tailgates in the parking lot.

When I came through the door, with the big grin on my face, Gina knew I'd passed. Her smile showed pride in me, her husband; something every man wants to see in the eyes of his timeless bride. I was proud of myself.

"Gina, I'm glad you signed me up for the course," I told her.

She said, "I knew you would be."

A few months later, I received my official Captains' License in the mail. That government parchment, issued from the Coast Guard, meant more to me than my two college degrees I'd stashed somewhere in back of a closet. I was an official *Captain*. Arrgh! I'm Capt. B.

Ironically, I sold my boat to Larry, the guy I was going fishing with, weeks before attending Sea School. So when I was licensed, I had no boat to captain. I had the ticket but no boat to go! It is now amusing, but at the time, it wasn't funny. I was a captain, but of what?

For months prior, I had been scouting around for a boat. I was looking for my dream boat, like every other guy searching for a new or new to him boat. The boat I wanted had to be center console, large enough to go offshore fishing safely, have room for four people, a large bait well, electronics, an excessive number of rod racks, and extra tackle storage, because I was prone to bring the tackle shop onboard. I was

293

constantly looking in the newspaper for boats, buying *Boat Trader* magazines, and I had formed a posse of friends looking for me. I had gone to look at numerous boats, however, none rang my bell well enough to have Gina come see it, in an effort to sell it to her. What's more, it took little time for the issue of price and affordability to crush my dream boat. Reality sucks on a budget.

Steve Wilson, a new friend I met at Sea School, told me he had a boat for sale. The boat was a twenty-five foot Robalo center console with twin 200 hp Mariners. He lived in Suwannee, Florida, the last blob of land before entering the mouth of the Suwannee River. He invited me over to look at the boat and go for a test drive. The next Saturday after Sea School, I went to Suwannee. Steve had the boat hanging in a slip in his backyard. He and his wife, Dallas, lived on a canal, which made boating most convenient compared to towing a boat. The boat was beautiful, set up for tournament fishing, with a lot of room, storage for fish and fishing gear. The test drive was awesome. I'd never gone that fast in a boat. It rang my bell.

"Hey, Babe, whatcha doing?" I asked over Steve's phone.

"Blah, blah, blah," we said, until I said, "I need you to come down to Suwannee and look at this boat of Steve's."

She knew the boat was the one I wanted; she could hear it in my voice. She had to come see it before we spent our money. I gave her directions and she was there in a couple of hours. The wait for her was time well spent; we talked of fishing and toured the boat Steve had recently bought. It was a huge 32-foot Sports Fisherman. His new, to him, boat was the reason he was selling the Robalo. He planned to use his new addition for charter fishing.

Gina arrived an hour before dark. We rushed her into the boat for a test ride. She loves to go fast, so when we were wide and clear in the Suwannee River, Steve said, "You drive," to Gina and pushed the throttles down for her; she was more and more sold, the faster the boat went.

After docking the boat, I got Gina off to the side for *the talk*.

"So… what do you think?" I asked.

She said, "It's you."

Steve and I shook hands. We took Gina in the house and introduced her to Dallas and then went back in the yard. We discussed where I could store the boat and more fish stories. That was the beginning of a good friendship.

In the meantime, in the house, Dallas and Gina were bonding over a litter of fresh puppies. They had mated their male Harlequin Great Dane with a stout Dane/Pit Bull mix and the puppies were adorable. We came inside.

Within the first two minutes, "Can I have…?" Gina asked.

I was already shaking my head no. She handed me the puppy. It was cute.

"Can we have…?" she began.

"No, I don't think so, honey," I said as kindly as possible, trying not to come off like a puppy hater.

She said, "But…" followed by an ever-increasing list of why we needed this puppy that ended with, "You're getting a new boat," then *the look*.

The puppy was solid black with a white patch on her chest; I named her Calcutta, a captain's purse money. The boat was a joy, but we have since sold it. The dog remains a joy for us. Calcutta is lying on an extra-large dog bed at my feet as I write. There is much more white on her now; she has given us years of love and remains a love. Calcutta gives licks to all coming to our house. Gina and I hope to follow the dog's example, well, with hugs and kisses, not licks, to those that visit.

In the next part of these stories you'll ride with me charter fishing, one story at a time. It will be real, the good and bad. Each story will be about a different fish. I'm looking forward to writing things down; hopefully, I can write a story half as well as my Uncle Tom could tell. I had a one of a kind mentor. Maybe, my Uncle Tom will live again on paper. He always lives in me.

God Bless.

About the Author

I fish because I love it, period. As far back as memory allows, I have fished. As a kid, I wet lines for bream, bass, crappie, striped bass, and catfish. Big fish in shallow water caught my attention immediately. Oh, that's just a carp, it's not something you'd want to eat said most. I didn't care about eating it, I just wanted to catch it. Bread balls, corn, and eventually a fly rod sold me on catching big fish. Yes, carp. But huge carp that made the drag scream. I realized the quality of the fish doesn't matter, it's the fight in the dog. Growing up in Virginia Beach, Virginia, I was eventually introduced to the big pond, the Chesapeake Bay and the Atlantic. When I gazed out across that endless body of water, I envisioned fish everywhere. Not having a boat, we fished from shore for spot, croaker, flounder, and sea trout. Those fish were great to eat but lacked in thrills. Over time I learned of shark fishing. I could catch a fish of great size and I didn't need a boat to do it. All that was required was spending endless hours, day and night on a pier, waiting for the big one to come along. Fond memories of youth.

I went to Virginia Tech to study agronomy. There I was somewhat distracted by studies and overly distracted by girls, but I did manage to catch many smallmouth bass in the New River before graduating. In 1986, I joined the Peace Corps and was sent to Honduras. We were allowed to bring sixty pounds of gear. I brought fifty-five pounds of stuff and five pounds of fishing tackle. Thank God I was stationed near a lake because the Honduran largemouth bass had never seen a black plastic worm before. I tried to introduce each and every one of them to it on an individual basis. When I returned to Virginia, I met a beautiful young lady who loved to fish. I put up a good struggle, but in short order, she had me in the cooler; I married her. In 1989 I came to Gainesville for graduate school. Within the first week I discovered Cedar Keys. The tug of the Gulf started on me at first sight of the salt marsh. I graduated, not exactly on schedule, due to spending a little too much time in the Gulf, but I did graduate.

The Center for Aquatic Plants in Gainesville was my first employment and last. The tug of the Gulf had become so intense that my wife said, "Why don't you go get your captains license and at least get paid for fishing?" She signed me up for sea school herself. I love her. Charter fishing was, at first, part time on the weekends out of Suwannee. Of course that is kind of like letting the fox in the hen house and telling the fox only to take one chicken. Within a year I was full time charter fishing. I have enjoyed it ever since. However, I have found out through hard times and costly repairs that there is far more to the charter business than just taking folks fishing. One has to love not only fishing but people from all walks of life, while handling the ebb and flow of money and repairs. An understanding wife is an absolute must, also. We moved to Steinhatchee in July 2000. The fishing out of Steinhatchee has been fantastic but the best thing here is the people. Gina and I have met some wonderful folks in Steinhatchee. We plan on staying here for a long time. I make no claim to be a fishing expert because regardless of countless hours on the water and the numerous books and magazines I've read, I learn something new every time I go fish and every time I speak to someone about fishing. Keeping both eyes and ears open is great way to improve one's fishing knowledge.

www.ingramcontent.com/pod-product-compliance
Lightning Source LLC
Chambersburg PA
CBHW021500240626
47154CB00002B/458